T0269469

**acclaim for NICK FOWLER's**

# A THING *(or Two)* ABOUT CURTIS

AND CAMILLA

"So what has changed since Hemingway and Fitzgerald and Cheever recorded the pressures and repression weighing down a sensitive middle-class man trying to make it in a capitalist world? As Fowler tells it, the pressures haven't changed much. . . . Nick Fowler is an expansive, lyrical, inventive writer. . . . His rueful, funny first novel is informed by a pretty irresistible delight in its own telling . . . and beautifully economical flashbacks. . . . Fowler's invocation of his literary heroes is a joy."

—*The New York Times Book Review*

"New York and young love in a fresh, form-bending voice."

—*Austin American-Statesman*

"A superior stylist, Fowler's writing pulses like a quartz crystal. . . . Sad, hopeful and taut, *A Thing (or Two)* demonstrates that life is worth living because it is hard. . . . Few novels, let alone first ones, deliver such wisdom with as much talent, humor and emotional force: Harper Lee's *To Kill a Mockingbird*, perhaps, comes to mind. . . . A frequently brilliant book." —*The Tallahassee Democrat*

"An honest and entertaining love story; Nick Fowler writes with Nick Hornby's sense of humor and Dave Eggers' playfulness with form." —*The Omaha Weekly Reader*

"Fowler's story aches with a hurt many people, who've loved and lost, should recognize. . . . Salinger created a similar scenario in his great story "For Esme—With Love and Squalor." And though we might be tempted to call homage such as this derivative, it seems likely that Fowler is behaving a lot like Hemingway, who often mimicked writers in order to display his talent. . . . In short, Fowler, as he ceaselessly strives to 'make it new,' transcends the limits of influence to create a solid, distinct and admirable work of art."

—*Pop Matters*

"Terrific—full of passion and energy, but at the same time literary, quirky and with the same oblique and self-mocking charm that makes *Breakfast at Tiffany's* such a hit."

—Joanne Harris, author of *Chocolat*

NICK FOWLER

# A THING *(or Two)* ABOUT CURTIS >

Nick Fowler, a musician, has written for *GQ*, *Metal Edge*, *Teen Beat*, and other illustrious magazines, and has appeared on *The Tonight Show* and *The Sopranos*. He grew up in Tallahassee, Florida, graduated from Cornell University, and now lives in New York City with his dog, Luigi. For professional inquiries only, contact nickfowler67@earthlink.net.

# A THING *(or Two)* ABOUT CURTIS

^AND CAMILLA

# A THING *(or Two)* ABOUT CURTIS >

AND CAMILLA

–NICK FOWLER

VINTAGE CONTEMPORARIES

Vintage Books A Division of Random House, Inc. New York

FIRST VINTAGE CONTEMPORARIES EDITION, JUNE 2003


Published in the United States by Vintage Books, a division of Random House, Inc., New York, and simultaneously in Canada by Random House of Canada Limited, Toronto. Originally published in hardcover in the United States by Pantheon Books, a division of Random House, Inc., New York, in 2002.



Permissions acknowledgments can be found at the end of the book.



The Library of Congress has cataloged the Pantheon edition as follows:
Fowler, Nick, 1967-.
A thing (or two) about Curtis and Camilla / Nick Fowler.–1st ed.
p. cm.
ISBN 0-375-42160-2
1. East Village (New York, N.Y.)–Fiction. I. Title
PS3606.O85 T48 2002
813'.6–dc21 2002190372

Vintage ISBN: 0-375-71323-0

AUTHOR PHOTOGRAPH © BEN BAKER
BOOK DESIGN BY JUSTIN SALVAS

www.vintagebooks.com

150098039

TO MY FATHER

—but the pang of tenderness remained, akin to
the vibrating outline of verses you know
you know but cannot recall.

—Vladimir Nabokov, *PNIN*

# A THING *(or Two)* ABOUT CURTIS >

# ONE >

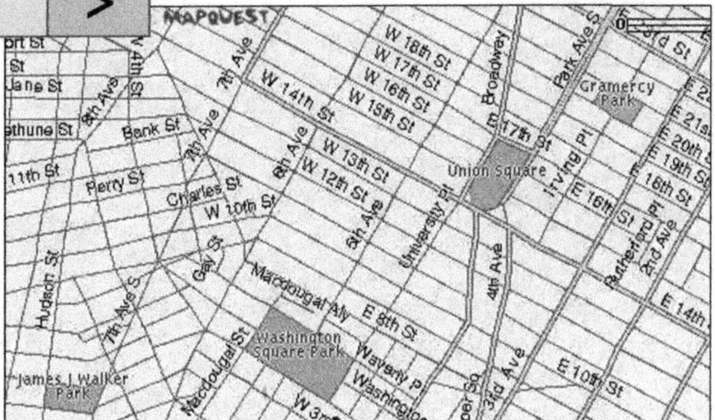

Map provided by www.mapquest.com

# Just a Little Green

“I’m Little Green,” she explained, in the ripe tone of Manhattan sophisticates. “Today I turned nine and a half and I’m your new neighbor.”

“I’m Curtis,” I admitted. “Happy half-birthday.”

I wriggled from the straps of my gig bag to shake an earnest, outstretched hand—and for just a fraction of a second longer than might’ve been necessary, I held the wee of her palm, still soft to this world.

Little Green gave me an appraising squint. “Um, why are there calluses on your fingertips?” she wanted to know, like she’d caught me in a lie.

I strummed an air guitar.

“Oh,” she went, slightly delighted, while we stood in the ’Nilla Wafer scent of her cardboard boxes. There were about a dozen of them blocking the dust-bunnied hall. I stepped over the largest and unlocked my Lilliputian studio, but as I was about to go inside, I felt Little Green looking into me.

“Were you named after that Joni Mitchell song?” I asked her over my shoulder.

“Yes,” she said gravely. “It’s about a girl who was given up for adoption, only I’m not adopted. It’s my mom’s favorite song.”

I left my door ajar and fully faced my new acquaintance.

“So how much do you charge for guitar lessons?” she continued, sizing me up.

"For you?" I rubbed my chin (which badly needed shaving). "I'll do one for twenty thousand dollars."

She rolled a set of voracious green eyes, looking far too large in her little blonde head. (I could see that the latter would catch up to the former as she began to break hearts.) "Come on, *really*," she insisted, all business.

"For the beautiful and talented Little Green? Make me blueberry pancakes someday and we'll call it a deal."

"All my *mom* can make is toast." She examined, then bit off, a cuticle. "Oh, and Cornish hens," she remembered, looking back up at me.

"Oh, they're tasty."

"Quite."

Little Green had on Diesel jeans, a tank top, and powder blue mules. She was gawky, nearly gorgeous—standing in that gangly limbo between girl and woman where they're still overwhelmed by their new, rude beauty.

And so wearing what someone (with whom I'll be overwhelming you and myself in just a minute) referred to as my *uniform* of black oil jeans and T-shirt, I asked my friend if she weren't married.

"*No,*" she said, with totality, her nostrils flaring to tame what I hoped was a smile.

"Divorced then?" I said—and I immediately wished I hadn't.

She gazed down at a mule, which she then began revolving in front of her, ballerina style. "No, but my parents have been considering one since I was six." She crossed her extended foot over the vertical leg. "My dad says that's why I'm an only child."

"I am too," I said, over-eagerly. But then, in my coolest Cary Grant: "I guess we have them to thank for your lovely eyes."

"Rather."

She yawned, covering a dainty mouth only as it was closing. "Have you been to London, England? U.K.?"

I told her I'd studied there.

"We just got back. They call parakeets *budgies*."

"I hope you brought along a warm *jumper,*" I said.

She gave me a shallow curtsy of a nod. "I get it." Then she looked at me carefully. "I write short stories, you know."

I told her that I'd actually just been thinking she was probably pretty gifted.

"I am. My dad says I'm extremely perceptive for my age. I have my own ascetic sense of abilities."

I asked her how she felt her writing was coming along.

"*Comme ci, comme ça.* That's French."

I told her I'd had a hunch it might've been.

"I've been in a bit of a writer's block, actually," she confided, inspecting her gnawed nails again. "Maybe you'd like to read a fairly recent rough draft of mine. I'd be kind of curious to get your take on it."

I told her I couldn't think of much else I'd rather do.

There was a pause. I thought I could see her eyes focusing on some far-off train of thought . . . and then, as it approached, ignoring it. "You have really thin lips, don't you?" she observed.

I cleared my throat and told her that I, personally, didn't really mind her saying so, but that someone with fewer tendencies to self-effacing might take offense to this kind of candor.

"I'm sorry," she mumbled, biting the corner of her own lower lip (which wasn't, for what it's worth, the least bit thin).

We stood there.

I looked at my wrist, where a watch would have been had I been a different kind of person.

"I'm sorry, Curtis," she said at last. "*Real*ly."

"Well, don't be," I suggested.

"Okay." She extended her little hand to me again.

"Okay, then," I said, shaking it, and we exchanged one of those stares that only The Movies would have us believe aren't useless.

"Can I call you Clyde?" she asked me, suddenly bouncing on her toes.

"Only if I can call you Stanley," I bargained.

"*Stanley?*" her nostrils dilated. "That's our *den*tist's name."

"Then in that case I guess it'll just have to be Walter."

"*Wal*ter?" she whined, but there was joy in her voice. "I bet you'll forget to," she reckoned.

"Why would you think that . . . *Walter?*"

At this, Little Green permitted me the first of what would be a long, bashful pageant of her beauty queen smiles. When it ended, she tilted her head . . .

"Are you lonely?"

I pretended to cough.

She shifted what slender weight she had from her left to right leg. Those emerald eyes were really sparkling at me. I sensed I wasn't going to get off so easy, what with having told her how unoffended I tended to get.

"Rather," I said, with a smile that felt more qualified than I'd wanted. "So, do you need help with those boxes?"

"Yes, actually. Thank you for offering." Reminded back to her task, my friend blew at her bangs. "And you should probably close your door," she suggested, tossing the bangs at it.

"Thanks," I said, closing it.

She swiped the glow from her brow with the back of an exquisite wrist, then hefted a box that dwarfed her, leaning back as she levered it into her empty apartment.

"Wow, you're really strong," I remarked, watching her waddle.

"I know," she sighed, dropping her box in the foyer before walking back to me. "Che Guevara Horowitz cried when I punched his arm in art. But he still wants to marry me."

"Who could blame him?"

Judging from her yuck mouth and trademark eye roll, Little Green could.

I slid my fingers under the bottom of a box—the largest—but stayed in my squat.

"And Che Guev always tries to *kiss* me," she continued, watching me.

"Who wouldn't?" I quickly wrinkled my brows into what I hoped was my most un-child-molesterish expression.

"Sammy Manna Sonnenberg. That's who. He's the only really sensible boy in my class. He's very much my type. But I explained to him that he'll just have to wait until I'm a bit more mature. Both physically and emotionally."

I told her that as far as things in this world being worth the wait went, I thought the above was probably right up there at the top of the list. Then I, an assiduous procrastinator, at last lifted my box with an affected grunt I'd sometimes heard my father make . . .

. . . and followed my companion inside.

"Anywhere is fine," she said, leading me into the living room. She flicked a pointer finger at nothing in particular. I dropped the box at my feet, where there was a dim, sound-effecty crunch of glass.

"Don't worry," she said, sounding more unconcerned than I suspected she was. "It was probably already broken."

"Will you let me know and I'll pay for it?"

"Okay," she lied.

I nodded and glanced around. The apartment had that demon sense of people fleeing old lives; a hopeful vacuum. There would be secrets discovered here, I thought. Sins dismissed.

"My mom told me not to let anyone but the super in here, but you don't look mean." She looked at me as though she needed my suit size. "You're like a big kid, Curtis."

I smiled, feeling my cheeks stretch back in a way that they hadn't in weeks. It was as unqualified as they come.

"Where *are* your parents?" I asked her.

Little Green twisted her neck, which audibly popped. "My mom's with the movers. And my dad just bought this phat loft on Crosby. That's why we had to move in here now. They're having a trial separation. It's just temporary." As she studied my face, her tongue darted once quick in and out of her mouth. She seemed to be auditioning something inside her. "Guess who lives in my father's new building, Curtis?"

I couldn't.

"Come *on*. Just one guess."

"David Hasselhoff."

"Wrong. Rupert Everett."

Fearing I'd now be thought irrevocably unhip, I admitted that I didn't have the foggiest.

"He's friends with Madonna."

"Oh," I said, shrewdly. "Oh. Okay." (Whatever *that* meant.)

"He just came out."

"Of what?"

"You know, *out*." Two annoyed blinks.

I gaped.

"Of the *clos*et," she rolled the famous eyes again.

"And it was about time," I conceded, not exactly sure of the tone I was supposed to be taking in these graceless days. But from the unfinished look Little Green gave me, I took it that I hadn't given quite the desired response. "That's too bad," I opted.

"No, no. It's really cool. He moved in with his boyfriend, Rialto. That's my friend Keanu's dad. Keanu's nice but a dork sometimes. He doesn't even know his times tables yet."

"Jesus," I scoffed, and "what about long division?"

"We're doing that next semester. But Harmony Downy's dad already taught her how," she grumbled. "Come on." She jerked her head in the direction of the kitchen, then led me there in a hopscotch formation that I suddenly remembered doing in another lifetime.

Little Green removed a takeout tin of hummus and pita from her otherwise empty fridge. She took what seemed to me an enormous bite for such a tiny mouth, then held the plate out to me, chewing, raising her eyebrows.

I refused out of reflex, I guess. We didn't speak for a while. I listened to her chomping her food, which made me realize I was actually very, very hungry. And that I hadn't had anything but coffee and Mentos since I could remember. I looked at my friend intensely then. She looked so a*part*. I wondered what the world would do about her. All at once I wanted to crush her to my chest.

Then the moment felt too posed, and I needed to deflect all the warmth advancing at me. I remember seeing myself as a foolish grin, suddenly discovering it has rotten teeth, if that makes any sense . . . there was just too much ugly in me now.

"Where are my manners? Would you like to sit down?" Little Green glanced around. "The only furniture that's unpacked is that, though." She walked back into the living room and collapsed into a corner chair of faded caramel leather. It fit her like a hug. "My dad made it for me when I was two." She looked up at me, nestled, her skinny arms flat on the rests. "All by himself. Do you like it, Curtis?"

I told her that it just might've been the most beautiful chair I'd ever seen. And I meant it.

"Would you like to sit in it?" she asked me, but this didn't exactly have the sound of a question. So I sat in it—or actually, wedged myself into it.

"Isn't it comfy?" she said.

I told her, in a constricted voice, that it certainly was.

"Should I bring you my most recent short story so you can read it in my chair?"

I nodded, trying, unsuccessfully, to cross my legs.

"Okay, cool," she said, then ran out of sight. I heard her rifling through boxes. "Don't move, okay, Curtis?" she yelled.

"Okay."

But I wasn't going anywhere. Not only because I was enjoying my new companion's company so much, but because I'd been up for over sixty hours, for a dim constellation of reasons I'll be rekindling in a minute. So I fell fast asleep . . . I'll never know for exactly how long. But when I awoke, I was watching Little Green walk, very cautiously, back into the room, holding only one piece of paper in her hand. Which, looking askance, she handed to me. "It's actually not a whole story yet. I've mainly been revising."

A single sentence, in bubbly script, had been scribbled, then crossed out, then shortened and expanded, for almost half the page.

~~Every body in my class.~~

Everybody in my Every body in my class wishes they had

While I was still reading, Little Green snatched the piece of paper from me.

. . . a delirious silence fell between us.

She gave me the full green brunt of her eyes.

"Everybody in my class," she said, "wishes *they* had a gay dad, too."

# Irony Kills

I just felt I should start this whole thing off by telling you that. It feels very central to me for some reason. That was what I was up against, encapsulated.

But now I'm going to lecture a little, if that's okay. Because more and more I've been hearing my own dad, the English Professor, speaking through me, inevitably, in that paternal ventriloquist's voice that makes so many dummies out of all us sons.

*Gay Dad.*

Okay. Think about the courage it must have taken our fathers to shoulder their colossal reversal. The pain that confessing this must have *cost* them, now reduced to a cute little catchphrase . . . an MTV sound bite. Jesus, I mean, the self-erasing burlesque of it all. Our *fa*thers, from whose loins we oozed, turning their backsides to the very process that gave us life. But still loving us, all the same . . . maybe all the more. Come on, isn't this the most relentless of ironies? Is the counterintuitive our new avant-garde?

So what black truths are left for this pop culture to plunder? Serial Killer Dad? Pedophile Pop? Kids'll be bragging over whose father has most profoundly molested them.

Okay. I won't go on. Because I'm not seeking sympathy anymore. Well, maybe I was expecting a little. But I think we know we're grown-ups when we stop resisting the urge to become a cliché. So I have to tell you, as corny as it may sound, that I really did it all for her.

Because this is a Love Story.

# And Then I Saw Her Face

I might as well start from the day that I met her . . . or from the day that I *fin*ally met her. That morning still burns in my memory, like a sunstruck Parthenon—white-hot and ancient—enshrining a battle I might have won in a dream.

Oh, God. Okay. Here goes.

Camilla.

I first accosted her on Sullivan Street, as Phillip, her dignified dachshund, tugged her through the self-conscious SoHo sunshine, throwing *Hurry up!* looks over his glossy little shoulder. I wanted to put him in a bun.

I'd actually promised myself I wasn't going to wish myself on anyone (house pets included) until I'd achieved some Success. But it was disturbing—how instantly starved for Camilla I was—and how she churned the memory of that gooey Love I hadn't felt since I was seventeen, and that I didn't think I could ever feel again.

Oh, Cammy . . .

I remember you so fiercely. As Manhattan lay sprawled under that first balmy day, hands clasped under its thawing head and its teeth no longer chattering, but chewing on a hayseed. Because it was Spring at last! April 1. The air soft with relief, bright with hope, and all the more precious because this teasing weather was always just an ellipsis between New York's stark winter prose and the hot drivel of its coming summer.

You see, during February, it's easy to let all the arctic apathy of this place erase us. Manhattan's too busy blowing on its own chapped hands to coddle any of its tenants.

But then the Angels unfold April . . .

. . . that warm, moist airplane towel. Reviving us (not to mention all the celebrities up there in First Class); breeding new awareness out of the couch-trained urbanist's fertile psyche. We all draft new plans, take our own inventories, and defrost our choicer portions. And, of course, we devise new lovers, usually denouncing the old ones. Then we feel a little guilty about the necessary transition. Because these loves aren't *Loves*.

Which reminds me that I'm digressing . . .

From my apartment on Thompson, I walked to West Houston. Past Aggie's and Arturo's, past all the starlets assaulting the Sunday . . . eager for sun, angry for Fame. I took a left on Sullivan by the steps of Saint Anthony's.*

And that's where I saw her . . . and stopped, struck. Camilla.

The first feeling I remember was being pissed off; at how this creature could be so reckless with her beauty. Couldn't she see how it could only punish those of us who couldn't possess It? I didn't even *want* to look at her; I feared she'd reduce me to something Neanderthal . . . disturb all those awful urges loitering in my genes like a billion hydrophobic rottweilers. I also felt there would've been something overly scripted if I, the mid-thirtyish hipster with carefully disheveled (and thinning) hair, calculated weekend stubble, and studied rock star blasé, had

FOOTNOTE >

*The Church of St. Anthony of Padua. There's a huge **PEACE TO THE WORLD** sign on top, and AA meetings held in the basement, which I'll get into later.

smiled at the nymphet I'd sighted, then walked hungrily toward her, while we both *did* SoHo.

But then I figured anyone who owned that doggy had to have a heart.

And so shamefully, admittedly, I first used little Phillip as a foil. Hoping he, fellow hound, would by instinct support me. (He had to have realized he'd won the dog owner lottery when he saw who was lugging him home from the pet shop.) I pretended *he* was my target, only glancing at his smashing mistress as if she were a happy afterthought.

I still don't know if Cammy saw through all this crap, even if she required its ritual, as we tend to do with the token plots of porno flicks. Because she seemed to insist that I gracefully scale all the walls she'd erected; that if I'd so much as hinted at the barbed-wire fact of her blockades, she'd have disappeared like a Snuffaluffagus.* I knew by then that Irony didn't even get a cameo in early Love Stories, and that, like all dramas that suspend disbelief, they cannot be acknowledged.

I was annoyed to discover that she was even *more* of a knockout up close than at the ten dueling paces from which she first shot through me. Camilla's eyes (oh, her *eyes*) had the cool, unsparing beauty of two cathode-blue security monitors. And while I admit this isn't the most Romantic image, I do feel it's apt, because (and I know this sounds like the rearview-mirror hindsight of that backseat driver narrators must so often become) I suddenly knew that no two things had, or would

FOOTNOTE >

*That elephantine creature on *Sesame Street* who would disappear whenever Big Bird, his only friend, tried to introduce him to anybody.

have, a more singular impact on my own perception of the world . . .

. . . or of myself.

That being clumsily said, I'll tell you that her mulatto skin was poreless, scoffing at Time, and that her faintly aquiline nose lent her a hawky sort of scorn. There were a few dirty-blonde tendrils woven through an amazed bush of hair, and under all this were a pink ribbon choker, lima-bean-green frock, and quietly expensive sandals.

I was crushed,* breathing in her vanilla scent as it came at me, as if Manhattan had removed that stick of straw from its teeth and were now blowing her pheromones into the wind like the fluffy spokes of a dandelion. I turned around so my better, less-balding profile would face her, then leaned over to scratch the old-goat scruff under Phillip's little chin, trying to think of something witty to say. Camilla stood back and considered me with what seemed both the fear and the defiance one reserves for vipers under glass. I wondered,

Who *is* this person? . . .

. . . Her few movements were so muted, but what I noticed most was a vast absenteeism in her eyes.

"I'm Curtis," I informed Phillip, now struggling to keep his black eyes open as I scratched him into a nap.

Camilla failed to drag him off the steps.

"And what's *your* name, sir?" I asked him, putting my hands on my knees.

He yawn-yelped, gave me a trembling stare—then yapped for

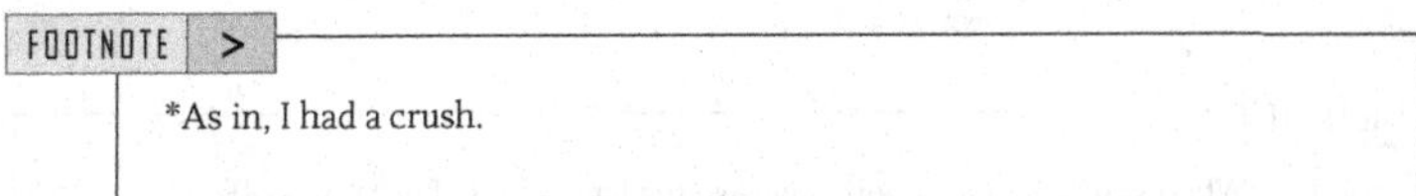


*As in, I had a crush.

more scratches. I didn't want them to think I was too easy—so the three of us just stood there in silence (dot, dot, dot) . . .

"A dog with no name," I said at last. "Sounds like a Neil Young song."

A pause. A distant siren sobbed.

"Phillip," she allowed.

Her voice was of a lower temperature than I'd expected. But somehow so familiar that it nearly upset me, revealed me, like those faintly shameful, undigested images that lie so deeply inside us that we hope they're only dreams and not memories.

At this point I also realized she was stuttering a flow of admiring male sidewalk traffic. And that they were actually giving each other flats* as they tried to get a Camilla-gander. Whether she was simply unwilling to acknowledge this or she assumed reality bent itself toward everyone in this way, I understood then, with a defeated relief, that *every* man drawn into her orbit probably assumed he'd been divinely plucked. Because one of beauty's delicate dangers lies in its implied conspiracy . . . we tend to feel that it *chose* us. So the pressure to fall in Love with her was off me. I was just like all the rest . . .

And here's a few reasons why:

A good two-thirds of her 5′9″ frame involved legs. Creamy, unscarred, and tan, like the skin on a new jar of Jiffy. And while she stood on these with a ballerina's diligent posture, they were slightly pigeon-toed. I knew I was a goner when I found this endearing. And thank God (or a certain Fairy) for that freak occurrence known as the "honest orthodontist." Camilla would later admit that this dentist foresaw how the buck of her girl-

FOOTNOTE >

*When you step on someone's heel so the back of his shoe comes off.

teeth would become the crowning charm on her lady-head, once her body caught up. But I wonder if he knew it would cause her faint frown, which she was making very available to me that first morning, as I stood there perspiring . . . lusting . . . scrambling for a next line, like,

"Phillip's a very serious little dog," because I had nothing better.

Suddenly I heard a wolf whistle. I gave its target a look meant to confirm the slapstick of all the spinning male heads—which she only glanced away from.

Still, I couldn't stop trying to decipher those eyes. I wondered if she was reading this whole guy-chats-up-girl-in-SoHo sketch inside the quotation marks that I was. I began to stroke Phillip madly, mostly out of Fear . . . or rather Fear's cousin once removed, Passion, displacing my Camilla lust right into her charge, who maintained his dreamy smile as I continued to burnish him.

When I stopped, however, and tried to talk to his mother, I couldn't help but feel that the sharp, black stare he was pinning me down with was a warning, from a Mafia midget relocated inside this witness-protection disguise—

*Buddy, don't you dare fuck with this one.*

And so, as if to peer inside, I checked his effective little teeth, then sniffed my fingers reflexively. *Great one, Curtis,* I thought. *She'll think you're some sort of dog pervert,* but,

"Do you like that smell too?" she asked.

"Yeah, and their feet smell like Fritos. If you're lucky."

"I thought that I thought of that."*

FOOTNOTE >

*I thought how odd it was that this would break her silence, and I remember imagining how I'd one day quiz her on this first question she'd asked me. (Talk about living in the moment.)

Phillip then sniffed my crotch . . . before deciding he'd taste it.

"Mind your own business, mister!" she snapped. "You don't know him yet."

Oops.

*Yet;* that runt adverb, so lost in promise, stepping as boldly into the future as a little boy trying on his father's Brooks Brothers suit.

Realizing what she'd said, I guess, Camilla watched her ankles and flushed a lovely salmon.

Had I met The One at last? I realized I was actually Happy, or at least his bastard son, Hopeful, as I squeezed surrogate Phillip like a tube of toothpaste.

"Are you sublimating into my dog as your objective correlative?" she said.

"Ooh, a Freudian who likes Eliot. Or is it Keats?"

(We were talking!)

"I lived next door to the house he died in when I was in Rome. *Truth is beauty and beauty is truth,*" she recited, and I imagined her sitting in some Romantics seminar, doodling swollen hearts around an unworthy jock's name, wishing she were really in the kind of Love she was studying.

"It's *Beauty is truth and truth beauty,*" I corrected, without wanting to, because my father was tutoring through me again.

"Oh." She looked sadly down.

"I'm sorry. God, I mean, Christ, I hate know-it-alls."

An appalling little silence fell. A hairy-calved, betunicked friar rushed down the steps of the church and tried to ignore us. Camilla kicked at some implicit street shmootz.

"What's it like going through life so beautiful?" I blurted. "I mean, God, I know it sounds like some cheesy pickup line, but I mean, like, scientifically, to have all that power? It must be strange. Am I being rude?"

"I can't look at it that way. It's like if I asked you what it's like to be white."

She looked at me hard. She seemed to be deciding on something. I felt like I was standing in a police lineup. And I waited (Cammy would later claim that I gulped). At last she stepped forward and shook my hand with an extra, delectable squeeze.

"I'm Camilla," she promised.

(Oh, ladies. You'll never know how welcome are these small gestures that give us huge hope, as well as hours of rewinding pleasure.)

Perhaps sensing the descending arc of our Love Scene, Phillip yawned, and, to conceal my elation, I bent down and, with renewed commitment, scratched at that special button on a dog's flank that can tilt his head and rotate a hind leg like a locomotive valve gear. I must've really won palsied Phillip over, because when I stopped, he clawed my leg in a death lock and, with M-16 intensity, began humping himself into oblivion.

Camilla peeled him off me.

And with residual quivers and quakes, he appeared as ashamed, if slaked, as that dinner guest who suddenly realizes he's outstayed his welcome.

"What are you thinking about?" I asked him.

I got no giggle from Camilla, but she did say,

"I'm sorry. Oh, God, his lipstick is out. But don't worry, he's a eunuch."

"Good, 'cause I've just run out of my RU-486."

"Ha," Camilla went, without smiling. "Ha, ha," then fell into a recollection of some similar dog incident that faded slowly behind my swelling inner narrative . . .

It didn't matter what she was saying . . . I was watching myself Fall in Love. And as my mind warped her words into the *womp-womp* garble of Charlie Brown's grown-ups, as I observed her pretty mouth making shapes, it seemed I'd known her forever.

". . . and he never likes men," she concluded, the peripheral drone of her voice taking center stage again. But there was a qualm in her eyes over this last fact she'd told me, as if she hoped I'd confess that I'd slipped randy Phillip a Roofie.

I looked into her brown leather purse, parched and cracked as an old catcher's mitt,* where I saw a book called ***Vocabulary Builder*** peeking out precociously, and whose title she then noticed me tilting my head at. She fired

"*Crepuscular!?*" at me.

"Occurring at twilight," I rattled off. "Either at dusk or at dawn." (It happened to be a favorite, and one that I'd devoted an index card to in high school.)

She bit her lower lip in a way that was at once pleased and pissed.

"*Catamite!*" I countered.

"Shit," she said, nibbling a nail, then looked at Phillip as if for a signal. He appeared just as stumped. "It's not that icicle thing," she squinted.

"I'll give you a hin–"

"No! God, I've looked this one up a million times."

And so I said, very slowly,

"A boy . . . kept . . . for . . ."

"Pederastic purposes," she said quickly. "God, we're dorks."

FOOTNOTE >

*I thought of Holden's brother Allie's mitt that he wrote poems on, realizing, as we do, that every little thing about this girl was in some way wonderfully connected to my deepest, fondest images.

*(We!)*

She looked me over then, grudgingly, as if she were about to fork over a very large sum of cash for a car-towing ticket. Then she poked the dog-eared copy of *White Noise** I'd been pretentiously carrying around back then. I felt a groggy erection yawning out of hibernation.

"Don't tell me you love this book," she warned me. Translation?: *Don't make me fall in Love with you.* "Is it your favorite book too?"

Making a mental note to marry this girl, yet trying not to seem eager, I said, at last,

"It was my undergrad thesis."

At that, Cammy grabbed a silver Tiffany pen from her purse and jotted something down—which I later learned was her AOL address—backwards on my forehead. Our eyes clashed briefly . . . she was close enough to drool on.

"Hey, da Vinci," she stepped back. "That's so no other girl will talk to you until you get back to your bathroom mirror."

(I didn't tell her how that wouldn't have exactly posed a problem.)

Noticing our notorious info exchange, a toothsome gaggle of French boys winked, kissed their fingers, and said very French things behind her. I ignored them and, feeling good about snubbing the *Fraahnge* for once, wrote my own e-mail address on the back of her hand . . . which I was delighted to find trembling as I held her wrist, like an injured sparrow.

FOOTNOTE >

*The novel by Don DeLillo,a big hero of mine. Here's a photo I downloaded and pasted into my little doodle/lyrics pad. Can you see the kindness in his eyes?

"By the way. What do you do?"* she asked me, reclaiming her fingers.

Oi . . .

Like the moment in *Midnight Express* when the drug-sniffing German shepherd starts barking just after we'd thought Brad Davis had made it past Turkish customs with his hash.

But,

"Are you a musician?" she offered, eyeing the gig bag on my back, the disgrace on my face.

I must have grunted.

"You have those hands," she said. "They're beautiful."

And with a final, irked glance, she was off.

I remember that the sky was suddenly smudged in storm cloud, and that there was the coughing of faraway thunder. I watched wingman Phillip trot off beside her, until he peeked back at me with a sad yodel over his shoulder. I gave him a half-mast wave, then walked off myself.

But after I crossed Houston, standing in front of Raffetto's Pasta, I couldn't help but glance back, where I caught Camilla doing the same.

We laughed.

FOOTNOTE >

**That's a complex question*, I once would have hedged. *Do you want to know what I do for the salvation of my soul, or for the solvency of my bank account?* God, what a load of horseshit I used to shovel. Girls would become so dizzied by my slacker equivocation that they were relieved to learn that I did anything at *all*. Other times, I'd go right for the old shame jugular . . .

*. . . I'm a janitor*

would tend to dampen any further sparks of interest, but this reverse snobbery was actually a good litmus for gold-diggers.

I realized that, until just then, I hadn't really seen her smile. It was a thin, unwilling thing . . . breathtaking, basically.*

I turned around and kept walking through steamy curtains of rain.

"I love you," I said, out loud. (Practice.)

I strolled along, getting soaked to the bone. I felt the surf of her crashing over, and echoing through me—pulling me under as I found my way home.

FOOTNOTE >

*Because Love is the Great Euphemizer.

# The Hollow Man

Well, first off, as you can see, I haven't exactly turned out the way I'd hoped. Or the way anybody else did, for that matter. That's an understatement. And I'll be the first to admit it. I might even be the odds-on favorite for the Vincent van Gogh Self-Esteem Award.

I've managed to get out of telling you a lot of the basic stuff, the big stuff, by huddling inside all of my pretty, hollow Easter egg words. I guess I've learned to live in them. But Reality, that relentless census taker, doesn't care where we reside.

So I know I'm escaping myself when I keep referencing my life against the Big Screen. And alluding to all the obsessively underlined pages in the broken-backed books of my boyhood; to all the leaning Pisa stacks of vinyl that I spun almost grooveless, and that are hopefully still in my father's garage, unless he tossed them. But more than any person, these things solved me. Shaped me. They conveyed me, conveyored me . . . away. (You see what I mean about the words?)

I felt cozy in Salinger's precious clubhouse on those stormy Sundays when my father wasn't quite feeling himself. Or, hungry for the hues the rain had washed from my world, I'd slip into some cinema's velvet shelter, communing in the blue confusion of Joe Buck's eyes.*

There I could dream in the silken fog of Never-Never, in my lonely only-childhood, suspended and fed by umbilical images.

But I don't dream in color anymore.

FOOTNOTE >

*The protagonist of *Midnight Cowboy*, the Academy's 1969 best picture.

# Dahmer Detector

For the first dizzy week I waited for Camilla to return my exploratory e-mail (*Just thought I'd say Hi*), Hope was an April robin, hopping inside me. And Camilla (because to me she was still a mere *Camilla,* without history or surname trailing behind her) was truly all I could, or would, think about.

Then, after one limping and another two crawling weeks, the narrative of our Love Story seemed to stall completely. Camilla hadn't contacted me. I convinced myself she was only resisting, because any new love promises both unexpected treasures and those things we'd hoped we left behind, like that grimy amalgam you find in the folds of men's sofas.

But then, after a soggy month of mooning around our monument,* hoping I'd "chance" on her and hound Phillip . . . of clicking my Hotmail in-box half-hourly, I told myself that I'd finally given up . . .

. . . When suddenly, on May 1, exactly one month to The Day, the following appeared on my computer monitor. I remember actually rubbing my hands together . . . I remember thinking, *May Day, May Day!* . . . I remember feeling life mattered again.

FOOTNOTE >

*St. Anthony's.

Curtis,

It was certainly very nice meeting you a month ago. Maybe too nice. But because a girl can't be too careful in Gotham, I've sent you this *Questionnaire.* It was developed by Vienna's foremost forensic psychologists as a screening device to identify serial rapists, mass murderers, cannibals, and the like. Phillip and I hope you're not offended. We're quite certain you'll do just swimmingly.

So please don't spindle, fold, or mutilate this test form . . . or me.

Good luck!

Camilla Fell

*Other than* White Noise, *what are some of your favorite books?*

SILENCE OF THE LAMBS, TED BUNDY: YOUTHFUL FOLLY, IN COLD BLOOD. (Only kidding.) All of Updike's RABBITS, NINE STORIES, THE MYSTERIES OF PITTSBURGH.

*Other than Phillip's breath, what are some smells you like?*

Napalm in the morning, clean sheets, suede, the scent of my father's face coming in from the winter when I was little, gasoline, new books, puppy breath.

*What piece were you in Monopoly? (I bet I know.)*

Bit iv cairse. Der schnauzer.

*Do you have health insurance?*

Why, did I look a bit peak•ed? Honestly, no, but I really should get some. I can't seem to find the gonorrhea ointment I fancy over the counter anymore.

*What are your three favorite movies?*

*Midnight Cowboy, Bonnie and Clyde, East of Eden.*

*Where do you consider home?*

Home is a face you know.

*If I called your apartment, what might I hear?*

A dozen or so teenage boys, tethered together, pleading for their lives. Just joshing again. Jeff Buckley.

*What are some foods you love?*

Slim Jims, Frankenberry, cold, coagulated sweet and sour pork, asparagus.

*What is something you hate to hear?*

"Everything," in response to "What kind of music do you like?"

*In* White Noise, *Murray tells Jack that his "wife has ______ hair."*

"important"

*What is something you say too often?*

"I'm fine."

*What are your favorite animals?*

Small, muscular dogs, otters. (I think the way they crack mussels on their chests against little rocks is awfully cute, no?)

*What annoys you?*

Slow walkers and people who claim they like to stroll in the rain. When people say, "My cat thinks he's a dog," and "My dog doesn't know he's a dog." People who trade in their passions for money.

*What makes you sad?*

The handicapped, burn victims, animal cruelty, lonely old people, *I'm Leaving on a Jet Plane.*

*Are you happy?*

Extremely.*

*In* White Noise *again, what does Jack do to his son Wilder's fingers when he's sitting in his father's lap, unable to stop crying? (Don't look at the book!)*

He uses them to practice counting from one to ten in German, through his mittens, mind you.†

*Do you have a scale?*

Somewhere.

*Any life lessons so far?*

People will never change for you.

*What is your favorite city?*

Paris.

*If you didn't answer Manhattan, have you or would you ever live there?*

FOOTNOTE >

*Technically, this really wasn't a lie, because, well, she'd contacted me. Sweeping me up, up and away into the ecstatic tornado the weathermen had, on Valentine's Day 2000 (which I'd spent alone), christened *Camilla.*

†I looked at the book.

I did, for a month, after finishing my Cornell Abroad semester in London.

*How do you feel about the song* "Night and Day"*?*
Haunted.

*What would you be sad to lose?*
My father, my virginity. (Ha, ha.) Your interest.

*What are the two easiest ways for someone to annoy you?*
Drop names, ignore me.

*If you could be someone for the weekend, who would it be?*
Elvis, circa '56.

*What grosses you out?*
Fake laughter, people who say "Ciao," girls who call themselves "actors."

*Back to basics: In* White Noise, *after Jack founded the Hitler Studies Department at the college he teaches at, the campus chancellor urged Jack to beef up his image. He told him to gain weight because he wanted him to "______ ______" into Hitler.*
"grow out." (I'm so glad you love that.)

*What is the only word in the English language that has opposing meanings?*
Love?

*Why did you pick me out of the crowd?*
Why don't you let me show you?

# Hello, Norma Jean

I guess you can see I did okay on the thing. I *bet*ter have. I worked on it from that morning into the little euphoric hours of the next one, as Camilla would later confess that she did as well. Only *I* spent the following and sleepless day totally overanalyzing and revising my reactions (big surprise), *ad neuroticum,* until the words on my monitor looked like meaningless mumble. Because I wanted very badly not so much to get Camilla's *Questionnaire* "right" but to make every aim of my answers utterly true to the angles inside me, however oblique.

Am I making any sense?

What I mean is, I wanted to confirm my feeling that this being, who'd seemed at the same time both more similar to and more unlike me than anyone I'd ever met, had sensed this intensity as well. And that, despite the well-founded fears that so often follow these conflicted inklings, she, like Marilyn M., that candle in the wind, would risk standing over a subway grate to feel the thrilling upgusts of New Love whoosh through her.

After I'd sufficiently obsessed over *Questionnaire,* I even wrote up my own set of questions (below), which I gave back to Camilla along with my answers to hers. But this time I sent the stuff by snail mail, as I actually wanted to see her handwriting. Or, I should say, her graffiti. Because it turned out to be, just as I'd hoped and feared, every inch as cryptic and lovely as its author. (Isn't it a ridiculous insignia of our love that I had to struggle to read every single word she'd ever write me?)

Camilla,

It really was great to meet you. However . . .

. . . I'll have you know that I too use a rather rigorous selection method to decide on such delicate (if beautiful) "matters." Hence, I feel it only fair to inform you that the answers you and Phillip so helpfully supply will be reviewed by myself and a judicious panel made up of my rabbi, one or two of my therapists, a handwriting analyst (would you please print?), Alex Trebek, his mustache, my college advisor, high school career counselor, and several other of the more discerning dachshunds whom Phillip had given as references.

So please be as candid as possible, and feel more than free to elaborate on or skip any questions you may find overly intimate.

I look forward to seeing you again.

Really.

Curtis

Are you related to Norman Fell, a.k.a. Mr. Roper on *Three's Company*?

*I hope not. He looks like a pervert. Oops. Didn't he just die?*

Do you believe in an aesthetic absolute, as in, say, Jane's Addiction is simply better than Kid Rock?

*Yes! I'm afraid I'm actually somewhat of an aesthetics Nazi. And I have to admit I believe in this absolute on both personal and quantitative levels. (How old are you anyway?)*

Do you consider yourself a <u>cynical</u>, disillusioned, squeamish, shy, <u>loyal</u>, <u>generous</u>, <u>adventurous</u>, self-centered, or <u>loving</u> person? (Please underline any or all of the above.)
*I think people mistake my introspection for shyness. But mostly, I try to be like my mother, who is the kindest, most generous person I've ever known. Although a little nutty at times; she drags poor Phillip to a special dog psychic every Christmas.*

Adore small children?
*Yes, and I want my own babies (someday), although I'm not one to go gaga over other people's.*

Believe people are innately monogamous?
*I would rather discuss this in depth and in person.* Although I do believe that monogamy is a necessary sacrifice, and the only way to maintain a relationship. It's the highest form of love.*

Ever spoken any of these phrases:
"He has good energy."
"He examined my chakras."
"It's all good."
"Peace out."
"Don't even go there."
"You go, girl!"
"Hel*lo*?"
"What sign are you?"

FOOTNOTE >

*In *person*!

*Only the last one, and only in polite response to the same daft question, but I'm so glad you've singled these out. Oh, wait! I hope you don't use these and that I haven't just totally insulted you. Drat! You've forbidden me to type so I can't delete or edit. But I guess this was your way of getting my gut reaction, eh, crafty Curtis?*

Snorted heroin?
*I only shoot. Just kidding. No, but I've watched others.*

Do your own laundry, or drop it off?
*Funny you should ask this.*
*Okay…*
*…I confess. When I moved here about nine months ago, I stopped doing wash for the first time in my life, and I feel like a spoiled little deb every time the sweet Korean family under my building opens their arms to my big bundle. But it seems to make them so happy, and they tie it all up so nicely into those little crisp packages, it's like getting a present, and I feel like time is so of the quintessence in NYC and all. But on the other hand, I do miss that feeling of accomplishment when you do your own laundry and carry the stack of jeans home and they're all warm and cozy…Oh, I can't believe I've just written an entire paragraph about this…I think you must've struck a particularly Catholic chord in me on that one.**

Worry about the future?
*I know this sounds like some New Aged kind of claptrap, but in a way, I feel it worries about me.*

FOOTNOTE >

*Later, I discovered that Camilla de- and refolded all her laundry anyway . . . even socks.

Sneak glances at yourself in mirrors?

*Not on purpose.*

Enjoy your own company?

*When that company isn't sad or cranky.*

Believe we live by a meaningful plan, or in a godless, random universe?

*The unfortunate latter. I just came out of a big Ingmar Bergman phase. Ugh! I feel like I sound like some gross NPR jockey. Can I use White-Out?*

In love at first sight?

*The jury is still out on That One. And I'm sensing it might've been hung.*

Respect Woody Allen's work (if not his sexual history)?

*I know it's probably artistically amateurish to say this, but I guess the two have become inextricable in my provincial little mind. I am, after all, from Connecticut. And it also really annoys me how he keeps casting himself opposite Hollywood's current It Girl.*

Confide in your father?

Have trouble sleeping?

*I can sleep through a pogrom.*

What piece were *you* in Monopoly?

*Woof, Woof! (I actually swallowed him once because I found him so cute.)*

Do you write down your dreams?

*Sometimes I draw them.*

What is your first memory?

*I seem to have blocked most of my early ones out.*

What are some of your favorite movies?

Man Holes One *and* Three. *No, honestly,* Breakfast at Tiffany's, Sling Blade *(brilliant sound track),* Judgment at Nuremberg *(Montgomery Clift's twenty minutes on-screen are the best acting I've ever seen),* The Jerk, Rushmore, Come Back Little Sheba.

Other than *W.N.*, name your five favorite books.

*Hmmmph! You are so cruel to limit me to five, and so I think I'm just going to have to break the rules.* She's Come Undone, The Great Gatsby, Glen Duncan's Hope, The Collector, Breakfast at Tiffany's, On Love, Madame Bovary *(can you define "Bovarism"?),* The Shipping News, The Book of Daniel, A Mother's Kisses.

Where did you go to college?

*What if I told you I didn't? Would you keep reading? Even if I'd really gone to Oxford?*

Why did you go there?

*To get far, far away...*

What was your major?

*English.*

Ever taken a feminist studies class?

*Yes. And although it was unforgivably required for my masters, and it's completely un-P.C. to say so, I found the "subject" boring and despotic.*

Do you love food? What are you digesting right now?

*Yes, I live for it (ha, ha). And I'm always highly suspect of those who claim not to. Let's see... right now, what am I digesting? Well, other than the memory of those strange minutes I spent with a particularly intriguing boy... are three slices of olive bread, a crisp, cold apple, goat cheese, and a Lazy Samantha.*

What is your favorite city?
*Paris, aussi.*

Do you like to flirt?
*I've actually been accused of not knowing how to.*

Are you more afraid of death, or failure?
*I guess it would depend on how painful and long the death is. I mean, I'll skip the job promotion and profit-sharing if it means being drawn and quartered.*

Favorite songs?
*"Night and Day" is my all-time favorite. But I love "Landslide" by Fleetwood Mac, "Silent Night," "Last Goodbye" by Jeff Buckley, "Are You Strong Enough to Be My Man?"*

Favorite painting?
Land of Make Believe *by Maxfield Parrish.*

Here's a foursome of *White Noise* questions for you:
What does Jack *say* when Murray tells him his wife has "important hair"? (Touché.)
*"I think I know what you mean."*

What is the shape of the anti-fear-of-death drug Dylar?
*Flying saucer.*

Who is Jack's son Heinlich playing chess by mail with?

*A convicted killer on death row.*

What does Murray pay a prostitute $25 to do?

*Let him perform the Heimlich maneuver on her. (En garde!)*

Have you:

Ever thrown something at a boyfriend?

*I guess you could call him that.*

Was it sharp?

*Not enough, but as sharp as bananas get.*

Did it hit him?

*Of course!*

Is there someone you'd die for?

*My mother, and my children, should I have them.*

Is freedom or happiness more important to you?

*I feel they're mutually inclusive.*

Would you trade your pinky to be famous?

*Yes, if I wanted to be famous.*

Do you like to stay up all hours?

*It depends on how those small hours are spent, as in, say, answering a set of very intelligent questions.*

Why did you wait exactly one month to e-mail me back?

*My mother always said it takes a month of Sundays to make a big decision.*

Bonus Trivia:

According to lore, what did Raphael do upon first seeing the Sistine Chapel?

*I know this! He fainted. How wonderful is that? It* has *to be true.*

Without, of course, consulting your reference materials, define . . .

. . . *Pulchritude.*

Hint: *You yourself* define it.

*You make me blush. Of course I had to look it up after that Tantalus clue. Or Blue Beard.*

(And at the bottom of the page, in a silvery ink so pale I almost didn't see it, Camilla had written . . .)

*By the way, my number is 529-9589*

# Rubber Gloves and Vaseline

At least I meet these days with a clear conscience. Or only a partly cloudy one. When I began doing hard drugs in my first dark, disappointed year in Manhattan, I'd wake up reviewing the mess of the previous night, glancing over a metaphorical shoulder for that stream of toilet paper trailing from my shoe. Then, when I eventually did become, for a while, a world-class drug addict, my reality was obscured by the illusion that it had some meaning, some direction. There was a drain-clumped-with-hair flow from cause to effect . . . things had to be fixed if they were forever getting fractured.

I'd curl up inside my narcotic eiderdown. Hoping the soft atrocity would eventually congeal into . . . *some*thing. Some finality, some ecstasy—an epiphany that would clarify me. Those who cared would have to help me, right? Stop me in my lazy race to Death. Drugs at first allowed me the easy green laughter of boyhood. But in the end all I could do was cry.

When I finally got myself unhooked, my life became a dial tone. A relentless, bored howl into infinity. And so I'd wank off a lot. A *lot*. Once I even tried to watch myself, which I hadn't done since puberty. But as I was dangling from that breathtaking orgasmic cliff, my face didn't reflect the adolescent rapture I'd expected, but the hesitant snarl we assume just before the doctor inspects our prostate.

All this time I still believed that by paying my dues, by sitting it out in Fame's game of Duck Duck Goose, the fickle fellow would one day finally decide to tap my receding hairline . . . appoint me as Rock Star . . . all so I could chase him around in circles, like my own tail.

And then I met her.

# So *This* Is Love?

Camilla was an hour and thirty-seven minutes late to our first date.

We'd agreed to meet at seven, outside, on that splendid veranda in front of Time Café—just next to Tower Records and Crunch, my gym—under those parasols, as crowded and cliqued as a whispering rugby scrum.

Anyway, I thought we'd agreed to this. Or really, I thought *she'd* agreed, because meeting there was my idea. I was surprised to hear the assertion in my voice, even as I tried to stop it from wavering over the phone.

It was a gentle, pink equinox evening. One of those extraordinary moments when the earth has no climate . . . when the atmosphere is the non-temperature of our own pumping blood. God must have really been on his toes that night, at least with His weather. Because . . .

. . . where *was* she?

Hadn't Cammy also been obsessively reviewing and rewriting the finer points of our opening Love Scene? I mean, do women even *do* that?*

FOOTNOTE >

*Ever since her debut, she'd remained perfect offstage, because I'd transformed my behind-the-scenes Camilla into a model philosophy, against which I held all the petty impediments of daily life in contempt. What I mean is, she was like a prospect, and a process, still unfolding . . . and hopefully in my direction.

I kept asking my actory waiter for the time, which he was very sweet about, actually. After he'd filled my cup with a fifth round of muddy coffee, he began giving me the hopeless looks one might offer a baby duck imprinting on the wrong mother. Suddenly I saw a movie montage of me spanning the next decade . . .

. . . sighing on the boisterous corner of Broadway and Astor . . . cursing under the awning of the Waverly Cinema . . . scowling in the drizzle outside of Veselka's Polish diner with some shitty little umbrella over me and Phillip, who looks annoyed, if rather dashing in a baby blue mac and matching hat. Me glancing at my watch-less wrist.

And waiting, always, for Camilla.

But as usual, I'm getting way ahead of myself.

So I sat there. Preparing, or rather, res*olv*ing to be heartbroken. Anticipation combusting into frenzy. Resentment swelling in my throat as the dusk gradually dyed The City. I remember thinking that it might have been like watching René Magritte paint his *Empire of Light* in accelerated frames. And how I'd tell Cammy all this when, or *if,* she ever decided to reappear.

I said a few anti-canker affirmations,* just in case. I stroked the Korean-deli orchid I'd bought her, which suddenly seemed, in light of her lateness, not only too pushy but downright pathetic. Then I pretended to read my copy of *White Noise* because, for one, the daylight was dying, and two, I couldn't con-

FOOTNOTE >

*I, of course, developed a cold sore (translation: *herpe*) on my upper lip, for which my New Age pharmacist, rather than suggesting medicine, sold me a book of Marianne Williamson affirmations. ("Re*lax* with it, accept it, don't give it so much power.") I ended up hiding it behind a little circular Band-Aid.

centrate. I mean, how could she *do* this? And did I really want someone this ruthless?

When I thought the coast was clear, I blew my breath against my palm and, although I couldn't actually smell anything, I ducked under the table like I was only sneaking a bump of blow, or tying a shoe. Where, under that starchy white canopy, I flossed with the spare container of Glide I always had handy. Back above table level, I tried to affect a *She'll-be-here-any-second-now* expression, which I don't think the few uber-hipsters under their parasols bought; I must have had that flammable look of the Guy Getting Stood Up, because they glanced not so much *at* me but over and *around* me, encircling me in a virtual tenderness so as not to embarrass me more. Basically, they were embarrassed *for* me.

(It can get, I'll have you know, however enviable the position, a bit taxing here at the Center of the Universe.*)

At a table next to me, alone and glancing incessantly at her wafer-thin watch, stubbing out one nervous cigarette after another, sat an aging model type. She had the clutching ethos of someone getting slowly edged out of her Beauty by a world it can no longer buy. I saw this a lot in these superchic bistros. I'd actually been feeling my own version of it lately. And so sensing, and *needing*, a kindred soul, I tried to reel the woman into a *fancy-that . . . us-both-getting-dissed* kind of smile. But she wouldn't bite. Instead, she glanced at the insensitive Time on her wrist as if it were a just-polished fingernail, then got out her compact and stabbed lipstick around her mouth in the swift weary stroke

FOOTNOTE >

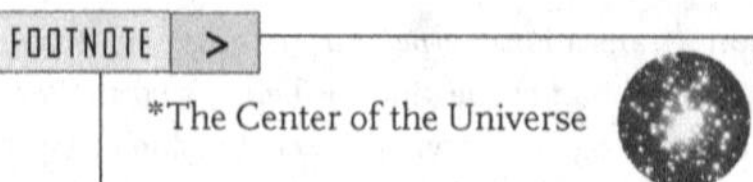

*The Center of the Universe

of a teacher circling her millionth misspelled *Connecticut*. Just when I'd caught her sneaking a look at me in the reflection, she stood up to greet a lean heir-apparent type approaching with irreproachable posture and an almost contrite, impossibly white, there-were-just-no-cabs-to-be-*had*-darling smile. As she whispered some forgiving thing into his ear, Ex Model used the moment to express to me, in a low-lidded scowl, how she was most certainly not in the same leaky Love Boat (or de-DiCaprioed *Titanic*) as I. She then gave me the final once-over, as if just to make completely sure I wasn't someone she should be nice to, and, satisfied with her initial suspicions about my value, she blinked me away like so much junk mail.

I told myself I'd give Cammy till forty-five after (a generous concession, I thought, compared to my standard half hour), and I managed to wait another seven seconds or so before I looked at the clock inside.

Seven fifty-six.

I didn't want to admit how upset I was. The twilight deepened a sudden, heartbreaking shade, as if God, suddenly bored with his dawdling dusk, had dimmed down his master switch one clumsy interval. At last, livid from another round of coffee and pitiful waiter glances, resisting a Lot's wife itch to look back at a no doubt victorious Ex Model, I closed my book without marking it. And in a caffeine huff, the orchid a damp, defused flare in my hand, I walked into the soft night. Without a plan. With a hummingbird's heart.

I just walked.

Cursing both Camilla and my idiocy for thinking she might've been different. Sneering at all the happy, handholding couples, who seemed like movie actors, mid-scene and camera rolling, their director whining . . .

***Show me love. I need more* love*, people!***

. . . through his bullhorn.

I almost offered one such couple the scorned orchid, as I twice circled the block, muttering Camilla curses from East Fourth to Broadway—then back to Great Jones, past Sheryl Crow's place and the fire station. Wondering why firemen are always so goddamn handsome.

Then, and you're going to hate me for this, I walked pathetically back and stood near Time Café.

*Near.*

Not right in front. Just to make sure she hadn't been sitting at another table or something. (Yeah, right.) I made sure, however, not to make eye contact with either Ex Model or my waiter.

And I was fuming. I could smell that alkaline fear sweat soaking my underarms. So I also made a mental note that if Camilla *did* show up (and Phillip's narcoleptic collision into a hydrant was about the only excuse I'd accept this late in our First Act), I'd keep my elbows at my sides, casually pretending I was just arriving as well.

*Oh, hey! Thank God you're running late too . . .*

. . . as I gave her cheeks double European kisses, then sat down to dine.

But when another twenty minutes of my squinting in the direction of any approaching female passed, I realized I was tearlessly crying . . . a dry-heaving sort of thing. I tossed the orchid atop an overflowing little trash can, picked it back out, threw it back in.

Then, recklessly rounding the corner of Bond Street, visually deleting her name from my Hotmail address book . . .

. . . I smashed into Camilla.

And Phillip. Whose leash coiled anticlimactically around me.

As I extricated myself, I instantly (and secretly) forgave these two. Mostly because, her lateness aside, Camilla Fell was a girl who knew a thing (or two) about getting ready for a first date. She was wearing a black, single-piece, body-hugging cat suit. The kind you might see on the artist formerly known as the Artist Formerly Known As Prince. In a hyphenated word, she was knee-buckling.

"Were you *leav*ing?" she asked me, innocently, and maybe even a bit accusingly, now that I think about it. With cruel understatement, arms glued to my sides,

I nodded.

Instead of saying she was sorry, Camilla seemed disappointed, impatient, like maybe I wasn't nearly as good-looking as she'd remembered. And to top all this off, it seemed that high-falutin Phillip was *snubb*ing me, the little stuffed shirt! As if he hadn't licked my face and other, more intimate areas on that (what I'd *thought* was a) fateful afternoon only thirty-six days ago. Apparently he had more pressing things to attend to, like the edifying, thirsty maple tree in front of Bond Street Café. Coy Phillip wasn't throwing me any eye contact to speak of. A lot, come to think of it, like his mistress. Who told me,

"I'm sorry," finally, a bit mechanically, as if she were excusing herself for a hiccup. But when I gave her my hard-boiled stare, I saw that her eyes held deep blue remorse.

Jesus.

The Eyes.

I'd forgotten (or *tried* to forget) just how final they were.

But,

"You're *sor*ry?" I said, trying to sound as pissed off as I'd been thirty-six seconds ago. "I'm leaving. I'm in a bad mood now. I wouldn't be any fun anyway."

"Please. Don't."

"We'll talk later. Maybe." Realizing her tardiness would steal focus from my abscess, I continued to pretend my boots were made for walking. (I was almost sure I was bluffing.)

"Wait. I'm sorry," she said, sounding awfully sorry. "Curtis."

Hearing my name in her mouth was manna, to muddle a metaphor, and it was at this moment that I suddenly saw, in one of those rare, clarifying flashes that align your world to where everything clicks, as when a magnet spins itself 180 degrees to kiss steel, that Camilla was the only truly honest person I had ever known.

"I mean," she said, batting long, demure lashes, "you knew I'd have to be late."*

To this day I'll swear Phillip nodded.

And then, sensing the distress in his mistress, he suddenly remembered who I was after all, prancing cordially forward to greet me.

But it was too late. I snubbed the snubber. Then plucked the disheartened orchid out of the brimming dustbin. I told Camilla

"I was pretty pissed"

by way of explanation, offering it to her as timidly as would a backstage fan to a post-matinee ingenue. She took it and, without even checking it for garbage slime, lodged it behind one lovely brown ear.

FOOTNOTE >

*So Camilla was breaking a capital rule by acknowledging that she was playing the romantic game. She was giving Irony, that unauthorized film biographer, the green light to comment on our Love Story . . . before the thing had even gone to edit. And without conferring with *me,* her costar . . . she was letting Irony watch the goddamn *dailies*!

"It was *cleave,*" she said.

"What?"

"The word. The only one with opposing meanings."

"Oh." I suppressed a smile.

We stood there. The usual sidewalk testosterone was beginning to accrete around her like cotton candy on a stick.

"Can't we cleave to*geth*er?" she said, half turning to the Time Café but looking back at me.

. . . Does Prince wear lifts?

# On the Nod

Peering over the gilt edge of her menu, Cammy offered me three more (muffled) apologies. But I realized her lateness had offered yet another element to our Love Story . . .

. . . *Con*flict.

"So why were you late?" I heard my jagged voice ask her.

"It really had nothing to do with my *Bovarism,*" she deflected, alluding to the stumper she'd thrown me in *Questionnaire.*

"Self-absorption?"

"Be more specific," she said, closing her menu . . . but I felt entitled to some facts, like

"What does your father do?"

The muscles along her jawline winked. She enmeshed two forks. "Anything he wants," she murmured.

"Oh. Um."

"He used to be a therapist."

"Okay then," I persisted. "Tell me about your girlhood. Was it happy?"

"Happy," she mused, as though she were trying the name out on a future child. "I guess–"

. . . Phillip was suddenly under the table, resuming his greedy woo of my shin with Elvis thrusts even deeper and more dedicated than on the first day, as if he were atoning for his earlier snubbing (or perhaps just making up for some precious lost hump time).

"You should be flattered," Cammy said, in a distant, bread-buttering way. "It's not just any old duffel bag he takes to like this." Her mouth tried and pretty much failed at a smile.

Great. I'd upset her, been too forward, as usual.

Mainly to dodge the moment, I again ducked under the table, as if to dislodge this dachshund, and although I have to admit that his rhythmic attentions were now almost lulling, I gave Phillip a firm gentle shove, then a beseeching stare, as if he could somehow convey where his mistress was drifting. To which he only glanced up, annoyed, his slender hips clenched as he tupped himself senseless.

I lifted my face just above the table and gave Camilla what I hoped was a helpless, Spencer Tracyish smirk.

"I missed you," she said.

"Really?" My throat got all lumpy. "I—"

"And I'm sorry." She pulled his leash. "Phillip thinks he's Mr. Clinton."

Despite the loud crowded night, ringing with sex and jealousy, a charged silence seemed to bulge between Camilla and me. The air had that fidgety, overly intimate quality among strangers cramped together on airplanes. As she kept rearranging her silverware, I saw that her fingers were bare but for one quiet diamond, smiling in the moonlight. . .

I'd learned long ago never to ask girls where they got their jewelry.

So I made myself ask her all the regular things that *Questionnaire* hadn't covered, like what she did for a living, hoping to God she wasn't going to tell me she was some actress—creating daily dramas meant to keep her chops up when she couldn't get work. But,

"I'm in PR," she said.

I gave The Wound some pensive pats. "Do you like it?"

"I do," she said, with pondering nods.

I nodded as well, flexing the brows.

I could tell she hated it.

A pause.

"Shaving," I answered, out of nowhere, my thumb on the Band-Aid.

She gave me several more helpful nods (we were doing a lot of nodding). Phillip leapt into her lap (the luckiest little man alive), where she back-folded his ears into a sleek new hairdo. I motioned to our thespian waiter for more water, and, refreshing my glass, he seemed relieved that I hadn't been abandoned after all, giving me a few maternal *at*ta-boy nods. (This nodding tends to be contagious.)

Inside the restaurant, Coltrane began braiding his wild flames of jazz. While inside my mouth, its tongue, that most ardent and clumsy of muscles, began a whispering chant of . . .

*Camilla, Camilla.*

God, I wanted to taste her.

From time to time I caught Ex Model reassessing me, my stock apparently having risen a few cool points now that I'd been endorsed by Camilla, at whom E.M. couldn't stop herself from staring with a weary, sterile longing.

Soon our waiter returned and wondered if "Madame" would care for some wine.

"Do you have Chardonnay?" Madame asked him, in that calm (but not peaceful) voice. "And water for him?" pointing to parched Phillip. Presently, two half-filled goblets arrived, of which Phillip got the virgin . . . while I turned my empty one over.

Camilla looked away in a way that I felt acknowledged everything I'd left unsaid.

During Caesar salads, she called herself a

"hopeless dork. I think we'll always consider ourselves how the popular kids treated us in high school."

I remember: "discovering" my Magritte observation, then stuttering away from the subject when I realized it was already dark; inserting a careful fork in my mouth to avoid the unmasking of Canker; how Camilla was allergic to half the nut-containing menu; that when she went to "the loo," Actory Waiter sang "Getting to Know You" at me . . .

I remember that I smiled non-committally.

Throughout dinner (she the seared swordfish, me the cheapest pasta), Phillip was at times the sullen teen, at times the crotchety codger. Taking fitful slobbering naps on my Nike, or sneaking off onto furtive little forays, from which he'd later resurface with his happy jaws locked around some grisly wet treasure, which Camilla would then extract while still nodding at my Date Talk.

After one such sortie, Phillip's eyes grew saucery, sliding back and forth à la vintage Alfalfa. Diners were standing up, napkins aloft, looking incensed (in an ultra-hip way).

Phillip had relieved himself on the patio . . . number two.

Camilla leapt up to snatch a groaning busboy's dust broom as disgruntled patrons, including Ex Model and continental companion, actually started leaving. I heard the word *complimentary* crooned several times from our stylishly starved hostess while, over a sweeping shoulder, Cammy asked, "Who did that?" a question whose rhetoric was not lost on Socratic Phillip, who then looked about him as if for corroboration, fairly shrugging his shoulders. "Don't play dumb," Cammy snorted.

"He won't be winning any Golden Globes this year," predicted Actory, grinding unwanted pepper on my penne.

"He's just jealous of you and he's doing it to piss me—as it were—off," she informed me,* gripping his scruffy chin as she shot him (what I assumed she assumed was) an ominous glare. Ham-it-up Phillip raised two slow, guilty eyes to his mistress, who told him, "Now, I don't want to do this," raising her hand into smack formation, under which Phillip cowered and squint-blinked . . . before making one last appeal to me.

I gave a hard nod.

"The waiting is worse," enlightened Actory, fists on his hips.

Wap!

Phillip yelped.

Hipsters applauded from under umbrellas, while Camilla told Phillip how sorry she was, cradling and cuddling him, kissing the spot she'd swatted.

"Mixed messages," clucked Actory, tying his apron.

But I was actually glad. This subplot was taking the pressure off our dialogue to be sparkling, and might make great *Remember when?* fodder later in our Love Story—assuming there'd *be* a later.

During crème brûlée I wondered, "What did that dog psychic tell your mom about him last time?"

"Phillip yearns for a baby blue sweater."

We glanced around for said fashion victim. We heard snoring. Which, we discovered, belonged to a derelict passed out among the green triangles of pine bush surrounding the candlelit hub-

FOOTNOTE >

*Wasn't Cammy's accusing Phillip of being jealous an admission that he had *grounds* to be?

bub. While nestled inside the crook of his swelled, infected arm was Phillip—also snoring (and perhaps playing a role in the unfortunate's own unconscious love story). But the seraphic couple was sundered when, tickled by Phillip's white whiskers, the bum awoke with a sneeze, his eyes round and yellow as no-hitter baseballs as he roared at Phillip, who looked back in terror as he trotted to our table.

"Gimme five dollars!" the vagabond commanded him, and then, smoothing back his Afro, casually asked if we

"happen(ed) to know the exact time?"

"Nine-twenty-seven," Cammy told him, then, sotto, "Why does he care? Does he have a conference call with Katzenberg and Ovitz?"

I giggled. Felt a little guilty. And saw that a handwritten cardboard

WiLL Fuck for Food

sign hung around his sooty neck. While Phillip, now in the clear, stretched himself out in a taunting posture, extending a front and hind leg as deftly as a little Baryshnikov . . . before he leapt onto the chair next to me. As if to discuss my intentions for his mistress, protean Phillip then sat back with his bandy legs flared, a father in his favorite La-Z-Boy. (I wanted to give him a pipe.) All this was just too much cuteness to bear, and I took him into my lap and rubbed his firm, toasty tummy.

Camilla was up to her adjust-the-cutlery routine again. And again that certain silence was rearing up inside the thrilled interval between us.

"What adjective," I asked, "best describes how you feel about me right now, at this moment, on our first date, ha, ha?" shielding my longing inside *Questionnaire*'s polished armor.

"Smitten."

People always say that Falling in Love lifts the heart, but it was my lungs that felt inflated. I realized how right the phrase *walking on air* was. I could barely sit still. I wanted to sing

*Oh, it's so nice to be with you*
*I love all the things you say and do.**

I wanted to rush into a bunch of SoHo boutiques and buy Cammy a bunch of tchotchkes. (While I secretly wondered what it was in me that she could possibly find smite-worthy.)

When a kneeling Actory gave me the check and a proud, conspiratorial eye roll, I half expected him to chuck me under the chin. I suppose my happiness was that palpable. Then I noticed Camilla staring at me with that strange blue drone in her eyes.

"Arf," I went, waving Phillip's front paw at her.†

And then the oddest thing: her left eye presented a single tear.

Frightened by the shrill and instant concern I felt for her, I said, "God, I'm sorry. What have I done?"

She circled her fingernail around the fallen drop on the tablecloth. "It's happened before."

"Was it me? Jesus, I'm always doing the wrong thing."

FOOTNOTE >

*I love this song. Gallery reached number four with it in the summer of '72.

†Caught in Camilla's nervous quiet, I stopped myself from making this stale joke: "The sound of silence, by Paw Simon and Arf Garfunkle."

"It's not you. I mean, well, it *is* you. This seems to happen—whenever I'm . . ."

"Whenever you're what?"

♥

We spoke a few shy parting words under a tawny, wise moon. There was some awkward eye contact, and we both said, "I'll call you," simultaneously, after which we both said, "Jinx."

I patted my sore, as if to explain why I wasn't trying to kiss her. I was actually relieved that I had an excuse not to Make the Move. But, because dogs are supposed to have those killer immune systems, I did bend down and plant one right onto Phillip's nose. Which was as wet, black, salty, and cold as a living hors d'oeuvre. He returned the gesture with deep and desperate French kisses as I hoisted him into the cab that Cammy had flagged. The backseat of which he immediately began to dig a hole through, much to the reluctant laughter of the mollusk-headed driver. I wondered what it was that dogs were getting at when they did that. I wondered in what deep blue forest of a dream I'd first heard her voice, which now wished me *Sweet dreams*.

I watched their cab wander into the wide, elegant din of Lafayette Street. Just as I was about to turn away, Camilla's head twisted back around. And as she looked at me through the dark shrinking rear window, the soft jewel of orchid aglow in her hair, she touched the glass.

This is that picture, *Empire of Light,* I was talking about.

# Would You Be My Girlfriend?



*Would you be my Girlfriend?*
*Would you be my girl*
*And we'll ignore the world*

*When you're my girl, friend*

*Would you be my world, friend*
*Won't you be my pearl*
*And we'll avoid the void*

*When I'm your boyfriend*

*Would you be my best friend?*
*Could you be my girl*
*Would you be my Girlfriend*

*(repeat and fade)*

# Killing Zoe

I scribbled that song in my notepad as I walked home that night. Because now there was a lovely new incentive for me to crack that bank safe of a business I'd been locked out of all these years, pressing my ear* to the ticking chambers of its black heart. Trying to cipher the secret to its successful entry. Only now I had a reason.

I had a Muse.

FOOTNOTE >

*Now totally tinnitic after a lifetime of playing loud music. Yet another nice little perk of the biz.

# In the Lamb White Days*

I couldn't believe she kept agreeing to go out with me.

Our fourth date filled the end of a long empty Sunday. Like a warm voice finally answering a ringing, ringing phone.

We met at Alonzo's, a swank old-school Italian place where the gloomy fawning owner let us bootleg little Phillip through the main room and into a secret cozy smoking den, from the days of Prohibition, within a glass gazebo. I think they only let us do this because of the business stolen by the early summer Hamptons set. Which left the weekend blank and tranquil but humming with abandoned magic, like Disney World after it closes.

We unwrapped our grumpy little contraband from Camilla's blue-jean jacket, then stuffed him under an ottoman. While outside, a slow purple dusk seeped into a courtyard of hanging laundry and thoughtful dogwoods. I was still (and always would be) fairly nervous around Camilla. She seemed fresher each time that I saw her. Sharper, more brilliant, as if she were being tweaked into focus by my growing affection.

*"Nothing I cared, in the lamb white days" is from Dylan Thomas's "Fern Hill," which was the reason I bought the fern that I'll show you in a minute.

We idled over a supper scattered with bitter salads, al dente starches, and little clouds of careful silence. Or actually, Camilla nibbled, while I tried not to gobble. And tried not to watch her. But we kept catching each other's glances. So I'd look off at a sad, unmatched wash-line sock in the breeze. Or drop damp sponges of focaccia onto a certain translucent tongue when it lolled out from under its hassock.

But it was impossible to keep my eyes off Cammy. And so she began returning my stares. Which grew longer, and braver. Until we played chicken, a visual footsie, with no sound but the nimble anxious racket of our cutlery.

It was all soap opera stuff. It was all wonderful.

I looked around at the few other couples, leaning into their stammering candles. They seemed to be conjuring spells, like when you'd pretend your spiritually unprompted hands moved over the Ouija board in high school. I watched them all play along. Fools. Because this wasn't the case with me, no . . . the falling need no pushing.

I'd barely been able to respond to the few things Camilla'd said during dinner. Like,

"Don't you hate it when people put an apostrophe in *CDs*?"

"*Christ,* yes!" I barked around a mouthful of fettuccine.

Or,

"When I was little, I thought all the songs you heard on the radio were performed live right there in the channel or, I mean, the station. So I imagined all the singers constantly rushing around the country to play their hits. It made the Jackson Five seem so unreal to me, like gods almost, that they could travel like that, so far and so fast."

"That," I told her, "just may be the cutest goddamn thing I've heard in my entire life."

I didn't tell her how it bothered me . . . how it diminished the aspiring Rock Star.

Not that I could've if I'd wanted to. Because I'd been dumbed down by Love.* As the candle wove its nervous embroidery on her skin, I just wanted to *kiss* her. Badly. As we'd yet to do this, or even to touch, save the usual glancing blows of early courtship skirmishes, those cramped *After-you-Alphonse* moments in doorjambs. We were still on our best behavior. Putting our best feet forward while trying not to step on each other's toes. Engaging in all that compliant nodding and hyperaccommodation you see in new waitresses. And when our own crabby one shoved us the check, Camilla'd insisted the dinner be dutch again. All at once I was pierced with a hideous and crystal thought; what if she was preparing to say the three most appalling words in the king's English?

***Let's Be* Friends.**

Great. Could I have misread all the signs, once again?

Whatever the case, I tossed a dejected (and borrowed) twenty onto the crumby table. We smuggled verboten Phillip back through the dim leather main room,† thanked our smiley glum owner, who bowed, and then confronted the twilight.

Now what?

As we walked along, somewhat woodenly, past Depression Modern, past Joe's Dairy, I was dreading Cammy's

*Well, I think I'll get a cab.*

But she was silent. I began to grow heavy with that same late-

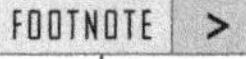


*Also the Great Equalizer.

†Which seemed fragrant with the *omertà* threats of Gotti's bored Mafiosi.

summer Sunday-night sadness I'd felt as a kid before beginning yet another new year at yet another new school . . . when suddenly, on the right, was **Saint Anthony's.**

I watched Camilla's face as we approached our Monument. And my sidelong suspicions were pretty much confirmed. Because her eyes, in all their strict beauty, would show me no sign. Would look only down. Where the asphalt twinkled sarcastically.

But Phillip huffed off and perched himself onto the very same second step he'd stood on that first day. Where now, windshield wiper tail on high, he seemed to be encouraging us with a

*Look, Ma, no hands!*

salute to the mastery of a task that had once seemed impossible.*

Cammy, however, didn't appear, or flatly refused, to notice all this. Until, after passing Il Bocconcino, Raffetto's, and L'Angolo, just as we came upon tour guide Phillip, her knuckles gently knocked mine . . . pulled away . . . then slid through my own in a trembling mesh.

For once in my life, I didn't feel the need to form a word. Just felt my pulse in her grasp, throbbing . . .

*Oh, God,*

as I led her to Thompson.

When we arrived at my building, I said,

"Hey! Here's where I *live,*" trying surprise.

We stopped. We awkwardly unwebbed ourselves.

"That's my fern," I pointed up at my window, as if purely for educational purposes.

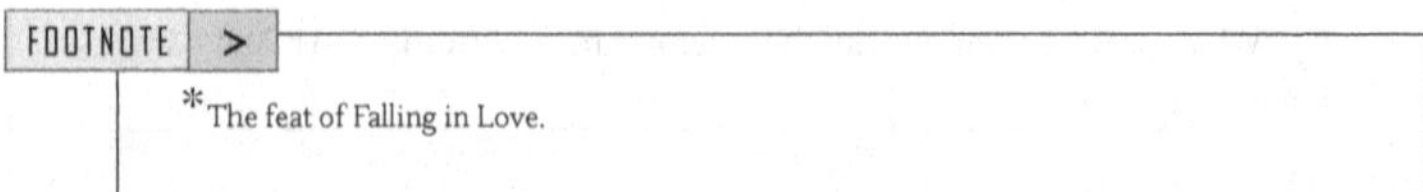


*The feat of Falling in Love.

"She looks a bit thirsty."

Through the last dregs of sunset, we stood there inspecting my plant, as if we might catch it trying to sneak in some photosynthesis. Camilla pointed at a timid sliver of moon. "It's two hundred and thirty-nine thousand miles above us," she explained. "Traveling in a car at sixty miles per hour, it would take us a hundred and sixty-five days to make the intersolar trip."

"Wow."

"Sarah Smile" wandered out of a distant radio.

I got up my courage and looked firm in her face. What did those precise, laughless eyes always seem to be deciding on? Did I even want to know? Maybe if I managed to capture their terrible light, her magic would fade, in the way that fireflies are only flies the morning after we've bottled them.

I exhaled. "So . . . Yeah." (Brilliant, Birnbaum.) "Well, um, again, I've had such a really wonder–"

"May I use your washroom?"

*Yes!*

"Sure," I said, V-ing my brows, as if mulling this over.

*Wash*room. I loved her. I scrounged for my keys, but,

"Actually," she said, rethinking . . .

"Really, please! I mean," I said softer, "it's fine."

After appearing to hold her breath, Camilla said, at last,

"Okay," decisively, as though, after every option had failed, she'd surrendered to some all-or-nothing course of chemotherapy.

And we walked into my Art Nouveau vestibule. Or rather, she walked and I floated. While, as if from above, I watched myself trotting eagerly to the elevator.

As we stood there, not looking at each other, I remember wanting to pull the fire alarm so that every one of my neighbors could see the goddess who was coming over to be with . . . *ME!* I must have pressed the already-lit UP↑ button five or six times. But as with elevators, Love, and all things that lift us away, we cannot speed their arrival by pushing.

My foot tapped out a 4/4 on the tiles.

"That's my mailbox," I pointed.

(Could she see it bulging with the threats of creditors?)*

"I bet that's where they put your mail."

"It is," I said. "Oh, I get it." And I laughed, dumb and hard.

Itchy silence.

From above, we heard the prehistoric screech of a baby pterodactyl. Then an electric sawish sound, which made Phillip's ears twist.

"Is someone building a coffin up there?" Cammy asked.

Phillip searched my face, then Cammy's, and made two piquey sounds that just fell short of being barks.

"I wonder if he has to poop," she said.

(How could she make this word sound so pretty?)

"You think?"

(Where was the goddamn elevator?)

"I must diagnose," she said, swiveling abruptly on a sandal with his leash behind her.

"Oh, okay, bye."

And they left. Great. I knew this couldn't last. Maybe I hadn't held her hand right. She'd probably felt calamity there. Of *course* she'd felt calamity there. And they'd no doubt rehearsed that little bowel number just to get out of scrapes like these. So

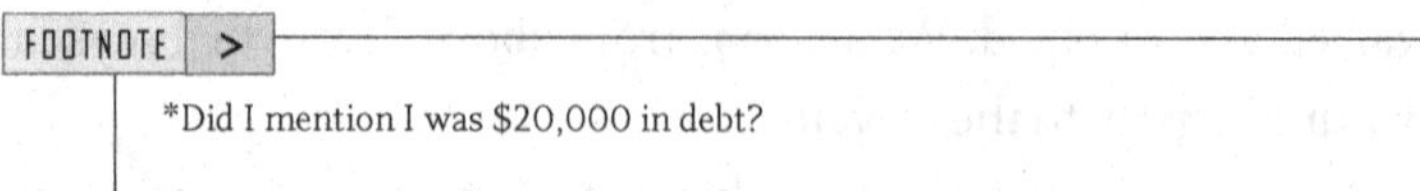


*Did I mention I was $20,000 in debt?

I'd never see them again. Perfect. Right now they were probably sprinting across Houston, glancing over their close-call shoulders. By morning her number'd be changed. My e-mails all blocked.

*Relax! She **likes** you (for some reason).*

The elevator opened.

If they *were* coming back, was I supposed to wait here for them? I didn't want her to think I was *guard*ing her. But I didn't want her to think I was rude, either.

The elevator started doddering shut, so I pried an arm in, looking back to see if they were coming, but the rubber door was gumming my elbow, so I wrestled my way inside.

I immediately began to clean my apartment.

Did it smell? I couldn't tell. Other than the roach guy, I hadn't had a visitor in, God, over six months, I guessed. So I lit these honeysuckle votives I'd stolen from a Christie's catering job,* which I'd been waiting forever to show off, then distributed them semistrategically around my living room. I shoved my favorite *Hustler* and my little notebook full of (mainly new, Camilla-centric) lyrics and doodles under my mattress. Paced (or tried to walk away from myself). Nibbled a frayed thumb cuticle into a wound. Turned my *Norton Anthology* to the Keats section, bled onto his "Grecian Urn," and thought, *Oh, how Romantic* as I displayed it on my coffee table. Turned my ringer off. Turned my dingy green fitted sheet over (because it was my only). Threw out the seven or six scattered scraps of paper I'd written Camilla's number on (safeties). Damp-wiped under the cush-

FOOTNOTE >

*And for which I'd been fired, which I'll get into later.

ions of the chocolate-Lab-brown faux-leather sofa on which I'd spent so many dawns Hoovering pricey fauxcaine. Sat down and crossed my legs. Sucked a bloody thumb. Remembered why the habit had been such a bitch to quit.* Recrossed my legs. Clasped my hands over my top knee and practiced a calm, nodding chat to the invisible Camilla beside me.

Paced.

Opened a window and leaned into the vacant lazy night to see if they were coming, then yanked myself back inside so they wouldn't catch me perched and waiting above them.

Then I went and stood in front of my bathroom mirror, where I washed my clotting thumb, flossed, Sonicared, and with a Murray's pomaded palm, smeared a cowlick over my balding spot. I realized I was sucking my sunken cheeks into that Bon Jovi sulk. I wished I'd earned the right to be vain. And I promised myself not to lie to Camilla, even whitely, *ever*.

Then she buzzed.

I dove at the intercom. Pressed the downstairs door button for at least thirty seconds.

As it buzzed through the building, floating up from outside and into my window, I improved some poor posture and made what I hoped was a jaunty, disarming smile at my mirror. Which I tried to keep on my face as I opened the door, where in front of me was . . .

FOOTNOTE >

*Sounds like a Keith Richard solo record. Actually, I'd sucked my thumb, but only when I slept, until I was thirteen, at camp, when I awoke to find my entire cabin laughing at me with the lights on. It was a real winner. My bunkmate, Sean Mahoney, the house bed wetter, would be forever indebted to me for stealing his unwanted thunder (or rather rain).

. . . nothing.

Except the anemic buzz and flicker of the ceiling's light fixture.

I sniffed. Smelled some kind of carnival food. Then looked down to find a tiny, misdirected Ecuadorian delivery boy.

"Wrong apartment," I sighed, actually gnawing my lip so I wouldn't scream at him. But he made a meek smile. And kept standing there.

"I just *ate,*" I told him, cranking the virtual fork in front of my face.

"*Sí,*" he said with enthusiasm.

"No, no. I'm *not* hungry."

"Jess, *mucho*!" his wide-open face understanding the last word.

And he was sweet. I saw how happy it made him just to connect, to be human and smiling. How the global white gesture disarmed me of questions in a language he had no means of mastering. So I figured I'd just pay him the $12.55 for the plastic bag of mystery food, handing him what I realized was a $26 tip only after he'd stepped back into the elevator. Which Camilla and Phillip stepped out of.

"Thank you, seeer!" his eyes wide on my money, the bright grin increasing.

"Sure," I said, clenching a smile, waving weakly to Cammy (she was actually going to come in*side*!) and Phillip, who then began snorting the delivery boy's groin, causing him dainty giggles, until Cammy said,

"No sir!" tugging the leash as the elevator closed and descended.

The three of us stood there for several tense and fluorescent seconds . . .

Until the spell was broken by the distant elevator's *Time's-up!* ping.

"How'd you guys get in?" I asked nonchalantly, my free arm draped from the top of the doorway in your basic Stanley Kowalski configuration.

"We heard the buzzer buzzing from the corner." She wrinkled her face at the bulging bag as she came to me.

"I got sort of a second wind." I patted my stomach, swinging the sack. "While you two were out, I figured I'd get in a good purge."

She made a wise *Ha*.

"Actually, well, it's a long story," I said.

Phillip took a few clever steps at me, performed a Walter Payton left/right juke, grabbed a mouthful of plastic, and squirmed though my knees and my door.

"No!" Cammy yelled, peering tiptoe and wistfully over my shoulder.

I looked back over it as well, where I saw Phillip in my living room, attempting to dig and chew through the bag (which was actually very cute). I was surprised at how unworried I was when I realized, from Camilla's taut pout, that her impeccable manners were preventing her from walking inside to prevent Phillip's mess.

"Oh, God, come *in*. *I'm* sorry," I said, stepping aside as she plowed immediately past me. I closed my eyes and breathed her calm cloudy scent, then opened them to see her shimmy from her knapsack (which I tried to help her out of), arching her back so she made a quivery shelf of her breasts before running over to Phillip just after he'd emptied a sopping hill of chili dogs onto my carpet. Which had been the shade of tofu.

"Oh, God, Curtis, I'm really sorry," she yelled, spanking his rump away from the coppery mound.

"Oh, well," I murmured, loving my name in her voice. "It's

fine. I'll just clean it up later." I walked to my bed, from which a jiggling, wagging Phillip was surveying the dog pile. "Or maybe just let him lick it off the rug," I proposed dreamily, petting his panting head. "Do you want something to drink?"

"Water, please?"

And I wasn't just being polite. As I turned on the kitchen sink's Aquapure filter, I found that I really couldn't have cared less about the mess he'd made. That I was just so happy to have these two vivid creatures blooming through the lackluster fact of my life.

Handing her the water, I also noticed that my Studio 54 track lighting was stadium bright, but I realized that dimming would look totally ridiculous while Cammy was cleaning. So,

"What would you like to listen to?" I asked, pointing at something you might call a *hi-fi* (if you were my father).

She sipped the water, her left hand still scouring. "Can we listen to that French Jeff Buckley bootleg you mentioned?"

"*Oui, Oui,*" I said, pronouncing *oui* "way."

"Any more paper towels?" she said, half a song deeper, still intent on the fading bronze stain, which was still the size of a laser disc and which still didn't bother me enough.

"Please, really, forget it," I told her from the sofa.

"May I take off my shoes?" she said, taking off her shoes.

"Sure, yeah, plea–," I tried to tell her, against three rapid sneezes, a messy little hat trick that used to happen when I'd become very aroused. Which Phillip, his eyes filmed over in food trance on the couch, roused himself to answer with a trio of barks.

"Bless you, sweetie," her last word bashful.

*Sweetie!*

I felt warm. I felt brave. I wanted to lick her feet.

"I'm a little chilly too," she told the rug.

"Oh, no. Um, do you think you want a sweatshirt or a coat or something? Long johns? Socks? I think I have space heater."

"Maybe a sweater?"

And I wanted to knit her one, to cuddle her up in quilts and pillows and play hooky from the world forever as, from my closet, I handed her my favorite old gray turtleneck. And while I watched it assume all her lovely curves and scents, I hoped that this was a very good sign. That this swapping of selves, this blurring of barriers and living in the other one's skin, would be the first of many. I then very gradually dimmed down the lights on the wall switch behind me, bracing myself for a *What's-the-big-idea?* look from either or both of them. But just then Phillip, as if prompted by darkness, snuck over and sniffed my speaker, glanced at me, then his mistress, and hoisted a nervous leg until she said,

"Don't even think about it, Pigpen! I'm really sorry about all this. I'll buy you a new rug."

I gave her an *I-wouldn't-have-it* scowl. And we watched sated Phillip slip under my bed.

A pause.

"Thanks for being so sweet about him," she said, shaking her head.

"I love him," I said, for the Word was all in me.

For a long hot second, Camilla gazed up at me. She patted the cushion beside her, twice . . . but then she looked down, drumming her fingers, as if the whole thing might've been a fidget. I chose the ambitious interpretation, then came over and sat down a Phillip's breadth away from her.

I tried to listen to Buckley. Blood rang in my ears. My cocaine heart was wheezing away.

"Did you know it's actually pronounced 'flak•sid'?" she said suddenly.

"*To*tally," I yelled, as if we'd just solved an Escher print, but the force of my *T* had blown out a votive on the coffee table in front of us, which I then relit and moved so it glowed over "Grecian Urn," hoping she'd notice.*

"I love the smell of honeysuckle," she said. "It reminds me of Benjy Compson."

"Caddy, Caddy," I mumbled.

We stared straight ahead. "Lilac Wine" ended, and there came that intolerant silence that I knew I should fill with a first kiss. I chickened out, grabbed my guitar, and began to pluck out the intro to "Grace," which came on next. Phillip, who'd apparently been watching all of this from under my bed, barged over and held a fragrant paw over my strings, looking over at Camilla before giving me a *Kiss-her-you-fool!* glare.

And I was a fool.

"Are you showing him a new chord, Phillip?" Cammy coolly asked him.

"Oh, come here, you little monkey," I dragged him into my lap and behind the guitar, my two-ply protection. Back on the old sublimation train, I kissed the small bumpy bone nugget on the top of his head, took his left hand in mine, smelled it, then held it to the fret board while I strummed with his other. Diversion

FOOTNOTE >

*She told me later that she had, of course, noticed, but that she was still embarrassed at getting the quote wrong on our First Day.

Phillip only looked back at me with an *I'm-really-not-amused* smirk before he squirmed out of my lap.

I stopped the shenanigans.

And so, as if falling through blue sky and cloud, I at last began my initial descent into Camilla. Edging toward her, making sticky Pleather groans. Until I smelled gentle milky things.

What if I tried to kiss her and she drew back in astonished laughter? What if our mouths didn't work together? I looked at hers then. Impossible, I thought. I could see by the way it sipped her water how thirsty for me she was.

Or *was* she?

She looked down at her glass, circling its rim with a pensive brown finger, which caused a slippery chime that dissolved into candlelight and Buckley. (And caused the wolf deep in Phillip to moan from my bed.) I lifted my hand to her face . . .

. . . and she got up!

Christ.

And went to the windowsill. Stood over its glowing row of votives, gazing out into the blurry neon tangle of Bleecker Street. From her glass, she spilled a careful inch of water into Fern, touching her leaves. Healing.* I got up and slowly moved to her, because, I felt, some bend of her invited me. She placed her glass on the ledge and a barrette in her teeth as she did up her hair in that gesture so rapt with all the things that men must never know. I glimpsed the tender flesh under her skinny raised arms, and my God, I was weak as I fell into her force field and that beautiful stupid tension.

FOOTNOTE >

*And the next day, I swear, Fern actually looked greener.

---

*Maybe I'm too young to keep good love from going wrong.*

She pulled something from her backpack and slipped it into her water glass—a crimson peony, still plump and unflowered.

"It's almost disturbing how soft this is," she said, turning to me.

I touched the peony, pretending it was my focus.

"Soft," I agreed. "Did you get that for me when you were out just now?"

"I might've." She kept her eyes on the closed velvet fist. "It looks so secretive."*

"I love the way you put things."

A pause.

"Why are you so nice to me?" I thought out loud.

She peeled off a petal. "Close your eyes."

And I did.

Feeling silly for a only a second, then just giddy and nude as she pulled the petal over my palm, making me imagine the little red tab unraveling my cellophane skin as she brushed the thing slow along that eager pulse of wrist where the razor knows best. I peeked very quickly as she whispered it over the embossed branch of vein along the crook of my arm, dragged it up to my neck, where I giggled till she slid it onto my forehead, falling over my lashes, down the bridge of my nose, till it stopped . . .

. . . on my mouth . . .

. . . I felt the cool feather of flesh. I parted my lips.

FOOTNOTE >

*She told me later that she knew Phillip didn't need to go but that she wanted to get me the flower, and that's what took her so long.

And then . . . it was gone.

I stood there. And yearned . . .

And then the petal was back—and it was her mouth.

Our first kiss, as I've discovered of all unmerciful things (hunger, addiction, Death), was irresistibly simple. But it also held thc healing symmetry of a kids' game of catch. A welcomed aphasia. That opiate earned when the self is forgotten. I realized, as we carved that oblivion out of the hope and regret between us, that, despite all the kissing clichés, this was really the language we should've been uttering all along. That the rest was all hearsay, a noisy corruption of the immaculate stuff humming between us. We were effortless together. Twinned. Every tease and bite seemed a foregone conclusion. We knew just what to do. At one point, Cammy laughed, airily, into my mouth. And I think, I thought, I knew just what she meant.

We fit.

It seemed like we'd been necking for fifteen or twenty minutes. But when I heard the faint preparatory flexing of my answering machine, which then began screening my dad's skittish

"ARE YOU THERE?" . . .

I learned from his lonely

"IT'S ELEVEN-FIFTEEN" . . .

. . . that we'd actually been at it for almost two hours. In a blissed daze, I looked around the room, hushed in blue moonlight. All the votives had died. Buckley had long ago given up serenading us, and my father's agile voice had undone the moment.

We stood back from each other, looking down at the shy hands we were just barely holding . . . nearly strangers again.

In the past, I'd noticed that a third, digital presence like this (my father) could actually lessen the tension. That an invasive phone call was just the thing to break the ice, the gate crasher who strengthens the insiders' alliance, imparting a sense of putting one over on the odd man out. But Camilla and I hadn't found this ease, and as my father's voice reached in to touch aboriginal things in me, I felt him pulling me away from her.

"IT'S YOUR RENAISSANCE MOM," his voice bright with new joke. "I'M LIKE THOSE MEDICI MOTHERS WHO WENT AROUND POISONING EVERYBODY FOR THEIR SONS' SUCCESS," with mock desperation. "I JUST WANT YOU TO BE HAPPY, CURTIS. ANY NEWS ON THE RECORD DEAL?"

"Excuse me," I told her, and tried not to run to the phone.

"Dad, I'm picking up," then softer . . . "Hey, it's not a good time. Can I call you back?" (My dad was now inaudible to her and Phillip.) "Because somebody's here," I whispered, glancing back at Cammy, who was looking out the window, rocking Phillip like she was burping a baby. "Yeah, Dad, my girlfriend."

Yep. It just came out. I felt my cheeks burn in the dark.

"Sorry, Dad. Tomorrow," and I hung up the phone.

"I hear a lot of you in his voice," she said as I came up behind her.

She turned to me.

"And you called me your girlfriend."

# A Rite of Passage Passage

*Girlfriend.*

It was like when the waitress had first called me *sir.* On that windless summer road trip I took with my father. In the first muddy wake of divorce. About a thousand years ago.

Amid distant mirages wiggling above the high-noon highway, we saw the bird-shot, green-on-white wooden

**PADUCAH, KENTUCKY**
(FIRST, LAST AND ONLY EXIT!)

sign and, both of us clenched for a rest room, swerved into a park whose shady marble table we'd spread Velveeta sandwiches and my birthday-present chess set across. Which, one careless and two precocious moves later, would be dappled crimson from the small leaking nose which my father had struck in the half second after its owner had for the first (and last) time checkmated him.*

I remember him walking on the parking lot's squishy tar next to me, beside himself with guilt over his misplaced rage, the

FOOTNOTE >

*We never played again.

messy chessboard under one penitent arm while the other one hugged my stunned bony shoulders.

And he was raw in my ear with,

"I'm sorry, God, I'm so sorry, Curtis, I just lost it, are you okay? Keep your head tilted back, yeah, like *that,* okay, hon? We'll go into that Denny's for some ice,"

As we hurried along, I was watching the fine white zipper a tiny jet was sealing the sky with, thinking,

Fly . . .

Fly . . .

"You know I love you, don't you? Well . . . don't you?"

"Yes, Dad."

"Well, Curtis, I really hope you do, because I really do love you, and I just lost my temper. I'm so sorry, it will never happen again. I think it's that maybe sometimes I look at your face and I see your goddamn cunt mother or something, ha. Okay?"

"It's okay," and I was thinking it had to be, embarrassed at the way his voice wobbled as I swallowed a chalky red gulp and we rushed through the heat.

"We're almost there, so just keep your head tilted back until we . . ."

. . . came into the slam of Denny's air-conditioning, where, as I looked up at a brown shoreline of water damage, I heard heads turn and gossip soften, and the scrape of a fork on porcelain. And then the woman's tuneful twang that enchanted me, only eight years old that yesterday, into a pleasant new perception of myself . . .

. . . *Sir.*

"Smoking or non? . . . Oh, Lordy, hold tight and let me get you a Kleenex, sir. Cecil, can you get him a Kleenex?"

"Ha. He just gets them sometimes," my father told her.

"I got one at home does too. But I 'spect hers's for another reason. Now hold your head back, sir, and keep applying pressure . . ."

with my right hand, while I noticed my left was still a fist around the little wooden king.

I've found it's often another's voice that explains some essential change inside us.

And just as that waitress had neatly soothed the wound of that day with her little Band-Aid labeled

*Sir,*

actually hearing Camilla say

*Girlfriend*

should have healed all those painful weeks of wondering how she felt about us.

But somehow the word didn't fit.

And so, like that crooked day with my dad, my Camilla-memories are always mixed. At once happy and wistful . . . but never entire.

# When We Were Good

Here's a typical early e-mail between Camilla and me.

ME: I mean, it's like you're from another planet.

CAM: I'll try not to be from another planet tonight.

ME: No, no, I *like* the other planet thing.

CAM: But what if you discover I'm only an ordinary girl?

ME: But you're not.

CAM: Yes, I am.

ME: Only in e-mails. I feel like you're way more communicative in e-mails. You're much more mysterious in person.

CAM: I don't think I like that. I feel like you'll eventually decode me and run away, my little darling. I mean, INXS didn't write a song called "Demystify Me."

ME: Never! But I also feel like I'll never really get to know you.

CAM: I hope not.

ME: Mmm?

CAM: Mmm.

ME: I'm sorry I was such a bummer the other night. Sometimes this music business gets me down, and I don't want to drag you through my moods and ruin things with you.

CAM: Don't think I can't handle some sadness, too. You're not going to ruin things unless you want to.

ME: So you still like me?

CAM: Stop it.

ME: *Do* you?

CAM: More than I care to admit.

ME: When did you actually *start* to?

CAM: Here we go again.

ME: I forget the details.

CAM: That's a paradox.

ME: Come on. *Please,* Cammy. This'll be the last time, I swear.

CAM: All right.

**You had my complete interest and attention from the moment you approached me.***

ME: I really did?

CAM: Yes! You were so cute and nervous.

ME: Okay. Now say the other thing.

CAM: Curtis! I'm at work.

ME: Please. Oh tiniest of the Tinies?!†

CAM: Jeeeeez. Okay.

**I knew it was a sign because it rained like a vengeance after you walked off.**

FOOTNOTE 

*Now. She actually bolded the font like this. Emphasizing, *I* felt, the historical importance of the Event. Or maybe this was only the spry hand of Irony using chiaroscuro to foreshadow the early mirages that in the final act can leave Love so blind?

†This was that critical chapter in a Love Story when you see if the other person's willing to do pet names, thereby hermetically sealing the narrative inside your own exclusive world of words. Sorry for all the pedantry. Back to the story.

ME: I've got goosepimples. I'm so nuts for you. When I'm drowning in you, and not myself, I can make myself believe the universe might just be smeared with something dewy like God.

CAM: I have a hard time with the god thing.

ME: Me too, actually. I was just trying to be all Gatsby.

CAM: Or Pynchon. I can't wait to fool around with you later. I feel very lucky to see you walk around naked, my little porn star.

# The Art of Living

Trips had often been deal breakers for me.

What I mean is, when I'd suddenly seen a traveling companion out of her depth and adrift in the sharky waters of foreign accents, cars, and customs, more often than not I'd discovered it was equal parts person and context that had distilled the particular potion I'd (once again) mistaken for Love. And so, dubbed into an alien tongue, that certain girl's song seemed to lose all its charm, no longer rhyme, to sound tin in my ear.

But Cammy, as they say of classic cinema, *traveled.*

And this, I see now, was because I'd not so much *met* Camilla Fell as discovered her within me. Because those blue eyes of hers, or their alias,* had been mounted somehow inside of my head. And in such an unshakable way that, like dream and memory, they resisted all conditions. Camilla, to me, was timeless and placeless. Even now it's not like I have to call her to mind exactly. But more to access her image, confess up her genie, which seems to have been looming inside me like a Princess Leia hologram all along.

We'd decided to take advantage of the outrageously low Euro-

FOOTNOTE >

*I mean like a computer-icon alias.

pean airfares and spend a weekend in Paris. This, I think both of us knew, would wordlessly and surely force an issue. (I see now that it was perhaps a good part of the reason why we went . . .)

. . . because Cammy and I had waited, on purpose, by unspoken pact, to make love. All through that cool ecstatic spring and into a muggy summer whose every other day seemed to break some sort of heat record, we'd lain naked in candlelight, exploring, revealing, but in the end always skirting the deep blissful issue. Until slowly, without hurry, we'd at last arrived at an expectant pause, like that which falls between songs on a favorite CD.

I didn't tell her I'd maxed out my MasterCard for the tickets; that I'd purchased hers with my Frequent Flier miles; or that, in exchange for five vocal lessons, the mother of a Dalton kid I taught up on Sutton Place lent me the brass, clumsy-quaint keys to their Place Saint-Michel atelier. Instead, I told Cammy it was the place of a friend. Which was, I know, only a yellow lie. But one that bent the vow I'd made a little while ago . . . and for which, as you'll see, I paid miserably.

A certain dachshund with abandonment issues had nearly made us miss our flight. But a frantic last-minute search found his mother's missing tooth-marked passport at the bottom of her hamper. And then, after we'd deposited him at the Gramercy walk-up of Camilla's best friend, Emily, orphan Phillip performed a slow-blinking guilt trip from her landing, up to which Cammy had then climbed the four flights bearing breathless bon voyage kisses, after I'd almost had her out the front door, twice.

Cammy and her eyelashes managed to convince the gentleman at check-in to reopen the Delta jet where the slow grouchy boarding line stalled us in the first-class section. Leaving us to stand in that moment when those *Medallion* members already seated behind expensive smiles and little *Preferred Passenger* cookies might still think we weren't headed for the lumpen Economy section. As I stood there, trying not (very successfully) to nuzzlekiss Camilla's neck, gig bag on my back while affecting my best *Mysterious and Rich Musician* pose, I noticed that Bob Liebenthal–former president of the Cornell fraternity he'd "asked" me to deactivate from, and now (I recalled a rumor) chief executive of some nebulous moneymaking machine–was a first-class passenger.

We loathed each other.

Liebo had the dark unctuous good looks of a young Tony Curtis, circa *Spartacus*. And was wearing a smart olive Agnes B. sharkskin suit, in which he was explaining something about his Apple Titanium laptop to a fortyish flight attendant. Her hair was fried chemical white, and she leaned in very close to him, all raised eyebrows, nods, and smiles. I immediately reached for the cheap Astor Place sunglasses I felt hiding my hairline, found only their ghost, and, glancing at Liebo, who looked crisp and effective as a new-minted fifty, I grabbed Cammy's hand and ducked into a forward charge.

"Sweetie, slow down!" she said, as I knocked us into a Hasid securing his multilocked briefcase* into the compartment above him.

FOOTNOTE >

*Diamonds are a Goy's best friend.

"Sorry," I told her, then him, smelling a damp asparagusy odor, *peyes* grazing our heads as I navigated around his potbelly. All the women snuck looks at Cammy, then double-took on me in their struggle to work out the odd aesthetic equation. This made me happy and sad, which, I was realizing, had become my prevailing mix of emotions around Camilla. And, I reminded myself, a fifty percent upgrade.

Just as we'd completed our walk of shame and made it safely back to coach,

Liebenthal quacked,

"Spermbaum!"

*Christ.*

"Here's our seats, Cam." I kissed her wrist. "Twenty-seven D and E."

"Cutie," she said, with soft caution, "I think someone's calling you."

"Really?" I said vaguely, stowing my guitar and relieving Cammy of her carry-on.

As was her way, she didn't pry. And we sat down.

Or rather, *I* did, because in Camilla's seat was a messy little person in a faded Jars of Clay* shirt.

"Excuse me," I told him, "I think this is our seat."

"Really?" He squinted up from his ticket to the seat number above him. "No," he said sweetly, "I think I'm in E."

There was something so luckless about him. So completely kaput. Of course I liked him immediately.

He was somewhere between seventeen and thirty, with the

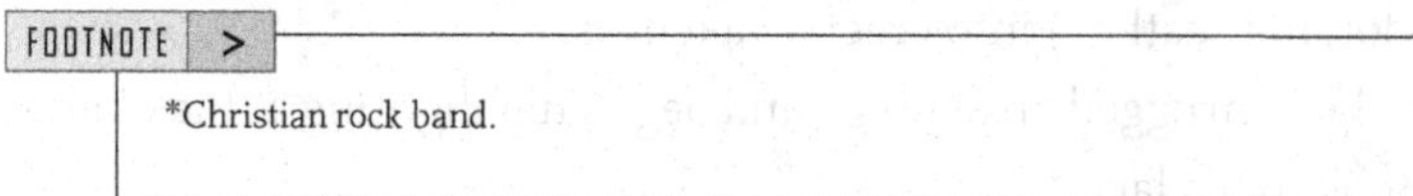


*Christian rock band.

rumpled appeal of a mini Danny Bonaduce, his right wrist a festoon of happy-colored strings.

I stood up in the aisle to inspect the seating situation, blocking the testy traffic behind us.

"Please take your seats," the peroxided stewardess snapped, stabbing me in the kidney–

"Oww!"

–with the corner of a drink dolly.

"*Excuse* me," she mumbled, stepping into the kitchenette beside us.

I looked back at about twenty impatient, craning faces. Cammy and I leaned out of the aisle to let everyone pass, while Jars of Clay peered up at my guitar with interest. Camilla said,

"Miss, actually, maybe you can help us. I think we might have the wrong seats."

Peroxide slammed shut an overhead cupboard, loudly, avoiding Cammy's winced eyes, then examined the three tickets that Jars, Cammy, and I were holding out in front of her in paper-rock-scissors formation. I watched her eyes amble over our ring fingers, Cammy made a moron face just behind Peroxide's, and I noticed that, under camouflage of powder, there was a hickey on the slack, hennish flesh of her neck.

"The seating is correct," she determined. "When you redeem Sky Mileage for multiple flights, Delta can't guarantee you adjacent seating unless you request it. Which you didn't. It says so on your ticket." She gave us a lipsticky smile, then pressed a button on the seat next to her, which jerked a snoring old Indian woman (dot, not feather) into erect awakeness.

Jars shrugged an apology and began highlighting a thick black Book in his lap.

"I'm so sorry about all this, sweetie," I said.

"It's not exactly your fault."

I was a little taken aback by her "exactly." We watched the last of the line pass.

Which was Bob Liebenthal.

"Are you a rock star yet, Birnbaum?" He extended his hand to me, his eyes to Camilla. Who began looking out the little round window at the earmuffed and baton-wielding workers on the tarmac.

Liebenthal worked my palm, assessing, grinning.

"Nice sideburns, Birnbaum," touching the left one. "How's the music biz?"

"I'm about to do a demo," I mumbled, pulling my face away, looking over at Cammy, whose cheeks, in the window light, clouded just perceptibly.

"That so? You should let me give it a listen. If you're not still pissed at me. I have some short friends in high places."

"Mmm."

A lull. The good-natured ding of the *Fasten Seat Belts* sign.

"So where are you headed?" he said.

"Paris."

"*Moi aussi.* But first I'm in Nîmes for an awards thing."

He let this one hang. Quick glance at Cammy behind me in the dust-moted cone of window light, then back to me with . . .

"If you're nice to me, maybe I'll let you crash at my condo on Ile Saint-Louis for the weekend."

"Thanks, we have a place."

"Where?"

"Place Saint-Michel."

"Oh. Very swank. Yours?"

"Sort of." I snuck a look at Cammy.

" '*Sort* of' . . . Gotcha. So what's doing with you, Turdis?" (My frat name.) His teeth blazed at Camilla.

"Actually, we have kind of a seating mix-up," I said, glad to talk of the neutral, reaching back for Cammy's hand.

"I guess I'm in Twenty-seven F," she said, looking from her ticket to an empty seat amidst a pillow-fighting row of teenagers.

"*The Bad News Bears Do Europe,*" said Leibo, as a befreckled girl got pinned and noogied by a fat laughing boy. "Hey, you can sit up front with me if you'd like," he said, to Camilla! "I always buy an extra seat for my PowerBook. That is, if it's jake with Turdbaum here."

She squeezed my hand—would not look at Liebo. I gave him my *that's-very-impressive-but-there's-no-way-in-hell-you'll-ever-sleep-with-her* smirk.

"We met at Cornell," he attempted. "I don't believe I've had the plea—"

"Please take your seat, sir," Perox said behind him, half-coyly, and just in time.

"Okay," he said, perusing his wallet 'til she walked away. "Here's my card with my cell number," which he shoved down my breast pocket. "Think it over," he said, more to Camilla. "I'll see you in the next time zone, Chief." (I was *Chief.*) And walked back to first class.

Cammy and I stood there an awful minute in the back of that plane, in the septic wake of its lavatory, while the captain told us his trusty name in his crusty voice through a crackly speaker. Camilla was looking away from me, batting languid, dark lashes, which always sent me, and

"Oh, Cammy," I said. "I'm so sorry about all this. Are you pissed?"

"Not at all."

It was a big fat lie.

"You can go sit with Liebo if you really want to," I tested her. "He's handsome, huh?"

"He's a tool." She fingered a sample life vest on the wall. "The last person I heard call somebody *Chief* was what's-his-name, Maurice, the elevator operator guy, to Holden."

And I was thinking . . .

. . . *This goddamn girl is perfect!*

as Camilla's pewter blue eyes slid back and forth from my own left, to my right, as if fitting me for contacts. "I'm not mad," she murmured, softly biting my ear. "I just wanted to snuggle with my cutie over the big pond, is all." (And I remember thinking this would end up as a *Best of Camilla* moment, which it did, and which I've been replaying in my mind on Heavy Rotation ever since.)

I've discovered that one couple's contentment is often a single person's nausea. And, standing downwind of all our revolting baby talk, Peroxide suddenly stomped up behind us, yowling,

"All passengers, please take your seats, fasten your seat belts, and return all trays and seatbacks to their upright positions . . ."

. . . right into my ear, which I jammed a finger in until she left us. We looked over at the antic youngsters.

"*I'll* sit there," I said.

"No, really, I–"

"Don't even try it." I noticed they all had on the same braided bracelets as Jars. Who said,

"No, *I'll* switch with you," standing up and smiling. "My manners must be seriously out to lunch."

He was no more than five foot.

"Are you sure?" we sang in stereo.

"*Tot*ally. I know them. We're all in CONNY," he waved his Book at the rioting teens. "The Church of the Now or Never Young. My Earth Name is Rip, by the way. I can't tell you my CONNY Nomino."

We introduced ourselves, Cammy bending to shake his tiny hand with deep, noncondescending nods. "You're the guys chanting in Tompkins Square Park every Saturday," she recalled, adding,

"with bongos,"

as if to musically validate it.

"That's us," he said, with a Barney Fife* sniff.

She angled her head at little Rip in a friendly way I hadn't yet seen in her catalogue of gestures (and I remember hoping I would never stop learning her).

The eyes of Peroxide glared at us over the oxygen mask she was now doing her little safety dance in. So me and Cammy sat down as Rip looked at the open luggage compartment above him, then made a touching little upward jump, at which Camilla tsked and said,

"Oohh!"

just under her breath. I leapt up to help him.

"That one, please," he pointed at a battered black briefcase. I had the sudden fear that Rip was going to ask me to transport it for him across customs, but after I handed him his attaché, he issued little pamphlets to both of us.

Camilla shot me a terrified side glance as I sat back down and feigned interest in the shoddy, typo-ridden dogma, as opposed to

FOOTNOTE >

*Don Knotts's character on *The Andy Griffith Show.*

the sudden visions I had of licking her inner thighs. Which I then laid a hand between.

"I saw your guitar," Rip said, standing in the aisle, his squirrelly head just level with my own. (I liked the way his hair smelled.) "Where do you perform?"

"Um, actually, I play almost every day in the Lafayette Street subway station." Cammy's knees budged. (I'd been a tad reluctant to tell her this.)

"I'll come check you out sometime after CONNY gets back from Burkina Faso."

I smelled my fingers. Rip cleared his throat in my ear.

"I used to have a drug problem," he said, in profile. Then very slowly turned and gave me a long, challenging look.

"Oh." I pretended to examine the barf bag in the pouch in front of me. I felt like I was betraying both him and Camilla by not 'fessing up.

"Then I let go and let God," he told me, turning to the window with a jut of a gallant chin. Peroxide began making shooing motions at him as we prepared for takeoff. But Rip began waxing about his *CONNY Conversion,* in the trancey way we explain our dreams, assuming they'll seem just as absorbing to others. I studied him. There was just no harmony in his little face. Most of the features had been crammed into its bottom margin, like the P.P.S.'s of a kid's postcard from camp. He finally went and sat down after Peroxide explained, over the speakers, that little Rip was the airplane's anchor—the one thing preventing our jet from ascending.

It turned out Cammy loved airplane food.

"I guess it's that sort of clean, freeze-dried taste, and the perfect economical portions in these cute little containers. Or maybe it's the thin air up here or something that makes me so hungry . . ."

. . . and she even asked a hassled Peroxide if she could possibly save her any leftover lasagnas. Suspiciously, there was not a one.

I was just so happy to escape New York, to soar through the frigid misty hither-and-yon with Camilla beside me, as our Parisian weekend sparkled under the clouds. I could barely sit still, or stop squeezing her, as if just to make sure she was true. Until someone began kicking the back of my chair, and I wheeled happily around in my seat, standing on my knees like I'd done as a kid. In the row right behind me were a father and son with matching brush haircuts. There was some poignant reversal in this, which I see now made me nostalgic for a thing that hadn't happened in my own life.

"Wheeler, what do you say?" the dad said, scruffing his boy's turfy head.

"I'm sorry," he told me, dutifully, shyly.

"It's quite all right," I assured him, "sir."

I remembered how I'd felt at his age, with Flight all new and coursing through me. And now I had my own version sitting beside me.

Later, over the dire ashen Atlantic, the recycled Delta air was beginning to drain us, make us edgy. I think all our expectations about the weekend caused the usual gaps in our conversation to stand out even more stridently, like the squeaks of guitar strings as fingers find chords. So, seeking structure, Cammy and I played our new *Simile Game* . . .

. . . "Europe," she said, her hand in mine and her eyes on the sky, "is a middle-aged dad in a silk robe and slippers, and he's too tired to argue with his rebellious son, America."

"Yes, excellent, Cutes, and, um, although America has become his own successful businessman, he still looks to his dad for approval."

She fell asleep during the Delta Presentation of *You've Got Mail.* I watched a dream flutter under her eyelids. (Wondering, of course, if I was its star.) And just feeling so lucky to have her calm beauty, and all of her goodness, there humming beside me.

I looked out upon a sun-blasted castle of cloud. And wondered when, and how, all this would end. It made me feel meaningless, but in some way exalted. All of us shot in this huge gleaming needle through the white heart of God. Then the pilot said we were now descending at 656 miles an hour.

Cammy whimpered, just barely, beside me, and I found myself swamped with Love as I took her dreaming hand in mine and watched her there in the drowsy window light, this dark gift I'd been given. Why? And then I saw, on her damp Delta napkin, next to her pretzels and sleep mask and headphones, that she'd drawn a little girl crawling through what looked like a vast shag carpet . . . each of its strands the size of an elm.

When the landing preparations woke her up, Camilla caught me staring at her. And (because this was the first occasion of what would become my nightly routine) I was completely embarrassed. I quickly put my finger in her yawn, which I rescued just before she could bite it . . .

. . . *Clack!*

And,

"We're landing!" I told her.

The corners of her lips tried to make a smile. She gave me a probing look, kissing my forehead, twice and slow and soft, then stared out the window. Suddenly, despite shrieking jet engines and the planeload of anxious chatter meant to disguise all our Gravity fear, there fell an eerie silence between us. Cammy blinked, so slowly that I thought I heard her lashes unstick.

"*Defenestrate,*" she said. "I think Nabokov uses it. I can't remember where, though."*

"The Defenestration of Prague." I knew what it meant. And I've since wished I'd asked about her bad dream. But,

"*Velleity,*" I said.

"Spell it." She rested her head on my shoulder.

I did, stroking her. Until she gave up. And before I could tell her the word's definition, we saw the sudden certainty of runway in front of us. Camilla nibbled my nails as we landed.

During deplaning, Peroxide stood and smiled by the captain and his cockpit. Churning out "Fly again's" with her bored courtesan's eyes. But saying nothing as *we* passed.

At the baggage carousel, Rip gave me a colored bracelet. And I actually felt my eyes welling up as I thanked him; while Cammy bent down to hug him, giving me a worried look as she administered motherly back pats.

"Goodbye, Sweet Pea," she said.

"I'll catch your act," Rip told me with a manly hand grip. "You guys are a beautiful couple with beautiful hearts."

When I saw a portion of Liebo advancing behind Rip, I scurried off with my luggage before he could see how cheap it was.

If New York is a **Number One** pop song, flashcatchy and instantly addictive, then Paris is a symphony, harmonically stu-

FOOTNOTE >

*PNIN, p. 108

pendous. As the Charles de Gaulle shuttle bus wound us through a foggy masterpiece of arches and monuments, every angle was supple, each moment a curve.

"It's so beautiful," I said as we walked off the bus into the damp Pigalle morning. "I think the only thing I don't like about France is the French."

"Maybe we can ask them to leave."

I had to restrain Cammy's hand from tapping the back of a gendarme in front of us, then from shoving my own fingers into the furry plumber's smile of a workman bent over a pothole. We were feeling wild and invisible, released from identity, and everything—the cars, the cement, the new faces—seemed laughably weightless, stage-propish, and exotic. As if they were all trying, for our sake alone, extremely hard to be Paris. I giggled like Bela Lugosi, while Cammy was, as usual, a brown study in deadpan. There was a rising, confident sun and the gin scent of juniper.

"I feel so free and so happy with you!" I said, and with my guitar on my back, I leapt up and clicked my heels, first my left, then my right, and we plunged into *le Métro.*

After we'd barely slipped into the train's sliding doors, all was suddenly dead calm and dead serious, as if God had just thrown the Gravity switch. A spruce elderly man sat down next to Camilla and gave her directions with his hands and brittle English. I fiddled with my Rip bracelet, because I had a surprise in mind. And then, having thanked the old gent with several tender *mercis*, Cammy wrote our address on the back of her hand and sat circling fun stuff on our Go Paris! map. Conferring with me softly, idly rubbing my thigh, while the man, clearly taken with her, rode on alone, looking lost, straight ahead, or maybe just back into his past, a carved ivory cane in his hands as he held on to the dignity that so often stands in for Love. And although these days I wish I'd savored every one of her touches, sucked every last bit of the marrow she'd (so briefly) instilled in my bones . . . I slid Camilla's hand from my leg and pretended to stretch.

As we stepped off the train, among the tunnel's dubbed American movie and campy French panty ads, a sudden urge for Camilla sang in my blood, was a chill in my loins. There was such a totality about her, as she walked in her sundress, without slouch or complaint under the strain of her bag. There seemed no desire to blackmail the world in that sensible stride, in her slender shoulder, which I kissed, and bit, saying

"You're so amazing, Camilla," I shook my head. "Whatever happens, I don't know, I guess I just hope I know you forever." She smiled her good rare untrusting smile.

And we rose into the radiant fountain spray of Place Saint-Michel, a cool neon city of lazy cafés and ripoffy postcard joints where a wondrous champagne bubble of Hope now enclosed us. Within this we began walking the noisy gilt block to the borrowed apartment. I looked invincibly at all the hotels with their smug *Complet* signs, and we fell behind a swarm of gossipy nuns. A situation that, again, seemed strictly out of Central Casting. While the Issue, our subtext, seemed just underfoot. So I nervously explained,

"French is so hard for me to understand. It's like the words disappear inside of their mouths or something." I did my dumb impression of their tape-rewindy inflections. At which a young pretty sister, like a Chinese waiter grown accustomed to customer ridicule, turned to freeze me with the look of God.

Camilla gave me a "busted" shrug, slowed our pace, then softly said,

"I know just what you mean." (Of *course* she did.) "French

sounds just as secret and withholding as they all are. I mean, I think all languages have to reflect the personalities of the people who made them. And I also think everyone secretly wishes they were French."

"That's so true, yeah, you're right. I never thought of it like that, but it's totally true. Being French is like the ultimate elitist club," I explained to her, needlessly, "because they're the biggest goddamn snobs. You know you really are brilliant."

She said a humble

"Welll . . ."

And we glared at all the pretty, dark people sitting with poodles and espressos. I felt a Phillip pang.

"Hey, there's la rue Cousin," I said. "I think our street's the next one."

"I think it is," she said, and her eyes dodged mine, went down on our map, which I noticed was turned to Nice.

We heard a woman yell,

"*Va te faire foutre!*"*

in the distance.

I was filled with a heavenly dread because, at least for me, the undertone of all this seemed to be buckling our discussion, like tree roots beneath a sidewalk. As we turned away from the din, into the shady rue de Goff, I tried to talk about general things, saying,

"It seems very un-American that there's a lack of graffiti here," with a pompous hand flourish at the high white walls. "I think graffiti must be some sort of manifestation of American

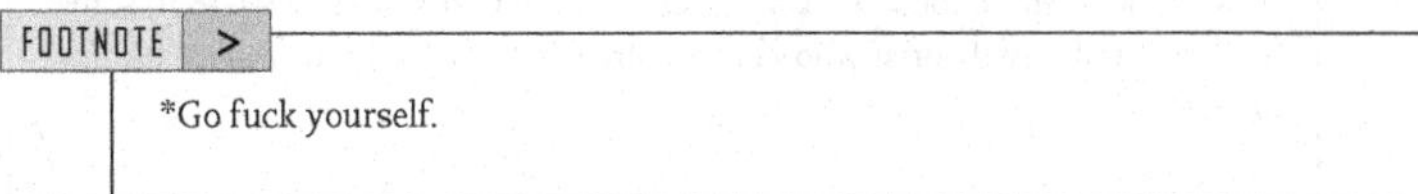


*Go fuck yourself.

ego, like a manifest destiny with nowhere to go, in that we all think we have the right to express ourselves, and so we'll even use defilement to do it. Um."

I snuck a look at her. She nodded. So I said, "It's like an extension of ego, but by other means," wondering what in the hell I was talking about.

And then the right wall was suddenly tangled with Jim Morrison graffiti.

She saved me with

"Clausewitz called war *an extension of diplomacy by other means,*" doing something to her camera.

"Oh, that's right" (like I knew who he was).*

To the left was a path bending into the cool leafy distance.

I said, "I think this is it."

"I think I dreamed this," Cammy muttered, tilting her head.

There was the yell of a robin.

A hush fell.

"Oh." I tried and failed to feel her déjà vu breezing through me.

Camilla paused a moment . . .

. . . then led my hand down the winding pleached lane.

Which ended in a towering gate about fifty yards ahead of us . . . another world.

To which we walked in astonished reverie, under a sun-dappled canopy of elm, and I was so dotty and glad, as if a beer commercial were going off in my head with the merry little

FOOTNOTE >

*Later I learned on the Net that he was Carl von Clausewitz, 1780–1831, some Prussian military theorist who's apparently mentioned a lot in *Gravity's Rainbow.*

cymbals of its opening cans, that I remember telling myself, as I looked into the quiet blue of her eyes, in the wickered shade, that in the Future, if I was ever without her, which on some blurred, awful level I knew I would be . . . I would have to remember how happy she'd made me. How, as I hunched in some dark Hell's Kitchen dive, relapsing in Tanqueray and self-pity, I would not let the fellow lush to my left convince me it was only memory's forgiving focus that had lit Camilla in this Technicolor nimbus.

She was that fantastic.

We arrived at the intricate wrought-iron entrance and opened it, creakless, with Hansel and Gretel wonder as we wandered onto a clearing of soft golden grass. Glancing at each other with a disbelieving magic that I still have stashed in some deep cozy pocket of me. Then the sky, which had grown bright and eager, was suddenly thundering late-summer sun showers, it was all Jacuzzi humid as one hysterical jag of white lightning knifed out of a cloud. And so, getting soaked, we ran at a stone bungalow where the old wooden numbers said 706, which Camilla checked against the smudged back of her hand as we hurried under an ivy-bearded portico guarded by gargoyles.*

"This is so surreal," she said.

We stood there panting, dripping, unshouldering bags. Cammy standing with the sunny storm behind her, the rain all silky on the tops of her breasts.

"You're so gorgeous," I said. "It's preposterous."

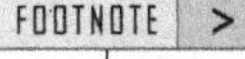


*There was water coming out of their mouths, and Camilla told me later that the words *gargoyle* and *gargle* are cognates, because of the gargling sound of the rain. I mean, do you see why I loved her?

"You're the sweetest." She licked rain off her chin.

"I don't want you to get a cold." I bent down to untie her Nike, and she balanced a hand on my head as I poured a Charlie Chaplin sluice of water out of her shoe. Just in front of me the cotton crotch of her dress clung in a damp triangle.

Oh God.

There was the happy gargle of rain in the gutters. I removed the other shoe, secretly inhaling the damp pong of her sock, which I peeled from her soft pallid arch. And kissed it, aroused toe to nose, before I stood up.

"Sweetie, this is unreal," she whispered. "Imagine slipping into the cool delicious sheets," swinging my hand a little.

"I can't *wait,*" kicking off my own shoes. "I just don't want to track up the carpet," which I could see waiting creamily inside the dim window.

"I think I'm kind of schnauzer."*

"My friend told me there's a huge bowl of fresh fruit and all sorts of cheeses and breads and stuff! And their maid just cleaned."

"Yummy."

I smiled, thinking how I'd give that kid a free voice lesson as I searched my pocket for the bulky brass keys, then . . .

"Oh my God," I said, slapping my pockets, rifling through my bag. I could feel my eyes widen . . .

. . . the water purring in the gutter . . .

. . . as suddenly I saw the keys on Camilla's wood kitchen

FOOTNOTE >

*This had become our own word for starving because, as Cammy revealed in *Questionnaire,* she'd once swallowed him when she was little.

table, just next to the Tabasco, and just where I'd left them when a most insatiable little dog had yapped for scraps of breakfast that day.

Jesus H.

I could see so clearly, so cruelly his impatient freckled tongue. As now, in my skull, came the stinging *almost* sound of a tennis ball smacking net tape . . .

. . . Smack!

Always *al*most.

"I'm sorry, Cammy." I pressed my eyelids. "I left the goddamn keys on your table. I can *see* them. Right by his leash . . ."

. . . and in the way a gas changes form in extreme pressures, I've found that a combustible relationship, in similar situations, will reveal itself in conclusive ways. But,

"It's okay," she said.

I couldn't look at her.

"Fuck! Fuck! Fuck!" I said, with three stomps of a heel. "I cannot *fuck*ing believe this. Hey, maybe we can pry open a window or something." We looked at the one by the door . . .

. . . where the rain was hurrying down the glass to a SONITROL ALARM SYSTEM sticker just above the sill.

"Perfect. Oh, God. I'm really just so, so sorry." I tried the locked doorhandle in a furious twist. "Fuck!"

The day, as if sensing our mood, grew gray and deflated; the rain went weak and the sun hid. Camilla looked off into the drizzle, her water-beaded back half to me. And we stood there a minute like that, under the stone ivied eaves of that cottage. The soft laughing rain . . . the ruin.

Then sudden lightning sizzled the sky.

"A bolt of lightning," Camilla said, softly, "is supposedly six times as hot as the sun," with her back still at me.

"Jesus. Look," I took her hand, turned her to face me. "Cammy, I insist that you let me pay for the nicest hotel . . ."

. . . but there was a taunting little *Complet* sign, swinging in my brain like the *No Dogs Allowed* one in Snoopy.

"Com*plet*," I mocked, with a fussy lip pucker, which Camilla ignored. I hurled my sneaker out into the yellow wet yard and watched it do its little racing-car roll into a juniper bush. "This is like some fucking Dante thing," I said, walking back to her.

Camilla nodded, with aplomb, but I saw the anguish in the rims of her nostrils.

Another cloud burst.

And then I said the unsayable: "Maybe we should call Liebenthal . . . ," with a dread in my voice, like I'd suggested *Darth Vader.*

Cammy looked down without responding. I persisted with

"You think?" leaning toward her a little, with a *Please-say-no* arch of the eyebrows.

She shrugged.

And then I lost it. I leaned against the wet wall behind me, slid down onto cement, letting the roof rain spill all down the back of my shirt.

"Simile Game," I said, raising a finger in the downpour. "It's like I've attached myself to you. And now I'm like that *challenged* wheel on your shopping cart, the one that keeps making you go off course. Totally holding you back. I'm really sorry, I seem to ruin ev—"

"Sh, sh, shhh." She sat down in the veil of rain, stroking water off my cheek, murmuring, kissing, her leg over my lap. We were soaked.

"I miss Phillip," I said, my voice beginning to shiver with the thrill of both hypothermia and, despite my resolve to feel very sorry for myself, tremendous lust.

But . . .

"This isn't exactly the place of a friend," I went on heroically, my hand on the warm wet small of her back. "This rich kid I give vocal lessons to's mother let us use it in exchange for a bunch of lessons I gave them." Another chill wiggled through me. "I mean, I'm not rich and powerful like Liebo," I warned her, holding her face away so she'd look at me.

A fat rude raindrop smashed itself against her forehead. Then a jagged something came into her face. Some promise she'd made, mostly to herself, seemed to be collapsing inside her. And making room for me.

"What are you getting out of this, us . . . I mean," I said. "I just can't believe how lucky I am to have you, I mean not that I *have* you. But, like, I just don't see what you're *gett*ing out of this. Of me, I mean, and I'm not fishing, but what exactly is it that you *like* about me?"

We heard the Cowardly Lion grumble of distant thunder.

"I like *this,*" she whispered, grazing her fingers, then her tongue, over my teeth. "And the sweet voice inside here, that lullabies me to sleep. And I like this too." She licked my tongue lightly. "Because it says all the perfect things that make me happier than I've been in a long, long, long time. And I like these," taking my wet feet in her lap and rubbing them as the rain fell over us. "The way you cried when you thought you wouldn't be able to fit them inside of your boots every morning before nursery school. And these," she said, "I especially like these," tracing her finger over my eyelids. "I think these might just be my favorites. I might like these more than both of us know. Maybe more than any two things I can think of . . . right now. The way they bore into me, and the way I have to look away from them sometimes because I don't know exactly what they want from me."

She saw my dumb worried look and shook her head, straddling me . . .

". . . And I like these," kissing each of my fingers. "The way they play guitar. The way you crack them when you're nervous. They way they touch me . . ."

"That reminds me," I said, feeling, among a million magnificent things, much warmer now. I reached under her legs and into my front jean pocket, with the fool's last hope that I might have missed the keys. Which I hadn't. But I did find the two rings I'd fashioned out of my Rip bracelet, one of which I slid onto Cammy's long wet finger.

She smiled her soft cynical smile. Rain gathered, hung, and fell from her chin. Then she slipped the other ring onto my own finger, and we made a pretzel of our newly ringed fingers, christened in rain.

Which she kissed.

". . . as I was saying; I like the way that they touch me. The way they touch me here." She took my finger and put it up inside her, so wet she was silken, then brought it back up and into my mouth . . .

The rain in the gutter politely guzzled, clearing its throat. I glanced over at a spewing gargoyle, who looked back at me, stonily, giving me the creeps, so I picked Cammy up, kissing her and kissing her as I carried her on bare feet across the wet blonde lawn until we came into a little garden at the back of the house, all misty-wet with rain, where I laid her down in the soft flaxen grass . . .

The first time was like one long inhalation of her. There

seemed to be no distinct moments, as we moved through one slippery position after another. It was just so . . . right. And the rightness of it eclipsed that usual sense of detachment. Of the

*Hey! I'm really* fucking *again*

Sensation.

It was undeniable. It was a completion. We'd shed our wet clothes, unzipping, unbuckling, tearing, biting. Ravenous, perhaps, for the people we'd always wanted (but had failed) to be. As the rain swelled and waned all that hothouse day, in our steamy charmed garden.

After, we dozed like waterlogged kids on a beach.

The lavender evening was deepening to plum. I watched Camilla yawn her way out of a dream. And the phrase, as phrases sometimes do, seemed for the first time to make improbable sense:

We'd *Made Love*.

I found myself preparing those three words I felt must follow our Act. But even as they crouched behind my teeth, waiting to pounce, the three words that came out were

"Who are you?

# She Said, She Said, But You Said . . .

Here's one of our instant message exchanges.

ME: Hello teensy-weensiest of cuties. Sorry I kept you up going through *Questionnaire* again last night. I hope it's not annoying how I keep referring to it.

CAM: No, I love it, Little. And the whole way it's lost its article. Like a little person.

ME: Like our child.

*(I know. I bit my tongue after I wrote that one. I knew I was really pushing it, because then she says . . . )*

CAM: Like our couples counselor.

ME: Wait. You mean you don't think things are going great with us?

CAM: No, silliest! I mean it's like our own personal *Constitution.* The way we're always citing it. We're like those constructionists or whatever they're called.

ME: I think it's *strict* constructionists, hon.

CAM: Yes, that's it, smarty pants. But really, I do the same thing. I look at *Questionnaire* when I'm alone all the time. I keep it right under my bed. I'm always comparing how I perceive you now to when we met.

ME: So what you're saying is that you're finding that I'm just not living up to the poetic first impression I'd tried so hard to perpetrate?

CAM: **STOP!** *No.* What I mean is, *Questionnaire*'s like the key that unlocks our own special, self-referential world. When I was a little girl, we used to mark how tall I was with a pencil on the inside of my closet. All those little marks had so much meaning to me, but if new people moved in, they'd probably just paint over all that scrawl. *Questionnaire* is kind of like a portable version of that to me.

ME: Totally. I love the way your mind works. I like to think *Questionnaire* wields the abstract power of myth. Right?

CAM: Yes, little goat. It's omniscient. Like our personal Google.

ME: And it's retroactively writing, producing, directing, and starring in our love* story.

CAM: Yes, cleverest. It's our own little Woody Allen.†

ME: I like you. We get all of each other's jokes.

CAM: You just get more wonderful the more I get to know you.

ME: And you get more beautiful.

CAM: That's because you make me glow.

ME: I'm so filled with affection for you that I feel like my head is going to pop off sometimes.

CAM: Me too. I loved seeing you play last week. Do you know how sexy you look onstage? And I love to wake up in your bed.‡

ME: I love the way your skin tastes. And the way your armpits smell.

FOOTNOTE >

*Uh oh. I knew I was really going out on a limb with this one. Because it was the first time that Word was mentioned in direct respect to us.

†She went with it.

‡Again, the L word, bursting with purpose and promise, like a new president, waiting in the wings to get formally sworn in.

CAM: I love to rub the soles of our feet together in bed.* I love the smell of your sheets. Even on that first night.† Although I have to admit I nearly giggled when you did that *Playgirl* pose in your doorway. Even if it did get me all hot and bothered.

ME: Would it be a terrible inconvenience if I arranged to spend this winter between your thighs?

CAM: Oh, goodie. Can we make a porno‡ later?

ME: Only if it's completely filthy. And we play my Barry White CD's.

CAM: You're my favorite person in the world.

FOOTNOTE >

*Was she sleeping in the same bed that as I was?

†Like a fool, I confessed to her later I hadn't washed them for months.

‡One of our expressions for sex.

# Little Chap. of Horror

Once we'd begun Making Love, it became the only Irony-free haven for Cammy and me. It was just too fantastic to mock, too wonderfully awkward. It would be like saying,

*That cartoon there isn't realistic.*

And, as with drugs and rock 'n' roll, our sex seemed inherently kamikaze. As though we were willing to sacrifice it all for the lovely, terrifying dive into our final fiery moment.

In it lived all the agony of birth, the ecstasy of shame. It was all so vivid, so revealing, so graphic . . . the wetness, the smells. I picture bloody organs filmed during surgery. (But then I would, wouldn't I?) Exposing all the gory detail of, and I hate to say it, the *Soul.*

It felt like the one place I might finally reach her. But even as I lay under Camilla, even as she, or we, brought her closer, closer . . . I saw something in those eyes.

What *was* it?

There seemed to be a vast traffic jammed behind them. Some thing I just knew I'd never dislodge.

# Swimming with Your Boots On

The days were getting shorter.

I could feel the first yearning hints of twilight in the air as we hauled Phillip, our laundry, and groceries down Clinton Street, then up the five moldy flights to Camilla's apartment.* A bit winded, and with her long careful fingers, she unlocked the door onto the airless dim, and the sun fell across our faces in warm venetian stripes.

But only two of us were a bit short on breath and blood sugar. Because Phillip had not an hour ago received a public spank for the *Gulp!*ing of an entire cruller off a neighboring table at Once Upon a Tart. (In those days, Cammy and I half expected to see felon Phillip's snooty **WANTED** mug in the windows of all our favorite SoHo cafés, from which he'd been so routinely eighty-sixed.)

Up until that, our afternoon had been breezy and lolling. We'd spent the Indian summer Sunday wanting things in the windows all up and down Fifth Avenue. In the host of all those otiose boutiques, from Tse to Betsy Johnson, amidst the worn, scornful smiles of the shoppe girls and their chilly pats for

FOOTNOTE >

*The vet had informed us that steep staircases were bad for lengthy Phillip's little back.

Phillip, he and I had lounged happily on a fleet of overstuffed, overpriced sofas. The little noodge nosing my palms for scratches as Cammy emerged from one dressing room after another, wondering which blouse, which boot, looked better. But somehow, through her sober, cool charms, Camilla managed to escape seeming vain. I think by posing all those choices with the dour deliberation of a lab technician, she'd made her aesthetic quest seem merely empirical—done in the name of some greater glory—as if she were asking us which smock we thought would prove the most hydrochloric acid-repellent.

Now, as her apartment grew darker, I lay back on her cool crispy sheets, feeling happy and exhausted as she opened a window and went to the bathroom. While Phillip, whose bedside manner was never exactly excelling, demanded his evening scratches with a special intensity (no doubt owing to his glucose overdose, which had left him as revved as a tiny idling lawn mower). I lifted him into my lap and serviced him, sitting next to the tidy gift of Korean laundry bound in its string. I looked around that midget studio, which had been barely able to contain the three of us and her kitchen table, with its bottle of Tabasco even now so vividly wedged in a neural nook of my memory. I remember Phillip's low, orgasmic moans, the jolly Mexican musics from the bodega downstairs, and above all this the grateful porcelain chime of Camilla's pee. It was distressing that even *this* could arouse me. I still felt totally lucky to be allowed in her apartment, half expecting her to suddenly rush out of the bathroom and, as if reeling from a head injury, scream . . .

Wait . . . Who are *you*?

Who let you *in* here?

**Raaaaape!**

I wondered just how much of her I'd invented. Had I only mastered some skill for awing myself? Or would this creature, Camilla, like a settler's incessant New World, keep increasing my capacity not only to marvel but to marvel at my*self* in the face of her?

I snuck a pair of her panties* out of the hamper and buried my face in them . . . gasping her luscious ripe scent until, hearing her flush, I stuffed them under the bed.

She opened the door and crossed through golden slats of sun, kissing the tops of both Phillip's head and mine before putting Del Amitri on her stereo.

*When you're driving with the brakes on,*
*It's hard to say you love someone.*

I flossed a stubborn hunk of cruller out of Phillip's front teeth. "I guess we left his Sonicare at my place."

"God, he's becoming a little butterball," she said, setting dishes in the sink.

"Shh!" I covered his ears.

A sudden gust of the muggy dusk blew through the blinds, sending Phillip, annoyed by the heat and my dental work, out of my lap and into the bathroom, where we heard him washing down dessert with boisterous laps of toilet water.

"Our little scatalogue," Cammy said, rinsing a bowl.

FOOTNOTE >

**Panties* . . . the word alone harbors such feminine mystery, such sway over me. What if Camilla had caught me, and I'd asked her if I could keep them, wear them over my face, like a gas mask, when I was away from her, as a memento?

And I wanted so much to make deep searching love to her, to look into those eyes for the rest the night, or into the next millennium if I still hadn't gotten to the bottom of her. I wanted to finally tell her I loved her.

"It's boiling in here. I'm all sweaty," she said, and walked to her dresser. As she peeled down to her tank top and panties, the sunlight gilt her downy outline; then, as she walked over to me, it winked through the notch between her thighs, which she straddled my leg with.

The glands under my tongue began leaking.

"Will you take a cool bath with me?" she asked, eyes down, shyly grinding into me.

"Sure," I said, as we both played down the fact of our first bath together.

"Okay." She twirled my cowlick. I felt her dampening heat. "Or do you like it very hot?"

"Scalding."

"I'll make sure we end up with some decent third-degree burns."

"Or at least get us completely dehydrated."

She went off to the bathroom, where I heard the wrench and groan of her turning the faucets. There is comfort in the sound of running baths.

I stripped naked in the long golden shadows, then timidly walked into her bathroom, where she'd half drawn the shade against the day's last light and arranged about a dozen lit vanilla candles along the rim of her tub, which was very deep and full of bubbles. As happened with everything Camilla, a private island had gathered around her, with its own whispered idioms and subdued magics. I plunked into the tub and fit myself in behind her, enclosing her, letting the forgiving hot bath begin melting the day.

Soon a certain third wheel crashed into the tub, briefly paddled about, only to slosh himself back out on the tiles, spraying us as he shook-wrung himself dry and flounced back out of the room with suds on his nostrils.

"Thanks for dropping in," Cammy yelled.

"*Jape,*" I said, quizzing her from ***Vocabulary Builder*** in the spluttering light.

"A joke, jest, quip, or jibe," she was certain.

"Wrong," I teased her, turning the page with wet fingers.

"Really?"

"No, just kidding, Cutie. You were right."

She leaned forward and bit my big toe, which peeked out of the fizz.

"Ouch!"

Underwater I goosed her ribs, recalling how Cammy was not in the least bit ticklish, which always made me a little sad, it seemed so emblematic.

"Party pooper," I said, which let me understand something happy. "*Simile Game,*" I murmured into her ear. "Having you in my life is so comforting, because it's like you feel and say all the same things that I always did, but hearing *you* say them somehow confirms them for me, the way it's impossible to feel the same pleasure from running your own fingers through your own hair. What I'm trying to say is, you just can't tickle yourself."

Looking forward, she brought my hand to her mouth and kissed it. With a bobby pin I drew up her hair–kissing the tiny sweat beads at the nape of her long tawny neck before soaping it. Then I noticed, among the three or four favorite waterlogged books she used to keep on her bath ledge, that her copy of *The Waste Land* was turned to a poem I didn't yet know.

"*Marina*,"* I said, and then, to myself, I read the first handsome words:

*What seas what shores what grey rocks . . .*

"This is haunting. Is it one of your favorites?"

I felt a dim quiver in her flank.

"In a manner of speaking," she said, in a flat voice. "Do you want to switch so I can soap *your* back now, sweetie?"

And I think we both knew, as I leaned back into her kindness, her warmth, felt her seeping into me with the slow-motion dye of a tea bag, what a big step this was for us. What could be more intimate, more placental? This steamy, candlelit cradle she'd made us, twins tied in the womb. Grooming each other, letting the soil and torment that is the world's indifference disappear down the drain. Here, at last, was my partner. Tucked behind the wet walls of our sanctum. Here we could gleam anew with infant vigor, could refuel each other . . . with the will to believe again.

*. . . the hope, the new ships.*

Del Amitri dwindled off in her bedroom. There was the flickering dark as she soaped me, the little wet noises freckling the silence.

And then, all at once, it was all way too much. Continents collided. Suddenly I had the lovely, harrowing sense of losing myself—in her. And, half turning my head back, I said,

"But I love you."

*A poem that'll play a too large role in my life.

# A Game of Chess

The next week Cammy opened my medicine chest.

I'd been flossing in front of the mirror, but now I had to look into the awkward angle at which she'd cracked it. Thinking how this rudeness was completely beneath her character, I suddenly saw what she was up to. Camilla was smuggling toiletries out of her little blue Dopp kit, then aligning them along my narrow crowded shelf. Kiehl's SPF 15 Face Saver, Chanel Eye Therapy, Phillip's antiseizure medication, the cylinder of Glide they shared.

I tried to trap her eyes in the mirror, but she'd only look down.

For once I tried not to overanalyze these little miracles Camilla was always shaping before me, tried not to deconstruct the magic show from the audience. I just observed her, per*ceived* her—and I think I understood for the first time how she was so totally self-contained, and so unlike me. That she seemed possessed by a private melody, utterly absorbed in the math of some internal sonata.*

FOOTNOTE >

*She just couldn't be paraphrased, and that's why I don't think I can ever really clarify her for you . . . or *me*. She was decor for decor's sake, made out of the same raw music as people like Dylan Thomas.

I sneezed three times.

"Bless you, honey," she said, still asserting her things onto the shelf with the timid persistence of someone assembling chess pieces for a windy seaside game.

Because Cammy and I had begun playing out the second act of our Love Story, in which each person wonders just how committed the other one really is to their role. We were still discovering which struggles would need which muscles, still a bit flustered by all our potential—by those invisible dramas poised before us—by the pieces of our chess game. We'd test each other through little invasions, plotting each careful move; then wait, teeth on edge, for the anxious aftermath after one claims, "Checkmate" . . . hoping we haven't presumed into some fatal queen trap.

As I watched her committing her task, I tugged on the sleeve of her little cropped blue jean jacket, which was hanging on the back of the bathroom door like a kid hiding from tag.

"Where'd you get this? I love this," I skirted the toiletry issue. "The little spandex give in the denim is so cool."

"A gift," she said briskly.

"From who? Sorry, sweetie, am I being nosy?"

"My father." She knocked my deodorant off the shelf. "Shit. I should buy you more Charmin," bending under the toilet paper thing to pick up the Secret, then coming back up and unloading more of her things.

I watched her trying not to look hesitant in her little mission. Then I thought, cruelly, what if I'd said,

*What the fuck do you think you're doing?*

The prospect of that, and of her packing her little Dopp kit that morning at her own bathroom sink, combined with the swelling tension of this unacknowledged event and Camilla's general shyness, all suddenly panged me . . . and I found myself squeezing her waist, inhaling her hair, kissing her eyelids . . .

"I wanna eat you up, I love you so," I told her, quoting *Where the Wild Things Are,** a favorite kids' book of ours that I'd often pretended she'd managed to read me to sleep with. Immersed in my hug, Cammy smiled her muffled smile, confirming the fact that we'd survived the moment.

Then she shimmied her arms out of my vise, so I was left holding her hips, and with a rascally smirk, she resumed unloading her items. Which included a variety of free condoms I'd watched her stuff into her purse at various fund-raisers and chic bistros—reading PETA, ASPSCA, GMHC, NoHo Star, Nobu. I was quickly kindled, unzipping her green jeans, scrabbling around in her purse for a trusty Trojan.

"Which one of the following condoms would you be most likely to use during intercourse?" I asked in *Questionnaire* format.

A smile bubbled up in her eyes as I fell to my knees, so hard that I winced, but not wanting to slow the momentum, I licked the white cloth hiding her and heard the tiny dry crackle of her hair under my tongue. Camilla leaned back, unsealing, unfolding, forgiving. And I was drugged between the slippery dank of her thighs—looking for myself at the end of the world inside her—when,

"What are these?" she said.

"What?" I looked up to see her holding what I'd been hiding in the hamper since we'd started dating.

FOOTNOTE >

*That wonderful book by Maurice Sendak, where the Wild Things beg child hero Max not to leave their island: "Oh, please don't go, we'll eat you up, we love you so!"

"Terrifster," I said, holding her knee to get to my feet.

*"These."*

"What?"

"The prescription bottles with your *name* on them."

"They're for anxiety. And a little depression."

"You said in *Questionnaire* that you were happy. So why are you taking these pills?"

"They make me happy." I grinned. My upper lip twitched.

"So this person I'm falling in love with isn't you, then?" Her voice was calm and appalled. "This is a chemical distortion of the real Curtis Birnbaum."

"A chemical en*hance*ment. Please, Little, it's still *me*. I would've told you, but I didn't want to scare you off."

I felt like I'd been caught reading CliffsNotes to a classic. Cammy shook her head in small, baffled jerks, then looked at her new row of toiletries like she might take them all back.

"Tiny, please!" I said. "I'll stop taking them. *You* make me happy. Enough."

"Obviously not," she said softly.

I grabbed the bottles and poured a Pezish torrent into the toilet, then flushed them all down. I looked up at Cammy, who looked away, so I flushed again. Then we both looked down at the water where . . .

. . . the little guests had all returned, anticlimactically, to retrieve forgotten coats after a long-dead party.

# When They Begin the Beguine

If this were, say, my own After School Special, the establishing shot might seem cloyed with a Jimmy Stewart glee. My father and I are having a catch. Looks sweet on paper, right? Or Kodachrome, rather. But instead of some perky *My Three Sons* Muzak, we hear the doomed flight of Cole Porter's "Night and Day."

You know this song.

*Night and day, you are the one.*

You have that tragic singularity of Love.

*Only you beneath the moon and under the sun.*
*In the roaring traffic boom. In the silence of my . . .*

Here the song arches its back so it . . . just . . . clears the high jump bar of

*Lonely room.*

We try to recover from the fall, but still we

*think of you . . .*

The resolution into the obsessive refrain . . . because all great melodies are circular.

*Night and Day.*

This gorgeous noise eclipses the conversation between a boy and his young dad, whose matinee idol beauty is curdled only by an insolent something around his mouth. Which, as we move in for a close-up, begins telling his son some impatient thing. The lips are pinched and already a little wrinkled at the corners from sucking too many unfiltered Camels.

Now the camera follows the arc of their baseball, drowning through the gathering night and into the father's college catcher's mitt. "Night and Day" fades enough for us to hear the father make a distracted whistle. Which wobbles in and out of that path cleared by "Night and Day" 's melody. Warbling slightly off time and under the pitch of the movie theme song, his whistle offers us the aural equivalent of a photo blurred by double exposure. We the lonesome TV viewers wink and nod to ourselves as this life leaches Art.

*Night and Day.*

If I could write just *one* tune like this, I'd never complain again. (Which is the greater feat?) It seems to me, like all great art, to have been not so much created as channeled.

So the father has a catch with his son. Whose fair, eight-year-old hair still gleams Warhol white under a streetlamp that has just blinked on in what's left of the evaporating lavender light. And because it isn't totally dark yet, this streetlamp looks out of place, overly bright, unnecessary. Like that nerdy new kid who stood apart from the other kids on his first day of yet another new school. Me.

Gradually, "Night and Day" fades—the cellos taper to one sad note that floats softly for a beat before landing, leaving us with the tranquil hysteria of cricket scream. Hypervigilant close-up on:

My face, filmed intimately enough for our viewers to see the whirling filigrees in my eyebrows. Which I knit in ripples, a needle gathering cloth, before asking my dad,

"Did you love me when I first came out of Mommy's rectum?"

"Vagina," he laughs.

You see, I never received the famous sit-down sex talk I'd seen on all the sitcoms. But I did work up a television appetite for it—anticipating the events in my world with the detached mistrust born of spin-offs, sequels, and killed-off characters. So all the crucial facts of my life piled up around me without any sense or sequence, jumbled in the cobwebbed corners of my mind like those derelict books you see donated to an apartment building's laundry room. For instance, I didn't learn *cunt* until the age of five, when I heard my father scream it at my sobbing mother one kitchen dawn. That same night I would hear him whisper, grunt, and finally sigh the same word in their bedroom, as I crouched with my ear against their door in the shag carpet dark.

Then suddenly *cunt* was everywhere.

The way a word you've just learned seems to leap cheerfully into every sentence, like a helpful *Sesame Street* grammar lesson. It was all over the magazines my dad liked to keep under the lawn mower in our garage. It seemed to apply to any of my mom's absent friends. I admired its multipurpose zest. It could produce tears or make love. Had a flair for chopping through and even stopping conversations. It felt clever as it sailed through my brand-new teeth.

*Cunt.*

The several times I asked my parents what it meant, they only gave each other sheepy looks and changed the subject. So I came to imagine it as some cunning kitchen utensil. Hot, sharp, and rounded. With the sly charm of a Chinese cleaver, or one of those patented wonder tools that the ranting announcer on wee-hour paid-TV-segments threatens will change our lives for only a C.O.D. money-back $19.99.

*Cunt* felt irresistible. (As it turned out, I was on to something.)

I began to employ my new word relentlessly, reaching that delirium when a little boy discovers that new device which can chafe his dad's patience to red anger.

*You cunt, you! Oh,* please *be a cunt, won't you, Pater?*

I guess I was flexing those first Oedipal muscles. Limbering up for just what I didn't know. Something big for sure. I *did* come to discover how this barb of a noun had a real knack for annoyance and, apparently, for anguish. Because it sent my sweetest, most Catholic babysitter sobbing into our bathroom, where she locked herself for an entire night against all my guilty pleas. And neither would Alvira tell me what *cunt* meant through the door, or come out until my parents finally returned two hours later than they'd promised, humming with booze. Alvira then emerged, eyes puffed and stained with vaporized pain, like a boxer punch-drunk on defeat. My parents' eyes were all shame, their *hellos* warped by alcohol, but even though they seemed to read the situation a bit blearily, I think they *did* sense that they couldn't exactly scold Alvira for ignoring me the whole evening. Which is now nostalgically called Cunt Night in my family. And which brings us back to our movie . . .

"Did you love me when I came out of Mommy's vagina?" I ask my dad again, as we continue our catch.

"Actually," he says, rubbing the baseball's faded red stitching like he's recalling the cause of a boyhood scar, "I didn't have any feeling for you one way or the other."

His gray eyes remind me in these moments of an angry bruised cloud, unsure if it wants to burst or scatter with the wind.

"Why didn't you love me, Doug?" I ask, using the Christian name he prefers I call him by.

He tosses the ball back to me and, true to cinematic pace, I miss it. I stand still. Again I want to shit, to come, to bite. Do *something* that will free this thing he breeds in me.

"Why?" I say.

The strings of me feel way too taut, groaning with discord—I'm an out-of-tune guitar suddenly struck. So I laugh. Just one sad chuckle. Then run over to retrieve the baseball from the sappy grip of a violet bush.

After we resume our catch, I wait a few moments, then ask him,

"Well, when did you start loving me?"

He's silent.

I feel one hot tear finally spill . . . spelling out things I won't understand for years, although I know somehow this moment will be defining. More tears come. Snot clots my throat. I spit, try to feel manly. "How long?" I ask my father.

"I guess about three weeks," he looks away. "Then I started to, well, feel like I do for you."

"What if I had been a retard?" I wonder, daring myself to

drink more of this delicious elixir of pain. Doug waits for the ball I throw to find his mitt with a small leather yelp.

"I would have drowned you," he explains.

I remember feeling as though I'd breathed saltwater through a snorkel.

# Blue Jean Baby

Friday night in Cammy's apartment, I watched her long sharp fingers try to peel off the Scotch tape I'd slopped on the saggy gift I'd just given her.

"I don't want to rip the pretty paper," she said, sitting next to me on her bed in her tank top and white panties. I could hear the weariness in her words, straining through hoarseness, an attempt to sound weekendy.

"Just rip it," I said, ripping it.

I caught her rolling her eyes before she unfolded and held up, with arms fighting fatigue, a little baby blue sweater. "It's so cute," she said softly. She tried to jam herself into it.

"No, no, it's for *Phill*ip," I said, feeling sad that she'd had her hopes up, until I saw she was relieved because the thing was so tiny. While Phillip, at our feet, wiggled and wriggled, swimming into the air until we lugged his little iron bones onto the bed and fitted him up like a married tailor team.

I closed his top button, which was too tight, so I unclasped it. "He looks *dyn*amite, right, Cam?"

Model Phillip stood dutifully still, fine-tuning his posture, checking his reflection in the grim antique mirror.

"Very handsome." She kissed his brow, then neatly folded the Kelly green wrapping paper. I wondered who would earn the present it would someday be wrapping.

"You are the sweetest," she said, lifting my hand to her mouth.

I watched her eyes digest something as she paused briefly with her lips on my skin, then reached under the bed and pulled out a Barney's box, black and sleek as an expensive chocolate. She humbly laid it on my lap.

"Otter! I can't *believe* this," I told her. "We both bought each other presents. This is like a little cutie Christmas. It must be some kind of telepathy." There was Camilla's weak smile, me straining, as usual, and jealous Phillip's glowering. "Thanks so much." I gave her neck a brief phrase of kisses.

"Open it, hon."

"I love this *box*."

"*O*pen it," she insisted, with a tickled giggle as I pecked at her neck again. I could tell she was proud of what she'd got me, but I felt embarrassed at getting a gift that was so obviously expensive. I didn't want to be indebted—or bought off.

Phillip began pumping my shin, as if with a new sense of pride in his official blue humping uniform. Preposterously, I realized I was not only growing fond of these throbbing little moments between us but that I'd actually begun to depend on them when I couldn't reach her.

"Stop always stealing the limelight," she told him, yanking him off by his thin little hips. He glanced up at me, a tiny werewolf changing back from the thing he so loathed becoming . . . as we all must.

I finally opened the box and pulled back the tissue.

"Oh my God. You *knew* I wanted this. You're so thoughtful. I love it," I said, trying on the same kind of stretchy little jean jacket that she always wore. "It's fan*tas*tic."

I laid my head in her lap, breathing in her blurry aroma.

"I thought you might like it," she said, running slow fingers through my hair.

"I *love* it!" I vaulted into the bathroom.

Snubbing weary eyes in the mirror, I yelled,

"Hey, we can all be twins, okay? Cammy? You me and the little one. When we go out tonight, right?"

She didn't answer.

"Mandy" drifted out of a distant car stereo, then decayed as sadly as the end of a summer. I breathed in Camilla's vanilla candles, molted around the rim of the bathtub we'd made so much flickering love in, and the triple-milled soaps, sage and rosemary, like candies wrapped bite-sized and luscious on her ebony shelves, and all her beautiful useless boxes, wondering if she thought they could make some sense of the Emptiness—capture and contain it—when something caught my eye.

On top of the toilet, jutting out of the little tumult of her leather purse, amid her Kiehl's lotion and the photos we'd taken in Kmart's InstaBooth that week, was another snapshot I'd never seen.

Sepiaed by Time, it featured all but the head of a little girl, astride a mechanical seahorse in front of what actually looked like a Kmart. Gangling out of her blue-checkered dress were two replicas of the knees in the other room . . . while just beneath them, on the sun-baked cement, was the rippled photographer's shadow.

"Curtis?"

I put the picture back and walked out of the bathroom. Cammy went about getting dressed. Phillip's tongue was draped between his two bottom incisors, so I filled his water bowl and told Camilla,

"I love my jacket. I can't wait to be twins with my tiny," sitting down on her bed to pull on my sneakers. She slipped into her sandals, attached Phillip's leash, then stood by the front door. I began to feel that same post-present letdown of so many past Christmases.

"Where should we eat?" she said, eyes on her keys.

"Wait." I got up. "Aren't you going to wear your jacket?"

"No, Curtis," she said, in a mannerly voice, walking out into to the hall.

"Why not?" I looked inside the closet and touched her jacket, growing more and more disgusted by the needy fawning boyfriend I knew I'd become.

"I'm not really that cold," she told me with a clean, bright Windex stare. "Come on. Let's go." Phillip, rearing to hit the town in his brand-new duds, grumbled. "I think he has to *mic•turate,*" she said.

"To pass water; urinate," I mumbled. "Good one, Cam."

A pause.

"Look," I said, "just admit you don't *want* to be twins. That's it, right? You think it's gay."

"I just don't see that we *need* to be."

"Come on, Tiny." I pulled the jacket from the hanger and held it out to her.

She took it, brushed "something" off it, and folded it over her forearm.

"*Simile Game,*" I said. "I feel like our whole relationship has been me lurking behind you, like a late-night taxi, desperate to get the fare, honking and honking, and just hoping you'll finally decide to climb inside me."

"That makes me very sad," she said. But she didn't put the coat on.

"Okay, forget it." I took the thing and hung it up. "I just thought it could be like me and you and him," I said, nodding at Phillip over my shoulder. "Like a little blue team or something. All for one and one for all, you know?" I raised a *rah-rah* fist.

"I think that's a lot of the problem with you . . . us," she said, in a mum voice, because of the neighbors. "It's like you don't know where you end and I begin."

"I thought that was the point."

# Shine On, You Sleazy Diamond

"Curtis, there's going to be someone at the party I really want you to meet."

The deepening dusk made a hesitant mirror of the cab window Camilla was staring out of. She bit her lip, then released it.

With me on her left, and armrest Phillip between us, I could just make out the milky ghosts of her eyes, which appeared more focused on some difficult thing within her than on the fast cement-and-neon narrative gushing past them.

We were rushing east over hectic, ugly Fourteenth Street. To a cocktail/auction affair she'd been invited to through her work, at an Upper East Side address that had sounded oddly familiar when she'd told it to the cabby. Daylight Savings had just ended, and there was that tapering sense of hope in the streets. Of the world's being pulled out from under us.

Wishing she'd tell me more about her *Someone,* I tried not to watch the meter, looking up instead at Virgin Megastore's enormous clock, on which Time is a digital countdown to doomsday, tabbed on God's calculator.

"He's a friend," she said softly. "He's one of the nicest people I know here. So please be nice to him, okay, sweetie?" taking my hand, still facing the twilight. "Not that you would ever *not* be."

Phillip made a smelly nest of my lap, then scratched his ear with the blurry wheel of a hind leg.

Was I about to meet an old boyfriend? An ex-*hus*band? Her gynecologist?

"Him?" I asked, with more of a whine than I'd wanted. "It's a *him*? Little?"

Our cabby's snooping eyes met mine in the rearview mirror, and the car careened sharp around Union Square onto Park Ave, spilling Phillip from my lap and into Camilla's as another passing taxi nearly sideswiped us from behind, then almost collided into a cab ahead of us, sending the whole honking Doppler flock swerving in yellow smudges through the dusk.

As we regained equilibrium, the driver said,

"I'm sahrry," in a twisted angry accent, looking stiffly ahead.

Cammy kissed Phillip's front paw and told him,

"It's okay,"

rolling her eyes at me.

We passed Barnes and Noble, Park Avalon, Lemon, and City Crab, where the sun's final klieg light slanted through their huge windows.

"This reminds me of a Maxfield Parrish painting they have in the Met," she said, gazing out her window. "That same golden time of the day. It's called *Land of Make Believe*."

"Maybe we can go there tomorrow. Or Sunday?"

She didn't answer. Then,

"No *D.O.G.*'s," she spelled. "But you're sweet to ask," squeezing my knuckles.

"Maybe we'll sneak you in," I told him, uncrusting some sleep from his eye, till he pawed it, as if batting a tear. "I love you," I told Cammy, hating how it always came out sounding like a question lately.

I watched her reflected eyes squeeze shut, then open. "I love you too."

And we drove on through the desolate glass-and-iron landscape of Midtown, through the wistful, zigzagging anonymity of all the red taillights, like the gestures of so many smokers in the dark—before plunging into the dingy vault under Grand Central, past the invisible eyes of the mole people who live there, then back up the through Helmsley's golden arcade and out along Park Avenue's grass divider, where jolly bronze rabbits hang in never-ending hops.

Suddenly it seemed I didn't know her at all. That I could sense her past ballooning between us, a huge overdue baby in her womb, preventing our embrace—and who I'd just discovered was not my own. Our lover's history always feels like a betrayal, I thought, which made me eerily aroused, so I bit her neck and slipped my hand along the silky thigh of her dinner dress, then over her ribs and under the buttons until I felt her soft nipple awaken in chilly bumps.

"Not now," she said, holding my hand still against her, eyes still out the window. "Please, Cutie, just not now."

I saw the avuncular rearview glint of our cabby. I removed my hand, feeling like I'd been caught on *Taxicab Confessions,* then pulled proxy Phillip in my lap and snuggled him close.

"Here is fine," Cammy told Uncle Bickle, and he pulled over to the curb in front of the Hotel Del Monico, where she paid him, refusing my money. Phillip's head periscoped out of the large leather Coach bag she'd slid him into as she got out.

I heard the cab guzzle off as we walked through Park Avenue's dying amethyst light. Just in front of me was Christie's auction house, where I'd worked for years.

"Wait. Oh, Jesus," I said, praying to God the party wasn't being catered by Richard Swamble, who'd fired me from his company last summer for stealing those honeysuckle votives I mentioned before—when a plush red concierge said,

"Good evening, Mizz Fell," opening the important bronze

door. "You look gorgeous, as always. Aren't you a little chilly without a–? Holy sh– . . . What *up*, Birnbaum?!" His big black face pulled together a smile.

I said, "It's good to see you, Hector."

It wasn't.

"I almost didn't recognize you without your monkey suit, man. I haven't seen you for ages. Since that"–he chuckled–"Donna Karan party where you got– . . ."

He looked over at Cammy, who glanced over at me, then down. Hector snuck me a *Yikes* face. Then said,

"Is everything coo?" leisurely, neglecting the *L*. "What's up with the record deal?"

"Um, I'm in negotiations." I felt Cammy's stare on my cheek. "Are you sure it's okay to let *him* in, Hector?" I raised my eyebrows and gave the Phillip satchel insistent little *Get it?!* nods.

"Not a prob," Hector said, "missing" my signal. "Mizz Fell brings him here all the time," and he bent down, hands on his knees, asking, "Doesn't she, wiener dog?"

Phillip gave Hector the kind of blasé expression his question deserved. We stood there on the sidewalk. The sun was all gone now. Cammy whispered,

"I'm cold, hon,"

barely nodding at Hector, who gave her his bribable smile as she walked in ahead of me with Phillip hinged from her shoulder. Hector shook out his on-fire fingers with a *She's-Smokin'* squint, and I gave him something between a smile and a wince as I followed Cammy into the Grande Ballroom.

Where I instantly broke into an icy sweat amid the sudden blast of chandelier and forced cheer and bad memories, which rose up along the spiral Plexiglas stairway that corkscrewed through floors of Fabergé eggs, Tibetan rugs, Gainsboroughs, and Ming Dynasty urns . . . and all the highborn, tinkling-glass chatter that was the prissy clamor of Christie's.

How I'd forgotten.

"Are you okay?" Cammy asked me, as with her wary grace she plucked a flute of Cliquot from a floating silver tray. "You look shaken. You're sweating, sweetie."

I snagged a bottle of Evian from another tray.

"I think I'm gonna puke,"

which was almost true, but I faked a little gag response, then groaned,

"Is this carbonated?"

. . . teetering a little as I held the bottle up in front of my face and pretended to read the label in order to hide from an approaching cater-waiter named Brad,* whom I'd known for years from Manhattan's little soirée circuit. I braced myself for Camilla's Hector questions as she felt my forehead, and I tried to put on a preheaving expression (realizing, pathetically, just how much I loved being mothered).

"Maybe you got carsick in that cab," she said.

"Yeah, maybe we should take me in another one home?"

"You *are* a little hot," she bit a nail, glancing around. "I wish there was someplace you could lie down."

"The backseat of a taxi?"

As I scanned the room for Swamble's big flabby head, thinking just how little I deserved Camilla, I noticed Phillip eyeballing

*I still couldn't tell if this was a Swamble affair because not only did his *challenging* work ethic cause tremendous employee turnover, but all of us cater-waiters freelanced for a lot of competing companies at the same time.

trays of salmon carpaccio with citron-dipped cucumber in a shaved-ice rosemary frappé.

(Swamble didn't sack me for a lack of trying.)

Cammy took my pulse. "Um, how do you know Hector?"

"I sort of, uh, did a couple of catering jobs here once, in a while, sometimes," I stammered, hoping for a kind of off-hand/delirious approach. By rolling the cold sweaty Evian bottle across my forehead, I was able to hide almost my entire face.

"Is your friend that you wanted to introduce me to here?" I glanced around before I brought the Evian to my lips with trembling hands.

"No," she said, daubing my forehead with a napkin, and I thought I could see her making some kind of a deal with herself inside her eyes.

"Let's go," she decided. "I'm really getting worried about you," rubbing my back, with real concern and disappointment in her voice.

Feeling guilty, I said "No, no! I think I just started to feel a little better, actually." I stood up straighter, massaging both of my temples with one veiling hand while peeping through my fingers for Swamble . . .

. . . whose big busy body was suddenly rushing down the spiral staircase, very much on display as he whispered side-of-the-mouth commands at Brad, who nodded up at him.

I moaned, "Oh, no."

"Who's that?" but she was looking at a girl with thick, brick-hued hair, smiling obscenely from the little coat-check booth in the Great Hall in back of us. Great. It was Rachel.

I used to sleep with her.

"I used to work with her," I said, and for once it was me avoiding Cammy's eyes. "Her name's Rachel," I explained, in a virtuous chirp, and after I gave Rachel a little *Aye, aye* salute, she started doing that little index-finger-only wave she always thought was so adorable.

Camilla said, "Oh," meaning: *Bitch*.

Rachel swiveled her hand so her index finger now told me . . .

. . . *Come hither.*

"I think I'm feeling really sick again. Maybe she can find me some Tylenol or something."

Phillip practically rolled his eyes.

"Or some Dramamine," I suggested in a more vomity voice.

I gave Cammy's cappuccino shoulder a guilty little squeeze before hobbling, head down, one hand over abdomen, over to Rachel.

"What's wrong with *you?*" she said, in the tough-love tenor of a wrestling coach. She fold-marked a yellow-highlighted page of her French's playbook before closing its cover (*Hurly Burly*).

"I don't feel so good," I said.

"Glad you're so happy to see me," touching the back of her hand to my cheek as she snuck a look at Camilla.

"Oh, stop. I just feel nauseous."

"Well, don't give it to *me*."

As we exchanged one of those little stiff back-patty hugs, I craned my head around at Cammy, who was trying not to watch me as she explained something to Phillip. I wanted to tell her how the *Guiding Light* pantomime she was watching actually consisted of *Divorce Court* dialogue, for instance,

"What are you *up* to these days?"

from Rachel, her apparently still-running double entendre for my performance on that last liquored night we'd spent enmeshed across the floor of that very closet. And another reason why I think I was fired.*

"You're a caution," I said.

"How's rock 'n' roll?"

"I'm talking with a few labels," I said, which was an outright lie, but I liked this new answer's crisp equivocation so much that I decided right then to make it my standard one.

"How's acting?" I made myself ask.

"In*cred*ible." She waited for a follow-up *Why?* Then added, "You got . . . ha . . . *balls* coming back here after what happened with Swindle."

(She'd made sure to tell me on a number of occasions just how tiny my nuts were.)

"Do you think he's still pissed about that night?" I asked her, using this as an excuse to look over my shoulder for Swamble, as well as Camilla, who glanced at her watch as Phillip shot me cynical scowls from out of his joey pouch.

"It's funny, but actually, he still talks about it sometimes," she said.

"In a nostalgic, fond kind of way?"

"Mmm, *litigious* is more the word I'd use. Isn't there a warrant out for your arrest or something?"

"*Is* there!?" I felt my lungs ice over.

But then I got an idea. Because on the floor next to Rachel was this dusty old derby which had been there since I'd started doing coat check ten years ago, still unclaimed, that

FOOTNOTE >

*Hector had found us with his flashlight, and I always had the hunch that he'd squealed on me to Swamble, but not on Rachel, who I actually heard gave him the occasional blowjob.

we'd used to stash hors d'oeuvres and cocktails and sometimes even a little terracotta bong under for those long dismal shifts.

"Hey, can you pass me the Homburg?" I said.

"I've got a mai tai under it."

"*Please.*" I glanced back at Cammy, who was talking to an enormous Anna Nicole Smith sort of person with phony torpedic boobs that nearly brushed the nose of a millionairy little yutz standing beneath her, whose shifting eyes held that embarrassed entitlement of someone waiting for their dog to piss on the sidewalk. Cammy snuck another glance at me, so I reeled a bit. Asking Rachel,

"Do you have any Dramamine?" with the back of my hand to my brow.

"Who's *that*?" she said, affecting, for Cammy's sake, a little Breck Girl toss of her auburn locks. "The big rock star's supermodel hottie?"

"Shut the fuck up."

Rachel's big red mouth tried to reply, but I told her,

"I'm sorry. Look, please, I beg you. I need the Homburg. Swamble'll probably have me sentenced if he recognizes me." I looked over my shoulder to see his full-tilt swagger down the long marble hall, then hurtled over the little half door of the coat check, nearly knocking Rachel over as I crawled on all fours at the Homburg, wanting very much to taste the pretty pink potion under it, then getting a mouthwatering whiff of marijuana when I pulled the hat onto my head and hid behind a warm curtain of coat. I smelled the cozy poison of mothballs and heard a hoarse woman ask for

"the old camelhair?"

as my ass, which was apparently sticking out in the breeze, received a swift little kick,

"Ow!"

before Rachel retrieved the fur, saying,

"Cheap old bitch,"

when she didn't like the tip which had chinked against some coins.

"Keep smiling, girlfriend," came Swamble's high nippy tenor and three finger snaps as he no doubt did that little indignant-diva-who-cranes-her-neck-like-a-belly-dancer thing. It was Brad's loud wet giggle followed by four receding marble footfalls until Rachel told me,

"The coast is clear, Curtis."

And I leaped over the little partition and walked though noisy smoke and gossip to Cammy and Phillip, with the Homburg pulled way down over my eyebrows.

Wary Phillip yapped once at me.

"It's *me,*" I told him, distractedly scratching behind his ears as they twitched out of her handbag.

"You feel better?" she asked, taking my hand, taking in the Homburg.

"Not really," I remembered, doubling over a little. "I mean, it seems to come and go," leaving my options open.

"Why are you wearing that hat, hon?"

"Um, well. What I'm trying to do is, see. What I'm trying to do is keep my body heat in. They say eighty percent of it escapes through your head, or something." I adjusted the Hat a bit.

"Seventy-five percent," she said. "And I think it's *all* of your extremities. Sweetie, do you smell like pot?" she asked politely, and quisling Phillip huffed the Homburg, which he then began licking until she finally pried him off. A woman walked by, stroking a silky tan Yorkie who sported a tiny white fur coat that replicated her own exactly. He and Phillip exchanged snotty glances. Cammy said,

"Are you sure you feel all right to stay?"

"I'm fine. You seem to really like it here, huh, Cutie? When did you start coming?"

"First I was invited through work, and then I guess Christie's put me on their list. I feel like Holly Golightly in here." She gazed around with guilty glee at this last wrinkled empire, the fine hard glint of Europe still in their eyes as they held off Death with the battered equipment of anecdote. "These people," she said, "are so fascinating to me. Their faces remind me of those grotesque Leonardo sketches."

"I know the ones you mean."

And I thought I'd had another rare glimpse at her essence just then. That where in anyone else there would have been spite, in Camilla there lived a deep, almost pleasant skepticism, honed out of so much pain that it might have been acceptance, if only that pain could be phrased.

"What did Hector mean about that night?" she said, loudly, as the Christie's din suddenly swelled a few decibels around an exciting new arrival at the chandeliered entrance.

"Well," I tried. "There *are* some things I've been—"

"Hello, Phillipe," roared a dry, manicured lady I'd seen a lot at these wingdings over the years. She gave his head an obligated little pat, from which he recoiled. She laughed musically, then gave Cammy her big ugly diamond of a smile, and one I'd been offered many times instead of a tip.

I guess she didn't recognize me in the Homburg.

"How *are* you, Camilla Fell?" she howled, giving a little *too-tle-loo* wave to the gloomy handsome man at the entrance who was causing all the fuss. Cammy said,

"I'm simply *mis*erable, Maggie."

"*Smashing,*" from Maggie, rising up on her toes to peer at the Somebody. "And you look stunning as ever. What have you been up to?"

"Well, for starters, I killed my grandmother last night."*

"Really?" said Maggie, now squinting in a more interesting direction.

"With a monogrammed ice pick," Cammy yelled through the racket.† "Right through her pancreas."

"Uh-huh," nodded Mag, and the ruckus subsided.

"And then I had to cut off her finger so I could get at a diamond as big as your fist."

Mag was "So glad to hear it."

"Are you flatulent, Mag?"

"Of course," she said, Stepford head revolving.

Cammy gestured at me. "I'd like you to meet the surviving half of Milli Van–"

"Might you get me a champagne?" Maggie asked me, tapping my shoulder as her hard little eyes prowled the room.

"Um, I don't really work here anymo–," I began, but she was already snatching a slender goblet off the tray of a waiter in front of us.

Who was Brad.

"I *wor*ship your dress, Camilla," he gushed. "Is it an Oldham?" (Brad was an aspiring designer.)

FOOTNOTE >

*F.D.R. tried this greeting line out at the White House one night to see how many people were actually listening.

†Cammy was alluding to one of our favorite Salinger lines, where Eloise, in "Uncle Wiggly in Connecticut," refers to such an ice pick.

"No, it's from APC," Cammy told him.

I pulled my hat down further. Mag hitched herself to a passing tray of shrimp. The auctioneer tap-tapped a feedbacking mic, triggering a hush in which he welcomed us all, in *Brideshead Revisited* inflections, to the renowned Christie's auction house. He began listing items:

> **"Commencing with lot number 372B.**
> **We have a Chanel white patent-leather Barbie case,**
> **circa 1980. Starts at eight hundred U.S. dollars . . ."**

Brad stage-whispered to Camilla, "Would you care for some roasted pheasant stuffed with pomegranates and persimmons or some brandied black terrapin?" with every ingredient braised in his Irony. And none of which seemed to catch Phillip's fancy as he scanned them.

> **". . . and next we have the eye patch**
> **worn by John Wayne in the motion picture *True Grit*,**
> **sold in tandem only with the gown**
> **Audrey Hepburn wore in *Roman Holiday*, current bid**
> **for both is fourteen thousand USD . . ."**

Camilla whispered, "No thank you, Brad. But I want you to meet—"

"Hello, Homburger," he said, loud and bored, not looking at me.

The room was now amurmur over the last item sold.

"Howdy," I mumbled, eyes down.

I felt Cammy's stare on me as Brad traded a whistling waiter his champagne tray for another one holding honeysuckle votives, which he began igniting in front of me with a wide gummy smile.

"I love that smell," Cammy murmured, squeezing my hand, remembering, and she excused herself to the Ladies' Room.

"What's wrong, Birnbaum?" wondered Brad, his last word in three syllables. "You've got that hangdog look. Like you just took a big hairy shit and you're walking out of the bathroom."

"Please don't tell Swamble I'm here, okay?"

"Why *are* you here?"

**". . . and a Carlton Fisk autographed baseball offered by RBI Sports Memorabilia . . ."**

"We were invited," I said, dodging his eyes as another hush fell.

"*We*?"

"Yeah, *we*," I said, which my voice got loud and cracked on. A painted lady with a puckered brow and a finger at her lips turned to

"Shush!"

me.

**". . . the collar in which Checkers, former president Richard Nixon's cocker spaniel, passed away. Starting at . . ."**

Brad breathed, "Camilla's gorgeous," right into my ear. "Are you sure you can afford her?" Then actually licked my lobe.

I twitched away and winced, saying,

"As a matter of fact, I'm about to receive a very sizable record deal advance," unslobbering my ear with the back of a wrist.

"It's funny how you've been a*bout* to receive that advance for the entire decade that I've known your sorry ass."

When I could no longer stand his stare, I found my hand

shooting up in fiscal self-justification, at which the auctioneer pointed—

"Going, going."

In hopes of finding another bidder, I turned my head a desperate, sitcom 360 degrees . . .

. . . Sold!

I was so flustered that I hadn't even heard how much I'd bid as all at once the room buzzed in tittle-tattle, and I was flanked by a familiar half-pint record-keeping creature and a security guard the size of a Coke machine. The first one pipsqueaked,

"Will that be cash, charge, check, or Christie's Credit Card, Birnbaum?"

"Um, I'll go get my checkbook. It's in my coat," I told them, the blood in my skull athump. I gazed up at Coke Machine, taking all of him in.*

"How much is it again?" I asked casually.

The tiny man wrote on a pink receipt, which he handed me.

I gave the number ($7,500) a few nonchalant nods, then told them I'd be back in a sec. As Brad, his tray of votives illuminating a criminal grin, walked backward through the vast swinging doors. Which Camilla came out of . . .

I made sure she saw me puff out my cheeks in a barf-suppressing expression as I lurched and ducked under trays of feta cheese profiteroles, past the Donald,† and out into an empty

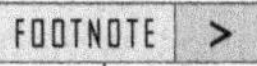

*I remember wanting to squeeze his thigh-like biceps.

†Trump was always at these little affairs.

marbled atrium in whose far corner bulged a black velvet chesterfield, behind which was a private little restroom that we all used to do blow in . . .

In the cool, abrupt, tiled calm, I left the lights off and locked the door. The room was lit only by a tube of pale blue moonlight that snuck through a Marlboro-sized hole in the shade. Which I'd made at the end of one very unhappy, coke-addled evening so long ago . . .

I collapsed on the toilet and cradled my face in my hands. I stayed there for some lost black minutes, I'll never know how many. Finally, I got up and looked into the huge, sumptuous mirror.

Great.

A cool $7,500. Add that to the grand tally.

"I'm not a bad person," I tried to convince my gloomy reflection.

*So what? You're going to lose her . . . Loser.*

Deep breath. Okay. Plan. Go fetch Cammy and Phillip, then exeunt. In the morning call up Christie's and, if need be, snivel and blubber my way out of this. And if that doesn't work, try and sell the collar on eBay—maybe even turn a profit.

I cracked the door. Cammy was rubbing supine Phillip's black tummy on the divan just in front of me, every now and then glancing up at my door. As I stood there and watched my little brown family, I sensed in this scene the end of an era. And, along with a vast sadness, I was flooded with tidal Love.

Still peering through the crack, I started making an elaborate combination of groans, wretches, whistles, and hockings, which immediately made soldier Phillip's tail and ears stand to attention. I gave it everything I had, pouring water in the toilet, and even shoving a finger down my throat to achieve that authentic visceral response before I ran water over the crown of the Homburg to make it look like I'd perspired right through the material. I staggered out, whispering,

"Tiny."

"Little, are you okay?" She grabbed my arm. "We saw you running over here and I was so worried." She sat me down on the sofa, stroking my pseudo-sweaty head as P.I. Phillip licked my wet fingers before cocking a suspicious head. I remember there was a Muzak version of that Britney Spears song "Oops" coming out of the speakers.

"You're soaked in sweat. Let's get you home right now."

"Please, thanks, yes," I shivered, looking around with hallucinatory glaze. "You're double-fisting?" I groaned, noting a pair of champagne glasses fizzing at her boots. "Who's the other drink for?"

The shadowy man who'd caused all the hullabaloo at the door before was smiling with extended palm above me.

"Curtis," said Camilla. "This is Stevers."

I stood up to shake a hand softer than any man's I'd ever. He was tall, dark, and fading, the wings of his patrician nose an atlas of broken capillaries and the amber of his wet, indulgent eyes mapped in minute scarlet vein. Yet I sensed that he'd once been very vigorous.

As he handed Cammy the silky white knuckle of an unblossomed rose, I noticed the diamond she'd always worn matched his exactly.

"I'm sorry to hear you're not well," he said. "I've heard so many lovely things about you." The voice rolled with the fluid precision of an expensive pen. And, as well as feeling confusion, humiliation, and something a little more cloudy than the gaudy greens of jealousy, I wanted him to talk to me forever . . .

But he didn't get a chance. Because Swamble was now charging down the long marble hall, in full fashion-runway strut, dishing out directives not only to Brad down at his left but up at Coke Machine to his right.

When the trio reached us, Swamble said,

"Hello, Stevers. Hello, Camilla," leaning in for the kiss; "Hello, Phillip." He offered him a fistful of fat oily cashews. Phillip sniffed and chose to abstain.

Swamble then turned with a scathing smile at me.

"Nice hat."

# Fly Me to the Moon

I said, "You told me in *Questionnaire* that you *liked* to stay up all night," as we lay in the dark on my bed. "Cammy?"

"I didn't mean every night."

There was an awful lack of accent on her *every*. Recently I'd started making her overdiscuss everything—struggling to fix Us with the desperate fluffs and pats a restless sleeper gives his pillow—flipping it over and over for the brief soothing cool side—before it goes flat and tepid again.

"I know you hate it when I ask you this," I asked her. "But are we getting along?"

"How can you not *know* that?"

"Because you never *tell* me anything. And would you please look at me for once?"

She flaunted the cobalt blue of her eyes at me in the moonlight. "It just scares me when you say that. It makes you sound so *insecure*."

"Cammy, if you haven't noticed by now, I *am* insecure. I used the word as my Hotmail password."

"I'm not sure I wanted to know that."

"Jesus. If I can't tell *you* stuff, then who can I? I mean, isn't there someplace where low self-esteem is re*war*ded?"

"Auschwitz."

And I actually laughed, relieved for some levity, as she lifted her head and looked over at the pale green glowing limbs of my alarm clock, then rolled over with a groan.

I tried to let the worried air around us subside awhile . . .

but silence with Cammy had become, at that point, like getting an itch on my nose with my hands tied . . .

"So, *are* we?" I said.

"What?"

"Getting *along*?"

"I've never been happier with you."

"Why don't I get that sense? Cutie?" I could see our pet names were now only cloying decorum, wilted corsages clutching at life. "Cutie?"

"It seems like you want to pick a fight with me or something, sweetie." She punched her pillow with the brutality of a blue-eyed rookie cop. "Like you have something else on your mind."

"Maybe you're right," I said, hoping she'd pursue this, which she didn't. And through the next damp batch of minutes, we drifted . . .

. . . into a tide, my bed as our raft, floating upon a kind and courteous sea—but one that grew gradually muscular, trying to convince me of some vital thing, as it began to dream *me,* as if *it* were the mind and I were the image. I was aware of needing to please this ocean, because I had an appetite for the words it was urging me on with, in the way we need a father's approval—until, from above, I watched a ghost of my body fall back into itself and onto my bed—where I awoke in a jerk, mouthing the word *avocado.*

Little sawing sounds were drifting out of Camilla.

I pressed her leg until it twitched awake, then immediately removed my hand. "I miss you," I said softly, frantically.

"How can you miss me?" her voice struggling out of a drowse, "I'm right here."

"I think it's a kind of preemptive nostalgia or something."

"That worries me," and she took my hand and spooned me, aligned me, strapping me in for another plunge into Sleep . . . but

"I promise I won't keep you up anymore after this, Otter, I swear," I said. "Just one more thing though, okay?" In the parlance of date rape, I took her lack of an answer as grounds to proceed: "Remember when we were growing up, that kid who supposedly died from eating too many Pop Rocks?"* I nudged her. "Cutes?"

She moaned something, half digested by a dream.

"So when did you finally realize Fonzie was a fag?"† I persisted, hoping this would amaze her back awake.

"Winkler's *gay*?"

"Damn straight. No pun."

"Oh, of *course* he is," she said, resigned. "Of course."

"Yessiree." I rolled over and ladled her sleepy soft haunches, and as they conformed to my own, I got totally aroused. "And remember when Rod Stewart passed out during that concert, and they pumped his stomach and found a pint of some guy's sperm?"

"I heard it was a quart, though," her voice slow with memory. "God, why do I still need to believe all that stuff? Remember the whole Richard Gere gerbil thing?"

FOOTNOTE >

*Those candies that would crackle in your mouth.

†I had no idea whether this was true or not.

"I never bought that one. I had a field mouse. Esme."

"That's cute," she said, "Cutie," in a sisterly tone, rolling away from me.

"Are you too tired for sexeroo? Cam?"

She let out a loud, guilty breath.

"Out of the following sex positions, which one . . ." I went on in *Questionnaire* mode, almost wanting her to turn me down so I could hold a grudge. "Um?"

"Sweetie, I'm just so exhausted."

"Okay, fine. Terrific."

Gradually, I watched a confining dream grasp her, causing her jaw to pulse in the moonlight.

"Did you see the new *TV Guide* with Travolta on the cover?" I asked her, loudly. "I gave my spot up in the express line at Gristede's just to read it."

"It's *fright*ening. I know. He's a *mon*ster," she rallied with surprising vigor. "He looks like Eddie Munster. There's just no way he approved that photo. His hair looks like a black helmet. Like a *work of Renaissance masonry,** as DeLillo would say."

"And his face is *huge* now, right?"

"*Huge*. He's a different person than Vinnie Barbarino on *Kotter.* He's got that moon face."

"Exactly!" I sat up, relieved to be agreeing on something. "These people *moon*. What *is* this phenomenon?"

"Well, several things are occurring," she explained with a practiced boredom, playing down our delight in her always astute celebrity perceptions. "First, your skin thickens and

FOOTNOTE >

*From *Great Jones Street.*

coarsens, and it loses a lot of its connective tissue, elasticity, and pigment, so you get that sagging white bloated look."

"Right," was my encouraging caesura in her rhythm.

"And the muscles around your jaws atrophy, so the sides of your face grow round, hence that moon effect. The skin around your eyes also thins, and the cartilage in your ears and nose continues to grow until you die. According to *Glamour,* there are fifteen muscles"—she was petering into a dream—"in your lips . . . alone."

In a minute she was drooling on my hand. I didn't move it, or even really *want* to. *Lovesickness,* I thought.

"So who else, Cutie?" I elbowed her. "Let's get to the bottom of this. Who else mooned?"

"Stevie Nicks," she mumbled.

"*Totally.* And Jimmy Page, right? Hey, maybe I should have my lips thickened. Rock stars just don't have thin lips. Tyler, Jagger, Elvis?"*

"I'll break up with you if you do," she promised into her pillow.

"Thanks."

A prickly pause.

"Hey, Henley's thin-lipped," I said. "And *he's* a sex symbol. Did you see his new album on the panel at Tower? It's called *Inside Job.*"

FOOTNOTE >

*These days, combing my star map for more mooners, I find Debbie Harry, the three less-interesting guys in Aerosmith, Paul McCartney, Mickey Rooney, Jon Voight, Cindy Lauper, Eddie Vedder, Anson Williams, the Boss, the King, of course . . .

"That's *so* Huey Lewis. And your lips are sexy, sweetie." With a blind hand she gave my penis an appeasing little squeeze.

"I have to get that goddamn lump looked at. You just felt it, right?"

She yawned. "Curtis, there *is* no lump. We've been through this. But if you're really worried, just go get it checked."

"I'm scared. They'll say they have to snip it off just to get my money."

"I can't believe you won't go."

"I can't af*ford* it." Another pause. "Tom Hanks. *Tot*al mooner."

"You mean you didn't get the health insurance yet?"

"I'm working on it. As soon as I get the record deal, Tiny."

"Have you started the demo yet?"

"Technically, no. Not yet. I'm still in preproduction."

Clenched, I let the statement fade off into the dark.

In a minute, she murmured "Moon Unit" in a departing watery helix of a voice.

"Moon Unit Zappa," I said. "She still goes by that name. They said it in *People*."

I sensed the troubled tentacles of her dreams beginning to grasp her, and I waited . . . needing them to reach out for me.

"I'm sorry I'm not famous for you," I didn't mean to say.

I thought I felt her stiffen.

"Look," I said, hoping she'd chime in from whatever level of consciousness she happened to be bobbing on. "I'm *trying*. I mean, is it so much to ask for to get a fucking panel at Tower? . . . And I just realized something," my eyes on the ceiling. "You don't think I'll get a record deal, do you? You always avoid the subject. It just occurred to me."

"I think it's very difficult," she said finally, matter-of-factly.

"Just admit you don't think I'll get one."

There was a long, windy silence, desolate as a stretch of midnight interstate. I looked out the window at a swollen, jaundiced moon. *How literary,* I thought. It was waning.

# I Do Want What I Haven't Got

That late summer Monday held Winter's first deadly breath.

I spent it busking in Lafayette Street's subway station with a raw throat and chilly stiff fingers, which had turned my singing and guitar work into a loose rusty mesh that jangled through the ruthless fluorescence of that gigantic refrigerator.

Around dawn I'd slipped from Cammy's drowsy warm clutches* to get in a good day of practice and pocket money. But my songs had only grazed the ears of my fellow New Yorkers as they squinted up into the squawk of the antique speakers, as if to better understand their garbled train announcements.

I'd spent those nippy eight hours competing with that and the rhesus-monkey screech of train breaks. There'd been the usual, random Cornell acquaintance from whom I turned a blushing face, as well as the occasional guy wearing his guitar on his back, bleeding heart on his sleeve, with whom I shared that weight-of-the-world sigh-and-eyebrow-raise of one Sisyphus to another.

Of course, I hadn't made a dime.

The echoing station seemed oddly drained that day, and the only money in my gig bag, lying open and pleading in front of me, was the three rumpled singles I'd baited myself. Finally,

FOOTNOTE >

*I lied and told her I was going in to temp as a proofreader.

after finishing my scratchy take on Sinéad's "Last Day of Our Acquaintance," I bent down in one last attempt to arrange those dollars to look somehow both forlorn and well spent—when suddenly a fiver fell on top of my ante, and, looking up, or rather *down*, who did I see but little Rip!

I realized I'd actually missed him, which I told him as we hugged, then gave him a Little Green–styled flyer to a distant upcoming gig at Baby Jupiter, for which he traded me one to his **CONNY No Commitment Open House**.* I saw him searching my wrist for the friendship bracelet he'd given me, so I told him the whole Camilla ring thing (minus a few details). He then offered me and my own ring a cautious little nod and asked me where "the soft brown soul with the beautiful energy" was anyway. I said I was actually supposed to be meeting her in a few minutes up at the Met . . . when suddenly he was yelling her name across the rat-filthy tracks to the opposite platform.

I ducked behind a sooty pillar, avoiding both her eyes and a strained good-bye to mystified little Rip as, in attempt to beat her uptown, I madly gathered my things and managed to pry an arm into the ❹ express train's shutting doors, which the invisible operator utilized in giving my ankle several savage and disciplinary bites before I managed to squirm my way inside of the car. I looked around at the delayed, scowling, sardined passengers, who seemed to consist of about one actual commuter to every ten homeless beggars—before I noticed, through finger-smudged windows, Cammy rushing down the stairs and stepping onto the local ❻ train.

Great.

FOOTNOTE >

*I pictured him feeding a ferret in his bedroom.

I crashed through armpit odor and *What the fuck?*s so I could save time and get to the train's front car, which stopped at the Museum's entrance, picking my way through knots of tourists betrayed by their colorful duds and lack of Manhattan pallor. I was sure that Cammy's widening eyes had met mine as her local train passed my creeping "express" at Twenty-third Street, so I leaped between cars. Where, in the clattering, flashing blackness, I heard the needle-on-vinyl squeal of my gig bag snagging something metal.

# Tut, Tut

Running late up the steps against kvetching, gray wind, and winded myself, I slowed into what I hoped was a Sunday-at-the-museum kind of stride as I came into the soaring gloom of the Met. Glancing around for Cammy, I had the sudden sense of a boy king stumbling onto his own mausoleum. I think this feeling of a fait accompli, combined with my general Camilla guilt, was deepened by the museum's vacancy that afternoon—which I suddenly understood when the cashier wished me a

"Happy Labor Day."

"Ohhh," I said, getting it. "Okay. Thanks."

And I hurried into the gift shop and bought her the poster of that Maxfield Parrish painting she'd mentioned, *The Land of Make Believe,* then mounted the immense cement staircase, taking three of its smooth, regal steps at a time until I reached the Rembrandt room. Which Camilla had picked as our rendezvous. And which she'd beaten me to, standing in there alone except for an old security guard with a paunch and a pistol.

"Why do you have your guitar?" was the first thing she asks me. "I thought you were proofreading." I realized I'd never once heard her voice glare, never seen her eyes these crushed shards of blue bottle.

I blinked, thought of a lie, and swallowed. "I thought, that, um, we could have a little picnic in the park later, and I could serenade you."

"It's fifty-five degrees out."

"I thought we could maybe build a fire or something," I smiled, disgusted with my own budding flair for deception.

"There's an 87 percent chance of rain."

"Oh. Where's our little man?" I said gaily.

"I snuck him in," she mumbled, rolling her eyes at the guard behind us, then down at her half-fastened backpack. There were two gleams and a blink in the leather dark.

"How did you get that rip in *your* bag?" she went on, with surprising tenacity.

I felt an odd obligation to really play up my role as the double-dealing boyfriend. "I was attacked by a pride of Chihuahuas in Chelsea."

Turning her back to the guard, she said, in a screaming whisper, "Look, I saw you on the subway, and I know you saw *me*. And I saw Rip. And you busking." She gave me the full bitter glitz of her eyes.

There was something so awfully satisfying about this alien state I'd caused in Camilla that I couldn't even speak. I just stared in her face, letting myself be pulled into the fatal magnet of the moment.

"It just hurts me so much that you would *lie* to me!" She looked down, shook her head. "That's what really hurts me the most," she said softly.

"Okay, okay, I was busking, Cutie. Look, I'm totally broke and I need to practice, so I figured, why not get paid? I'm really sorry I lied to you, Cammy." I took her hand, which stayed limp. I released it. "It's just, I always feel like if I don't lie to you, I'll lose you."

She was silent, glancing over at the guard. He began pacing, giving us "Strangers in the Night" in a trilling witty whistle.

"But I already seemed to have done that," I said. "A while ago, actually. I guess we've both been pretending, but neither one of us had the guts to say anything, huh?"

I looked at the self-portrait on the wall next to me, at two lovely pallid hands that Rembrandt had painted with one of them—I knew I was making a memory.

"Things aren't working out, are they?" I said.

There was a long, adhesive pause, in which Camilla still couldn't look at me. The guard clasped his hands behind his back and strolled all the way to the other side of the huge, silent room.

"*Are* they?" I said.

"They don't seem to be," she said, in half whisper, head bowed.

"Can you please look at me, Cammy?"

She did.

"I mean," I said. "At least until you're done breaking up with me," hoping she'd say, *I'm not breaking up with you . . .*

. . . which she didn't.

And then, as Hope and Despair faced off, there was that utterly still, at-the-top-of-the-roller-coaster moment . . . before the screaming fall.

"So you're breaking up with me, then, aren't you?"

"I don't know." She shook her hanging head. "Yes. I think I am."

A mercury tear rolled into my mouth. "Is this a definite decision, or is there room for me to negotiate here?"

"I guess—I guess I really don't know yet."

"When do you think you might get a clearer picture?"

"Please, this isn't funny." She took my hand, slamming her eyes shut. "This is extremely hard for me."

"I'm the one who's crying." I retrieved my hand to wipe my

cheeks, then glanced back at the guard, who took sudden interest in his foot, which he started to tap. I kept my eyes on him until I'd stared him right out of the room. Cammy said,

"This would be a good way to pull a heist," with all her calm moxie still intact in the face of disaster.

"Maybe *you* could cry a little too, maybe. For once. I mean, do you have *any* feelings for me at *all*?" Because now I just wanted her reaction, some intensity again.

"I do! You *know* I do. The deepest possible feelings. That's what makes this so disgusting. I just don't feel them as publicly as you do."

"So basically, we're breaking up over busking? Is that the deal?"

"It's bigger than that." Her face wrinkled with deep pain and concentration. "But yes, it's definitely part of it."

"How?"

She bit her bottom lip.

"How?" I repeated.

"You didn't make me feel safe," she said, in a delicate voice.

"You're already using the past tense. Great. 'Safe'? Okay, so I'll stop busking."

"But I don't *want* you to change. It's who you are. And it's really not just that one thing."

"About how many things is it?" I said, with a teary giggle. "Just an estimate."

She didn't respond. Her backpack bulged. I stroked it.

"Really, how many, Cammy? I can totally change them all. Let's go through them one by one, okay? . . . Please?"

"Okay." She looked at me bluntly. "The whole thing in Paris, where you forgot the keys. I mean, I know you had a lot on your mind, but . . . and all the medication you take. And the night at Christie's—"

"You made a list today, didn't you?"

She didn't deny it.

I said,

"Which one of the following traits would you say contributed most to your ultimately dumping me?" in *Questionnaire* format.

"You lied to me about the thing at Christie's, Curtis."

"Cutie, I was so broke back then that I couldn't *eat*. And I also knew I'd need those votives to woo you with six months later."

"And I want a family."

"I do, too!"

"But sweetie," she said, which I could tell she hadn't meant to let herself say, "you don't have a steady job. And it's not that I'm *ask*ing you to get—"

"Look, I'm busking because I love music. But also so I can practice performing and get a huge record deal, which I *am* going to get, whether you believe it or not, and ultimately have a gigantic family. I *love* kids. I wanna have tons of them. With *you*. Five or six, if you're up for it. Climbing all over us like little monkeys." I could see her eyes going soft as she tried not to imagine this, so I came at her fast with, "I've always had this vision of us on some big ranch, full of our little brats with strawberry jam all over their faces, and a whole goddamn squadron of dachshunds." I gave the leather lump an *Exhibit A* hand flourish. "I mean, don't you think I'd be a good father? . . . *Don't* you?"

Behind her narrowed eyes I could tell she was hunting around for a euphemism. "I—I think you'd be like, the magic. But"—she sighed out of her nose, steeling herself—"I don't think you'd be strong enough."

"Wow. Wow. That really hurts. Jesus. I think you're completely fucking wrong, by the way. I'd totally rise to the occasion."

"But it's—also, it's—we're very different. I think you refuse to see it. You put me on a pedestal. You're so obsessive. You have an addictive personality, and that whole thing scares me too. I just feel like I know deep down it would just be fatal for us in the long run. I'm not blaming you, but I'm exhausted because of your insomnia. I haven't slept for months. I feel like I've traded day for night . . ."

And her words were coming quicker and quicker, spaced closer and closer, a quarter spinning on a glass table, as frantically falling she went on with,

"And don't you see how incredibly helpless and upset it makes me when I see you so unhappy about your career and I can't do a thing?!"

"But you wrote in that early e-mail, quote, 'Don't think I can't handle some sadness too. You're not going to ruin things unless you want to.' Re*mem*ber?"

"But you took it so far. You made all of your problems mine."

"I'm sorry, okay? You never told me any of this. So now I know, okay? I won't do it anymore, I promise."

"Please," she said. "That's not—it's just—not *right*."

"Jesus, why am I crying and you're totally stone-faced? Why do I always—or why *did* I always—feel like the woman in our relationship? Or not even the woman, exactly. More like some marginal little elf or something. And why do I have to make *you* feel safe? What am I, a *fire*man? Why can't you make *me* feel safe? I always feel like I'm grade-grubbing for your affection. What happened to me being your favorite goddamn person in the world? E-mail session eight, I believe, near the middle. The one taped to my fridge. Me and your mother, you said."

"Maybe you still are."

" '*Maybe*'? And what about *you*? And all your secrets? You never told me the whole deal with that Stevers character. And those matching *Wonder-Twin-Powers-Activate!* rings. I mean, do you trade rings with *every*body?"

She looked down. "We do things," she said privately. "We go on drives together, through Westchester. He's very lonely."

"Does he make you feel safe?"

A pause.

"Yes. He does. But there's other things."

"Like what?"

"His daughter killed herself last year. She had HIV. Stevers feels completely responsible. We share the same—he and I seem to fill some kind of—I tried to tell you that time what he means to me, but you got so jealous. He was why I was late to our first date."

A young couple came in, nodding and rigid with early courtship, forcing themselves to look a little longer than normal at each painting before they moved on. I watched them with an ironic nostalgia that I hoped Cammy would notice, but some central gear of her was otherwise engaged.

"Where *are* you now?" I asked her. "You're doing your receding thing. And right in the middle of our breakup."

"I'm sorry," she said, coming back only somewhat.

"I always wondered, Cam; where is it that you *go*?"

Staring at the floor—in a dense, secluded voice that seemed not her own—she said,

"There are things, from a long time ago. And I go to that place, where they happened, looking for her. For that little girl. Who could cry."

"What happened? Cammy, please tell me."

She was silent.

"Why won't you let me love you? Cammy? I *love* you."

"I always felt—feel like you want me to *prom*ise you something when you say that."

"Look, do you love me or not?"

The wooing couple traded looks and listened, grateful to be bonded by our breakup, grist for their new mill.

"Fuck them," I said. "Yes, or no?"

"I don't *know.*" She lowered her voice. "I don't feel like it's exactly love we're in. It's different."

"How different?"

"It's sharper. Maybe it was *more.*"

"I think that's what scares you, that somebody can feel this intensely about you. Cammy?"

"It does scare me," she said, almost to herself. "I've learned there's such a thing as too much love."

For the first time I felt that Camilla, for some long-ago reason, had been expending the whole of her being into a vast, blind resistance. And that this resistance, as well as the reason that aroused it, would do its best to exclude me. I knew it was over.

I sniffled, in a completed way that reminded me of a bullfight's cleanup crew.

"I got you this," I remembered, handing her the poster.

As she unrolled it, Cammy gave me the only truly honest *You-shouldn't-have* look I'd ever seen. "You're so good," she said, looking down at the picture. "That's why this is so sickening. You're just so good."

We walked out through dark chalky catacombs and treasures that didn't look much like treasures; past the mummies and pyramids and the ivory bust of Caligula with his ravenous lips; and finally past a Gilbert and George exhibit of grainy graphic paintings with titles like *Piss, Shit,* and *Cunt*. I looked at Camilla, walking ahead of me, away, thinking how much more valuable she was than all of it put together. Then she turned back to me, with a glance that made me say, in my stunned despair,

"*Simile Game:* You just gave me a look full of both a kind of entitlement and guilt, like an airplane passenger in the seat right in front of me, about to lean back and ruin my flight."

Outside on the steps was the damp gusting night. This winter was supposedly going to be the most atrocious since 1916 or something. I didn't feel exactly up for one of those.

Phillip made a smothered whimper and we freed him.

"I'm going to miss you and your mommy very, very much," I told him, framing his sharp little head in my hands. I was fighting back tears so fierce that zones of my face were now going numb and twitchy from overload. I kissed his moist nose goodbye.

"Cammy," I said against the chilly windsong. "The worst part of all this is that not only did I lose you, but I know deep down that you're actually right about a lot of this. And so I know I really can't, in any good conscience, talk you into me." I wiped my nose with the back of a wrist. "I mean, you're the best thing that I ruined. And there's been a lot of things."

She sighed "Oh," or maybe it was "No."

There was the glum jingle of a soda can getting blown down the steps. I lifted her chin and, out of a last-ditch denial, some animal desperation, I leaned in to kiss her. And she let me. Until I began moving my tongue inside her indifferent mouth, and she gently pushed my chest away, shaking her head, her eyes sealed.

When they opened, I stood there. Searching them a last time.

"I wish you heaven," she said.

We took different subways downtown.

## TWO

The Angel

I Dreamt a Dream! what can it mean?
And that I was a maiden Queen:
Guarded by an Angel mild:
Witless woe, was neer beguil'd!

And I wept both night and day
And he wip'd my tears away
And I wept both day and night
And hid from him my hearts delight

So he took his wings and fled:
Then the morn blush'd rosy red:
I dried my tears & armd my fears,
With ten thousand shields and spears.

Soon my Angel came again;
I was arm'd, he came in vain:
For the time of youth was fled
And grey hairs were on my head

# Under Sleep

Oh, Camilla.

Her tenderfoot soul. My gossamer girl. Shredded in the engines of all my ambition. In Love's bitter mystery.*

I lost her.

Now, as I wander through shelterless days, I'm still not exactly sure what went wrong. The idea of her seems so impractical now. Did she actually happen to me? Had Cammy really managed to love the wretch of me so deeply? I keep poring over *Questionnaire,* attempting to reinterpret every subsequent event—to shuffle some of this blame around—by, you could say, perusing the fine print of our contract for a loophole that might lead me back to her. I mean it's obvious that I, with all my impossible need, tried to get her to mommy me, fix me, dismantle the grenade I'd become before I inevitably lobbed it onto the altar of our Love. Still, I always feel there was something buried, something more. Something *other.*

But when these insomniac nights† finally fade to first

FOOTNOTE >

*In Yeats's "Who Goes with Fergus?" he says "And no more turn aside and brood upon love's bitter mystery." I wish.

†It was on one of those distorted morning-afters that I met Little Green, my new neighbor and soon-to-be star guitar student.

light . . . She comes back to me. Or actually, I come to *her.* Because the Camilla riddle is scribbled on the backs of my eyelids just as soon as I close them. A hieroglyphic in the twinkling tints of dragonfly wings.

And then last night, I felt like I finally fathomed Her. Her essence. You know that sensation, when somebody just *dawns* on you? For the first time she seemed to make consummate sense—as I lay suspended in that elastic lesson of half-dream, just before day broke—and saw that not only was she just so . . . *sane.* But I think I also understood, at last, what her eyes were so flustered for.

*Order.*

That was it. Every inch of her ached for it. From the unlenient blue stare, to the scrupulous mouth.

Order.

# A Hint of Hieronymus Bosch . . .
# A Splash of Norman Rockwell

I'd spent the night treading filthy rotten milk at the bottom of a well. The Dream Gestapo said I could stop only after I'd counted aloud to a thousand, in German, which I discovered I was surprisingly fluent in. But of course I kept losing track and having to begin all over again. Finally, after many black rancid hours, the day broke above me. I was no more than a wallowing cramp at that point, fading fast, my mouth counting in gasps just above the surface—

—until suddenly, I managed to clutch at the sunlit mouth of the well above me . . . because in it was the silhouette of Camilla (Oh, blessed Uvula!). She yelled down to me then, but I couldn't understand a thing she was saying; her words became cold drizzle as they fell in my left ear, which, in straining to hear her, I'd managed to hoist just above the curdled surface.

It didn't matter anyway. I knew I was drowning. And it struck me as horribly apt that, tragicomic to The End, my ear would be Cammy's last memory of me—an alert little nautilus, gurgling into oblivion.

All this, however, was rudely interrupted when Reality, that dogged door-to-door salesman, came knocking on my unconscious. And so, lying somewhat awake in a gray wedge of dawn (and the appropriate cold sweat), I began to groggily understand that the raps had been at the actual front door of my apartment. I freed myself from a damp tangle of sheet and dream, and as I was fumbling into my clothes, there came a couple of much softer knocks—a hopeful little pause—and then a sad *Oh well* tap.

"Just a second!" I croaked, almost tripping over the still-empty leg of my jeans as I limped to the front door's fisheye . . .

. . . which, I noticed, had turned the figure outside into a long green parenthesis.

I blinked.

The parenthesis poked a finger at the peephole.

Great. I'd forgotten Little Green's Monday-morning guitar lesson. Again.

Opening the door, now fully dressed, I sucked in my lungs and rose up on tiptoe as my student, eyes down, lugged a guitar case as tall as herself (but several years ahead of her in curves) past me down the cramped foyer. She wore Nikes, green tartan pajamas, and her hair drawn up into a central geyser.

I followed her into the shady room, where she sat on the couch in a ray of mild sun. She instantly crossed a pair of very long legs and, without a word, began to examine the chord chart in her hand ("Black Bird"), which I'd made for her as homework—all the while offering me her profile as though I'd asked to sketch it.

I just stood there, about two guitar lengths away from her, feeling incredibly guilty. The latest Camillanightmare had left a bad taste in my mouth, and I was betting my breath was probably pretty horrendous—so I waved.

My pupil, still reading, waved back; but it was strictly from the wrist.

The room was totally silent except for the busybody hum of

the fridge behind us. Finally, I did a little *So-let-us-begin* clap of the hands, but I realized all the lights were still off, so in the hopes of brightening room morale, I yanked the dimmer up to a blazing O.R. level. At which point my pupil, bending forward to unbuckle the case at her feet, winced those tremendous eyes. I dimmed the lights a bit and, with my back at the wall, cleared my throat and said,

"I've got Earl Grey or English Breakfast, Sweet Pea. Are you hungry at all?"

A pause.

"Not especially, thanks," she said, deeply absorbed in lifting her guitar out of its red velvet vault.

I plowed on with

"And the honey's almost empty, so we can turn the bear into another squirt gun!"

I waited five heartbeats—eyebrows high—until she muttered

"Cool," now attending to a blemish she'd apparently just discovered on the back of her guitar's neck, which she'd clamped between her knees.

"Cool," I agreed, just audibly.

My visitor took her time placing the guitar on the sofa cushion to her left. I fished a pitch pipe out of the front pocket of my jeans. I looked at it. And then I could've sworn I'd seen a peripheral pack of Kools* as she leaned forward to snatch a pick out of her case's little storage cubby (and snuck her first glance at

FOOTNOTE >

*They'd been the brand that looked the koolest to *me* when I'd secured my first furtive pack from the empty mall's vending machine on that long-ago Sunday—reaching down into the dark slot as if for some delicious wicked mints.

me)—before slamming it shut. Obviously, I was in no position to grill her right then, but I did put my hands on my hips and, for a long akimbo moment, watched her raise the guitar strap over that blonde spray of hair and down onto the back of her neck.

"Gimme your A?" she asked casually, indicating my pitch pipe with a glance that just might've achieved its full cucumber cool had she not been nibbling a nail right under it.

I blew the obliging note.

In severe concentration, my young apprentice began tuning her guitar, which, now in her lap, hid almost all of her except the extremities.

In The End, I think most of us'll find ourselves clutching only that handful of trusty images which, for whatever ineffable reason, never failed to leave us speechless. But I suppose I've gone and made it my own fragile task to tell you how I stood there and watched my friend's small solemn fingers, their nails gnawed to the quick, wrestling with the strings. Or how, after a full minute of tweaking her final E string (which hadn't needed it), Little Green finally looked up and, putting me on the business end of those eyes, said

"You forgot again, Clyde."

The fridge came to an eavesdropping silence.

"I'm so, so sorry, Walter," I said, as quietly as I could.

Little Green looked down at her fret board. She swallowed. After a second, she tried to say something—but she could only swallow again. With her head still down, she played the first clumsy notes of a scale she'd been struggling with that winter—then, giving up, she let her hand drop.

"You promised," she said, shaking her head as she looked back up at me.

There was an excruciating lack of accusation in her voice; a weary, fact-stating flatness.

"*Je*sus," I said. "I overslept again." I rubbed the back of my neck. "I can't believe what a *jerk* I am!"

She knit her brows and made slight, judicious nods. "Maybe it's best if we let my mom start renumerating you."

"No, no, sweetie!" I lunged forward and knelt in front of her. "I *swear* it's not that." I told her (out of the side of my mouth) how our time together had become "the absolute highpoint of my week," a fact that I then tried to squeeze into her cautious half of our secret handshake.*

"Really?" she reflected, gazing out the window. "I'd of thought it was your *na*dir." She let her guitar's neck serve as a wrist-rest for the hand I kept pumping, until, "Hey," she said, clamping my fingers. "Your hands are kind of clammy, Clyde." She shoved her meowing guitar aside and, standing up on the couch, motioned me to get up as well. I obeyed (with knee-cracking accompaniment), and she touched my forehead, furrowing her own. "You *are* a little *warm*." She bit her lower lip as she dabbed at what was left of my hairline with the flannel mitten she'd made out of her sleeve cuff. "And you're all sweaty," she said. "Are you sure you're okay, Clyde?"

"I was doing my pushups right before you came in," I lied. "But I just realized something."

"What?"

"*Some*one's getting *cal*luses."

"*Really!?*" she beamed . . .

. . . then immediately reknit her brows.

The immense green of her uncompromising eyes was now just level with my own (a first). I wondered if the unrequited

FOOTNOTE >

*An elaborate thing that ended with us cracking each other's knuckles.

nostalgia we seemed to be sharing was what we call déjà vu—and quite possibly the closest, heaven help me, I would ever come to God.

"I really am sorry, Walter," I said, not quite as gently as I'd wanted. "I guess I've been a bit under the weather lately."

"No biggie." She lowered her eyes. "Oh, God. *Sorry,*" she said, gritting guilty teeth as she noticed her Nikes on my sofa.

"No biggie." I held her hand as she hopped to the floor and skipped into the kitchen, where the fridge shuddered abruptly back on duty.

I sat down in the La-Z-Boy across from the couch and strapped on my own guitar. The sun had been slowly devouring a lumpy oatmeal sky, so the room was cheering up a little. My friend came back and handed me a measuring cup* full of ancient green Gatorade ("You need your electric lights, Clyde") and then, with her back to me, began taking very slow, heel-to-toe Breathalyzer-test steps to the window. She was silent as I tuned the first string and a half. Then,

"Hey, you know, I've been thinking," she said.

"Fill me in."

"According to my calculations, Clyde, we will have been acquainted exactly six months when my birthday comes."

"And when might that be, my love?"

"I just wrote it down in there on your calendar." Peering back at me over a tartan shoulder, my companion paused her advance until she obtained an authorizing nod. "And also," she said, stepping window-ward again, "I started writing lyrics for that Major 7 thing I showed you last week."

FOOTNOTE >

*My only clean glass.

"Mmm," I replied. (I was tongue-tied in a way that perhaps only a guitarist in the dissonant midst of tuning-up can appreciate.)

"So don't you wanna know what my song's going to be about, Clyde?"

I stopped tuning to say "I'm *dying* to, I just didn't want to pry," then continued.

"It's about the day we met."

The young motorist in question extended a horizontal arm and, after some teetering difficulty, managed to touch her nose as she walked. "Remember?" she paused, watching her feet.

"*Please,* Miz Green." I made an offended tsk. "Do I strike you as the type who just goes around forgetting fateful days?" (Twang, twang.) "Well?"

"*Nooo,*" she said, long and shy. And from the precise aerial leap she then executed, I gathered that my friend was now on a balance beam. "Question," she said, revolving on a toe to face me.

"Shoot."

"Can you babysit me after school on Thursdays?"

"What happened to what's-her-name? Rory?"

"I told her I thought we needed a little break from each other."

"And how did she take it?"

"She seems okay with it," she nodded. "And also she said you were cute but you should reconsider the retro sideburns. Anyway, my mom is really only home on the weekends now. And if you babysit, you can meet Calley Corbin next Thursday."

"Calley Corbin?" I said, straining to hear my A string.

"She's the new kid. I already *told* you about her." She kept her eyes on me as she divided herself into a split. Still tuning, I cocked an at-a-loss head. "Who nobody will be friends with because she *stutt*ers?" she said.

"Oh, right, Calley *Cor*bin."

"Well, she's nice and I invited her over to watch *Survivor* reruns."

"Good."

"Then after, we're gonna shmush bananas in our hair. The potassium," she explained. "will leave it silky-soft to the touch." She yawned. "There was a thing about it in *Cosmo Girl*."

"Well, be *care*ful," I said ("*Care*ful"?). Done with tuning, I moved on to noodling.

Little Green rolled over on her stomach and, supporting her chin with a pillar of fists, she lay there watching me with her shins scissoring the sunlight. After a minute she coughed and said,

"Anyway, Clyde, regarding Thursdays; not to be pushy, but can I get a commitment?"

"I think I can work it in. How *is* school, anyway?"*

My playmate sighed. "The whole school thing is getting a little tired, actually. Like, Che Guevara barely even *talks* to me now after I beat him in arm wrestling. Which was *his* idea in the first place. But then Sammy Manna informs me that Cheg only did it because he bet Sammy a week of chocolate-milk money that I'd let him hold my hand by Winter Break, which technically he *did,* I guess. Then, if *that* wasn't enough, last week, when everyone was saying what they want for Christmas and Hanukkah . . . Clyde?"

"Right?" I looked up.

"Well, half the class got totally mad at me when I told them

FOOTNOTE >

* I remembered too late how dull *I'd* found this question as a kid.

how Santa Claus was fake." She paused with a look meant to establish whether or not I'd been living under similar misinformation. I remained poker-faced. "Then," she continued, "they got even madder when I said that *God* was fake, too." She stared at the rug. "My dad says I'm lucky that he'll never lie to me."

She yanked herself to her feet and went to the windowsill, where, chewing a nail, she began probing sick Fern with her other hand.

"We better get started," I said. "You're not even dressed for school yet, Sunshine."

"No, I'm *wear*ing this," she told me, a bit wildly, picking up the framed Kmart InstaBooth shot of Camilla, me, and Phillip. "Sleepwear is fashion-forward. Tree Rabinowitz even copied me last Friday and wore his bunny suit, without the shoes. Just the footies."

I strummed gently as she studied the photo. From my angle I could just see the swollen, sullen jut of her lower lip, and with a not so dull pang, I foresaw that it was going to endure far more than its share of unwanted, as well as wanted, kisses.

"Clyde?" she said.

"Yes, love?"

"If I give you a picture, will you frame it? And I'll totally understand if you don't feel like we're there yet."

"*Frame* it? I'll blow it up and wallpaper the place. But come on, hon, what song should we add to your arsenal today?"

She turned around. "What song were you just playing?" She aimed the frame at its source. "That was totally cool."

"It's called 'Night and Day.' But Cole Porter isn't really rock and roll, honeybee. How about a classic? 'Round About?' 'Smoke on the Water'?"

"Well . . . I'd *like* to think we're pushing the envelope, Clyde."

Carefully, my friend set the frame down exactly where it had been. "I mean, Beck says crossed-pollination is what keeps music evolvingly vibrant. The *Beast*ie Boys sample Cole Porter."

And so, detached at first, I watched my fingers make chords I'd forgotten they knew, landing like break-dancers in a parade of impossible positions. For the first time in years, I noticed the pleasant sting of the strings cutting into my virtuous fingertips; the tiny shrieks of aluminum laughter they made as I slid up and down the neck; the hum of the hollow wood torso ebbing into my lungs . . .

*And this torment won't be through*
*Till I spend my life making love to you*

While I sang and played that essential psalm of longing, with its melody that reluctantly climbs the hopeful majors because it knows it must soon dive through the bitter minors, I realized I'd taken all of it for granted. I remembered, in my rusty vocal cords, in the sweet cramps of my fingers, why I'd decided to make music my life; how it could distill all the world's bottled-up yearning, then spill it through me or any number of other (less weather-beaten) instruments; how, within a few bars, it seemed to weave all of the uproar–the jackhammers, hollers, horns, sirens, and car alarms–into harmony; to make splendid sense of despair and confusion, in the way high altitudes make toy soldiers of war. I'll even risk saying I felt a part of the Universe again, and the possibility crossed my mind that its center might just rest outside of myself. I felt so free, I wondered why everyone wasn't *always* singing. It seemed like the most obvious, cathartic way to communicate, and that talk was only its vulgar, guttural abbreviation . . . its Yiddish.

Little Green and I lost ourselves somewhere inside of that song. When it was over, the sun smiled and the light in the room grew silvery. Outside, birds were beginning to swap last night's gossip. Then all at once it was unbearable.

"What's wrong, Clyde? Don't be sad. This is great!" She took a stab at "Night and Day" 's first chord. "It's why we want to be rock stars . . . right?"

I nodded, setting my guitar on its stand next to my chair. She walked to the window and rested her elbows on the ledge (without having to lean over), her chin on the joined heels of her hands.

"Don't you still want to be a rock star?" she asked me.

"I'm not sure," I said, in falsetto—I'd had my voice up so high during the song that I'd forgotten to bring it back down.

We were silent for a sunny wistful minute.

"Clyde, can I get your opinion on something?"

"Of course."

"Are divorces final?"

I got to my feet and came up behind her. "I've been wondering that myself, honey."

We stared into the morning. There was a single star left on from last night, and I remembered something I'd learned at around her age—that its shine was actually a million years old.

"But I guess I'd still like to think that only one thing is final. Which reminds me," I said. "Is there, by any chance, a pack of cigarettes in your case? . . . Um, Walter?"

"Not that I'm a*ware* of." Still looking out the window, she cracked her neck to the right and then—sneaking a sidelong glance up at me—to the left.

I tapped her shoulder, but she wouldn't turn around. "The pack of *Kools?*" I said, shaking her stalk of hair as if to jog her memory.

"Oh, *those,*" she said, nodding out the window. "I'm just holding them for a friend."

# I Read the News Today, Oh Boy

The low autumn sun washes my Art Deco lobby in dirty dishwater light. Although I've grown more and more terrified of what's sneering in my mailbox, I still force myself to check it once a week, with the same dread we get before facing that shocking gunk clumped under our fridges. And it's something I do only because I promised the mailman I'd clear out my box so he wouldn't have to keep cramming all my letters in. He was flabbergasted when, just recently, I asked him if I could even extend my weekly grace period to a *month*ly one, I guess because most of my neighbors hover around him as he distributes their mail, like a guy tossing chum to the screechy dolphins at Sea World.

My first letter today congratulates me on my honorable mention in one of the songwriting contests I spend around a grand entering annually. And I think, Hey, maybe my luck's changing. Maybe Karma's a kind of cheerful, task-happy old Aunt Jemima who's willing to wash behind my ears, not to mention those sheets I've been tossing and turning in, leaving me scrubbed and ready to step into a smart new wardrobe. I actually assume that I won some money—*validation!*

But no.

They're telling me I just missed the cutoff for cash prizes, and they've enclosed the bounced $50 check I paid for the competition fee.

Next up we have this month's student loan payment, on which, of course, I'll be defaulting again. Then I see an abusive-looking envelope, which contains an invoice and a note that reads:

> Curtis,
> Because of your delinquency in repaying your debt, your account will now be charged the standard annual interest rate. If by the first of the month you do not comply with the plan by which you agreed to repay the $15,000 you borrowed from me for the down payment of your co-op unit, legal action will be taken.
>
> Love, Mom

These days her letters arrive missing those little *xx*s and *o*s, which I now realize were maybe not so annoying after all. After I kept missing my payments, she said she wouldn't talk to me until I fully reimbursed her . . . which doesn't exactly bode well—barring a six-figure recording advance or some massive injury settlement, my mom and I have already spoken our last out-of-court words. Because now she's mentioned litigation. So why not incarceration? Who would have guessed that she, my own *mother,* from whose breasts I suckled primeval vaccine, that original shield and selfless guardian, would one day install me as someone's prison bitch?

Yet somehow it had to be, and I can only side against myself as I find a septic blue "Cancellation Notice!" from Verizon.

Maybe next week I can look forward to an audit.

As a final encore, I see a Nationwide Life Insurance policy offer—somehow this doesn't strike me as their wisest investment.

Leaving the lobby, I spot Andy Bish—the fastidious president of the co-op board to which I'm also in "abysmal arrearage"—on the sidewalk. I dive headlong into a dusty stairwell no one uses where, through the door's little window, I watch Bish yelling at some poor old lady for not curbing her Jack Russell.* The tiny, frightened woman nods up at Bish as she bare-hands the wet dog turds, with Bish all the while bent over his prey in a red-faced tirade. She attempts to restrain her hotheaded little hound from lunging at him as they try to out-yap each other, and it's only when the little lady looks on the verge of tears that triumphant Bish sashays into the lobby.

He checks his mail, then quickly glances around as he relocks his box and walks away empty-handed. Waiting for the elevator, he looks around again before sneaking a crotch scratch. Bish has the flaccid look of those yo-yo dieters you see always losing and gaining a third of their weight on *Oprah*—a leaky beanbag of a person.

He suddenly steps out of eyeshot, and as I wait for the elevator ping, squinting through the window so I can see what he's up to, I'm stunned by the ghostly semireflection of my own face. Is this how the world perceives me? With the teeth-bared expression of a cornered rodent? No wonder I've been making such stellar impressions.

I relax. Unhunch my shoulders. Unziploc my insides. I realize I haven't breathed deeply in weeks. The muscles knotted around my spine are a chain of frozen pretzels. But it's soothing and secret in this stairwell, and I discover that I don't really want

FOOTNOTE >

* Of course, I wondered if he'd ever met Phillip, sniffed his bum in the dog run.

to leave it. I figure I can also use the downtime to do a few vocal exercises . . .

*Merrily, merrily, merrily, merrily, life is but a dream.*

. . . there's a cool reverb in here.

*Merrily, merrily, merrily . . .*

"I *will* get a record deal," I try and convince my reluctant reflection.

As I begin a new voice exercise, I hear a peevish little scrape on the floor, where I see that a piece of paper has been slipped under the door. Chinese delivery menu? Those bastards never let up. But as I stoop down, I read some numbers that someone has scrawled across what I realize is my mom's little love note, which I must've dropped on the lobby floor. And this figure seems very famil–oh, it's the total of the maintenance payments I owe the co-op board–as I rise out of my squat to see Bish's stagy face in the window . . .

Our lips are not an inch apart. My throat issues a ticklish noise, almost a whinny, as Bish stands there scowling. I can see the follicles standing out from his nose.

"Please don't litter," he lisps in that starchy voice, sounding semisupernatural through the glass.

I remember being sad that he was missing some molars.

# Little Lamb
## (One of God's Own Flock)



*Since you were a little lamb*
*The world was spinning way too fast for you*
*And did it ever seem to you*
*That people always grew too fast for you?*
*I know it too*

*Then I found me a friend*
*Who taught me to bend*
*So one could be two*
*But soon we tore each other down*
*Why I never knew*

*The reason*

*Now I can't find another lamb*
*With eyes that undo*
*My reason*

# Tyger, Tyger

The next day, at the bathroom mirror, I apply my Rogaine, with its sinless little syringe. I gulp down my morning cocktail of Wellbutrin and Centrum Daily One. I look hard at myself. I guess I just never dreamed, in the wild faith of my youth, that my ravaging ambition would leave me *here*—thirty-three years old, the Catch 33 of myself, with no credit, no credentials, no career . . . and no Camilla. Not that I feel sorry for myself or anything. Maturity is what I've done with my disappointments. I guess I had to store them all somewhere.

God, I'm really not aging gracefully. The elastic in my cheeks is losing support like a seasoned jockstrap. I've been groaning at Gravity's stamina more than ever lately. The bastard never seems to take five. No, the reigning *heavy*weight just keeps at it with his one-handed pushups, while the rest of us paunch and sag. Apparently, he's still got a lot of pull around here, hardy har har.

Do you see how, in my devout masochism, I've even assumed *Gravity*, as in Einstein-Space-Time-Contingent, as my own personal antitrainer? He's like that vague friend who for years had been only a shadow on the margins of your life, and then one day materializes on your doorstep to tell you he's homeless.

# Listen to the Lion

Which is a perfect entrée, because I actually did have a houseguest, who was yelling

"Hurry up, fuckstick!" outside of my bathroom. "Are you throwing a private jack in there?"

Meet Gary Shapiro, with whom I . . . *consent* is actually a pretty apt verb . . . to my most stubborn and complex friendship. This thing we've managed to build is dented with resentments, corroded with secrets, and highly combustible. But for some reason, the jalopy of our love just refuses to die.

Through a crack in the door Gary nudges his nose job, which is almost too literal, too much like a nose. (Like your father's girlfriend, you don't want them looking *that* good.)

"It reeks in here," he scrunches. "Did you shit in your pants?"

"You barged in on *me*. I'm only trying to pee. You know that I'm pee-shy."

"Then why are you sitting down like a pansy?" He steps up to the bathroom mirror* and pounces on a pimple. "Come on, 'fess up."

"Okay. I read in **PAPER** that Jeff Buckley pissed like this."

FOOTNOTE >

*Gary's Favorite Place in the Universe, which I'll from now on refer to as GFPITU.

"Did you also read that he was an all-state swimming champ?"*

I think a lot of Gary's appeal for me was in his refusal to hold anything holy. I suppose I'd felt safely pickled in that elitist love of his, which always seemed so hard won, because he'd suddenly persuade himself to go sour on something, in the way the tyrannical clique of the popular kids in my high school would get so bored with their own power that they'd decide to oust a member.

Through a tacit arrangement to live in my apartment until he finds his own, Gary's promised to produce for me a demo he feels certain will win me that elusive urban legend . . . the **Record Deal** (Grail). After having defected to the "industry" camp of the biz, Gary had been quickly ascending into the upper echelon of A&R guys—that same species of weasel he and I swore we'd never befriend when they all wheedled our band into signing their contracts. Back then, Gary and I knew we wanted Geffen from the get-go, but every label was willing to bribe us with New York Strips at Le Cirque. He wanted to wait out the bidding war and keep upping the ante—"we" ended up blowing the deal. So these days it's just a little odd to hear my alleged best friend and ex-bassist, with whom I pissed on the desk of Polygram president ________† when we snuck into Worldwide Plaza one midnight, babbling about "indie cred" and "moving units." It's probably a lot like seeing an old girlfriend post transgender op.

"I've been thinking, Jew Boy. You're just going to have to lose the name Curtis Birnbaum if you want to make it in music."

FOOTNOTE >

*In the summer of 1998, Jeff Buckley, the singer/songwriter son of sixties minstrel Tim Buckley, who overdosed on heroin, drowned in the Memphis River.

†I omitted the guy's name to avoid litigation.

"What about *your* name?"

"It's different for me." He regards his reflection, running fat little fingers through a massive head of hair which is dark as soot, prickly as pubes, and two heads lower than my own. "I'm be*hind* the scenes now. You're still the artist. Jews can't be the actual rock stars."

"There's plenty of Jewish rock stars. Look at Kiss."

"I've been toying with some names for you. What do you think of Hitler Vicious?"

"Mmm," I said, hating it. "Let me sit with it. But don't you think Curtis Birnbaum's a nice name?"

"Exactly. *Nice*," he says, rummaging through his nose with a Kleenexed index finger. "But rock stars aren't *nice,* retardo. The thirteen-to-seventeen-year-old white trash female comprises today's largest unit-buying demographic. She wants to hump a Hells Angel, preferably a statutory rapist, or at least a dude who looks like he's done some respectable maximum-security prison time. Kids these days gobble down death like it's Ecstasy. As long as something's extreme, they'll consume it. They can't tell the difference between Auschwitz footage and the old *Ed Sullivan* Elvis stuff. The serial killer is society's new superockstar. He's the only one who can still terrify these teenagers. Charles Manson was our first. He had the total rock 'n' roll mentality down cold. Now we have Axl Rose, a famous incest survivor. As well as Trent Reznor and Marilyn Manson. Just look at the similarities . . . both the superkiller and the superockstar are classically single-minded, media-crazed, and fame-hungry."

"That's so true," I say, egging him on with my customary inquisitive blinks. I can tell he's digging in for one of his postmodern dialectics . . .

"Both types," he delves into the other nostril, "are ruthless in their ambition, immune to fear, inherently short-lived. Because they know instinctively when to turn themselves in so as to achieve maximum media saturation. Look at Cobain." Gary places a little octagonal pill in my palm that reads *Propecia.* I ask,

"Doesn't this stuff cause pregnant women to miscarry if they even touch one or something?"

"Are you expecting?" He shoves me a bottle of wheat grass juice from my medicine chest.

"Expecting what?" I wash down the tablet with something that tastes a lot like, I imagine, skim milk mixed with cheap white wine. Gary asks,

"Do you think Elvis obsessed over which pills he was taking? Just do what I say. And as I was saying, if Elvis hadn't made it big, is it so difficult to see him as the sexy rural murderer? Square-jawed and sloe-eyed? The Byronic stud, brooding like Ted Bundy? Both of them with their teen idol good looks and their mommies at home, overweening them. And Dick and Perry were total rock stars, right? They had that classic Sonny and Cher, light and dark, Dionysian/Apollonian dichotomy down pat. Didn't Capote know how to exploit the spectacular marketing potential in those sex symbols?" He shakes an approving head. "Do you think they were *nice*? A rock star is the dude who *fucks* the mensch's girlfriend, then eats her corpse. There's still something very ex-boyfriend about you, Birnbaum. We'll have to work on that. We'll start you off with the standard Lenny Kravitz nose ring. That guy gets enough ass to choke a llama."

"*He's* a Jew," I tell him, politely, attempting to swallow away the awful wheat grass aftertaste.

"But he's *black,* so it cancels out. We'll also cover you up in tattoos."

"No way. I can't do tattoos," I say.

"Look, you're my cash cow now. Do you want to cash out or not, cash cow?"

"Yeah, of *course*. But I can't even af*ford* a tattoo. You don't seem to understand the financial nightmare I'm in. I owe my mom fifteen grand and my co-op board thirteen months' maintenance! They're going to foreclose on this apart–"

"Tattoos suggest that you're utterly committed to the rock 'n' roll aesthetic at the expense of your own. You've sold your soul, so to speak. Hey, maybe we'll even put one over your face," tracing a shape around my left eye.

"Maybe," I sigh, actually trying to picture this while I walk out into the living room.

"Look, cash cow," he says, waddling behind me, "people *want* to be fooled these days. The truth's become so goddamn painful it's boring. We want to dream the implausible dream. We *need* Scott Weiland* to relapse. That's what a rock star is *supposed* to do. He plays his role to a tee because he knows his image is more important than his life. In rock 'n' roll, pretense, bluster, and arrogance are re*war*ded. This is the culture of the counterfeit. That's why Donnie" (Gary's therapist) "says all you singers want to slit your wrists whenever you're not onstage. Because all art is only a kind of neurotic reaction to a world we're not satisfied with. The other two choices are, change the world around you, like Hitler did, or compromise yourself, like everyone else does. But the artist rein*vents* the world, building his own fiction to live in. Or at least he tries to. That's why guys like you don't know what to do with yourselves when you're out of the spot-

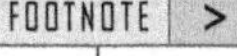

*The invariably drug-busted frontman of Stone Temple Pilots.

light. You can't strut around the Wiz like a rooster. Donnie says if we understand where all this Id is coming from, we can 'secure you the historically slippery record deal' in no time. But hey, if this fails, there may be a stellar career waiting for you as a professional wrestler."

"I can easily see myself ending up as that, actually."

"That's exactly what I . . ."

As I walk to the window, I hear Gary's voice, scraping away, sharpening itself against the silence . . . until it recedes like a distant power tool.

My little Fern still sits on her sill. I guess I've really depressed her. These days her tendrils frown over the pot rim, the troubled limbs of Ophelia, drooping from a creek-side. As I lean down and breathe in her resonant death scent, of course I picture Cammy watering her that first night we kissed.

I gaze into the mizzling morning, the sky a sodden gray quilt of down. The church bells of St. Anthony's plead six times . . .

*The bells out in the church tower chime,*
*burning clues into this heart of mine**

I wonder if this ringing is really some programmed CD, the modern machine mimicking grace . . . and speaking of Grace . . .

She's out there. Somewhere.

I discover I'm staring at Andy Bish, who, from under his humongous umbrella, is standing on the sidewalk across Thomp-

FOOTNOTE >

*From Jeff Buckley's "Last Goodbye," my favorite song.

son Street, inspecting something on the face of our building . . . until his eyes find mine in the mist. I drop to the floor in a pushup position . . . then figure I might as well get in a good twenty, but as I'm pumping, the chilidog memory wafts from out of the faint brown stain just under my nose, and I can barely do a pushup as I'm suffused with the spicy ghost of that night.

"Stay away from the window," I warn Gary as I collapse. "Bish on the loose," but Gary walks to the window anyway and tells me,

". . . of course we can't tell these A&R guys that you're pushing fifty," taking out his goatskin wallet as I tug on his shirt cuff until he's down in a squat. He yanks his sleeve back, removing invisible lint.

"Please, dude," I say. "They're going to foreclose on me."

"Stop living in fear. Here. I altered your driver's license. You're twenty-seven."

"That's my only valid ID," shuffling backward and jerking my head toward the center of the room so he'll follow me away from the window.

"You know who croaked at *that* age, right?" He stands up, his flabby back in full street view.

"Janis, Jimi, Kurt, Jimbo," I rattle off, grabbing his thick left ankle as, in reverse, I crawl crabwise toward the bathroom, towing him behind me.

Once inside, he becomes immediately distracted by GFPITU.

"I still really miss her," I say, sitting down on the closed lid of the toilet.

Mid-primp, Gary explains "It's a very difficult process" in the even tone adults often use on their mothers. "Donnie says it takes at least a year to get over any real relationship."

"All I do is think about Her."

"You know it's bad when all they need is pronouns."

"Like God."

"Or a ship," checking his teeth in the mirror.

"I really miss her," I repeat, hoping he'll take the bait, but Gary has a knack for detaching himself, as if he's got me on permanent speakerphone. So,

"She's so spectacular," I continue, knowing this will get him going.

"She was a spectacular . . . *prag*matist."

"Good song title." I ignore his past tense. "But you feel she's a little rigid, right?"

"Is Courtney Love ambitious? Look, she was never really on your side. Your partner is supposed to be your *part*ner. Camilla was just waiting for you either to fall or become famous. She'll be kicking herself when you're a big rich rock star."

I toss an easy lob—"She's not like that."

"Oh, yeah? You're fooling yourself if you think women don't care about status. They may not *want* to, but they do."

"She's different. She never complained. She was so sweet and low-maintenance."

"Another good song title, so's a cactus," he counters, and we fall into our old menstrual conversational rhythm, in which each moment's an extension of our ongoing shtick.

"She had such lovely posture," I continue.

"Stiff." He taps a razor against the wall of the sink and leans into the mirror.

"Such a beautiful back."

"But she never applied the small of it to your relationship," making a long O of his mouth so he can shave the hairs in its corners with my new Mach 3 razor. "And you're forgetting all the bad stuff. You were always bitching about how she couldn't communicate."

"Exactly. Keep talking. This is good for me. I tend to forget all this."

"That's an evolutionary tactic that allows us to move on. If we remembered all the shitty stuff, we'd all be too depressed to screw."

"Who's screwing? Who's not depressed? I'm not exactly up for the Franz Kafka Rosy Disposition Award, you know."

"Look. You *are* forgetting the bad side. When someone is that good-looking, it's easy to. Beauty of that magnitude can drive you crazy. It's like hearing some goddamn fugue twenty-four hours a day. She was fucked up, if you ask me. Looking like that can do it. All that attention, Jesus Christ. And for doing nothing. We're always insulted to find out that very good-looking people can be very unhappy, too. It's like the opposite of when you get pissed off when a real ugly girl has the gall to think she can pursue you."

"I miss her so much."

"I know. It really sucks. How long has it been since you've talked to her now?"

"I don't know. Twenty-eight days."

"Well, this is actually good. Silence is the great punisher. It's building you up to mythical proportions in her mind. And vice versa. It's *good* you're so unhappy. You'll write better songs. And you're saving yourself from a lot of laugh lines," he pats around my eyes as I start to floss. "And you should get your teeth bleached."

"Ca*mill*a had teeth."

I can tell he wants to get off the subject, but we both know that sympathy is the lion's share of his rent check. "Hey, did you shave your balls again in here? Or your *nose* hairs? It's all ova a oilet," my phrasing sawed by floss.

"Both," by way of apology. "But those must be yours because

they're all gray," he says, taking the impeccable pause of a Catskills stand-up. "So we'll get you some Just for Nuts so your groupies won't know you're an old man."

"And would you please try not to piss on the rim?" I ask him, weakly.

Gary waits a few I'll-piss-anywhere-I-want-to seconds, then takes a vague swipe at the bowl with a garment hanging off the toilet tank.

"That's my Radiohead T-shirt," I tell him, through bleeding gums.

"It made you look fat. And it has piss stains on it."

Once again Gary's pushing all of my buttons, just for kicks, like the kid who presses every floor in the elevator before he gets out.

"Do you really think I'll get a record deal?" I ask him for the zillionth time.

"I wouldn't be doing your demo if I didn't. But we don't want to do too much grooming. These A&R guys want you to be all grungy."

"Be honest. Am I losing my looks?"

"Hey, now. I'll say it one more time, fuckass . . . nobody likes a victim. Or a whiner. These days the execs want to think they're caging some wild animal. Discovering priceless exotica and displaying it to the world. So put up a fight. Act like a prick. Josh Epstein just signed this rapper kid from the South Bronx who told his wife she was a cunt. This makes him a legitimate hood in Josh's eyes. There's even a song the kid wrote for them called 'Greedy Motherfucking Music Biz Jew Suit and His Bull-Dyking-Ass Bitch.' And Josh is executive producing the track him*self!* It's amazing. I heard that he actually asked his wife if she would give this little prick a blowjob so he could win the bidding war and sign him. So you can't be so fucking compliant.

These A&R guys hate it when you're needy. You have to promise me you'll really be rude to the ones I bring down to your shows."

I give him three somber nods.

"You can start practicing at your big Baby Jupiter gig," he says. "Just keep in mind that they want authenticity. Arrogance. We'll zone you as the brooding Jim Morrison type. Lots of potent B.O. Did you shower today?"

"No," I lie.

"Good. Don't do it till after the gig. And work up a good sweat at the gym right before. Give these A&R shmucks some good flimsy handshakes. And *never ever* make eye contact with them. We'll buy you some mirrored shades for when you take meetings in their plush corporate digs. Let me do all the air-hugging. Stand behind me, aloof. Remember: rock stars are *rude*. Think adolescent tormented by the hypocritical paradox he's become. Resentful of the very success you craved. John Lennon. Kurt Cobain. These are your models . . ."

Gary's cell phone makes its bratty little noise, he holds up a stubby index finger and, recognizing the displayed number, decides to screen the caller. We listen to the thing giggling with its secret data.

"Useless," he scoffs, meaning his screenee. "That guy has about as much juice left as O.J."*

Wondering how many times he's screened my calls like that, I ask,

FOOTNOTE >

*And I had to face the fact that Gary was becoming just another Head-Honcho-Hit-Record-Executive-Producing-Credit-Thefter who always asks for No-Dairy-in-That-but-Do-You-Have-Any-Soy-Milk-'Cause-I-Have-My-Pilates-Class-Now-So-My-People-Will-Be-Calling-Your-People-Just-As-Soon-As-You-Sign-the-Deal-Memo-and-Can-I-Get-a-Plus-One-with-That-Please?

"You're my friend, right, Gary?"

This only earns me an eye roll, so I say, "I mean, you *care* about me, right?"

"You've been asking me that for a decade. It's irrelevant. I'm going to make you a star."

# Let Us Go Then, You and I . . . A Reflective Moment

So you would think, from the elaborate way I drivel on and on, that the architecture of all my self-centered fear would have castled me in something noble. Calamitous. Some candlelit kind of depression, dirged in monk chant.

But it wasn't really like that.

My misery limped along. Cleared its throat.

Think Prufrock here.

# So, to Paraphrase . . .

I show my NYU I.D. card to the big sloppy security guard on West Fourth Street. As he slits leaky, tired eyes at me, I try and make a wholesome smile.

Last year I stole this I.D. from the lost-and-found at Crunch, my gym, so I could sneak into the NYU computer lab to whittle away at my lyrics. Then I actually used this same card to obtain the student discount on my renewed Crunch membership because, in addition to being flat broke, the fluid ruse of stealth at least adds a little intrigue to the humdrum I've become.

I pick a monitor and check my e-mail, where the usual collection agencies have been unleashed to hound me through cyberspace. And oh, God . . . there's one from Emily, Camilla's best friend.

Jesus H.

I cup my genitals reflexively, another alluring little habit I've acquired of late, but I quickly remove my hand when I notice the delicate Asian girl at the next terminal pretending not to notice.

What does Emily want with me? We haven't spoken for eons, in Camilla time. I decide that maybe I'll wait a few days before I even open her e-mail (or at least thirty seconds), so I can savor the delectable hope that Cammy, bedridden since the day she'd dumped me, fired from her job, can now do nothing but mumble my name as she flits in and out of tormented dreams. That is until yesterday, in a rare moment of febrile clarity, when she'd at last called Emily to her bedside and formed her first coherent phrase in six months . . .

"I just can't go on without him," she'd whimpered, rolling her head from side to side on her sweat-soaked pillow. But, still too weak from her diet of woe to even lift a phone, much less log on to the Internet, she'd begged Emily to do her bidding for her—to inform me that she could no longer spend another moment away from me, whining and all, health insurance be damned.

Or maybe no. Maybe Emily's informing me that Camilla's expecting (perhaps with one of those Oasis brothers) and Emily just didn't want me to see it first on Page Six.

I was surprised that Em didn't ally in disgust against me after our breakup. This was actually a small victory for my identity, like when the phone company lets you keep the same number after a move. And yet, undertaking, as always, the ongoing project of becoming Adults, Emily promised she'd keep in touch with me, under the proviso that we wouldn't mention Camilla, and that she wouldn't speak to Cammy about me. Of course my real hope was that through that best friend osmosis, Camilla would somehow sense just how far along I'd progressed toward safety and Success. And, conversely, it turned out that Emily had managed to suggest, through the gist of her omissions, the occasional shape that Cammy's life had taken . . . her silhouette, photo negative . . . a lonely Camilla echo like the ghost sensation at the stump of an amputated limb. (Me.)

The few early e-mails that Emily and I had exchanged went something like this:

ME: So what's new, Emily, anything?

*(Subtext: Come on, Em, has she met someone?)*

EMILY: Not much. Same-old same-old, really.

*(Wishful translation: Of course not, silly. Camilla's initial fears that you'd be sexually, aesthetically, and intellectually peerless have been painfully confirmed for her. She's come to her senses and now understands that she'll always be impossibly in love with you, Curtis.)*

ME: So what's new with you?

*(Subtext: Really. I can take the truth. Has some hot young rocker with a lightning metabolism, James Brolinesque hairline, and a three-record deal on Sony complete with a monstrous health/401k plan been sharing her bed?)*

EMILY: Nothing much. I'm dating a new guy who I think I might like.

*(Wishful translation: Don't worry! Cammy only had one blind date with this boring Merrill Lynch guy who apparently came up after to use her bathroom . . . and left the seat up.)*

ME: That's great. I'm really happy for you.

*(Was he taller than me?)*

But my de facto/default camaraderie with Emily was soon only a clumsy waltz around the black hole that Cammy had left in my universe as door prize, an exercise as forced and semi-incestuous as slow-dancing with a stepsister.

Now, as I sit here wavering over whether to open Emily's e-mail, I'm reminded of those soft, unsullied dawns after a night of my blathering in bed to Camilla, as if I'd been prepping her for some special-edition *Jeopardy*! tournament based on my life; cramming that lovely, jittery silence between us with the entire minutiae of me, which included *The Allegory of Debbie Lagorie,* who merrily showcased for me and a ring of ecstatic boys the blood she'd peed into our Montessori school toilet . . . my father's fairly recent admission that the reason I was encouraged to sleep between him and my mother (until I was twelve) was because I was in fact a treasured partition between enemy lines . . . as well as the toenail I'd clipped to the quick that afternoon. All this, of course, as the warm-up act before slated headliner: *My Most Disfiguring Fears.*

Imagine the windfall for me, chatterbox only child who'd recently quarried self-pity unto uncharted depths, unloading myself into this beautiful new human ear as we lay adrift in the fathomless sea of what I'd thought was New Love.

# A Month of Sunless Days

I've now endured thirty Camillaless days.

After a thankless afternoon busking, I approach my building in the dour autumn sunset. I notice Gary swagger-waddling back and forth in my window above me, scheming into my phone, clad in nothing but my favorite J. Crew flannel boxer-briefs.

Bastard.

In the doorway there's a couple of scrawny young guys in doctorly smocks interviewing my co-op board president about something, on camera. Only finicky Bish would waste his time with these vultures. Or red herrings, rather, because at least they avert his attention as I scamper past him and into my building.

Under my doormat is a note.

Clyde, I'm thinking about the name Nanny Nanny Boo Boo for my girl band for which some day I hope to front and for which I want to say thank you once again for being always so supportive of, Clyde. And did you know that astronomy is a totally different deal from astrology? I hadn't. What sign are you anyway? Please get back to me about this stuff ASAP.

Yours forever,

Walter L. Green

When I walk in, Gary, still pacing with phone, shoves a *Village Voice* at me with circled offers claiming I can . . .

**EARN BIG $$$**

Participate in a six-week, outpatient FDA-pending double-blind placebo clinical trial of a new Hair Loss Deterrent, already approved for European consumption. Email inquiries to stopreceding@mindspring.com

and

**Increase BOTH Length and Girth! Because Size Matters!!!**

If you've been told it doesn't, it was only because you lack it. Participate in clinical tests for a pioneering new surgical procedure and walk away with new confidence . . . not to mention a new penis. Email our discreet, friendly staff of medical professionals at Timetogethung@hotmail.com.

# My Life As Conceit

Okay. Though I was well aware I'd become high travesty, for some reason (whose name I think I might've mentioned once or twice), I kept stuffing myself—like a Demerol-era Elvis into his becaped, stonewashed-denim jumpsuit—into the rock 'n' roll aesthetic. For this I led a dog's life, sacrificing steady paychecks and holidays, all of which, ironically, had managed to murder the one Love that had finally allowed me to live. I just couldn't afford to wander from the Iditarod I'd long ago planned to lead me to the finish line of . . . *Fame*.

I think our generation will always hear the word shrieked in Irene Cara's hungry soprano.* I'd always thought it would be the supreme revenge; could barely wait until the popular clique of the Deep Southern private high school (into which I'd transferred from a progressive Free School with no rules) read about me in **SPIN**. The same kids who made a yellow bow-tied present of a possum head and left it in my locker; who stared with savage adolescent hush as the school's peculiar new arrival carried his tray to the only empty cafeteria table for another lunch alone

FOOTNOTE >

*God, where is *she* now? Didn't the *Star* claim that she and the *Eight Is Enough*'s gang were running a midget-wrestling ring in Reno?

with the deaf girl . . . (I'm *not* a victim) . . . who held me down on the scummy shower floor so lacrosse captain Saxon Proctor could get a good aim at my tonsils; who wrote

TRANSFER BACK, BIRNBALLS!

in Crayola's Burnt Sienna (I've been waiting thirty-three years to spell that one) across the hood of my old white VW Bug, an embarrassed bare buttock among the parking lot's martial rows of automotive splendor.

I can still see myself sitting alone at the top of the dark gym bleachers, the only stag at the senior prom, vowing, in my tuxedo of shifting disco ball stars, that one day I'd really show them all . . .

Of course it's very handy to claim all this drove me to enroll myself in the Elvis Presley Independent Pharmacology Study. But even after getting clean on my thirty-first birthday, I discovered there wasn't much left to bamboozle me out of myself. Until . . .

So now, in these Camilla-free days, the only altered states left for me are the pillowy cheat of antidepressants and the grim euphoria of obsessive exercise.

# Cap'n Crunch

I belong to the Crunch on Lafayette Street, a 24-hour singles bar fitness equivalent, where, out front on this freak hot autumn afternoon, the teenage staff sit frowning through a cigarette break. As they squint against smoke and sun, quenching potbellies with Whoppers, I wonder how these louts get hired by a *gym,* thinking it's a little like a publishing house neglecting to run spell checks on its own dictionaries.

I make a senseless smile, giving them a little obedient wave as I walk through a silence I know is only a preamble to the anecdote I'll become after I get inside. The biggest, lardiest kid glances back at me like I've just asked to watch him jerk off. Why do these salt-of-the-earth types always despise me?

At the check-in counter (nametag shouting) *Dominic* demands my I.D. number, which I recite, adding,

"And Dominic? May I have a towel, please?" assuming an underprivileged grimace.

"Large or small?" he grunts, taking lots of precaution to avoid my eyes, like he's flushing a public toilet with his elbow.

"Small," I say, because it's a dollar less, and for some reason, Dominic looks disgusted as he hands me the lavender cloth.

On my right, a girl with an insistent false chest whom I've seen in AA marches on a treadmill. Standing in line, I watch her blink coyly, averting herself, aware that I'm watching. People are always a lot more indented by our presence than we think, I think. Because last week I watched this same woman weeping peacefully through my Wednesday meeting. There was a sort of laborious beauty about it, so I sat down beside her, only to have her refuse the (stolen) yogurt-covered raisins I'd offered, probably thinking I was hitting on her.

Which I *was* . . .

But only because I was hoping to prove to myself that Cammy hadn't taken my entire libido along with her—that she hadn't demolished all the sexual curiosity I'd been constructing since I ran in to show my napping father my first lonesome pubic hair.

The fact was, I wasn't even the least bit open to the idea of another love. Like one of those old file cabinets that can have only one drawer open at a time, I was nowhere near ready to close my Camilla chapter. I didn't want to believe I could get over Cammy—because wouldn't that mean she could get over *me?* A Love Story can't end without the consent of its co-protagonist . . . can it?

Unless there was a new leading man. Great.

Today this woman looks away from my nod, then decides to wave to me when I'm pretending not to notice her—all the crossed radar that builds a neurosis.

Which seems to be quite an area of expertise to a lot of downtown's atoned addicts, who, untoned if still methadone thin, enlist here at Crunch to tune up. Here we overhaul and derust the chemically-glutted engines; for us, Crunch is the Emerald City spa where they all got revamped in *Oz*.

As I enter the gym from the check-in line, this woman and I at last find a yielding moment to swap timid nods, which are meant to endorse our mutual recovery; to say,

*We've staggered out of our own wreckage, but let's not linger in the choking smoke. We're all about progress, not perfection.*

The Weeper is extremely exercise-accessorized, color-coordinated in full cardiac costume, and thereby distracted gaily from internal debris. Around her waist, she's tied the obligatory sweatshirt in transparent attempt to conceal her ample rear end.

The guys in here wear anything.

Our locker room bulges with the entire spectrum of manly contour today. We all try hard not to size up each other's members, so there's a lot of staring at the floor and virile brow-knitting.

Of course I get stuck with a bottom locker, which I fasten with a shitty little lock I ripped off my suitcase after I kept forgetting the combinations to my other ones. A sinewy Wall Street sort combs his costly hair at the locker above me. He gives me a testy sideglance, like I'm trying to read his diary over his shoulder, then looks at my violet towel as if it were a come rag. What is it with these *tow*els?

I step onto the scale, watching its little needle's wiggling decision. How could I possibly have *gained* a pound?

"Is this thing weighing heavy?" I ask anyone who'll listen, then glance over my shoulder to see Wall Street rolling his eyes.

"I thought it was weighing light," yells a genderless voice.

"Really? Thanks," I shout, peering around the lockers to catch the source of it.

Great. What a week. Can't anything *ev*er go my way? I'm not asking for an MTV Award here. The fact that I can't even locate the person who answered me is somehow too much to bear, and I discover that my eyes are actually tearing. (At least I'm shedding water weight.)

The phrase

*Suicide/Success*

floods my skull in a celestial chorus, the latest addition from my inner voice, and one whose pith I actually still admire.

*Suicide/Success.*

Okay. Deep breath. Things could be a lot worse, right? Cortical aneurysm . . . Bolivian prison gang sodomy. Although right now the whole gratitude concept feels largely academic.

I squat on the bench to remove my decomposing Nikes, one of which Wall Street catches me lifting to my nose and sniffing. I laugh, inclusively, in an obvious *Ha-ha-haven't-we-all-done-that?* kind of way.

Apparently he hasn't, because he narrows his eyes at me as he smacks Armani cologne onto his despicable little fat-free physique. I decide to invest in a voice lesson this week instead of a fresh pair of sneakers, even if the soles are worn thin. I realize Conceit just won't leave me alone.

A musical kid on my right looks up at the ceiling when I catch his eyes. Which are mystically green, swimming in a luscious spill of chocolate locks. (Wondering how I'm going to pay for my next bottle of Rogaine), I notice the kid's forearm is a sleeve of elaborate tattoos, the largest reading *Limp Bizkit*. He clangs his skateboard into his own bottom locker, then opens it ninety degrees, I assume, to shield himself as he undresses.

The Gary coffee is beginning to nudge at my bowels, so I walk into the muggy men's room and lock myself into the wheelchair-accessible stall I always use because it's so roomy. And believe it or not, this cheers me up a little . . . this long damp moment has become a highlight of these desolate days. Pathetic, I know, but I look forward to the Zenish calm, sitting alone among the echoey tiles and re-re-reading my frazzled *White Noise*. I always find myself drawn to Murray's kill-to-live thing:

*I believe, Jack, there are two kinds of people in the world. Killers and diers. Most of us are diers. We lie down and die. But think of how exciting it is to a kill a person in direct confrontation. To kill him is to gain life-credit. Kill to live.*

I'm actually thinking of trying the passage out as a kind of between-song monologue at my next Baby Jupiter gig. Its shameless embrace of brutality, its Darwinian disgust with the petty reasonable, its challenge to cool ourselves in Death's looming shadow—all seem so completely rock 'n' roll to me. Then again, it probably wouldn't be such a hit with the groupies, would it? (Like I have any.) An aging rocker publicly grooming himself for mass murder.

Sometimes I actually sit in this stall for an hour, confirmed by the manly scuffle outside. I feel a part of the great food chain, in a way; listening, reading, gleaning, excreting. Information; in, out.

Today I figure I'll work on some lyrics.

## Elvis Costelloish song idea—

*Gravity, the nag, that universal Jewish mother.*
*Weight's guilty conscience, pulling each and every one*
*back to the source.*

New song I must work on: *If Camilla Fell.*

My little reverie's punctured by three tetchy knocks on the buffed-metal partition, under which I suddenly notice a wheelchair.

"God, sorry, just a sec, I'm really sorry," I say. And as I'm flushing and feeling totally guilty, I hear three far more angrier knocks, and a looming African-American voice yelling,

"Hey, bro. He's fucking disabled!"

"Thank you," a near and softer voice says.

"I'm coming. I'm really sorry," I say, but my boxers snag on my sneaker, and I fumble *White Noise* into the toilet.

A violent silence is flowering outside.

"Just a sec, sorry," I say, and as I'm wiping the wet book against my T-shirt . . .

"Look, you selfish motherfucker!!" roars the black voice, and the walls of my stall suddenly thunder with fists.

"I'm sorry," I say, stepping out of the stall, and with one hand I hold the dripping DeLillo, while I offer my other to the Asian guy in the wheelchair, who rolls jerkily past me and into the stall.

"Prick," he says, slamming the door.

A powerful black man with a salt-and-pepper beard and black turtleneck glares at me through John Lennon specs, blocking my path with potent arms folded.

"Sorry," I say, stepping neatly around him, and in the mirror I meet the reverse scowl of the ever-primping Wall Street. They both watch me as I wash my hands a lot more thoroughly than I would've normally and scurry into the gym.

Great start to my day . . . making friends again.

As I parade past the immense collection of today's most recommended self-torture devices, the women erect towering walls of indifference before me. Maybe I'm flattering myself, but they seem to go to a lot of trouble to crinkle their brows, to appear purposeful, preoccupied, looking into any direction but my own.

On the treadmills next to me I hear one of them tell her friend,

"The only reason why I still come here is because I've been obsessed with my personal trainer. I practically begged him to fuck me for two years," panting. "But he said he was celibate. That he was preparing to enter some monastery upstate. Then, last night," more pants, "I find out from Vanessa that the whole time he's been fucking her friend . . . Kevin. He just didn't want me to lose interest and quit. It worked. Why can't I get laid?"

Her deeply thonged friend has a tip: she should wear her skimpiest gear here, minus panties, as well as her headphones, minus sound, so she can hear what all the guys are whispering.

Not exactly Camilla caliber.

The music in here evokes some massive metallic monster whose gearish teeth devour a flat black diva, yowling in orgasmic soprano. Real Twilo* vibe. Soldierly rows of Lifecycles stand hooked in to the vast, invisible fact of the World Wide Web. Our faces slicked in sweat, we make smug little half-smiles as we gossip through e-mail, purchase pornography, monitor stocks (I wish), research a new, discreet kind of Death at the many disease sites. But this bright Microsoft life seems to me only the rind of an abandoned dream.

I inhale the air today. Even this smells clinical and cool, deathly as the skin of a snake.

And there's the usual rubble of former celebrities, sweating it out among the plebes. We all feign indifference to them, because ogling these embers would confess us as lessers. Then I see Anthony Everyoung . . . as in Dumper, from the famed and eponymous seventies sitcom. Dumper's hooded in a ratty old sweatshirt. Dumper! I look around for someone to share my find with, as if to peep with me into the bedroom of a copulating neighbor. Another guy I know from AA is doing reps on a weight bench beside me.

"Hey, John," I say, stooping next to him.

He sits up panting, inflamed, his boxy Norse head bulging and

FOOTNOTE >

*A gay Manhattan nightclub.

veined. John has a scrambling face that always looks like it's just about to deny an accusation.

Solemn handshake.

He peers into me with the pious insight of the fellow fallen . . . we have to get all the twelve-step compassion out of the way before we can proceed with any secular stuff.

"How *are* you?" He looks at me, gingerly, like he's guessing my weight.

"Spectacular. Truly suicidal, but look," yanking my head in the Dumper direction.

"What?"

"Don't you know who that *is*?"

"Who?" he says.

"Dumper."

"Who?"

"Anthony *Ever*young," I say, discreetly hushing the "young."

"Oh, yeah, *I* know, so what?" But as John bends down to heft a barbell, I see him sneak an Anthony glance.

"It's *Dumper,*" I insist.

"He's just another discontinued star," working a bicep. "I mean, that thing transcends the term *Has-Been.*"

"But that's Dumper"—the word like a charm.

"Fuck him. I see him all the time at the SoHo meetings. Wearing his sunglasses inside like he's fucking Brad Pitt," in his interrogatory Scandinavian whine.

"*Real*ly? *An*thony? Anthony's an addict?"

(Definitely a hit song title here.)

"Addiction doesn't discriminate, Curtis."

"Please, John, no AA-speak this early in the day, okay?"

John shrugs, then begins arranging his face to say something, so, sensing a lecture, I say,

"Just look at everyone trying not to look at Anthony."

"That's 'cause nobody *gives* a fuck, Birnbaum. For God's sake, stop staring at the dude. He'll think you want to suck his dick."

I give Anthony a thumbs-up as he mounts a Life Fitness Elliptical, but he looks away. Suddenly I feel very sorry for him, almost covetous. I decide that in my first *Rolling Stone* in-depth interview, I'll single-handedly revive his career, just like Tarantino brought back Travolta with *Pulp Fiction*.

> CB (WITH A DEFLECTING SMILE): Let's just say the song "*Anthony's an Addict*" is a kind of metaphor.
>
> RS: *You mean for the addiction to fame in general, or for Everyoung's substance abuse problems?*
>
> CB: Well, both, I guess, but . . . wait, I really can't comment on Anthony's chemical dependency. Not that there *is* one! Hey, can you scratch that from the rec . . . (inaudible).
>
> Look, Anthony's a cherished friend. And a living American memorial to popular culture.

"At least he did it," I tell John.

"Did what?" admiring his tricep as it pops out with each pump of his barbell.

"*Made* it."

"Made what?"

"You know. *It*."

"I'd rather *not* have made it than be Anthony Everyoung."

We watch Anthony's sunken eyes fidget as he struggles with the machine. He looks abandoned, hanging on to a long-lost purpose, a derelict padlock clinging to a fence.

"Not me," I say. "Everyoung lived the American Dream. He enriched a lot of people's lives."

"Name one."

"Mine."

"Yeah, and the rest are now housewives in Boise." (John's an actor.)

"You're just a jaded New Yorker," I tell him.

"Thank *God*. Jesus, just look at the poor fuck. He's got those desperate, house-counting eyes."

As the AA Weeper steps onto the machine next to Anthony, he gives her a wobbly smile, his face tilted, tentative, as if expecting derision. But when the Weeper ignores him, he looks surly, like he was guarding his privacy anyway.

"Just look at him go," John says, in the vigorous voice of a sports announcer, because Anthony has suddenly begun wheezing. Stumbling off the machine, folded into coughing spasms.

"Does he think he's getting in shape for some pathetic comeback role or something?" from John.

"I hope he's okay," I say, and I find myself moving toward him when a paunchy black female trainer, nibbling from a sack of french fries, walks over and puts a concerned hand on Anthony's shoulder. She offers a fry, to which he shakes his head. With both hands on his knees, he looks up purple-faced to ask her something and glancing both ways, she stabs a cigarette into his mouth before he walks outside and lights it.

We diffuse into our separate workouts, but we're oddly combined. A kind of ballet seems to embroider every addict together. I'm reminded of Esther Williams as all of us preen in the myriad mirrors, pulsing, pumping . . . ever on the verge of becoming the newly-improved versions of ourselves, which we excavate from under all those flabby years of self-abuse—that lean muscle of a person we give pep talks to, whom we coaxed back from the ledge, our rescued platonic ideal, for whom we are forever chiseling, honing, sculpting.

Me and John rediscover each other at the ab machines. Even though neither of us can think of a damn thing to say, there's at least a tacit allegiance among addicts; we, the righteous wounded, delivered miraculously back from the dead, can now laugh at the living . . . just as authentic ghosts stuck in a haunted house might scoff at the mechanical phantoms.

"Do you guys know where there's a meeting soon?" says a voice suddenly next to us. It belongs to another guy I've seen a lot in AA, who's known for the bushy toupee he's sporting today. Sadly, it's dubbed him the Mongoose.

Hearty handshakes are traded. John nods at him cautiously and says

"Are you okay, brother?"

"Not exactly," he admits, giving me the twice-over.

"Do you know Curtis?" John asks him. "He's in 'the Club,' " he confides, with the indecent smile of someone who's just made a killing at a garage sale.

"You don't look that fucked up," the Mongoose tells me, accusingly.

"Thanks, I guess."

The question of whether we are all still sober hovers unspoken between us, waiting to escape like pant-trapped gas.

"I picked up a drink last night," the Mongoose admits suddenly.

John extends inverted palms and flutters his middle fingers in that guiding-a-parallel-parker-backwards gesture. "Come on, give me some sugar," he urges the Mongoose.

Who, somewhat reluctantly, walks into John's embrace. John then enfolds him, rubbing his back, purring and rocking him. I try to sneak off, but John gives me a panicked, *Don't-leave-me-now* look. At last the Mongoose attempts to free himself, but

John just won't have it—he keeps squeezing him, squashing him, clasping him closer, kissing his neck as he whispers secret things into his ear. Finally, when he's certain his prey has been stilled, John slowly releases him, then steps back and nods at him warily.

"You have my number," he reminds the Mongoose. "So use it. And expect a miracle," sending him off with a spank on the ass.

Secretly relieved it wasn't me who relapsed, I look closely at John looking pleased with himself, wondering if he feels the same; that the Mongoose vice actually earned us a virtue coupon. Kill to live.

"John, that was really cool of you, I think."

"I never liked that prick. And who does he think he's fooling with that rodent?"

"Hey, *you* look fantastic," I say, hoping to change the tune of this.

"Really? Thanks, brother."

I'm lying. Although Iggy Pop slender, his massive cubed skull now dwarfs his slight frame, achieving an overall sledgehammery effect. His skin looks parched, his hair dull and brittle.

"Have you lost weight?" I ask him.

"Yeah. I'm on this great new grain diet!" shaking his head like he just can't believe his good fortune. "The one sort of controversial thing about it, though, is that the only fluid you can have is one cup of coffee a day."

"And isn't that a diuretic?"

"Bingo," he smiles.

*John, there's a reason every civilization in the history of mankind has centered itself around a major water source,* I don't have the heart to tell him.

"I feel like I'm in the body of a teenager," he says. "That's what it's all about—taking care of that temple. Hey, you should come with me to the Sex Addicts Anonymous meeting tonight."

"You're a sex addict?"

"No, but it's an easy lay," leering.

"Oh. No thanks. But it was good seeing you. Thanks for being nice to me."

John gives me a fishy squint and says, "It's not a hard gig, Birnbaum. You're a good guy."

"Really? Thanks."

"But you look totally worn-out and pale. Come with me to the sun bed downstairs."

"I think I'm going to try out the new steam room. You wanna come?"

"Yeah, but not in *there.*" John hoists an eyebrow. "I see you've got the purple towel and everything."

"Whattya mean?"

Through steamy fog, the men are gooey specters . . . their hands hectic and groping as hungry guppies. I figure they're all probably muddled into some sort of New Age yoga poses. As my eyes adjust, I notice they all wear the sculpted, economic torsos of GI Joes, that the *pecs* appear as detachable as the chest plates of mediaeval knights, and that the guy next to me is smiling, expansively. I decide this might just be a chummy atmosphere.

"I feel great," I tell him. "I think I'm going to come in here after *every* workout."

"Please *do,*" he smiles. "Can't you just feel all the toxins being expelled?"

"Exactly."

The grin widens as he removes his purple towel, unveiling a

Speedo symbol, tattooed on his lower left hip, just as it appears on the swimsuit. I notice a throbbing, wolfish creature in the corner, and I assume that these guys are wrestling–when suddenly there's a callused hand on my thigh, which I realize belongs to Smiles. I hear groans and oinks from the wrestlers. And,

"I see you've got yourself a lilac towel *too*," says observant Smiles, sliding his hand inside it.

Of *course*.

How could I have been so *dense*?

I sit there a minute paralyzed in his caress, as the rapid flames of tongues twitch in the mist. I hear moist grunts and guy giggles. Then I realize *everyone*'s wearing these little purple towels! Smiles prods a tongue through my teeth and jostles it around, so I try pushing him away–but he's very tenacious. I don't want to hurt his feelings. Suddenly I understand what girls must go through . . . all that tardy guilt, like they've led us on. But, all the same, I can't say this sensation is entirely unwelcome. Nobody's really been this tender with me since Cammy. I try and tell Smiles,

"My name is–"

"Hush," he puts a finger to my lips, shakes a wise head.

But I figure I'll go with it a while; let myself recline into his bristly embrace. And the swampy fog actually begins to relax me. I realize I wish Camilla were watching . . . that she could see how she's reduced me to a grudge gayness . . . that I'm growing slowly erect. Wicked Smiles grins as he works and works my crotch. I don't remember anyone managing me (no pun) with such authority, such subtlety.

"We call him Hans," says Smiles, kissing the tip of my nose as he gestures through miasma to one of the Oinkers, now crawling on all fours at me. He arrives at my crotch, crouched and beaming, and starts licking my knee with a shrewd gaze into my eyes.

Suddenly I imagine my father watching all this on his mammoth TV, tossing back a fistful of Planter's Mixed Nuts, as if he'd accidentally channel-surfed on to some gay porn network.

This is what makes me finally bolt out of there.

As my erection and I stand shivering outside the steam room, I wonder if I've been repressing solely for my father's sake; what would happen if he were dead? Or *gay*? Would I find myself at the bottom of a different glory hole every night, crawling under the stalls of the Port Authority men's room?

Or maybe, like a thoroughbred, my member's only been yearning for some honest exercise after so many months of neglect. It elicits a few double takes from passing purple-towel wearers.

And I realize I've forgotten mine inside the steam room as Wall Street, now shaving his expensive face at his own little mirror, mounted up in his locker, catches my eye. Shrugging, I cross my wrists over my boner. As I'm about to open the steam room to fetch my towel, I notice a sign threatening . . .

**MEMBERSHIP REVOCATION WITHOUT REFUND**
**FOR ANY UNTOWARDLY BEHAVIOR DISCOVERED IN STEAM ROOM**

I open the door onto the hot swirling fervor. All hell's broken loose in here. Jesus! I see foggy rows of erections, heads bobbing, slurping, groaning.

Smiles eyeballs my erection with a meaningful grin before dragging me back into the riotous vapor. But I manage to slip from his grip and back through the door, where, palming my hard-on, I tiptoe to the showers, figuring a good cold one should extinguish me, right?

As I stand under the icy gush, I notice those little round, sea foam blue antislip stickers on the floor. And just guess whose eyes they remind me of . . .

Hey. *Good!* Maybe I'm really gay after all. That would certainly resolve a lot of past and future pain. So how would She take it? Isn't that the supreme refusal of a woman's sexual identity? I find myself actually wishing she'd get wind of all this somehow, as I look around the room for a soaped-up mutual acquaintance. No luck.

Still erect, I make the shower colder, which only seems to foment my arousal, even as my testicles cower and pucker.

Such an odd couple.

I realize it's been a while since I've examined these two. They look starved and refugeed, especially the smaller left one—a Sally Struthers child-hunger victim with his sicker, younger brother. But when I touch the latter, I notice that the soft bump I'd mentioned earlier has matured into a stubborn little nugget.

Great. Why don't I just get dressed, for God's sake? Cut my losses.

I step out of the shower where, from the dispenser, I unroll a brown (sand) paper towel for a fig leaf, then collapse onto my bench, cupping myself, when I notice Wall Street's genitals hanging only inches from my face. His nuts are enormous, as pendulous as hypnotist baubles. And my eyes idle on them two moments longer than I'd intended as I try to recall my lock combo, then look up to see Wall Street's slitted stare, as if I'd strategically posted myself right at his groin.

I try to cover my erection.

"Christ!" he hisses, hiding himself in a luxuriant towel, which isn't purple, before slamming his locker and huffing away. With the hand not shielding my penis, I dial and curse my lock because, in all my confusion, I've totally forgotten the combo. I drive five furious knuckles into the metal. Soon my teeth begin to clatter from the chill, and I realize that the mystical Limp Bizkit boy is suddenly beside me.

"I'm locked out of my locker," I tell him, still clutching the dissolving paper towel to my privates.

He gives his head a baffled tilt . . .

"Can't remember my combo," I say. "Ha, ha."

Then I realize, despite his American tattoos, that he must be one of those foreigners branded blindly in American culture.

"My *com•bin•ation,*" I say, dialing a fantasy lock. "To my *lock.* You wouldn't have an extra *tow•el, would* you?" pointing to the one around his waist.

Limp Bizkit recoils one homophobic step, then looks down at my erection as it strains through the wet paper. I attempt to pat it down.

"No, no," I say, smiling in what I hope is a sensible, macho manner. "I've been locked out of my locker."

"Rocker?"

"*Lock*er."

"Rock 'n' roll?"

"How can you have that tattoo and not speak the fucking language?" I find myself yelling, feeling instantly horrible when his eyes, needing no translation, appear obviously injured.

"Look, I'm sorry," I say, but as I step consolingly toward him, he leaps back again to tighten his towel.

"Forget it," I say (as if he'll understand).

I stand there in a dripping, towel-less tremble. At least I'm beginning to finally go flaccid. Then I notice that Wall Street's locker's ajar. Which I open . . . and while I'm rooting around for a towel, a goatskin wallet falls to the floor. As I pick it up with the hand not pressing the soggy paper to my crotch, I can't help but finger its buttery hide when I turn around to see Wall Street, the backs of his wrists on his hips, fuming behind me.

"Give me that," he whispers, snatching his billfold as he elbows past me to his locker and begins to gather his things.

"I'm sorry. Really. I was just looking for a towel." I drop what's now a wet tatter from my member. "I can't remember my combo."

"This guy's a thief," Wall Street informs a knot of men tightening around me, arms folded over chiseled chests.

"I'm really not," I claim.

"I'm calling management," he decides.

"And he prevented this disabled individual from using the designated facilities," says the bearded Black Defender, making a place for the wheelchaired man in the little ring around me.

"I'm sorry," I tell the glowering Asian. "I swear I wasn't trying to rip you off, sir," I promise Wall Street, but he twirls on a heel and hauls off.

A pause.

"Please, can somebody ask them to bring the bolt cutters?" My voice makes a pleading, pubescent crack as I look into each of their faces.

They assess me, disgusted . . . this betrayer of the manly sanctum where we are most exposed and trusting.

"Do any of you guys have an extra *tow*el?" I ask, a five-finger fan shielding my penis, which is suddenly riled again. The Black Defender spits on my chest and walks away.

Not so surprisingly, no one offers me a towel to wipe it off.

---

After what seems like an hour of shivering, Dominic finally appears with lethal lock-cutting jaws.

"Hi, Dominic," I chirp, and when he discovers that it's me who's caused him all the inconvenience, he gets a badgered look.

"He was stealing my wallet," Wall Street tells him, standing in tow, combing the hair.

"Goddamn thief," someone whispers behind me.

"I'm not a fucking thief," I call over my shoulder. "I was just looking for a towel," I say softly to Dominic. "I'll take a lie detector test if you want. Jesus! I'm freezing. Can someone give me a goddamn towel? I've had a bad day."

"I've had a bad *year*," Dominic says.

Our eyes meet, and something in him seems to surrender.

"Cancel his membership," suggests a man who I realize is Hans from the steam room. I catch his eye and he looks away.

"Nobody's canceling anything," claims Dominic, jutting then folding down the corners of his underlip in the indignant ethnic grimace that De Niro and Pacino made famous. After a few seconds, the crush of men adjourn with a disappointed sigh.

Dominic squats down and tries to bite my lock with the bolt cutters, but it's too small for the massive steel teeth to get a grip on.

"That's ironic, right?" I say, bending over him, my hands on eager knees.

"Huh?" he says, refusing to look at me.

"It's *ironic*. And how about the little moment we shared before?"

No response. After a minute, he gives up on the lock and stands up.

"What are my options?" I ask him.

"You'll have to wait for the guy with the blowtorch."

"And when does he come?"

"Tomorrow morning," turning away from me.

"But all I have to wear are these socks." I hold up a pink polyester pair I'd stolen from Camilla. (I had no money for laundry and they smelled like her feet.)

I'd be exaggerating if I said that he shrugged.

"Can't you give me *some*thing to wear?" I beg him through rattling teeth. "Or can I at least get a hug?" just to see his reaction. I catch him squelching a smile.

"I'll check the lost-and-found," and he leaves.

"Pickpocket," someone mumbles behind the lockers.

Naked and quaking I sniff the socks a last time before throwing them out.

Maybe ten minutes later, Dominic tosses me a tiny pair of white satin shorts.

"These look like they're for girls," I say, stretching the elastic waist.

# Who Wears Short Shorts?

Outside is the inside of a soup thermos. As I wait for a cab, which I'm willing to splurge on only because I'm now many job-threatening minutes late to the drawing class I nude model for, I have to keep bouncing from one bare foot to the next so the sidewalk can't char them. Still cabless, I hop, skip, and jump in front of the old Time Café, a half block from Crunch, where the chicly skeletal hostess gives me a nauseous glare from her podium. As I continue my little soft-shoe, all the parasol-shaded patrons regard me, it seems, more with amusement than hostility.

"Nice buns," a droll voice notes.

Ignoring it, I raise my left arm for a cab, arching my back as my tiny, shiny shorts *cleave* my buttocks, which are now soaked in sweat as the airborne grime discovers every one of my crevices.

Someone whistles at me.

"Eat shit," I mumble, but I'm too chicken to actually look over at them.

Of course I remember my first date here with Cammy. If you would have told me that only half a year later I'd be . . .

Or maybe Cammy's approaching me now in her own taxi, gazing with weary reminiscence out of her window as she nears our sacred meeting ground.

*Poor unfortunate soul,*

she'll think, spying the sideburned cross-dresser rocking back and forth on bare feet in what appears to be some kind of jittery crack withdrawal; peddling his ass in his white satin Marilyns to the closeted Wall Streeters who've snuck away on their lunch breaks for a little afternoon chicken hawk. All to pay for his habit, and God only knows what other debts . . . perhaps the money he owes on his co-op–

She visibly shudders.

"What's wrong, Milla?" the dusky man at her side asks in the trillish whisper of his exotic homeland. He enfolds her hand in his own manicured, comprehensively health-insured one.

"It's nothing, really, um, Otto," she stammers. "This city can be so fraught with those ghosts you'd thought you'd at last eluded, can it not? Cabby, can you in any way speed things up? And are you certain you know your way to the West Side heliport?"

But every taxi today seems to be taken or off-duty. I suddenly remember how Dr. Feete, the nude-modeling instructor, told me if I was late again I'd be fired, when finally a taxi slows down . . . only to spurt off when the beturbaned driver sees the creature about to slither into his car, bouncing from foot to foot in nothing but platinum short shorts and plush, sweaty chest hair.

Can you blame him?

I give him the finger for show anyway. From the tables behind me I'm hit with scattered laughter as cold as water from a spinning sprinkler. I turn around to find every face in a menu. Then I gaze over at the panels of Tower Records.

Call me a pessimist, but Success has never seemed more hypothetical.

Fifteen blistering minutes later (ten of which were, by then, elapsed class time), a cab steered by the hands of Irony himself finally stops and ejects a gaggle of giggling young ladies I happened to know from a School of Visual Arts sculpting class I'd posed for that previous semester!

"I'm actually late for a class, girls," I laugh, swapping places with them as I tell the cabby,

"One-eighty Thompson, please."

"Your sweater's all wet," one of them sniggers, sending the others into manufactured hysterics.

"Ha, ha," I play along, baffled and smiling as I pull the door closed, and it's only after we stop in front of my building that I realize she'd meant my sweaty chest hair.

My plan is to shed the mini shorts and score some of the $800 Gary owes me to pay for the taxi, but Bish (who for months I'd been successfully evading by means of a ski mask I'd worn whenever I was within a six-block radius of my building, until Gary borrowed and then lost it at some kind of group-sex-S&M-record-executive-thing he said Puff Daddy was at) is standing outside, his ear to the bricks. I crouch on the floor and ask the cabby to go to SVA directly. And as we pull away, I watch Gary assume shrinking tai chi poses through my window. Wearing what looks like a white loincloth.

When we arrive at SVA and I inform the cabby that I'll have to go inside to get his money from "my professor," he locks all the doors and calls over a cop, who ends up giving me a handcuffed escort through the ghostly halls, all the while looking down at what he describes, snickering into his walkie-talkie, as my "raisin smugglers."* Then, through the classroom window, I

FOOTNOTE >

*Again with the tiny testicle references.

see another, more "gifted" nude model. I assume I've been sacked until I notice a sign on the door saying that the room has been switched, and when I finally arrive at the right room, Professor Feete huffily agrees to lend me the cab fare, which ends up being twice what I would've earned for the session.

After talking Feete into unfiring me (yet again), I remember that I'd once carved the combination to my lock into the wall of the handicapped stall at Crunch . . .

just in case I ever forgot it.

# In a Model World

As you may've gathered, in addition to my demeaning array of odd jobs, I was a figure model for the School of Visual Arts. Imagine shivering through eight hours of nude poses in the brutal AC of a drawing class. *Why* did I do this?

Good question.

Certainly not for the six-fifty an hour. I think since my heart had become so sad and distorted, I figured, why not arrange the flesh likewise? Why not wind myself into a series of torturous squats and crouches a few times a week? If I was going to take a stab at this self-humiliation thing, why not go all out for varsity? Because in those divested days, after I'd been stripped of any self-respect to speak of, it seemed only logical that I should peel back all the falsity. De-bark myself for all the kids to carve their initials in . . . for every doggy to pee on. What could be more detached than a still life? And, inversely, wasn't my posturing only another way to feed the gut of that insatiable piranha . . . Vanity?

Hey, I'll take any stage that'll have me.

And what an alluring suitor résumé. Imagine the glowing impression I would've made on Cammy's mother. The thirty-three-year-old wannabe rock star with an Ivy League degree who spent his afternoons exposing himself to coeds.

*How exciting, Curtis. What* kind *of a model?*

Oh, the one who lies around with a prostrate prostate. Genitals flapping and hollows gaping before a dozen or so teens not much younger, come to think of it, than *your* lovely daughter.

So perhaps you're wondering how my life could possibly get any more pathetic?

Here's how it gets more pathetic . . .

Today, bathed in the lovely ashen Vermeer light of the warehousey classroom, as I switch to a discus-thrower pose, I feel the hot waves of diarrhea splashing against the walls of my intestines. This had been the focal point of many a nude-modeling nightmare. So who ever said my dreams wouldn't come true? As an icing of cold sweat begins to cover my skin, I grind my teeth and constrict my sphincter with all my powers.

The kids are silent, save the flinty scrapes of their pencils, and I wonder if they can hear the little dishwashery noises coming out of me. Suddenly I realize I'm just not going to be able to contain this one. It feels too vicious, explosive . . . Biblical.

"Notice the lovely vein now standing out on our model's forehead," notes Dr. Feete, who after eleven years still won't acknowledge that I actually own a name.

I'm glad I can help broaden the aesthetic sensibilities of today's creative youth, but let's face it, folks: there's a naked, hairy man in his mid-thirties who's about to unleash a steaming load all over your children.

"Dr. Feete, can I take a break now?" I whimper.

"Speak up, model!"

Fearing the muscles I'll need to repeat this might release the churning tide, I finally manage a "Break?" in a cracking, adolescent voice.

"It's only another eight minutes. And your face is turning a wonderful pallor. Class, notice how model looks like one of Rembrandt's sick studies?"

Straining every tendon, I moan,

"Pleassse."

The word echoes through the dim room. Feete ignores me. I start making all the obligatory God bargains . . .

*I swear I'll never bitch about Camilla again if You'll just gag this liquid magma.*

*Please! These children are the creative future of this Nation.*

(Is there a Whitney Houston song in this?)

I need a plan. I can't really sprint to the bathroom because every one of my muscles must remain utterly taut. Okay. Worst-case scenario: I unload as I make a run for it, then grab my robe and dash into the urinal, washing myself off a bit before vaulting out the window. *Never ever* to return. Get in touch with one of the better witness protection plans.

Still in my Grecian pose, I feel one hot drip on my ankle. Terrific. I dismantle my stance and, clenching my buttocks, begin a slow shuffle off the stage.

"Model, you still have six minutes!" screams Feete.

I can't even muster a grunt. I just waddle along with my feet splayed, chin tucked to my chest, all at a tortoise velocity. The kids are too polite to speak. They gaze, dumbfounded.

"What in God's name do you think you are *doing?*" cries Feete.

Why bother trying to explain this? I plod onward in this ridiculous duck walk, impossibly slow. Arranging the whole thing in my head as an amusing anecdote I'll be chuckling over one day on VH-1's *Before They Were Rock Stars*.

---

I guess the class finally caught on when they heard the noises squirting from the bathroom I'd finally reached. I then spent the lunch break alone in the refrigerated gloom because I didn't want to be caught too far from a toilet.* Draped in the dirty robe the school had provided, I sat huddled against the grate of a rattling space heater that Feete had finally given me after the kids kept complaining of my distracting sneezes.

*Suicide/Success.*

Listening to the students' sunny laughter outside, my teeth chattering in Loony Toon proportions, and a sore throat hatching as I gnawed the tofu slab Gary had told me was a great low-fat source of protein, somehow I didn't think Cammy would've been exactly kicking herself if she saw me. She was always such a stickler for details.

FOOTNOTE >

*Would I be eligible for workers' comp if it happened again?

# And Our Survey Says . . .

On my way home from class, lost in the hurrying hordes, I gush out of the subway* into humid Union Square. Sluggish behind beige rush-hour smog, the New York sun fails to thaw me. That immense Virgin Megastore's clock, on which Time is revealed as a never-ending digital game-show answer, gloats above me. But I realize just how irrelevant It is. Because my own internal clock now interprets the world in terms of B.C. and A.C.—Before and After Camilla.

I limp over to Third Avenue. This job is killing me; my vertebrae are twelve angry little fists, all cramped with carpal tunnel. Which reminds me of how She used to massage my back right after the weekly shavings.

Christ! Why can't she just love me?

(No, don't answer that.)

I walk South past Kiehl's, and that old movie house where Jodi Foster turned tricks in *Taxi Driver*. By the time I reach St. Marks I'm so lonely and attention-starved that I actually stop and *ask* if I can answer a survey being conducted in front of *Stomp*. Sud-

FOOTNOTE >

*whose East 23rd Street turnstile I, mini-shorted and tokenless, unlawfully vaulted over.

denly I recognize those same two bony med-schoolish kids I'd seen doing the on-camera Bish survey. And they can barely believe their good fortune: that a New Yorker has interrupted his life, unsolicited, to do something, without compensation. Astonished, they fumble with audiovisual gear before I can change my mind. I discover I'm actually getting excited by the unusual interest someone is taking in me, that I can hardly wait to start answering their questions. I neaten my hair and ask them if I have anything lodged in my teeth. Which I do (tofu), so I get them to wait while I fingernail it out. Pedestrians glance back at me. I haven't enjoyed this much eye contact in quite a while.

Then I realize the survey is about testicular cancer.

And that as the kid goes down the list of the questions, I have every single one of the symptoms.

My little horse rears its head with this new information, this spur in its hoof.

"Wait, sir, wait!" both of them yell as I stumble off, head down, massaging my genitals (through the damp satin of my minis). "Please, sir. We're almost done!"

I shake my head without looking back. My mind is a sports car screaming in a too-low gear. I shuffle past the old Fillmore East, Dempsey's Pub . . . crumpled into a mobile crouch, in attempt to ascertain the natty little lump—when someone's elbow gives me a sharp kidney jab. I wince and stagger.

"Watch it, pervert!" from an Aussie accent.

Terrific. Testicular cancer. Why doesn't this surprise me?

# Tower of Label

I plod along, pausing for occasional groin-gropes, past Indochine and the Blue Man Group, until I realize I'm right in front of Crunch. Still slightly bent over, I look up . . .

All the great white dopes are slugging it out with Gravity in there. And right in the front window is Anthony Everyoung. He's still here! But now he's trotting on a massively gadgeted treadmill and wearing some kind of heart monitor, with the machine on a very steep incline. I'm reminded of a lab chimp inside his own little rocket, dazzled with red-lit data, tilted to the stars.

I trudge on.* As the sun is snuffed out behind me. As Time Café twinkles fifty feet ahead.

There it is. The Big Bang of my Love Story . . . now a smoldering star . . . soon to collapse into entropy.†

FOOTNOTE >

*Too mortified to go back inside Crunch during peak hours, I waited until four-thirty that sleepless morning to go get my stuff back.

†Okay. Stars become vacuous black holes when they implode. And entropy is, I'm pretty sure, the second law of thermodynamics. Which says that total disorder and dissipation await all coherent structures, which I'll admit is quite a stretch if we apply that last term to Love. But basically, entropy means that heat and Death will reign in the universe when everything is the same temperature. If there are any metaphor enthusiasts left out there, I, ever-tiresome English major, am just trying to create a kind of Astronomy/Star/Love/Fame conceit.

Where *is* She?

As I reach a bouquet of umbrellas, I suddenly become terrified that, under one of them, I'll actually see Her hand, clinking flutes of Cliquot through the hemorrhaged sunset. I turn off at the Tower Records right there on East Fourth Street.

I think I've mentioned that electric shrine of panels which the record labels rent out for their Artists. A row of small bright monuments to the Stars that has, over the last decade, become my beacon, my torment. I've reduced all my dreams to achieving one of these.

*Suicide/Success*

washes into my head, like the chorus of some breathy old Barry White number.

I mean, is that too much to ask for? A shitty little panel at Tower? Everyone would see I'd finally carved something vivid out of all these dismal years.

*I will get a record deal,* I chant. *I'm* not *a bad person.*

And for a second, as I skulk along the row of artists with the latent lechery of a kid fondling his rich cousin's Christmas toys, I almost forget about the fatal little polyp in my pants.

*Metallica, Wilco, Jeff Buckley, Don Henley's Inside Job, Gay Dad.*

Wait. Has my Little Green seen this?

# Water Sports

Because of the Feete class fiasco, I was hoping to just hop right into the shower, but I find Gary taking one of his marathons. As usual the steam is keen with the insect-repellentish vapor from the multi-level-marketing-opportunity hair products his dad sold him.*

"Hi, buddy," I yell into the mist, coughing a little. He doesn't answer. So I say,

"Not that I'm rushing you," hack, "but how much longer do you think you'll be in there? I had sort of a bad day. I think there's a tumor on one of my balls. Actually, maybe you could give it a feel . . ."

"Yo, what's shaking?" his voice moist and low through the plastic curtain, but kinder than usual, so I immediately feel my face unknot, my lungs lighten.

"You're not going to believe this, dude," I say. "I'm nude modeling today, okay? And I soil myself. This tremendous ocea–"

"Sony offered you the contract."

What?

FOOTNOTE >

*His dad's the number two man in one of those pyramid schemes that cause people to lose all their friends when they invariably attempt and fail to recruit them.

This can't be true. I must be experiencing some kind of fevery visions that follow Montezuma's Revenge, or a post-traumatic stress delusion from the bad nut news. But,

"Yeah," Gary goes on. "I just spoke to Josh Epstein."

"You're shitting me."

"They're giving you two albums. Firm. With Gary B. in the producer's chair!"

Oh my God.

I would've shit myself every day for eleven years just to hear this. Maybe even have given up a testicle, which, when I feel it now, seems totally smooth again, making me think it was just a kind of stress knot. I tear off my sweaty minis and stand there naked . . . newborn and free at last! I elbow some steam off the mirror and nod shrewdly at my foggy face . . .

So I did it. All the toil finally paid off, it was all for a reason. No more Dumpster rummaging and ransacking trash piles for appliances to hock and clothes to consign. I can stop snagging the occasional single from the basket they pass around at AA, not to mention their free coffee, milk, and Oreos. Just wait until Cammy gets wind of this! I'll buy her a big rock this afternoon and appear at her door on bent knee.

"Is it really true?" I ask.

"They faxed me the deal memo an hour ago."

Jesus.

All these years . . . the thousands of dollars I wasted—no, in*vest*ed—on voice lessons; the thousands of hours I sat practicing guitar to a metronome (whose clicks still managed to infiltrate the customized earplugs Cammy had to get). The whole grueling Crunch regimen and all of Gary's emaciation/dehydration diets. All the—well, I could go on, but what I'm saying is that the Greek god Consecutivus has finally shined down upon me!

*Suicide/Success.*

Well, it looks like it's gonna be the latter after all, now doesn't it? Victory or Death, and

"Gary. I just can't thank you enou–"

"Yeah, it's a half-million-dollar deal," he says in his congested nose-picking voice.

"Gary, I can't wait to tell Cam–"

"Sony has options on seven records. We get three-fourths of the merch and we can always renegosh."

"She'll finally see I'm not such a loser." I'm inflamed with sudden virility. "And I can pay my mom back and–"

"Plus a greatest hits."

". . . now Bish won't foreclo–"

"Plus a six-figure publishing deal with EMI."

"Maybe I'll just sell this shit hole and buy a massive loft for me and Cammy and Phillip."

"With bumps of fifty K for every time you go gold."

"Gary, I never told you," I chuckle, "but all those bagels we've been eating were from out of the garbage bin outside Au Bon Pain."

Silence.

"Gary?" my voice getting sloppy in tears. "Gary? I love you, dude," as I yank back the curtain, bringing down the shower rod and not even caring as I cast my arms around him. We stand there embraced, under the flood, two hairy naked men–beautiful.

"I love you," I reiterate (feeling stubble on his back), but as I begin to kiss his cheek he frees an arm and holds up the finger.

"Uh-huh, uh-huh," he says into a little mouthpiece attached to a headset. He attempts to wriggle out of my arms. "Okay, yeah. I'll call you on your cell just as soon as they cut the check. Okay, ciao."

My eyes are tearing, partly from his shampoo fumes, as I feel Gary's heart strike against mine.

"Feel free to let me go anytime now, fucko," he says, the water gushing down on our hug and onto the floor.

"I thought you were talking to me," I mumble into his ear.

I release him and step back, as he palms his crotch, with all but his face frothed in soap. I stand there mute, stunned, beginning to shiver. "Don't electrocute yourself," I say, stepping out of the shower into the warm inch of water on the floor.

"It's waterproof." He re-wedges the shower rod and yanks the curtain closed. "Hey, can you shut the door?" his plastic voice asks me. "There's a draft."

"Yeah, sorry." I close it, sending a little weak wave into the hardwood hall.

"Don't worry, cash cow. You'll cash out, too."

I sit down on the toilet, my feet submerged on the marinated floor, from which I then feel the pounding of furious fists and the cartoony collapsing of plaster.

"Birnbaum!" come muffled Bish shrieks. "You're flooding my (unintelligible) . . . eviction!"

"I'm thinking there must be a way to market you crapping yourself," Gary muses over the subcommotion. "Do you think you could pull that off onstage? Like a Marilyn Manson kind of thing?"

Pause.

"I guess I could try."

"And what was that you were saying about the bagels?"

And on the eighth day, God created anticlimax.
And He saw that it was good. This so being because now all
His other works would appear all the more miraculous.
—The Apocrypha?*

FOOTNOTE >

*Tower of Bagel

God

# If Camilla Fell



*If Camilla Fell*

*Then what could she have done?*
*This I wonder on those days of Heaven's*
*Shades*
*of dreams a scrim before my mind*
*That dims the lazy things we said*
*all warm upon our Sunday bed*
*still linger as I wonder*

*If Camilla Fell*

*As I ride this subway train*
*Hoping I'll refrain*
*From writing one more*
*Song about if*

*Camilla Fell*

*I could've saved her from herself and me*

*The winter, she is coming*
*And I feel my will is crumbling*
*'Cause living in this City makes you strange*
*I miss your touch it kept me sane*
*But*
*What could I have really done*

*If Camilla Fell*

# Asylum

This morning I awoke with tears in my throat. The word *Home* on my lips. I really didn't know whether my crying was happy or sad, exactly. It didn't matter. For once I was glad just to wake into day. Surrender to something as big and blazing as the afternoon into which we walk from a dark movie matinee . . . melting the lie we'd just watched in the true stunning light.

*Home.*

There's so much friction in the word for me now. The obscene scents of jealousy and bacon grease . . . the inkling stench of incest.

And Camilla was in the dream, of course. She was almost a fragrance this time. I kept trying to place her. Sniffing her, until she became a long thread of pale blue smoke, with her face at the end as a cobra's—curling into all the rooms of the house I grew up in. Surveying things below her in her slight unflinching squint as my parents and I played Scrabble at the kitchen table. I kept pointing up at Cammy, but my mom was coming up with all these great triples. I was the only one who could see her.

Then I was a grownup, walking around the desolate rooms of my old house, where the walls were now charred from a fire; my Zeppelin posters curling and scorched at the edges. And all the while Cammy was hovering, a snake of baby blue smoke, bridging these chapters of me.

*Home.*

We need these puzzles to persist, I think. Death can't untangle the human things so snarled in us. All the conflicts we create, those textures at once coarse and forgiving. We think abstraction is a detour, but maybe it's our saving grace.

# Little Judas

## (TOP 40 PHENOMENON ONCE PRIAPIC)

I was thinking, nothing could be worse than what happened last time.

Well . . .

Despite the frigid air Professor Feete swore averted A.D.D., the Crunch erection revisits with a vengeance. And what a remarkable little encore. This time it's even angrier, and actually painful. So thank God I'm sitting on the floor with my back to the class.

"Model, please face us," Feete yaps.

I glare at it, warningly—it twitches, willfully. I don't want to piss it off, as it were. Maybe it'll eventually exhaust itself if I can just wait it out.

"*Mod*el," Feete whines. "Model, please turn a*round*."

I try wedging it between my legs, but it wriggles right out. The more I subdue it, the more it squirms, like when you shield a kid's eyes from a slasher movie scene—it doesn't seem to know if it's excited or terrified.

"*Mod*el, would you please take a *fac*ing pose?!"

Slowly, I swivel around, my head hanging, forearms folded over the culprit. But nobody's fooled by this variation on the old math-book-over-the-boner-in-class maneuver. It's peek-a-booing out.

All the pencils stop scratching. There's a lone burst of strangled laughter. A rubber band hits my thigh.

I look up, only to find all eyes on sketchpads. But I realize I'm actually disap*point*ed, that a good degrading round of cackling was maybe just what the thwarted artiste in me needed. There would've at least been something unruly and rockstar about it.

"Let's break for lunch now," Feete concedes—and of course, as everyone leaves, it starts wilting.

Feete moseys over. "Model, there's two things I want—"

"I'll totally understand if you fire m—"

Feete ignores me, saying, "One. There have been numerous complaints about your, um, body hair." He bends down and runs a leisurely fingernail along my shin. "Would you mind trimming?"

"I guess. I mean, does that mean you want me to shave my actual nuts?"

"No, no," he says, raising a halting hand. "Not the nuts."

"No? No, then. I mean, no, then I wouldn't mind, I guess."

"Splendid. *Two.* Can you do that on command?" nibbling the tip of a curious index finger, which he then points at the memory of my erection.

I knot my brows, confused.

He arcs one of his own.

"There's a private seminar I conduct on the weekends which could really use your talent," he says, in a voice that manages to meld self-loathing with lust. "You could earn from *one* of them what you make freezing your *tuchis* off in this cave all month. Nine bills a throw. Cash."

"When can I start?"

"Next week, if you're naughty."

# Coordinates

The autumn sky was dying above, in a last reprise, extravagant with clouds, the ruffled pink collar of an aging Ziggy Stardust.

The end of an era.

I walked home west down Bleecker behind a squat, swarthy guy.

"I'm almost at Mercer," he said into his cell phone's headset, but we were actually at Broadway. "Really, I'll be there in two seconds, sexy," in a shiny toy gun of a voice.

He had tremendous thighs, straining out of what looked like Gap khakis.

"Now I'm about to cross La Guardia," he made himself sound out-of-breath, as we very slowly crossed Mercer.

I stayed about a Ping-Pong table's length behind this guy, watching those massive thighs, trying to hear him.

"No, she's a cunt," he explained. "Well, that's what she *is,*" with a feigned grunty laugh. "I've *told* you, I haven't seen her forever, and nor do I *want* to. Yes, just that time on the Upper East Side. Okay, cool your jets. I'm crossing Thompson," though we were fifty yards from it.

"Wouldn't I have told you? I haven't *seen* her. I don't give a fuck what *Jes*sica told you. Or Andrea. No," shaking his head, looking around, as if for understanding. "We were never in love," he said, a little tender. "At least, I wasn't. Look, we'll talk in a minute, okay? I'm crossing Macdougal."

I turned home on Thompson.

# Bingein' and a-Purgin'

I'd resolved not to take (quite so much) shit from Gary.

As, standing at the fridge, I hear him flush the toilet and stamp into the kitchen.

"And we still need to lose some weight," he announces, parenthetically, as if we'd been discussing a related topic.

"*We?* You mean *me*," I say, going weak on the *me*, "while you eat your wheels of Brie," but the *Brie* comes out cautious, and I can't meet his eyes.

"Okay, *you* still need to lose seventeen pounds,"* he says, pinching implied fat above my waist. I smack his wrist away and say,

"Look, I want to talk, okay? There's a lot of stuff that's been building up,"

at which Gary gives me a *let's-hear-it* eye roll.

"I just feel like you don't care about me," I say. "Like I'm just some product."

"Dude, I'm looking *out* for you. I'm the only one who doesn't bullshit you. *You're a rock star, Curtis,*" he whines, in a sycophant mimic, his mouth an inverted simper. He waddles over

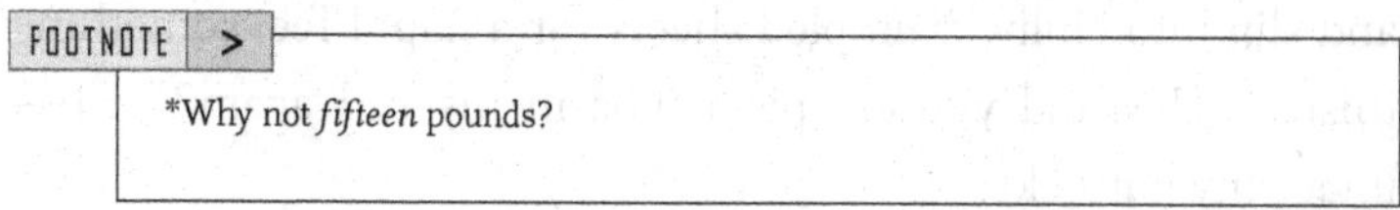
FOOTNOTE >

*Why not *fifteen* pounds?

and sits on the couch, failing to turn on the TV with a remote that's missing batteries I can't afford. "Seventeen pounds," he recaps, evenly.

"Seventeen pounds? I'll look like fucking Karen Carpenter."

"You should *be* so lucky. Look how many number one hits she had. KC had her own look and it worked wonders for her investment portfolio. Donnie says neuroses can be channeled into gimmicks. You don't think that was a genius marketing ploy? That anorexia nervosa just *happened* to be a really nice hook for Karen's career? It sounds brutal, but it's all strategy. Wake up, Birnbaum."

"It *killed* her."

"But first it put her on the toppermost of the poppermost. Listen, cash cow, you could take it one step further and be the first bulimic male rock star. I'm totally serious. Donnie says you have to get your priorities straight. What do you *really* want: happiness and health . . . or Fame?"

"I didn't know they were mutually exclusive. In fact, I thought they sort of went hand in hand."

"Donnie says happiness is overrated. That artists like you 'need friction to make sparks.' And smiling causes wrinkles anyway. Which reminds me—remind me later that I have a very expensive present for you."

"Wait. I mean, thanks, but can we get back to the bulimia?"

"Look, all I'm saying is, it would be a nice way for me to pitch you to the A&R boys. Why don't you think of *my* position for a change?"

"You're actually serious, aren't you?" As I turn off the light and slip into chilly, crumpled sheets for a nap, I feel something thistly. "Hey, did you eat pistachios in my bed again?" I feel under my buttocks.

"No," he says absently, and starts outfitting the arms of my couch/his bed in white doilies. "My grandmother left me these in her will." As he stands back to appraise them, stroking his chin, I realize it's his nail clippings that are in my bed again.

"Dude, please, I asked you not to cut your fingernails in my bed, remember?"

"Oh, those are my toenails, sorry."

Astonished, I watch him remove planks of wood from out of my closet and stack them inside what he's unspokenly appropriated as his own little district of my apartment.

"Are you going to come back here after your workout?" he asks me, measuring a board with my tape ruler.

"I was actually going to try and nap before I went busking. What are you build–?"

The screams of his hand drill bury my question. I watch a lovely little blizzard of sawdust. When the drill whines down to a whir I ask, "Hey buddy, what is that?!"

"Wall unit," he says. "It's cool, right?"

"I like it," I lie.

"Look, um, I was wondering if you could make yourself scarce for about an hour when this singer chick I'm thinking of working with comes over to play me her stuff. I might even get a hummer."

"Sure," and I get out of bed. But when I look for a sweater in my dresser, all I find is Gary's bikini underwear. "Have you seen all my sweaters?"

"I put them in winter storage, so I could have more room."

Then I just decide to come out with it . . .

"Hey, um, Gary? Sorry to hound you. I really appreciate what you're doing for me, and I love your company and all. But when exactly, and I'm not rushing you, because if you've decided you don't want to do it anymore I'm totally cool with that too, but when do you think we'll be getting around to doing my demo?"

"Oh yeah," he says, breezily, like I've reminded him of some tentative plans we'd made to spend a Saturday tie-dyeing. "We actually need to talk about that . . ."

But his cell phone does its cranky little alert, and he holds up the index finger while he scampers back into the kitchen. "What's up, kid?" I hear him say softly. I watch his fat, chuckling back as he stands at the sink.

"Cool, yeah, then sell 'em," he murmurs, and hangs up. His eye scans my direction from his semiprofile before he begins brewing up the jumbo iced coffee he insists I drink before my daily Crunch punishment.

"You were saying? About the demo?" I say.

"Yeah, um, there's been some delays." As he glances over his shoulder at me, it looks like he's zipping up his fly. I sneak up behind him as he wrenches something out of his front Armani jean pocket, and,

"Hey, I saw that!" I say. "What are you stirring into my coffee?"

Gary casually drops a little beige bottle into the garbage.

"Excuse me," I say, politely, as he blocks the trash, his cheeks bulging with Au Bon Pain bagel, at which point I drop to my knees and attempt to pry open the vise of his thick little shins . . . and he says,

"What, are you going to *blow* me?" in Jackie Mason's Transylvanian intonation. When I finally slither through his legs, he walks off on them.

And so, scummy with coffee grounds, I first discover some shredded copyright forms for my songs, one of which I notice is signed only by Gary. But I'm even more alarmed when, after digging through the slimy dregs of the rubbish, I extract the little demon phial, slick with blueberry yogurt, and,

"This is a laxative," I realize, wiping clean the label and absently licking my finger as I read . . .

**In the rare case of heart palpitations, severe diarrhea, or priapism, consult physician IMMEDIATELY!**

"No wonder I keep getting all these boners," I say, getting to my feet and following him to GFPITU. "How could you do this to me? And you used the whole *thing*!" as I douse out invisible fluid. "How long have you been sneaking this stuff into my coffee?" I try and sound more angry than hurt. "No wonder I always have the runs."

"It's all natural," he says, working a toothpick as he exits the bathroom, and then the apartment.

My heart relents a little when I walk out into the hall and see a note slipped under my front door. On the back of a Bowlmor Lanes one-player score sheet is written . . .

Monsieur Clyde,
May we please switch our guitar lesson, which will be our 14th, to 2 pm instead of before school next Monday as I've been necessarily detained. And the reason of which I will at further lengths explain upon our lesson. I hope this does not prove exceedingly unconvenient or untimely for you, Clyde. Please advise, si vous plait? And also, on Sunday my dad and I daytripped to Scarsdale to see my grandmother with bad breath and we got to drive through a car wash.
Warm Regards,
Walter
p.s. You are a mook and I miss you.

p.p.s. We learned in science that only bees and dogs can smell fear.

While under this was the drawing of a man, all in slapdash features, except for an obvious bald spot conveyed as an erasure smudge where she'd at first been too generous with his hair, but which she'd compensated for with the addition of massive sideburns, and hands that play a guitar whose treble clefs sing out of four curvy, unevenly spaced strings. These notes fly up into a periwinkle sky complete with both smirking sun and scowling Blakean moon.

And, of course, this blue sky makes me think of . . .

I leave my apartment to face the broad day. With only Her ghost to guide me.

# Only One Fell Swoop

I wanted to believe this fated sensation that we'd be reunited was enough to make it true. Because Love, I think, must live with the illusion, true or false, that it can't be avoided.

I wondered if she'd ever seen me. Ducked into some morning deli, the tidy Korean owners trying (and failing) to frown as this timid gazelle hid among their flowers, as in the foliage of that lush Rousseau painting. While the singing rocker outside moved through his noisy moment, keening off-key Zeppelin, wearing huge goofy headphones.

What could she have been feeling—or trying *not* to feel? Relief? Guilt? Thwarted maternal urges?

Nothing?

Not seeing Camilla for so long felt like a favor someone owed me. Or a debt they'd welched on, weighing on me more heavily each interest-bearing second. I had that short-winded sense of being cheated.

Yet I always felt I was just on the verge of her. When I'd wander east down St. Marks in the first chill breaths of autumn, with that rugged hickory death in the air that everyone swears makes them feel so alive. Composing my face to look happy without her . . . but not *per*fectly happy. In case she might round the sidewalk at Gem Spa.*

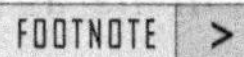

*Newsstand pictured on the back of the New York Dolls' legendary first album.

So where *was* she?

At first I knew she hadn't moved because I'd call her machine every day when she was at work. And on lonely days (a redundant statement), I'd sometimes call her back five or six times just to get that tart gist of her again.

And then the obsessing would start, as I searched for veiled meaning in her every stutter and breath.

Did I hear a kind of longing in her

PLEASE

before

LEAVE A MESSAGE?

Or a faint, farcical lilt in her vowels, aimed directly at *me* of course, admitting the hell her life had become through our distance. A kind of

*Okay, Curtis, can we please stop the bullshit already?*

Or was it a stoicism? Because why had she recorded that new OGM anyway? Isn't that a modern symptom of things improving? A release from the past? Had Cammy's life turned some sunny corner? Did she sound more assured? Contented?

Of *course*.

She'd met someone. That's why there were never any hangups on *my* machine anymore. Probably engaged by now. Something in her voice made me think *architect*.

And now, nearly every day, some creature catches my wild eye. Who almost moves with Cammy's frugal footstep. Her rigorous posture.

*Almost* being the operative word here.

Because they were always *near*ly Camillas. Camilla puzzles, shy a few crucial pieces. A nose less noble, a mouth less moody. At which I'd squint as I passed them on the sidewalk, usually startling their owners into rape-fearing steps away from me, as I tried to chisel Camilla's memory out of their faces.

Then the other day I saw Her.

In Union Square.

I was looking up at the Virgin Megastore's clock, recalling our taxi ride to Christie's, through that distant, late-summer dusk, when suddenly there she was . . .

Walking swiftly, about a bowling lane's length ahead of me in her green jeans and Nikes. Looking eager for something, it seemed. I immediately found myself hunting her through the blatant, concrete day. Over the steps at Fourteenth Street, through the postcard stands and that overpriced, straining-to-be-quaint farmers' market. Weaving through the slow navy blue menace of cops and the wearied commuter lunch girls sweating through polyester. Still on the run, I plucked a scarlet peony from the flower patch in front of the dog run, which I quickly scanned for Phillip. Then,

"Cutie!" I couldn't help but yell, softening the last syllable when I heard how loud it came out, as she (and several other not-as-cute people) half turned her face back as she kept on walking.

I finally swooped down on Cammy in the shade of the subway kiosk (the tyranny of the mundane ever-pressing as I remembered my Metrocard was empty). There was a kind of younger, taller, thicker-lipped, and in general sexier version of me leaning against the railing, checking his watch. But when he saw me, he smiled. My thinner lips almost curled into a grin as well. Because I guessed we were confirming our resemblance, participating in a living smile, with me a bit lesser, passing on the torch.

Wait.

He was smiling at Ca*mill*a—who actually squealed and broke into a little skip right into his arms.

Oh, my God.

Better Me slid two lucky hands over Cammy's ass, and she kissed him.

She *kissed* him. I saw tongue(s)!

I ran over and, using the peonyless hand, the Cro-Magnon man living within me grabbed her birdy shoulder with a sense of entitlement that alarmed me. As Cammy spun around, I remember the taffy moment taking forever, stretching out in front of me as I watched myself grab her lank arm, which, turning, she yanked out of my grasp. The tinnitic roar in my skull became so thunderous that I was thinking (or *not* thinking) inside a giant seashell. Better Me's face creased with testosterone obligation, preparing for battle, all systems adrenal—but *her* face looked more annoyed now than frightened, really, what with him there, I guess, and . . .

. . . it wasn't Camilla.

No.

For a second I didn't quite understand what was happening. Although I was aware of some awful, displaced familiarity occurring, like reading your childhood phone number within an escaped serial killer's prison inmate number printed in the newspaper. The whole thing felt like one of those S.A.T. relationship questions: Better Me is to Quasi Camilla as Curtis is to ——.

I looked at her mutely. It was always the eyes that gave these bogus Cammies away. They never quite held her queer azure stare. Never looked as suspicious of the very space they were thinking through. Never promised the consummate pain.

It was like, in struggling to reconstruct the real deal, some special Camilla interpreter had tried to explain those blue problems to the cloning technician, but of course all their resistant subtlety got lost in translation. So the answer was always a little wrong.

Strangely enough, my first response wasn't shock. Or even embarrassment, really. It was anger. By *not* seeing Camilla, I'd suddenly fallen yet another notch deeper in love with her. The situation just reminded me in a new way of how matchless she was. I mean, how could this girl have the gall to mimic her? And to do it so goddamn *well*. While at the same time totally missing her essence. The whole thing was as cheap and pathetic as an Elvis impersonation.

"What the fuck?" said the impostress.

"Yeah, what the fuck?" agreed dutiful Better Me.

A little black kid lifted a puckish eyebrow at me as he descended into the subway.

"Forget it," I told ersatz Camilla, as if *she* were the one who owed *me* an apology. "I thought you were someone else," I allowed, generously. "Sorry," I told Better Me, because I actually liked him. (Of *course* I did. I mean, think about it.)

But the poor girl must've been stunned—that this yutz, who'd wrenched her into his own reality boat and then just as carelessly tossed her back out, was rolling his eyes instead of apologizing like a madman.

"Sorry to disappoint you," she said, with a voice, by the way, nothing like Camilla's. (Smoker.)

"It's okay," I said, grudgingly, still not getting it, oblivious to the Olympian heights of my Camillacism, until I sensed the peripheral blue presence of a policeman, plodding toward me.

"I'm sorry," I told the girl, more because I was scared now. "I thought you were my old girlfriend," I added, realizing too late how stalkerish I sounded.

Anyway, to make a short story shorter, the cop came closer. In a neutral way, I gave the non-Camilla the red peony I was holding. She didn't smile or even take it from me. But Better Me did, before he threw a consoling arm around her and led her down the steps. The cop walked off (but only after he looked at me for a few *I-could-haul-your-ass-in-right-now-if-I-wanted-to* seconds). I breathed deeply. Then, as Better Me and his girl disappeared into the whooshing indifference of things, he looked over his shoulder at me.

"I'm sorry," he mouthed.

# De Plane, De Plane

ST. MARK'S TATTOO stank of dirty human hair and bad homegrown reefer. Its walls were a regimented bedlam of bumper stickers insisting on the Cycle Sluts from Hell, Blitzpear, Korn, Cum Guzzler, Straight Fuck, Hated Youth, Clit, Faux Leather Donut . . . and other bands in that general warm-and-fuzzy vein.

Gary'd spent months convincing me to brand, of all things, a yin/yang into my shoulder because Donnie felt its power lay "in the very self-admission of that stupidity and cliché so intrinsically and historically rock 'n' roll." And that "an icon so tired" would "appeal to society's lowest common denominator, who in fact embody the bulk of your record-purchasing public."

Sitting down, I noticed that the little gun they used to inject the kind of nose-stud Gary had suggested I "warm up" with was kept in a dish of what looked very much to me like filthy brown water. But when I timidly asked the tattoo artiste if this were indeed sanitary, Gary raised a curt hand and told me to

"Let the dude do his fucking job."

Although I had the sneaking suspicion that *no* design we came up with would've impressed our talented specialist, just as no teeth can be clean enough for the tsking dental hygienist, it wasn't so easy to interpret his take on Gary's aesthetic decisions.

This not only because of the tattooist's less-than-chatty manner that afternoon, but also because his face was a pincushion for numerous hoops, rings, trinkets, and studs, while below all this his skin was inked with important-looking barbs and tangles. And while the facial tattoo in particular failed to strike me as the wisest move should the fellow ever fancy a change in occupation, all of it seemed to convey some extremely meaningful and esoteric East Village philosophy. As I sat there getting disfigured amid the chainsaw assault of New York's cutting-edge Emo-Core,* I yelled,

"Your face looks cool! Is there some kind of symbolism in all of it?"

But my attempt at friendly banter yielded only a shrug from the chap, apparently absorbed in his craft as he suckled a rat tail of intricate braids.

Amid all the rumpus, I thought I'd heard occasional faint-but-spine-tingling howls, when at last a crew-cut and bowlegged young gal emerged from the back with a yelping pit bull in her arms. As she lugged the poor thing out the front door, I saw there was a bloody bandage over his genitals.

"What just happened to that dog?" I yelled through the racket.

After the tattoo guy ignored me, I stood up, turned down the jam box volume, and demanded to know,

"What the fuck just *hap*pened to him!?"

After a long, glaring silence, he mumbled,

"Meat pierce," working his tongue in the back of his mouth on some morsel of food (?) as he turned the "music" back up,

FOOTNOTE >

*Emotional Hardcore.

now even louder, then renewed his tattooing with a seemingly much sharper needle.

"They drive a stud right through their dicks and clits," explained a girl who'd just entered in a black-leather-Elvis-'68-Special-style jumpsuit. "Last week I had Stench (our tattooist) M.P. both of my rotties, Fetus and Cletus. And they fucking *love* it!"

All told, it was the most excruciating $375 I'd ever put on my MasterCard. I think I endured more physical pain in that half hour than in all the years leading up to it. But the real coup de grâce came when, through the actual tears of agony caused when Stench scoured my just-finished yin/yang with an alcohol swab, I noticed a swastika tattooed on his forearm as he rolled up his sleeve and went to the bathroom. At which Gary, seeing me dumbstruck, assured me that

"*Man*son had a swastika. And he was the fifth fucking Beatle."

The strapping, sexy leather girl told us we should call her Groupie as we walked out with her onto wintry St. Marks Place. "And your tatt's corny as shit," she added, poking it. "Totally passé."

Gary told her it was *retro,* then grabbed my arm, asking her, "And don't you know who this *is*?"

"I was thinking it was," she said, with slow, acquisitive nods.

Gary pulled me aside, explaining how Groupie might take my mind off Camilla by "draining" my "balls." As he hailed a cab, I caught him giving her a wily wink. Thinking, *At least she owns dogs*.

We walked. I noticed Groupie had the exaggerated features of a former child star; once cute, but now verging on the monstrous. Her amber sunglasses hid frantic black eyes, like wasps trapped in bottles, and they were clotted in Priscilla Presley mascara. As we turned the corner at Third Avenue, the skate punks sprawled in front of The Continental caroled

"Spare some change for drugs?"

and I realized that, just as "Groupie" embraced the shame in the name, confession-as weapon had come into vogue.

A guy walked past us with a foot-long blue beard swinging from only one side of his face, simultaneously lighting a smoke and hocking snot.

"I gave that asshole a hand job in the bathroom at Niagara," she thumbed back at him. "And I fucked Turd," she bragged, counting fingers. "The singer from Jerry Lee Loser. And L. L. Cool J's dad. Plus I gave really good, sloppy hummers to all the guys in Meat Whistle. Except the new drummer, who I'm pretty sure's a fag."

"I think the tattoo made me nauseous or something," I lied, stopping.

"Really? Oh, okay," she said, very quickly. "I hope you feel better. I'll let you be alone."

She'd heard this before.

"Well, you seemed really sweet," she said after our all-thumbs good-bye hug. "I was just wondering what your apartment would've looked like."

So I said what the hell and decided to show her.

# Bonnie and Clyde

With the concern of someone asking me if I'd remembered to turn off the oven, Groupie said,

"Do you want to fuck this?" pointing between the long legs she'd spread over the vinyl arms of my La-Z-Boy. I walked out of my bathroom, holding a shy condom in the gray boring daylight. I thought of how people's genitals were a lot like their owners. These hidden raw badges. Because hers was all slack-jawed . . . a sad crooked mouth . . . wanting, gaping. While above it her wayward breasts stared off in opposite directions.

And so I struggled to at least make my *face* seem aroused, as I glanced nervously over at the coffee table where Gary's day-old deli sandwich stood an inch thick in ham.* Which put me in mind of Camilla's pink folds, all tightly packed and deliciously mysterious. Realizing it wasn't exactly the sort of image one builds an Elizabethan emblem poem around.

Seeing my halfhearted erection, Groupie said,

"Maybe you'd like it *this* way," rolling over on all fours in the lounger. I placed an obligated hand over the snarl of ink at the small of her back. But I just couldn't do it. I said I needed to go

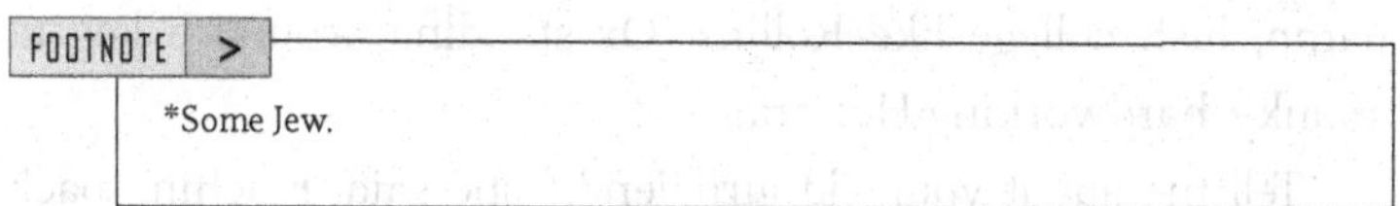
FOOTNOTE >

*Some Jew.

slower, and so, a bit stiffly, she let me pull her into my lap in the recliner.

I tried to comprehend her, asking her questions. She said she'd recently

"quit the business,"

whatever *that* meant, and had worked all last winter at a Seminole reservation in North Dakota without heat or running water. When I asked her how that had panned out, she said,

"Fucking a*maz*ing," staring off out the window. "I really evolved. It was all guys, which was totally righteous, because I'm not friends with women."

"Hey, can you remove those for the interview, Axl?"

She obliged and finally took off her yellow-tinted specs. Then I led her to bed, where, on top, she straddled me with all the rampant beauty of a Frank Frazetta huntress. I looked into the dark of those muddled eyes—what was so sexy-brutal about her now would in ten years, I figured, appear only impatient.

Who was I fooling? What was I doing?

With her still astride me, I told her I was totally exhausted because I'd had insomnia for months, but she missed the hint and said I should go to her Indian hypnotist/doctor over in Alphabet City. And when, half considering this, I asked her what happened when she went under, she said

"All I know is I wake up and he's zipping his fly."

*Simile Game,* I thought:

Groupie was like hard, wet candy . . . which had rolled into the grime under its own vending machine. Suddenly I wanted this nineteen-year-old to be far away from this City, at some damp, lush college like Rollins. Or standing around a keg at spunky, hardworking Hofstra.

"Tell me about your old girlfriend," she said, reaching back and trying to revive me. "Is she hot?"

I didn't answer. I wondered how she even knew I'd had one. But as she began to go down on me, I finally hardened enough for her to suddenly shove me inside her, without a condom, and when I tried to pull out and say something wise, she said,

"Don't fucking lecture me," clenching me, grinding me, contorting her face in the pained satisfaction of a guitarist getting off on his own solo. I was only an instrument, a means to her friction. And of course, I missed *Her* tremendously . . . pinned under this poor girl but stranded in the blue memory mists of Camilla Fell.

"Hey, rock star?" I said. "Remember me? I'm right down here."

And then something odd happened. A connection was made. There was a wild and gun-molly glint in her eyes. I felt in that moment like she was wholly on my side, that there was a once-and-for-allness and an all-for-oneness about us, just us, configured this way, and that the world didn't matter because we were going down together . . . I saw what was missing with Camilla.

The whole thing was over in a minute. I kept apologizing for coming so quickly, but Groupie told me it was

"All good,"

a phrase that seemed like a sort of

*Let them eat cake*.

"Peace," she wished me as she walked out the door.

"Peace," I said, surprised to feel my mouth close around the cliché.

# So You Wanna Be a Rock 'n' Roll Star?

Later that week I come home to find all the lights off. For once Gary's not here. Thank God.

. . . but as I adapt to the dark, I see his legs on my bed, hairy and folded Indian style inside a quivery little funnel of votive light–on my pillow . . . nude.

"Dude," I say, "could you please . . ."

"Shhhhh!" holding up the finger–and I see that he's on his cell phone.

I wait in shuddering, tawny darkness till he's done with the call. Then I say,

"Hey, it's okay that you sit on my pillow, but can you at least wear some underw–?"

"You broke my fucking concentration, Birnbaum! I was in a yogic phone analysis with Donnie. We were trying to access unfortunate muscle memories, and you fucked it all up just when I was starting to experience *Toxic Father Recall.*"

"I'm sorry. Should I leave? I'll leave." I'm amazed that I'm actually walking to the door when he says,

"No, for*get* it. Donnie said he could tell I'd lost my chi anyway." He pinches out the candle, flicks on the lights, and stalk-waddles into my bathroom.

Gary's been here for six months now. Slowly his unfolding possessions are strangling my own. We have yet to record one note of my demo.

I hint at this after he storms out of the bathroom.

"Donnie says I have to resolve some major Daddy Issues before I can even start on any new project," he says, crawling back into my bed, on which he's apparently been enjoying one of his sumptuous, three-course diner-style spreads. "So I'll keep you posted. But I'm bumping Therapy up to four sessions a week, so I should be making some solid progress pretty soon. And your songs are still too schmaltzy anyway. These days the kids want songs about butt sex. Murdering and mutilating and then sodomizing their parents. You should listen to Death Metal and all these rappers."

I tell him I write about what I feel.

"Nobody gives a fuck about what you *feel,* Birnbaum. Do you want to be a rock star, or a method acting coach!?"

Still butt-naked and prone, he opens a tin container of eggs and sponges a sun of placenta with a bagel that was lying right on my sheets, then folds the whole wad into his mouth.

"Hungry?" I say.

"Mmm," with hamster cheeks bulging. "Donnie got me stoned again today and I have the wicked munchies."

"Hey, buddy, can I have a little bite of your bagel, please? I'm schnauzer."

"You're looking a little jowly." He slaps my hand away. "What's *schnauzer?*"

"That's the word Camilla and I had for *starving.*"

"Please, not while I'm eating."

I notice he's using a stack of my mail as his iced-coffee coaster. The top letter reads **SUBPOENA** . . . and it's postmarked **LAGUNA BEACH**—balmy home of my beloved mother.

"Sorry to bug you about the whole demo thing again, Gar, but I guess I have some Mommy issues. Can you believe she's taking me to court? My own *moth*er? I *have* to get a record deal so I can pay her back."

"Stop whining. You want to write about what you '*feel*'? Then channel all this into your songs. But show some goddamn agro for once. Turn MADD around. DDAM. Driven Dudes Against their Mothers."

He slurps from a cardboard cup of matzo ball soup, which trickles lumpily down his chin. He looks up and catches me making an "ick" face.

"Fuck you, Mr. Manners," with sudden ferocity. "I'm practicing my vulgar-third-generation-Jewish-nouveau-riche-immigrant-music-mogul persona. It's been Donnie-approved." Gary lovingly suckles each one of his fingers, then wipes them all on my pillow.

There's the huffy buzz of his cell phone.

Gary, taking Donnie's advice that he try to "unwind his mortal coil," had been reading a bit of poetry, and as I sit down in front of the coffee table, I notice my *Norton* opened to "Grecian Urn," with its little rusty blemish of my blood. And the steamy whistle of the heater sounds like a Phillip whine . . . and from the votive I smell the snuffed memory of honeysuckle . . . and I look off out the winter window, where a bony tree branch is bent against the glass like the back of a hand on a lover's cheek—all these Camilla-recollections coming at me with the persistence of J. Crew catalogues.

And somewhere beyond that frosty glass, she's out there.

"I heard the guy's fucking *dem*os," Gary bawls into his phone. "They were excre*ment*al! I could've gotten a point on the album, but I just couldn't make myself give his tape to Atlantic. It was a total piece of shit. Now Kid Rock is as big as Vanilla Ice was. White trash is still America's platinum." He wads a mucoused tissue and arcs it at the garbage.

But it lands in my lap.

"Sorry," he mouths, silently, almost emphatically, as the tiny metal voice squawks out of his cell phone.

# You Are My Sunshine?

*You are my sunshine*
*my only sunshine*
*you make me happy when skies are gray*

I remember singing this once to Camilla, as I stood at her bathroom sink. There was something so unearthly about it—that a love could be so cloudless, so bare.

"Please don't call me that," she'd said, in a dull voice, just behind the closed door.

"Why, Cam?" I came and rested my face against it. "You take my serenading for granted."

"Please. Just don't."

# Mohled Again

I wake up the next day to find another Little Green note under my door:

Clyde, we just learned in bioscience that a duck's quack has no echo but that nobody can actually explain this strange phenomena. Do you have a best friend?

I also find, as I look into GFPITU, that the hole of my left ear is now fuzzed with a fringe of coarse, hoary hair. Great. That's really sexy—total rock 'n' roll. In the shower last week I felt a kinky black tuft sprouting out of my right shoulder—my own little daddy longlegs. That's a huge turn-on too, right? Teenaged groupies swoon over the stuff. Just the sort of trivia they love to read about in *Sassy:*

When dreamy power-pop rocker Curtis Birnbaum's not crafting catchy, thought-provoking love songs, the Manhattan superneurotic likes to spend his infrequent downtime tweezing and waxing unsightly back hair. Upcoming plans include developing a hump.

The thing that depresses me most about all this is that I could've gotten Cammy to shave it off in the shower.

I look down into the Tidy-Bowl-blue toilet water, and I see that it's shuddering, almost invisibly, from some untold convulsion in the heart of the building.

I study my face again.

Let's face it, I'm just too old for this now. I look like the rock Muzak version of my old self—softer, droopier, even kinder, perhaps the most gravid (pun intended) offense in the realm of rock 'n' roll.

Because now that I've been pared down to the cadaver Gary had requested, my face looks somehow even thicker. As if I'd been slowly dripping into myself, like the glass of mediaeval cathedrals, bulged at the bottom, oppressed under centuries. Perhaps not quite so majestic, but you see what I'm saying. Or maybe my face has finally begun its first phase of mooning. Not that I could get Camilla's take on it.

If she saw me now she'd probably be shocked at how badly I've decomposed anyway. I think this whole leisurely meltdown of my facial features has followed the volcanic one of my brain. So the Time/Gravity tandem must be pretty psyched about the way I'm progressing . . . all the while keeping commandant Death abreast of my satisfactory deterioration. Especially now.

*Vee heff a nahss new development,*

they'll say. Because lately I've been having more and more frequent ideations about lending them a hand in their handiwork—saving them some of the bother.

The narcissist's Bris.*

FOOTNOTE >

*Suicide.

# Sunday in the Park with Sores

On this grubby December Sunday, as I walk into Washington Square Park's mini Arc de Triomphe, I tell myself I'm not longing desperately to see a particular dachshund and his bodyguardess in the dog run. The air is full of false spring and the phlegmy purr of pigeons, sounding as hollow as those pull-cord toys I had as a kid. And for one moment I meet the amber eyes of a Rasta with a face rutted in ritual scars, bent over and cuffed by a cop, who makes me feel vaguely guilty, as they always seem to. I straighten up into a gait I hope appears nonperpetrating and try to put a law-abiding squint on my face as I listen to the lonesome drama going on inside his police radio. Some lovely vulgar Hispanic girls are wearing hoop earrings the size of bracelets, and mustaches that they're far too proud to wax as they watch a shirtless man inside the dehydrated fountain pretending to enjoy the enormous python coiled around his neck, taming Death. And as I make my way through the drab guitar jangle of an aging hippy whose voice chafes out a version of "Signs," I realize that it's far too close to home.

I reach the crooked little gate of the dog run, where I haven't been since she left me.

One hundred and one nights ago.

I remember one idle bright afternoon here when Phillip bluffed out his little chest, sneaking expectant glances back at me and Cammy, until she "restrained" him from bickering with that beagle. Despite its painful history, I still really love this place. All the honest music and muscle of the dogs. I sit on a bench and let their eager rhythms lull me, and for once, in these days so derailed, I tag along on a simple train of thought that leads me out of myself. Watching the dogs play, so easy, complete—one of nature's few and perfect inventions, like snowflakes and bananas. But for the first time I sense an erotic undertone here in the cheerful dust and gravel. How the owners trading doggy notes is almost a fetish, a kind of humble pornography. I see that the dog run is yet another modern dating venue. Where the pets are both ploys for conversation and confessions of loneliness. That the cur is both a cure and code for isolation, a living flare sent up, and suddenly, stripped of Cammy and Phillip, I see the dismal irony of owning this ancient mascot to Love, and Love given without cost or expectation in a city where whores and thieves make out like bandits.

And I miss them more than ever.

As I watch a pit bull lift his leg to piss on a bench next to me, I notice that his testicles are swollen. When I look up I realize that his mistress is the same bullish woman I saw at St. Mark's Tattoo. I find myself walking over to examine his genitals, whose two piercing sores have grown extremely infected in attempt to heal around a dangling silver female symbol.* The woman, her crew cut now modified to a Travis Bickle-model Mohawk, yanks his tooled-leather studded leash away and yells,

"Get your fucking hands off his cock, pervert!"

FOOTNOTE >

*My nose piercing was getting infected as well.

"His penis is all infected!" I tell her. "I was just worried–I saw you at St. Mark's Tattoo." I try to remember what's-his-name, Stink(?), the tattooist, to find a common ground, but she's now flanked by a little militia of women wearing Harley gear, as well as other, more slight and frightened-looking ones who bring up the rear, and who all seem to own drooling, snarling Dobermans.

# No Wire Hangers!

A few days later, I reach into my mailbox, looking away and wincing as if it's the hole of a rabid badger.* But then I think, hey. Maybe there'll be a nice surprise for me, some extravagant turn of events for the better. Like . . .

Cammy's decided to write me a sonnet. She'd just felt nothing short of the classic format could do justice to her sudden change of heart. Fourteen lines listing (just some of) *The Things She Misses Most About Curtis*. Bedtime being the theme she's picked for this first installment.

I'm betting she'll mention my consideration in remembering to share *all* of my problems, no matter how small or complex, or how tired I might have been, just as soon as we turned down the sheets . . . which by the time we awoke to greet the new morn were usually soaked in my night sweats. She'll probably also want to include my nocturnal "Mommy" murmurs, as I crushed her all night in my thighs, something Cammy now no doubt realizes was pretty darn endearing (in a *Mommy Dearest* sort of way). And I'm sure she'll want to mention how on the rare nights we did sleep apart, I'd insist, after our last phone conver-

FOOTNOTE >

*Sounds like a Sex Pistol–era band name . . . but I was actually reading about dachshunds the other day, and apparently the reason they're so sausagey is because they were originally bred to furrow badgers out of their holes.

sation, that we leave both of our receivers off the hook so I'd feel more "connected."

Basically, her poem will be a kind of "How did I love Curtis, let me count the ways?" thing, all building, in the final couplet, to a climactic (and, I'm guessing, a bit maudlin) plea for my forgiveness.

Or I think I'd even consider accepting a particularly well-executed haiku from her at this point.

But alas, there's no verse for me today—only the usual collectors.

Each time their take-no-shit envelopes look more likely to, well . . . take less shit. Each time their tone is just a little less courteous, and a little more intimidating. The *please*s tend to be more and more on the scarce side, while the font appears darker and increasingly impatient.

Actually, this time the phone company has reverted back to a look-we-understand-how-difficult-things-can-get tactic. Probably thinking they'll catch me off guard with a change-up . . .

*Surely we can resolve this rationally, Mr. Birnbaum.*

It's my mother who's the most venomous. Now she's claiming there's a way she can have my wages *garnished.* I know her—she just loved that she'd finally found an opportunity to apply that word to this lifetime.

I usually don't even open the other junk mail, but being a proofreader at heart (and by rare employment), my eye catches a curious-looking letter from the ASPSCA. I assume the extra *S* must be a typo, until . . .

***Dear Dog Molester,***

***This will be your first and final warning. You have been reported to the American Society for the Prevention of Sexual Cruelty to Animals because one of our members witnessed you***

*fondling a collie in the Washington Square Park dog run last week.*

(First off, it wasn't a fucking *collie*. Not that I fondled him.)

*As we are a still un-funded and unchartered organization, we do not at this time have the necessary resources to prosecute you. But rest assured: If you set foot on those premises again, you* will *be arrested. You are under surveillance! Our association exists for the sole purpose of protecting helpless animals from the roving fingers of abusers like you.*

KEEP YOUR PAWS OFF THE PUPPIES!

Great. I hope Phillip didn't get wind of this. Scratch the dog run off my list of last solaces. And these things seem to come in clusters, because next there's a Gay and Lesbian Coalition request for donations and volunteers for their AIDS Walk.

I fill in Cammy's name for both of these.

Not only do I get a little sadistic glee when I imagine these people harassing her, but I know she'll be too embarrassed, and really just too *de*cent, not to fulfill both "her" $50 pledge and the all-Saturday commitment she's promised them every weekend this winter. Then I realize that my real and underlying hope is that they actually might succeed in converting Camilla. For some reason, it's a lot easier for me to stomach her rolling around naked on a polar bearskin rug with another girl—as hair-tufts peek out from under all four of their armpits and sweat gleams across their fingernail-clawed backs, which are pinked by the furious fire beside them—than holding hands with some real estate mogul who waxes his chest. And trims his testicles (with a special shaver). Who makes in a day what I make in a month. Who won't admit he bleaches his teeth, but always asks for no ice in his drinks, which are never well brand, and which he often makes in a blender at his house in Southampton. Who adds a hundred points to his S.A.T. score (while I only add fifty). Who doesn't remember his Mexican maid's name but lets her see him step naked from his marbled shower if she's lucky. Who secretly suspects that every woman wants to sleep with him. (Do I seem a tad envious?) Who's been known to call his girlfriends "champ," once even while his last one gave him a blowjob. Who owns a boxer, even though he doesn't really like dogs, whose leash he jerks just a little too hard when he's sure nobody's looking. Who refers to New York as "this town" and De Niro as "Bobby." Who calls athletes "ballplayers." Who yaks on his cell phone from his floor seat through entire Lakers games, hoping the camera will catch him . . . because that's where he met "Jack" (Nicholson), with whom he did lines right on the bar last summer when they closed down Odeon together. Who uses *weekend* and *summer* as verbs. Who strokes Camilla's cheeks with the bushy back of his hand as he explains how, when they're legally wed this June in Quogue, she'll be added to his $100-deductible-no-copay-pick-your-own-out-of-network-physician health plan. Who looks at the future not as a threat, or even a challenge, but as a respite, a promise, a venture.

Okay. I'll spare you. I'm sorry. I realize I'm only indulging myself with all this. Because Camilla's taste is (with the exception of a recent and momentary lapse of reason) far too impeccable to let her end up with this kind of putz. And that's the hardest part for me, because I know that the guy she'll find, or (dear God) has *found,* will be a far better man than me—or rather, he'll *be* a man.

The last thing in my box is another Nationwide Life Insurance offer.

If they only knew.

# Feete Fête

Well, it turned out the Feete "seminar" was being conducted in a Christopher Street garret by about a dozen smirky middle-aged gentlemen dispensing rations of admittedly-Ecstasy-spiked Shirley Temples to a troop of shirtless, fatless fellows who all seemed to be about a decade younger than me. And who were modeling, with apparent gusto, such standard Chelsea-boy ensembles as the Mickey-Mouse-Hat-and-Bunny-Tail or that fetching old reliable, the gas-mask-and-diaper. All of these outfits were complemented by the evidently de rigueur ruby pumps.

As I walked inside, I sensed something painstakingly premeditated about the whole occasion's bacchanalian air of abandon, a sort of rigorous disarray, as evinced in the numerous hanging cucumbers that were draped in prophylactics, not to mention the swollen piñatas lovingly rendered in the form of enormous hard-ons. And while the tiny lilac Speedo held up against my pelvis by a grinning, greeting Feete was somewhat disconcerting, it was only after he'd tied the yellow Cub Scout kerchief around my neck that I just turned around and walked out.

# Allies

Even though I knew Phillip Fell would be utterly beside himself if he ever found out . . . even though Gary told me it would look "totally un-rock 'n' roll on tour" . . .

. . . I decided to get a puppy.

Little Green kept telling me how lonesome I looked, and although she'd promised me she'd dog-sit, I figured she wouldn't even need to because, if I bought one of those little snuggly packs people carry their babies around in, I could just take the dog with me everywhere I went.

At the Pet Express on Thirteenth and Sixth Avenue, I walked into the gamy jumbled aroma of birdseed, dirty fur, pissed-on gerbil trail, and, of course, the suspended memories of Cammy and me buying Phillip all the gourmet treats, toys, accessories, and up-to-the-minute pet apparel he'd always been so adamant about having.

Hoping, as ever and ever, I might just "bump into" those two.

But what caught my attention was these two tiny monkeys, who I instantly realized were mates as they performed a kind of tandem aerial-ballet-on-bars for a small enchanted audience of mostly kids eating popcorn. And so I stopped to witness an outrageous midair recital, in which every impulse was mutual, twinned in effortless motion, as this living symphony of leaping, swinging, diving, and flying just went on and on. Until the little simian gymnasts would halt their main event to take the occasional grooming intermission, which they'd always end in a general checkup on each other, tilting their severe little faces in *Is-everything-okay-hon?* exchanges, one of which was even followed by a heartbreaking little kiss.

And even though the routine appeared all the more poignant because it was delivered in miniature (just as technology always seems to cost a lot more when it's small), I think the real poetry was in a certain Word left unspoken, but that I think we all sensed, and this perhaps most intensely by a little boy with melted Milk Dud on his chin, when he actually burst into tears in the face of this display of affection so vivid, so frank and acute; a display to which his older sister reached out, dreamily, as if to capture. But those two ancient acrobats were blind to us—their world was each other. Which made me think of Elvis's pet chimp, Scatter, and how he died, they say, of loneliness, trapped in a golden cage, in a dank corner of Graceland's basement, after he too had in the end failed to distract the King from himself.

These two today, however, were in this thing together. The tiny binary miracle was not in the show, no . . . but the Love.

Waiting in line to ask about the purchase of a pooch, who do I see but the pit bull lady, her Mohawk now grown out into gelled solar spikes. I also noticed an **ALL PET PURCHASES WILL BE MONITORED BY THE ASPSCA** sticker.

Great. I was probably at the top of their (dog) shit list.

I bolted out of there.

Puppyless.

# Elizabethan Collar

Do you see how my life teemed with nonevent? Yet how there was something comic about my unique talent for self-crippling? Hey, they say everyone has a special gift. *Simile Game:*

If I were a metaphor, I'd be one of those lampshade things that dogs wear over their heads so they won't nip off their own stitches.

Let's cut to a wide shot of: me, crawling along the sidewalk with one around my neck.

# Return to Sender

At the sperm bank, having just mastered my task, I walked out of the sweaty little room where they had all the *Hustlers*, *Hardly Lawfuls*, and *Hungs*. And, although thoroughly drained, I was nevertheless brimming over with that post-orgasmic self-hatred women should never know.

Even though I'd had to restrict my wanks to these biweekly visits, this gig did at least allow me to have Repro Lab mail the money I, well . . . *harv*ested directly to my mother. I figured that way I couldn't spend the sixty bucks a toss they paid me. So if she thought it was the least bit odd that a sperm bank was sending her checks in my name, my mother certainly wasn't complaining. Or, apparently, even all that alarmed that she might in a few years be refusing Girl Scout cookies from a kid she had no idea was her own granddaughter.

Because this whole sending-it-back-to-the-source thing did seem to suggest some massive symbolic reversal. A kind of retrograde flow and end-of-the-reign. For instance, someday, if I was still around, I might be sweating it out on one of Crunch's Life Fitness Cross Trainers right next to a kid who seemed to have the old Birnbaum longing in his eyes. And we'd share a half-knowing moment. Or maybe still other stray zygotes would come claiming my rock star fortune, as bastard heirs, like so many alleged sons of Elvis.

Yeah, right. As Gary would sing, in Steven Tyler's whiskey rasp,

*Dream on! Birn Baum!*

And speaking of Presley, at *this* rate I'd pay my mom back in full about the time Britney Spears signed her first six-matinees-a-week contract at Caesar's.

As I sat on the shoddy little pseudo-leather loveseat, waiting for the semen experts to give my sample a microscopic once-over before they authorized my paycheck, I opened a copy of *Field and Stream* and wondered why Repro didn't just put the "fuck books"* out here as a warm-up, or at least to maintain a consistent decorative motif. The Dominican receptionist and I ignored each other as usual, pretending not to ponder the thing I'd just done. Then all of the sudden she tells me . . .

"I'm afraid we have some bad news, Mr. Birnbaum. Your sperm count is, um, a little low."

"How low?"

"Almost nonexistent."

"What does *that* mean?"

"It could be a number of things."

"Name some."

"Diet, disease, stress. Are you under a lot of it?"

"A bit. Yes," I conceded. "But let's get back to the disease thing. What kind are we talking about here?"

"Again, it could be a number of things," giving me the old paper shuffle.

"What sort of number?"

"I'd really prefer not to discuss this without fur–"

"So you're telling me it's probably testicular cancer?"

She gets a besieged look, then says,

FOOTNOTE >

*Gary's term for dirty magazines.

"Have you taken any recent medications other than the ones you listed?"

"No," but then I remembered that godforsaken hair-loss drug study Gary had talked me into, and the phrase ***Reduced Sperm Motility*** memory-flashed out of a waiver they'd made me sign.

My brain was suddenly a leg attempting to stand after it's fallen asleep. "Look," I pleaded. "Please. *Is* there any chance that this could be caused by testicular cancer?"

"Theoretically? Yes."

# Ah, You're All Wet

So we beat on, boats against the current.

—Francis Scott Fitzgerald

And the currents picked his bones in whispers.

—Thomas Stearns Eliot

No man is an island.

—John Donne

Water, water every where, nor any drop to drink.

—Samuel Taylor Coleridge

Expect poison from standing water.

—William Blake

And a blood-dimmed tide is loosed upon the world.

—William Butler Yeats.

She gave me water.

—Victor Hugo

Mud-luscious and puddle-wonderful.

—Edward Estlin Cummings

For I am but a mud puddle, shrunken to half the circumference I was, and the sun, afire, is yet to hit high noon.

—Curtis Irving Birnbaum

# La Giaconde

The little brass sign on the door read:

**SANJAY SINGH**

**Doctor of** Naturopathy/Homeopathy/Macrobiotica/Holistic and Nutritional-Therapies/Hypnosis/Acupuncture/Colonics/Kinesthesia . . .

followed by a quackish tangle of New Age initials.

Yep. This was the right building: 111 Avenue D.

Maybe not the poshest address for a Manhattan physician, but the only one I could find who would accept my insurance. All the ones I'd called up on Park Avenue seemed to shy away from Medicaid.

I came into the dank office, which was apparently a little lacking in light and a receptionist, and so silent that I could hear the moldy foam sofa's pneumatic *poooff* when I sat down. I set my gig bag aside. Soon I heard a grief-stricken wheezing, then noticed a pair of Birkenstocks protruding from a cot in a darkened corner room, the door of which slammed when I began to approach it. I looked around, where under a hanging, smugly plastic plant was an ancient black and white TV set showing, in the midst of its little snowstorm, one of those real-life court dramas. With the remote, I unmuted the program and heard a rangy old man with the face of someone who'd spent a large portion of his life earnings on lottery tickets say,

*"Your Honor, it all started off innocently enough. You see, I'm actually one of those rare individuals who* like *Girl Scout cookies. . . ."*

I switched channels to Drew Barrymore talking into a microphone and flashbulbs outside an awards ceremony, looking like she could barely stop her mouth from spreading into a teenybopper grin over her latest crush, which made me wonder if Cammy might be watching this right now from somebody's enormously pension-planned lap . . . and just how it might strike her to hear old Drew cooing over the new love of her life, for whom she'd decided to indefinitely give up the screen, so she could pop out about a baker's dozen babies with this up-and-coming rock god by the name of Curtis Birnbaum, who apparently the world would soon be hearing quite a bit about.

Yeah.

I got out my little lyrics pad so I could polish up the last verse to "Your Beloved Second Thought," tapping the armrest in Camilla Morse code, when a depleted voice said,

"Don't strike your fingers so hard."

I peered into the shadows across the room, out of which a dim, fortyish woman leaned forward. With a sigh and a wry smile she got up and slouched over in her stripy leggings and dirty brown orthopedics.

"You probably already have it, from what I can see," she said.

Then sat down next to me, chemo slender, with that self-righteous sadness you sometimes see in the chronically unwell. Telling me she had

"carpal tunnel syndrome," with the hard-won martyr's pride of a kid inside a sleeping bag explaining to a curious adult the name of the band he's been camping out all night in the cold to get tickets for.

"Really?" I said, hoping to look obedient in my new doom

role, which seemed to be suiting me more and more snugly, as I thought of my afflicted right nut, realizing I'd just bitten my cuticle down to the quick again when she glanced at it and told me,

"You're bleeding"—sounding annoyed, as with a tiny nylon scream she unzipped her fanny pack spangled with buttons reading ***Undereaters Anonymous*** and **Only Organic**, to name but a couple. She clawed around inside it and held out around six different faded shapes of Band-Aids. I chose a little round one in a blue wrapper, the size of an iris, which reminded me of a certain girl's . . .

"You should disinfect that," she said. "I know someone that had to have his hand amputated because . . ."

I faded out as I looked at her face, the pallor of Brie, under crisps of short, tintless hair. The whites of her eyes were the faintly browned flesh of left-out apple slices.

"Sit up straight and relax your shoulders," Carpal commanded. "And don't grip your pen so tight. Do your hands hurt?"

"Actually . . ." As I considered this, I noticed she was one of those people who start nodding before you even begin talking. She blushed, perhaps over how excited I saw her getting . . . and there was a pause.

Then, sneaking a look at my lyrics, she lifted her nose a little and asked me,

"Are those poems?"

Because my notebook was turned to a rough version of "Emily's E-Mail," the real one of which I'd still been too chicken to even open. I told her they were

"Just some song ideas," which she looked at, asking me,

"Who's Camilla?" offhanded, and even though I was dying to download on someone, I sensed I shouldn't with Carpal. I heard myself tell her it was

"My mother," to which she replied, "I have to call mine today," and I wondered at what age people stopped needing their parents. She told me her mom had passed "congenital chronic fatigue syndrome" down to her, and how she was noticing I had a lot of the symptoms. When she went to the bathroom, I jotted down some words for a Monkees song send-up called "I'm a Fatiguer (I Couldn't Leave Here If I Tried)."

Just then a receptionist/nurse sort of person, who looked even more anemic than Carpal, appeared behind the desk and told me to take off my shirt and wait in the little room where I'd seen the napping Birkenstocks.

I sat alone in the suddenly harsh light. God, I'd lost weight. My ribs sang like a Hank Williams lament through my thin pasty skin. I looked away. On the wall was a big bulletin board featuring about fifty snapshots of an Indian male, presumably Herr Doctor Singh, from his lanky boyhood to the paunched present, standing arm-in-arm with the owners of what seemed to be every single restaurant he'd ever eaten at.

Through the door, I could hear him talking to the nurse with the kind of honky voice that in aging Indian men gathers husk. When he entered I realized I was actually glad he'd kept me waiting, because his worth had inflated, which reminded me of how Cammy had come semiclean about how she'd actually meant to be late to our first date.

He was wearing the Birkenstocks. Had Singh been napping? Meditating? Sleeping off a hangover?

"So, what seems to be problem, young stud?" slapping my thigh.

"Just a checkup," I said, assuming a robust voice. (*Stud?*)

"Nurse said you sound full of fear."

"Yeah, well, just in general, I guess, ha, ha." I noticed his cheeks held the pitted memory of adolescent acne.

"Yes, you are correct. I had pimples," he frowned. Then, with sudden glee, "You present extremely pale and thin! How is appetite?"

"Appetite for what?"

He laughed loud and through his nose. "Ah, you use Jewish judo on Doctor. Do not think it goes unappreciated." He snuck a look at his teeth in a little mirrored utensil before shoving it into my own mouth. "Do you have specific complaints?"

"Uh-uh," I said, shaking my head.

"Any ringing in ears?" He probed, then actually blew into them.

"I have tinnitus."

"I will give you herbal gel for that, as well as for slight nose-piercing infection. Any venereal syndrome? Oozing abscess? Hideous sores?"

"Not that I know of."

He ticked off a set of boxes on a blood test form. "What else?" beaming at me.

"Well, I do have insomnia."

"You use caffeine?"

"Not that much."

"How much? Wait . . . let me guess. One or two Starbucks delicious new Mocha Cappuccino Grandes, daily?" He winked.

"Ten or twelve cups. Just regular coffee," I said.

"You must be pissing like racehorse. You take any Western allopathic medication?"

"Not really. Just a couple of things."

"Please enumerate for elegant Eastern doctor sitting effeminately cross-legged in front of you."

"Rogaine, Propecia, Retin-A, Alpha Hydroxy. Sometimes a little Wellbutrin."

"Oh, you are clinically depressed!" he said, as if he'd discovered I was a fellow Packers fan. "Your muscles have retained traumatic childhood episodes. We will massage them out of Curtis. Majority no doubt reside in his buttocks, sphincter, and perineum. Do you have questions for multi-degreed, internationally esteemed physician?"

"Do you remove tattoos?"

"Doctor shall train your skin to eliminate ink through hypnosis," checking off the list. "Anything else?"

"Um, can you thicken my lips?"

"Doctor was actually just noticing how uninviting and thin they were. I will give you homeopathic ointment. Anything else Mr. Birnbaum worrying himself silly about?" he asked, almost hopefully, I thought.

"No, I guess that's it," I got up. Then I mumbled, "I think I may have some sort of a lump on one of my balls," quickly, casually. "But it's probably just stress. Thanks for your time," and I started out the door.

"Wait. Please sit back down, Mr. Curtis."

"Why?"

"Can you remove stylish black oil jeans please?" setting aside his pen.

"Why?"

"Why, so Doctor can ex*am*ine."

"Examine what?"

"Penis and sack. Unit."

"Why would you want to see those?"

"You just told Doctor you . . . ah, you are joking?"

"Yeah, I was just kidding," I faked a laugh, reaching for the doorknob.

"Wait, thirty-something Birnbaum. Please, you just confessed you have lump."

"I said I thought I *may* have lump."

"But you did use word *lump,* did you not?"

"Okay, I used *lump.*"

"So you've felt something in nads, then?"

"Only in one. But it seems to come and go with stress, I think."

"Mmm, hmm," he said, writing with ominous precision.

"You're acting like this is some massive tumor."

"Can I see it?" cracking his knuckles.

"What do you mean, 'it'?' Look, can't you just give me a prog*nosis?*"

"But would-be rocker dude won't even let Doctor obtain diag*nos*is."

"I'm getting a second opinion," I said, opening the door.

"What was first one?" he giggled.

"You said I have a giant lump in my balls."

"Okay, off with them. Mr. Curtis is obviously quite upset, and with much reason." He seemed truly concerned. Suddenly I wanted to throw my arms around his neck.

"I feel like you really care," I said, loosening my belt as if Singh were my first hooker.

"I do." He stared at my zipper. "I bet you're well-hung."

"Not really," I said, watching his eyes. I stopped undressing.

Seeing my hands halt, he looked up at my face, then back down to the zipper, making the *Come on* motion with his fingers.

And so, reluctantly, I unzipped, turning away from him, which made him tsk.

"Will I still be able to have children with one ball?" I asked him over my shoulder.

"Let us not get ahead of ourselves. No pun, of course, intended," as he papered the examination table. "Please recline," he whispered, pulling down my boxers, and with a little spray-mist bottle he applied some sort of cold remedy to my crotch. Then hefted my right and left testicles, taking each in his fingers and rolling them around, safecracker fashion. I winced, with an irrational fear that he'd crush them between his fingers.

"It's cancer, right? I told you," I said, lifting my head.

"You may get dressed now, Birnbaum." (Why did everybody have to end up *call*ing me that?) "Clearly, you have small balls. But a very special little penis. Charming, actually," writing all of this down.

"Pardon?" I said.

"Very handsome dong. Lovely coloring. Nicely marked," and he dotted an *i*.

Was I dreaming?

He smiled at me, nodding. "I say that purely clinically, Curtis. Your pecker is first rate. Nuts, however, a little under par."

"So you've said. But thanks, I guess."

"Mm, hmm," he said, writing. Was he logging my responses as well?

"So what's the upshot of all this?" I said.

"Of what?"

"The nuts?"

"Yes, nuts," he said, looking up dreamily with the tip of the pen in his mouth. "They are relatively small."

This was taking on a kind of *Who's-on-First* patter. Was all this some cruelly elaborate practical joke Gary was having on me?

"But what about the lump?" I muttered. "Not that it's actually a *lump,* per se."

"We shall know about lump from blood tests. Nurse will give you instructions on yeast-free diet. Till then, Practitioner wants

Curtis to keep these chutney-sack crystals in his sporty J. Crew Boxer Briefs," removing little cheesecloth sachets from a paint-flaking drawer. "They have foul odor, but they will depolarize lump. You may fasten the largest crystal around shaft. And remove it only for bathing and fucking. After I receive results tomorrow, Doctor and Birnbaum will convene for follow-up colloquium. Nurse will lead aging rock guy back into this very room. He will wonder if she and Doctor are having torrid affair, just as one wonders about pilots and stewardesses–or rather, flight attendants. Both gold diggers trying to bridge social class gap. But you will be more concerned about your own nut results, and there will be expectation, wringing of hands. Much like a scene in *Quincy,* the seventies medical television drama starring Jack Klugman, formerly Felix on the TV adaptation of Neil Simon's Broadway breakthrough, *The Odd Couple.*"

"Oscar," I corrected him.

"Damn," he sighed.*

On my way to the carpeted bathroom, he told me to check out his "work of art." I wondered why, of all things, he'd tried to capture the elusive smile of the *Mona Lisa.* Doctors playing God, I thought. Because he'd got it all wrong. The inexpressible expression came off as the wise-guy smirk of some fifties sitcom gal, like Trixie on *The Honeymooners.* And at the bottom of the little oil painting were his initials . . .

*S.S.*

In the mirror, my eyes were bruisey sockets. I smelled some

FOOTNOTE >

*I wondered if Singh had memorized all this for some sort of Americanization visa application quiz, and didn't want all his facts to go to waste.

sort of organic stench, masked by a synthetic deodorizer, and when I washed my hands there wasn't any soap in the dispenser. A *doc*tor's office! But as I unlocked the door, I noticed a closet, which, in my search for soap, I saw contained towers of (free) Charmin. For weeks I'd been so broke that I'd been forced to use Bounty in my bathroom, so now I crammed a couple of rolls in the pouch of my gig bag, the zipper of which of course got caught when I tried to close it. Just then the sickly receptionist opened the door . . . her mouth in a snit.

"Sorry," I said, looking up from a squat. "I'm broke. Are you going to tell Singh?"

"Of course I have to tell *Doc*tor," attempting to get into the doorway.

"Please don't," I blocked the entrance (wondering why nobody at this office used modifying articles).

"But I *must,*" almost flirtatiously.

"Please," I begged her. "I beg you."

"Very well," she said, probably just to get me out of the way, but we engaged in that sideways mirror dance for a second, the neck of my guitar wedging the door until she actually gave me a little shove.

"Promise you won't tell?" I said.

"Receptionist never makes promise."

Attempting hygienic blackmail, I said

"You guys don't have any soap."

# Cyberaffliction

I haven't seen her in 121 days.

I'm slumped at the historic terminal in the NYU computer lab where I sent and received *Questionnaire*...

My Magna Carta. My death sentence.

I realize I'm literally brooding *in,* and not even *on,* the past these days. Really healthy, right? I guess my theory is that I should stick around the few spots I've actually had some luck in. Like God might take pity on the poor lingering shnook below and strike him with Love lightning twice.

*For Christ's sake, enough already,*

he'll say, in his James Earl Jones voice-over:

*Will one of you putti throw that mongrel a bone? Or a bolt, ha, ha.*

While His cherubs smile politely at their Boss's little funny, hesitant to remind Him that only yesterday His own *Mercy Kill: From the Stork to Kevorkian* proposal was passed.

As I polish up the lyrics to "Little Lamb—One of God's Own Flock" (tough guess who that one's about), trying to let myself be lulled into the Mac monitor's sapphire trance, I suddenly get the guts to just open Emily's e-mail, which I'd managed to write a whiny song about without even mustering up the courage to open. Basically, it's this: Emily breaks her policy of non-involvement because she feels I should know that Camilla may be leaving New York.

My tinnitus blares on in the metallic bleat of a TV station signing off after the national anthem. Reading on, hyperventilating, I realize Emily leaves the reason for Cammy's defection dangling ominously . . .

no doubt using Omission, that dead language people speak to the spurned. Because Cammy's starting a new life . . .

. . . with *Somebody Else*.

My neck goes slack, chin onto my chest. I feel like one of those abandoned umbrellas you see on the street, blown inside-out by a rainstorm, its spine smashed.

"Who is this prick?" I hear myself asking the room in general, my head still hanging. Peripherally I notice all the kids, their nervy eyes like spooked little ponies', wondering how they should deal with the madman.

All right. I'll stop whimpering. I need a novel approach here:

Maybe Cammy wasn't all that goddamn wonderful after all. Maybe it's just because she's remained off the stage of our Love Story for so long, lurking behind the curtains in the shadow plot, that she's managed to acquire this Oz-like status. Like when the Beatles stopped touring. Because I think the more I hold my lighter up in the dark, the more her potential encore seems about as likely as the arrival of a deus ex machina. Maybe if I actually *saw* her, it would weaken her sway, which gives me an idea. I'll work myself into a frenzy of contempt with a snapshot I keep in my wallet. Taken in the automatic three-for-a-buck InstaBooth at the Kmart on Astor,* the famed photo features Phillip, dapper as ever in the baby blue cardigan I'd surprised him with on his

FOOTNOTE >

*Of the remaining InstaPhotos from that original triptych, Cammy kept one in her purse, while the other framed one kept Fern company on my windowsill.

fourth birthday. Which is tastefully coordinated with the salmon clip-on bowtie Cammy and I had just borrowed from Men's Fashion for the shoot—a sort of Mr. Rogers ensemble. Child-Star Phillip is flanked between his stage-door parents, as we both plant kisses on his whiskers, cheating our profiles to the camera, whose flashbulb has turned Phillip's black eyes to a ghostly blind man's green.

Nevertheless, he looks, as usual, like he could, frankly, take us or leave us.

Wait. This isn't exactly working. It's not so much venom I'm growing full of for those two as heart-piercing, soul-crushing love and affection. I rip the photo in halves, then hysterical fourths and eighths.

Ten seconds later I find my eyes at the plastic sea-blue bottom of the recycling bin, scavenging for scraps, for the shredded pages of our Love Story, when . . .

"Are you still working on Mac number thirty-three?" asks a rigid voice above me.

"Oh, Jesus, yeah," I say, still bent over the canister, discovering I'm actually beginning to like it down here in all the blue safety.

"There's a macro on your hard drive," the voice tells me. "You're endangering all the other users. Please move it before it infects the mainframe."

"Oh, sorry," I say, squirming out and pretending I understand what he just told me.

Standing in front of me is Micro Softy, chief of the NYU Computer Student Aides.

"I lost a really important picture in there," I tell him, hoping, like a new parent, that he'll ask to see the snapshot I've just reconstructed in pieces on my palm like the buckled tiles of a tiny patio. "Apparently she's eloping," I continue as Micros clamps on a set of headphones, which, never mind how, I end up snagging on my hand, sending the attached Discman shattering across the floor. The word BANKRUPTCY towers in my mind like the beaming **HOLLYWOOD** monument, whose white paint at close range is revealed to be scabbed and scratched with forlorn graffiti, including **ICM Nazis!** Until the symbol goes suddenly creaking forward with nails shrieking and dust clouds billowing from the ground while the word's **B** tumbles into a twirling descent through Beverly Hills, whizzing past the breakfast nook window of bathrobed Brad and Jennifer, then churning a giant horseshoe shadow over the pool where Ron Jeremy, in black Speedo, takes his afternoon lap before the **B** spins straight into the eye of the camera, now the center of a SPIN headline that announces, in close-up, **SONY FINALLY BREAKS BIRNBAUM!**

As I'm crouching over the disheveled appliance, replacing batteries and a Kid Rock CD, I realize it'll probably cost me an arm and a leg to replace it . . . or a testicle.

"I'll buy you another one," I swear to Micro as I make a little heap of the pieces on his desk.

"He can fix anything," I hear a passing girl say.

"As I have asked you," he says, oddly ignoring the Discman issue, "please shut Mac thirty-three down so the virus will stay on your files only."

"What do you mean, *virus*?"

"The macro? On your *disc*?"

I leap at the monitor, where the frisky Macintosh script tells me a virus has "corrupted" my Zip disc and basically, I'll learn in a minute, vaporized eleven years of my lyrics and chord charts.

My palms clammy up and my testicles begin to feel achy. I wonder why all the agony of the world seems to flock to my nuts, and why I didn't make any hard copies of my data, despite all of Camilla's humble hints.

I follow Micros back to his desk. "Is there any way you can fix my disk? I mean, these things are pretty simple, right?"

He gets the offended look of someone who's been mistakenly asked, *Do you work here?* at Kmart. "That depends on about a billion factors," he says, licking the bone of contention that connects my skeletal grasp of this problem to his vast body of knowledge. He marches off and begins chatting up another student aide wearing heart-shaped, rose-tinted glasses, who, I remember thinking, had probably just finished reading *Lolita.*

Back at my desk, I shiatsu my temples and try to convince myself it's Camilla's indifferent hand that has dropped me into this abyss, and that if she'd only held on I'd be writing at her laptop, instead of in this electric petri dish . . . sipping hot cocoa as she tried to stump me with *Nine Stories* esoterica from her soft bed beside me, where we'd just made love, her socked feet hot and happy in my lap as Phillip lay snoring over my own.

Gone now are all the lyrics I wrote about her, which could've felled her with guilt, and maybe even second guesses, as "Emily's E-Mail" jangled out of a radio on some nude beach in Nice where she's spending her sunny honeymoon.

"Please. God. Somebody help me?" I blurt, in rhythmic android monotone.

Glances get swapped around the speechless room. To Lolita, I hear Micros say, "Viral situation," and then something about "irretrievably lost."

Jesus. My life's work . . . the formal geometry of every emotion that had ever moved through me . . . how would I get a Record Deal *now?*

Micros then tells Lolita, "Excuse me," with a gallant bow, watching her face, and she falls for his sham chivalry and smiles.

Behind thick lenses, M.S. fixes me with a Freon stare, hitches his belt up to where grandfathers wear them, and walks slowly back to my terminal. He flicks his wrist in two rapid backhands and, after I leap up, takes my seat with a sigh.

"Thanks so much," I say. "Really. I'll replace the Discman. Just let me know how much, okay?"

He actually almost nods. Then he stretches and, with a dirty thumbnail, scrapes a knuckle of spine just below his neck. He sneaks a look back at Lolita, who's now talking to a toothy boy with a lacrosse stick, then cracks his knuckles over the keyboard, a virtuoso clearing his tux tails to sit down for the opus.

"The fuckers who make these things should be castrated, right?" I suggest, and a breakable-looking Asian girl at the next terminal fires me a look of real alarm. (Castration apparently not the most apparent image to everyone.) Micros opens a menu on something called the Norton Disc Rescue.

"So what do you think?" I ask him. "The situation's really not so bad, huh?"

"Ashes to ashes."

"You mean all my *song* lyrics are gone?" I say, stressing the *song*, hoping he'll note that I'm an *artiste*. (*I write the songs, I write the songs.*) But he says,

"Bye, bye," in a cute voice, waving to the screen before he looks at his watch, which I notice displays the time zones of three different countries.

Suddenly I'm breathing barbed wire. Micro opens my Zip disc and I see the cordial letters asking me to . . .

PLEASE INITIALIZE DISC.*

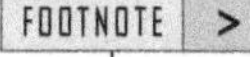


*Which means that it's all been erased.

"Jesus fucking Christ!" I moan, scratching at my scalp as naive eyes trade *Who's-the-psycho?* side-looks.

"There *is* one option." He turns to me for the first time and, in the irritated clip of somebody's who's just discovered me on their call waiting, asks, "Are you listening?"

"It has to be someone who knows your password," Lolita interrupts, arriving behind us. "Or someone who has unrestricted access to these computers," gliding the bridge of her heart specs back up her nose.

"What kind of insects make these goddamn viruses?" I wonder.

Sticky pause.

"Brilliant," nods Micros, beheading something on the back of his arm. "We'll see what we can do."

He and Lo walk off with my disc, holding it between them in a loving little burial rite. I tap at the keys, just to do something.

Just to do nothing.

# Hello, Cleveland!

In Baby Jupiter's dressing room (urinal), I told Gary,

"I just got a bunch of wonderful news. It looks like I've come down with testicular cancer after all. Then I finally opened Emily's e-mail, and apparently Camilla's eloping. And today I find out I probably just lost eleven years of my lyrics to some kind of fucking computer virus."

"It's actually your fault," he tells me over a shoulder as he pees. "Try to sympathize with this virus. Because Donnie believes we've 'inbred technology so deeply that it's come back to bite the seat of our own smarty-pants. Each microchip,' he says, 'is like a zillion syphilitic brains encoded in the congenital death we've only brought back on ourselves.' "

"Great, Gary. How does that help *me*?" I was surprised at the take-no-guff in my tone.

"Hey, all your lyrics sucked anyway."

"Thanks."

"I'm trying to make you feel *better,* asswipe. And I got you some presents." He does a little shake-and-one-legged-zip-hop before producing a tiny syringe from a leather medical bag. Then he informs me how he's actually going to shoot me up in the face with some medicine his dermatologist sister got him at cost, called

"Botox. It's a tiny, harmless dose of *Clostridium botulinum,* the thing that causes botulism. This is going to freeze up the area right around your eyes so there won't be any wrinkles when you smile."

"Terrific. Sounds like a lot of good, safe fun."

"It's for when you talk to all the A&R guys after the show, jackass," snatching a tatter of toilet paper off the floor and dabbing my temple, the injection accomplished. "So they won't think they're signing Methuselah."

"But it's *dark* out there," my face a sudden mask of a thousand tiny icicles. "And there's nobody even out there anyway."

"It's early. They're playing it cool. All their BMW limos will be pulling up just as soon as you take the stage. And here, I got you this cell phone. I'm going to call you onstage, right after you finish "If Camilla Fell," so you'll look like you got it goin' on."

When I told him I'd invited Anthony from Crunch (who, after I'd finally got the guts up to chat with him on the treadmills, had told me about his new-artist-signing production company), Gary called him a "talentless and hokey erstwhile." Then got even madder when, removing my shirt in what he called the *Jim-Morrison-bared-chest-and-leathers tradition,* he noticed the nicotine Patch hiding my idiotic tattoo.

"And where's your nose stud!?" he yelled over the sudden fuzzy thud of the first band.

"It's inside here," I hollered, pointing to my nostril. "I guess the infected flesh has actually closed up over it now."

"Don't worry!" he screamed up at me. "None of the A&R boys will notice because you'll be wearing these," clamping a set of enormous sunglasses onto my face. In the mirror I notice that each lens is a little Telecaster whose neck is pointing upward and outward, like something Elton wore in the height of his "Yellow Brick Road" epoch. So I said,

"You're kidding, right?"

But Gary shouts,

"It's total classic glam rock," now painting my fingernails robin's egg blue. "There's no room for any of your shit-eating Ivy League irony up there. And you better not read that stupid, abstract DeLillo monologue thing. You have to look larger than life and act like you're playing the Garden, no matter *where* you are. It's all about passion. So remember to make those tortured faces we talked about, like you're taking a big shit. And stop playing the goddamn air drums," he yells, seizing my wrists. "That's *tot*ally gay. You think Bono plays *air* drums?"

I could hardly keep my hands still because, as occurred before every gig, I was obsessed with an unfounded fear that I'd get up there and just start howling out the most unthinkable taboos and profanities. But,

"Relax," Gary whispers, right up into my ear, kneading my naked shoulders.* "It's all going to be cool. You'll open up with 'Fonzie Was a Fag,' then segue right into 'Donnie Was a Jungian.' So let's get rid of all this nervous energy right now by dropping and giving me twenty pushups." He claps his hands with Richard Simmons vim. "Pump up for your people!"

As I fell to the floor, my pitch pipe came out of my pocket and spun under a stall. Gary looks at me, then points at it . . . so I crawled back behind a toilet and emerged holding the dripping thing dead-mouse-tail manner.

"Great," I said. "And I really needed this onstage, too."

"Urine is completely sterile. Didn't you know Jeff Buckley drank his own piss?"

FOOTNOTE >

*Later, I discovered he'd rubbed this liquid sparkle all over me. Old Gary Glitter.

"Really?" I lifted the thing to my lips—then spat. "Forget it!" I said, throwing it down.

"Where's your *elec*tric tuner?"

"You hocked it."

"Oh, yeah. I did, didn't I?"

I spent the entire set tuning up. Then peering out into the inky silence and asking, in the hesitant tremble of a caller who suspects he's being screened by an answering machine, for

"More vocals, please."

"It's fine," came the curt, disembodied words of a soundman whose face I hadn't seen once in the eleven years I'd been playing there.*

By the end of the set my Botox jaw had seized up to where I could barely enunciate, which Gary later claimed was actually "cool because rock 'n' roll is all about slurring. Just listen to Jagger, or Stipe on *Murmur.* Nobody wants to hear some English Major fag from Cornell overarticulating."

As it turned out, none of this was really an issue.

Because the only people who showed up were

. . . get ready for this . . . Rip and Carpal. To*geth*er! (Apparently she was a *Founding CONNY Sentinel* as well.) From the first, dissonant instant, Rip stood right at the stage lip, just under my nose, pumping his fist through my entire solo acoustic set with the zeal of a diehard Dokken fan. And I could swear

FOOTNOTE >

*Suddenly I recognized his voice from my long-standing SoHo Monday AA meeting.

Carpal was mouthing some of the lyrics, which after the show she admitted she'd Xeroxed from my notebook when I'd been called in for my *Singh Symposium*. And so, suddenly relieved that I hadn't in fact lost *all* of my lyrics, I explained the whole virus debacle.* But she said she'd only copied "Sad But True," which I could certainly get back from her this week over lunch at Angelica's,† a suggestion I saw grab Rip's attention as he fiddled with my foot pedals. I wondered if it was he or I who'd inspired the rouge I suddenly noticed staining Carpal's wan cheeks, which made me sad either way as she inquired about the results of my blood work, which I confessed I hadn't yet called Singh for, omitting, of course, the fact that I hadn't called only because of the whole Charmin larceny. Then, in the inadvertent way a woman can make anything appear, Carpal gave me a little anticramp hand brace because, she said, my fingers appeared *beleaguered* onstage. But that I "was blessed with the voice of Gebrail,"‡ for which, truly touched, I thanked her at length, as I did Rip for all his musical enthusiasm, until I realized he was trying to campaign me into CONNY with the low-key ferocity of a rush chairman whose fraternity is about to lose its charter. The pathetic part was that I was almost considering joining.

Gary cut our conversation short by giving me a kind of Secret

FOOTNOTE >

*The pages she'd apparently Xeroxed came from a batch of lyrics I'd just transcribed from my notepad to a Zip disc. Having done that, I'd ripped out the pages and left them on the fusty sofa in Dr. Singh's waiting room, where I'd meant to throw them away.

†Famous for their tasteless vegan gruel.

‡The Lord's angel who dictated the Koran to Mohammed.

Service escort "backstage," pretending to coordinate with someone via cell phone. Once inside, he told me never to

"talk to the fans after the show. Maintain the mystique. You're the star. They're lucky they witnessed you play before your meteoric ascension."

"They? It's only Carpal and Rip. Did any A&R guys show up?"

"About twenty."

"I didn't see any."

"They were in the back. And they left near the end because all these guys want to make each other think that you suck, so they can sign you themselves. Trust me, there'll be about twenty messages on our machine when we get home." (*Our* machine.) "We'll tell all the magazines that you'll only talk if they give you the cover."

"What magazines?"

"Bel*ieve,* Birnbaum."

Gary also told me the chutney lump in my pants had me looking "about as well endowed as Robert Plant, circa 'Song Remains the Same,' " even though I watched him blab through my entire set to the guys in Hanging Door Chad, the band that followed a thrash metal outfit from Oneonta named Cloacae.

As we left, I realized I was actually disappointed that Groupie, whom Gary said he'd invited, hadn't shown, which made me dimly wonder how he'd gotten in touch with her.

When I asked the bouncer outside for my money, he said I owed the club ten bucks for the DAT Gary had them record the show with.

"Why'd you do that? I asked Gary, getting out my wallet.

"Don't you want it documented?"

"You can have it. It's not exactly going to be a hot bootleg item."

"Bad attitude, Birnbaum."

"Wait," the doorman said, grabbing my wrist. "You actually still owe us another nine. Your partner here had a drink and curly pumpkin fries."

"I'll get you back," Gary said, looking down, hands in his pockets.

He bounced once on his toes.

# Humbert

It's been nine months and twenty-six days since I met her. I realize we actually could've had a kid by now. Or maybe she's just beginning contractions with Eddie Vedder's baby.

In either case, I'm back at the mailbox, wondering what goodies await me.

Well, first off, I'm now on some carpal tunnel mailing list . . .

**FEAR IN A HANDFUL OF DUST**

**Official CTS Newsletter**

**In this issue:** ***How to know when you're cramping, hampering and overpampering your phalanges.***

I discover that Carpal herself has sent me reams of info she feels "will illuminate me" on every conceivable strain of computer virus borne out of Cyberspace. And that one White-Out-happy Mr. Cyrus Vaughn has taken the time to drop me a little typewritten note explaining how his stepdaughter, "who's gone and changed her God-given name to Groupy" (sic), has, after having run away from mobile home on the eve of her sweet sixteen party (last month!), recently sent him her live-in boyfriend's address (mine). Inquiring Cyrus apparently discovered her diary and now has "a big list of other rich and famous rock stars who besmirched my baby. Including your colleagues

Sebastian Bach, Twiggy Ramirez, Snoop Dogg, and Mr. Cool J, Sr."

Not so elliptically, Mr. Vaughn has made known to me his blackmailing objectives.

Excellent. Add statutory rape to the mix.

On actual parchment, there's a kind of formal bid from CONNY.

And, oh joy—another friendly memo from the folks over at the ASPSCA. Along with some sort of aerial photo of a balding guy, his legs crossed, on a bench in the dog run.

Wait . . . it's *me*!

**"WE'VE ALREADY WARNED YOU ABOUT REENTERING THE SITE OF YOUR FIRST FONDLING OFFENSE."**

Apparently they've now received funding to the tune of black helicopters and surveillance cameras.

Let's see, what else? There's a pleasant reminder from my fans over at Christie's. As well as an actual *court* order from my mother. And guess what the date is . . . my next birthday. She must've pulled some strings.

Is there any way out from under all this? Maybe I'll go home to Florida and live with my dad. What a power move *that* would be. Send Camilla crawling right back to me.

# She

I dreamed wildly about her all last night. Cammy was an antique locket that I found in my pocket. I held her and hefted her. Tried and tried to open her. But she was cool and complex in my hands. And made of a silver so pure it was blue.

Maybe that was the most developed part of her . . . the baffling crooks of her. The distance from which she knew the world was her real advantage. It made her precious, perfected her. Like the older kids' secret you keep thinking you'll learn.

So I held her. This locket. Ageless in its patience. Resistant to the stupid revolution of Time. Then I tried to sing into it, because I knew in the dream that somehow this was the only way inside her. That nothing but the most honest sliver of song, with a minor melody of jagged intervals, could hum its way in and make sense of her.

# The Poor Son of a Bitch

It was my thirty-fourth year to heaven.

As I walked toward the fuzzy peach of a sunset to the hostess podium at Time Café, it not only occurred to me that I'd outlived both Jesus and Elvis at his '68 Special apogee, but more how weird it was that I considered these moments the two equally towering landmarks in Western Civ.

I stood in line on that patio, guitar lashed to my back—my sword, my shield

. . . my albatross.

Gary had wondered where I'd wanted to have my birthday get-together, and so—where else? Talk about loitering around the Calvary.

On the sidewalk I saw Dumper walk by me, *see* me, then duck the same embarrassed head that hadn't been among those of my Baby Jupiter "crowd"—before slipping it into Crunch. Then the Black Defender ushered the Asian man's wheelchair* into the restaurant, the latter with a loathing salute as he passed me, and

FOOTNOTE >

*I know it might seem miraculous that I was always bumping into these same people, but Manhattan is actually a pretty small island, and when you "live" there as long as I did, it becomes a lot like Mayberry.

I was about to tell the thin, hard hostess I'd pick up his tab when she hissed,

"How many?"

"I need a big table," I claimed, victoriously. I glanced at all the diners gloating with that certain impertinent health that blooms out of Success.

"How *many*?" she insisted, jutting her neck an ostrich inch forward. "Give me a *num*ber?" blink, blink.

"A *lot,*" I said, just to bug her, wondering if she remembered me. (I'm the feller who rocked those little white satins!) "I guess we should probably even put a few tables together," I suggested, which she accepted, skeptically, letting me see the tweezed lift of a brow as she led me over to a set of vacant tables. Which I scraped together really loudly, causing slim hipsters to side-glance at me with their stalled forks stabbing seared swordfish. Hostess threw a stack of menus at me, then teetered off on her sharp black pumps.

I was thinking how people take after their shoes and their dogs, getting myself drunk on that scrumptious wine produced when we crush our own hearts, when Actory Waiter approached me, surprise going through him in a water bubbler gulp. I wondered if he was actually happy to see me, or merely being tip-minded. Apparently he'd undergone some sort of follicular grafting since last time, because his scalp was now rowed with the tiny holes of a Barbie doll's. I resisted asking him if he'd recommend the procedure and told him I'd wait for the large party I was expecting before I started ordering.

All around me were hands holding colorful drinks, which made me remember how, in the Past, once I'd gotten good and drunk, I still had to have the full glass in my fist—the comfort of clutching that cool wet weapon—just as some of us can't read without the poised pen. I kept glancing behind me for approaching friends, then wondered what friends, exactly, I was *expecting*. Gary had promised he'd meet me here at seven, with a surprise in tow. Was that a *good* thing?

I opened an olive envelope Little Green had slipped under my door.

Clyde,
Happy Birthday. I know you have been extremely sad lately, even though you don't tell me. I heard you crying the other night through the bathroom wall and this makes me very upset as well.
Please do not cry, Clyde.
I think you are perhaps the sweetest person I've come in close acquaintance with and also a highly gifted and talented guitarist/songwriter. I for one am certainly very glad I met you. I think Camila has made a gravest mistake and that she is highly ignorant of what she is now truly and sorely missing. You would be an awesome father.
I relayed this sentiment to my mom as well and also told her that sometimes I pretend you are mine. But please don't feel weird about this during our lesson tomorrow, which is I'm assuming at our customary time okay? SET YOUR ALARM!
Your pal, forever and ever and even when I go off to Harvard, or now I might actually be considering Sarah Lawrence in addition. Are you at all familiar with their curricula?
Walter

p.s. I've taken the liberty to construct this present for you in art.

She'd included a plasticized guitar pick made out of a snapshot, its size suitably reduced, that we'd once taken of her in my lap, sharing my guitar.

I looked up to catch Hostess complaining to a sleek managerial guy in a quiet black suit and smarmy dark hair. As she pointed the side of her head at me, I could tell from the suffered way he was nodding, one hairy hand assuring the small of her backless dress, that he'd slept with her. I looked intensely into my menu, hoping to affect a kind of *I'm-just-in-the-mood-to-run-up-a-massive-tab* air.

At a far table I recognized some pretty young things from the NYU computer lab, all giggles and gossip. I tried to fall slightly in love with the most stunning one (or fall a little out of it with Camilla). She was half Asian or something, so hard to tell in these mongrel days, and she got a panicky look when she caught me ogling. It was actually maddening how I couldn't have cared less. How, as ever, I was undone over how essentially Cammy still dwelled, dwells, in me.

Over the speakers, Bonnie Raitt realized "I Can't Make You Love Me" (the lonely heart makes every torch song its bonfire), while above this came the pleasant sky-tearing sound of a jet. Its tiny shadow wiggled over my knuckles. I thought of Paris, how we'd been hunched together in the gut of our own silver death bird. In a galaxy, it seemed, so far, far . . .

. . . so where was she right this second? Maybe she'd already left Manhattan and was hitchhiking on the side of I-10, blue jean jacket now with matching cutoff shorts riding high as she held a homemade cardboard sign saying . . .

Hell, *yes*, I'm a trucker fucker!

How pathetic is it that every road in my mind's tangled heap of interstate overpasses leads to Her?

And where the hell was Gary?

I snuck a peek over the undulate* edge of the *White Noise* page I'd begun to read about twenty-five times, at some hipsters in line with increasingly sugar-poor blood draining out of their faces as they pointed droopy arms at my four empty tables. When the hostess noticed them flaring up into hypoglycemic bickering, she pulled Actory behind her podium and flicked her hand at me, side-armed.

Where was Gary?

The third time I got up to see if he'd left me a message, I stood at the pay phone, searching *my* blue jean jacket pocket for another quarter, when I found the Gregg Liebenthal card. I actually considered calling him to come to my "party." Maybe I could even guilt him into some kind of a birthday loan. Then it just happened. I broke down and called Her—hanging up on the fourth, heart-pounding ring.

Still not hearing a message from Gary, I did hold a one-way conversation about a change in my birthday plans, then interrupted Actory's easy laugh with a busboy to borrow his pencil so I could take down some phantom info.

"They meant the *other* Time Café," I told Actory, hanging up.

"The one on Seventh Avenue?" he asked, relieved for me.

FOOTNOTE >

*Because of the handicapped submergence incident at Crunch.

"Yeah."

"Your friends are *there?*" wondered Hostess, clacking up behind me.

"Yeah, thank God."

"They're closed for a private party," she was delighted to inform me.

"Oh, um. That's probably *mine.*"

She gave me slow nods.

When I told her my friends were all coming here now, she said,

"We're going to have to move you to another table until they arrive."

Sitting alone at a small, darkened table near the bathroom, I looked out the window at the hard-core kids skating around Astor's giant spinnable cube. Then into the pink winter gloam over Kmart. For so long I'd been begging Eternity to take note of me, jot me down on her rich vellum skies, before I became illegible. Fame had seemed the only way to get a leg up on Death; to heal that most convincing, impossibly endless wound of all.

A woman sat down a few tables away from me. In a matte green dress, she was long, slender, and chilly, coming to a point in a pleated bun. This stalk of asparagus was Ex Model.

I almost called out to her. But her face looked lippy—from recent collagen shots? And even in the dim, I could tell she'd declined. That her former, slow-blinking sex appeal now verged on exhaustion. And while again she was alone and smoking a chain of worried cigarettes, there was no longer any waiting in her eyes. I watched them sampling the room, slowly, without exigency, and looking (for old Time's sake) anywhere but into my own.

Where was Gary?

I figured I'd get started on some apps, then noticed how every one of them was fried. But then I thought, Hey. You know what? It's my goddam *birth*day, and probably my last one with both gonads intact. I'm sick of this whole tofu-and-wheat-grass routine Gary's got me on. *Fuck* Gary! Where was he anyway? And who were all these "fans" I was starving myself for? Carpal? Rip? A disembodied soundman who, like a Bananafish, might very well have wedged himself for good in that sound booth after having eating a tad too many deep-fried delights himself. I ordered the calamari, onion fries, chicken-fried steak with bacon strips, and a milk shake. Extra lard all around.

"Good gracious," marveled Actory. "*Some*one's going to Crunch tomorrow. Actually, you could stand a few pounds. You've lost a lot since I saw you. What have you been eating?"

"Regret."

"I hear you," he said, and then, vaguely making the connection, "And where *is* that girl? *God,* she was gorgeous. Did I see her in a Jill Stewart ad? I trust you're still together?"

"She's coming," I said, with a cringing grin. And as I glanced over at the door, I almost believed she'd walk in.

But then it hit me. Of course!

Rip and Gary had organized a surprise party during the Baby Jupiter gig. And now they were just making me sweat it out a bit. Because soon Little Green would be rolling in a giant carrot cake-on-wheels, out of which Camilla would leap. Our reconciliation would be my birthday present. To really throw me off, they'd all chipped in and tipped the hostess handsomely so she'd act like an absolute bitch.

It worked.

But no. The pit at the core of the peach evening was the fact that . . . nobody came.

"You look like you could use some sleep," offered Actory, giving me the check.

"I could use a blood transfusion."

Need I add that my credit card was rejected?* Or that they wouldn't allow me to leave my guitar as collateral until, after asking me instead to see another I.D., Actory noticed that it was my birthday?† Telling me, because of my "mother-loving face," that I could pay him back tomorrow. Even Hostess understood how pathetic I was and wished me a patient "Happy Birthday," as if her own mother had, under the table, kicked her into saying it. She giggled coolly as Actory sang a breathless Marilyn Monroe version of the song in my ear.

"I can't even give you a tip," I blubbered, hugging Actory far too hard and too long.

"That's okay, sweetheart." He softly pried me off him, then handed me an oily brown doggy bag. "Say hello to that hound."

FOOTNOTE >

*Because, I would learn later, Gary had finally pulled the plug on my critically injured credit with the purchase of a $600 bidet he'd charged to my MasterCard, telling me, "The girls'll love you for it. And you them." I also realized, as I left the restaurant, that I'd forgotten to postpone the court date my mom had arranged for that day.

†Telling me I looked great for twenty-eight, as per Gary's revision.

# Pantheon

With darkness came arctic winds, bitching around the corner of Lafayette and East Fourth Street. I saw a sobby, arguing adolescent couple, sealed off and on display in their own private bubble of pain.

Love.

As usual, I walked past the panels at Tower Records, with the envy of a boy clacking his stick along the just-painted slats of that rich-neighbor-kid's fence.

Yanni, Matt Whyte, Green Day, Thisway, Moby, Björk, Tupac, Britney Spears, Kid Rock, Eminem, Christina Aguilera . . .

And then I saw it.

A panel that featured the Hollywood Squares, with each one of them lodging a different Rock deity, from Presley to Costello, and in the middle . . .

. . . was a drawing of me. With the bold-faced promise that

**CURTIS BIRNBAUM IS COMING!**

I must have stood there an hour in that wind, just watching my Panel, even yelling,

"That's me!" to a few hurried smiles.

Finally, in a sleepwalker's daze, I shuffled inside to find out who'd done this, assuming it was Gary's big surprise. But when I asked the sullen girl behind Refunds—who, perusing an off-track betting sheet, pretended not to hear me until I asked her again—she opened up a ledger and said,

"Camilla Fall. They put the order in nine months ago."

# Late Addition

The next day, as I walked east on Bleecker through a cool Ides-of-March noon, the world, for once, seemed unruffled. I heard the glad hand bell of a distant bike, its singular rings blurred into a bright sonic smile. While just in front of me, the empty bag of Doritos sighing on the sidewalk with each breath of breeze was a happy, colorful lung.*

I felt like I was at least on the boards now. (Or the Panels.) And the best part was that Camilla, although retroactively, had installed me there. So I knew she must have been thinking of me yesterday. Somehow Success, both musical and Camillical, didn't seem so aloof now.

Then I realized I didn't have anyone I could show my panel to because Gary had been mysteriously misplaced since my birthday. So, after reimbursing Actory,† I tugged him around the corner to look at Take Five, Prodigy, 'N Sync, Madonna, Hanson, and, yes . . .

. . . But *no*!

FOOTNOTE >

*Dizzy Gillespie tribute album?

†With cash I'd just acquired from hocking CDs.

Apparently there'd been some last-minute presentational fine-tuning because below

**CURTIS BIRNBAUM IS COMING!**

was spray-painted

*As he sucks your fat hairy cock!*

While I stood there and body-blocked this little P.S. from onlookers, Actory, blushing for both of us, ran back into Time to get me some turpentine while Hostess, who'd been mincing over to retrieve him, told me I'd left my driver's license on her podium last night. I thanked her and told her I'd come and get it just as soon as I was done leaning against this window. Then Actory returned with only a Sharpie, but one with which I immediately began to make a few editorial tweaks. Which happened to catch the navy blue attentions of a cop, who, waddling over, baton atwirl, also happened to look very familiar. When I tried to ingratiate myself by telling him this, I found that I'd only incriminated myself, i.e.,

"Hey, you're the guard from the School of Visual Arts, right?"

"That is correct," he said (a phrase I suspected he'd rehearsed in a mirror). "I moonlight there for extra mon–"

I watched the memory of his whole short-short escort congeal in his eyes. "Hey! You're the little homo– What the fuck do you think you're doing?"

"Me? It's actually a long story."

"Well I don't *want* a long story. We just got a vandalism call from that young lady right there," he pointed to the window behind me, which featured the OTB girl. "Are you Curtis Birnbaum?"

I confessed as much.

"And is it true?" he grinned, indicating the spray-painted afterthought. The gathering crowd tittered. At which point Dominic, the (failed) Bolt Cutter, perceiving the scene from the cigarette break he was taking in front of Crunch, proved a lot more successful as informant when he loped over and told the cop something that was news to both of us:

"We just canceled this asshole's Crunch membership after complaints of his attempted theft and abuse of disabled restroom facilities."

(At least he didn't mention the whole steam room thing.)

"And we also had to close down the steam room after someone reported to the Board of Health that he was giving some dude a blowjob."

"I was getting a *hand* job," I explained, a legal nuance that went largely unappreciated by the cop (although it enchanted the crowd), who then demanded my driver's license, which, as I said, was still in Hostess custody. So in a panic, I handed him my NYU I.D.

"This," he said, "don't say 'Curtis Birnbaum.' "

# Speak, Memory

Great.

The hourly interest on my shrooming deficit was probably more than the $75 "defacement" fine my recurring cop buddy gave me. And now that I was Crunchless, how in the hell was I supposed to remain Rock Star Skinny? Which actually seemed like a pretty good title for my memoirs, even if* they were going to be posthumously ghostwritten.

Later that afternoon, I looked through the wire-diamond-mesh window of my usual SVA classroom to find another (far less furry) nude model. Which only made me assume, as last time, that the room had been switched. But, already enraged over the erection, diarrhea, and "inappropriate exodus" from his "seminar," Feete finally fired me for my "artless tattoo." ("Maybe if you'd exhibited just a little inspiration, things would've been different.")

Thanks again, Gary.

Who was still oddly missing when I came home to find a phone message from a disinfected female voice:

FOOTNOTE >

*Testicular outcome pending.

"If Mr. Seth Gold* would please stop by the NYU computer lab ASAP. We have information regarding your viruses." (Plural.)

I realized this was Lolita speaking. And it struck me as strange that she hadn't left a number but, having for many days ducked the Micro Softy Discman issue, I decided to finally face the music, as it were. Which turned out to be a Sting composition, because apparently Dominic had called the lab after he'd discovered that the student discount I'd enjoyed on my Crunch membership was finagled with the sham NYU I.D. he saw me offer my peacemaking acquaintance, who I began to call Chronic Cop after I discovered him waiting for me, open-armed, a trespassing warrant in one hand and a misappropriation-of-instrument writ in the other.

On top of all this, Micro Softy had been fired and arrested when it was revealed that he† was the villain who had devised my virus. Softy was, however, now attempting to plea-bargain himself out of the allegations by "divulging prophylactic information about the growing viral epidemic." Info which, explained Lolita, light of my life, might assist in the recovery of my lyrics.

FOOTNOTE >

*The name on "my" NYU student I.D.

†So Gary, breaking the rigid rules of plot payoff, had not committed the deed after all.

# We!

Coming home after losing my little confidence game, I found the chilidog (mis)delivery boy at my door. But, in light of my life's increasingly ludicrous leitmotifs, it didn't exactly faze me. He was standing on the next handwritten inventory of songs Little Green had wanted me to teach her, including, as she styled them, "WILD 🐴s," "Fall Down," "It's My Party," and "FAKE PLASTIC 🌳s." When I told him, gently, that he in fact *still* had the wrong apartment, it became "apparent" through a series of nods, shrugs, and grunts* that he was actually here to collect the change *Gary* had shorted him (double pun) only a few minutes ago. After I sent him away with my last five in the world, expecting to see Gary cowering on the other side of my door, I discovered that not only was *he* absent–

–but that all his stuff was as well.

And he hadn't even left a footnote to follow what I suddenly knew, as I walked through the gloomy apartment, was the end of a chapter.

I played a message from my father:

FOOTNOTE >

*For the first time in my New York life, I was grateful that somebody *couldn't* speak English, because at least it meant I'd be spared another *So-where's-your-gorgeous-girlfriend?* inquiry.

"HEY, I WAS THINKING. DON'T PAY YOUR MOTHER BACK. BY THE TRANSITIVE PROPERTY OF EQUALITY, YOU'LL BE PAYING ME BACK FOR ALL THE FUCKING ALIMONY SHE STOLE. DID YOU SIGN THAT RECORD CONTRACT THEY WERE FAXING YOU?" (I'd lied.) "OH. I HAD THIS DREAM THAT YOUR GUMS WERE BLEEDING. MAKE SURE YOU'RE EATING ENOUGH FRUIT, OKAY? I GUESS I HAVE NO MORE NARRATIVE CONTENT. FIGHT ON AGAINST IMPOSSIBLE ODDS IN A WORLD YOU NEVER MADE. SUCCESS IS THE ONLY WAY OUT. AND REMEMBER, IT'S NEVER TOO LATE TO GO TO GRAD SCHOOL."

I went to my window. I tried to make sense of the past few impossible days; to get a handle on something familiar amidst the strange jumbled baggage whirling just out of my grasp on the carousel around me.

It was impossible.

A profound, apathetic fatigue washed over me. I saw that the moon was already hung. A sad, slender white crescent, eroded in places, like a half-sucked Certs. And, of course, *she* was out there. Watching this same world that I was.

How could Cammy not sense me?

The fact that we were apart seemed like a celestial injustice. Didn't *her* universe revolve around the corpse of our aborted Love? Wasn't it haunting her every thought? Why should I have to perform this goddamn autopsy alone?

But then I thought, Hey—if she was going to punk out on me, she could damn well find me a substitute! Or at least an understudy. Didn't I deserve some compensation? It would be like her alimony. She must know some nice girls, right?

Yeah, right. A Camillareplacement . . . how utterly oxymoronic.

I looked down at Fern. I knew I couldn't keep pretending she was going to make it. Her crispy fronds were the bitter color of coffee. When I touched them, they turned to powder. And of course, I remembered Cammy feeding her on our chilidog date. I looked down on the carpet at the relevant stain and . . . I was at it again. Savoring the exquisite torture of breaking my own heart. I realized this loss was really all I had left now. But at least it felt big, crucial, and gnawing. Like God. Or cancer.

And speaking of Death, I decided I'd just get the balls to, no pun, call Dr. Singh for my gonad diagnosis . . .

"Doctor insists Birnbaum come in to office," Anemic Nurse told me.

Great. This meant either a testicular death sentence or that Chronic Cop had set up a Singh Sting to nab me for the toilet paper robbery.

"You told him, didn't you?" I said.

"*No*, Birnbaum."

I could tell she'd immediately known what I meant. When I asked her if I could speak to Singh directly, she put me on hold forever. I heard the ending of "Don't Pull Your Love Out on Me Baby," followed by "Shannon," that song about the dog who dies. As Holden would say, it was a real picker-upper. Then a very familiar tune came on, yet somehow different. Suddenly I knew what it was; "Emily's E-Mail" had been butchered into a cheesy dance hit for Britney Spears, complete with those little police whistles and synthetic drum loops! I hadn't recognized it at first because her *people* had apparently changed the title to "Cecilia's E-Mail," so they could sample the chorus of the Simon and Garfunkel classic, which Britney now "rapped" over.

How would I tell Gary that somebody had stolen our—

Wait. That little *vantz*!* *That's* why he was MIA. And that explained the copyright forms I'd seen in the garbage.

Singh came on the phone muttering, "Bump de bump de dum," flipping through papers. "Very good, then. I have sent results over to magnetic therapy urologist colleague Dr. Robinder Agravat. The three of us will now converge in a room with immense X ray of your prick and gonads on wall—"

"Look, is it good news, or bad news?"

"Um, Birnbaum may want to sit down for this doozie."

I hung up in terror.

So it was true. Testicular cancer. Jesus. Let's think here. To a slacker like me, there's always some hidden benefit in sickness. Okay. First off, next to Death, it's the ultimate excuse for failure. People would have no choice but to be nice to me. And there's just no way my mom would ever take me to the cleaners *now*. Is there? Maybe even my icy alma mater would cancel my student loans through some amputation clause.

I yanked my pants down, thinking I might as well spend some good quality time with my condemned nut before they began hacking away at him.

Then it occurred to me . . . how could Cammy in good conscience ever abandon me now? She'd have to come sweeping back into my life in the role of a sick nurse. Perfect. But then again, what would she want with a castrato? Still, this was a life-and-death matter. Even if she'd already skipped town, there'd have to be a forwarding number. So I called her . . .

"Hi, we're not home now, but . . ."

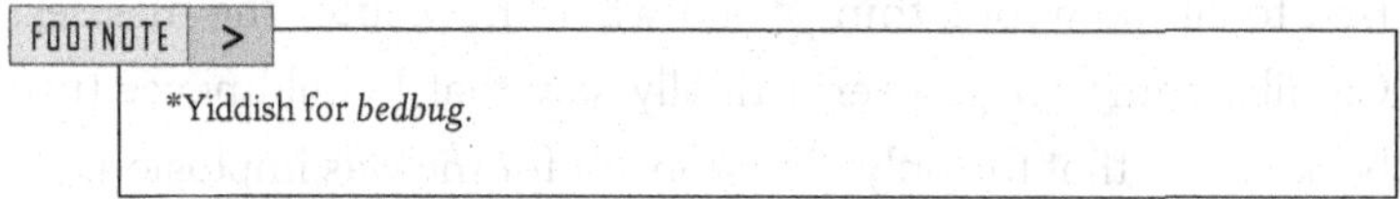


*Yiddish for *bedbug*.

# A Place in the Sun

WE.

Maybe she'd acquired a roommate. Or maybe she'd only meant Phillip.

Yeah, right.

I ruptured then. The next few days would be whipped into a damp, gray gibberish. From which, half lucid, half liquid, I finally dribbled out of my building into a chilly March twilight, unknowing if the sky were a dusk or a dawn as I checked sidewalk eyes for either sleep crusts and glints of pre-work worry—or post-work ennui. Walking east up Bleecker, I decided it was a Friday because fewer mouths were frowning, and then I knew it was A.M. as, turning right onto Mercer, the sky came grouchily awake, a vast smudgy gray erasure ready to wipe me off and turn the Eternal Page.

Basically, as far as suicide weather went, it seemed pretty promising.

And so this, I thought, is where it would end—in Manhattan, the dazzling jagged puzzle where the solutions for me had proved merely virtual. Where after all these gaunt years my internal compass had only grown more rusted, misgauged, and magnetized to all the wrong things; and where now, after the messiest Camilla hemorrhage ever, I finally saw that I could never turn back to her; that the only direction left for me was implosion.

And I hadn't even cracked the *Billboard 100*.

I made myself do a little farewell self-pity walk along Time Café. All the umbrellas now slept collapsed in a pile, still down for the winter. On the bench out front sat the Will-Fuck-For-Food bum, who lifted his ass to free unabashed gas. I envied him, actually, thinking what a blessing it must have been not to care like that.

Then I realized I no longer had to care either.

I went and stood gaping into the window at the warm-lit world of wealth and contentment . . . at a young rosy brunch couple who gave me nervous looks that I finally walked away from, over to a man sitting in a shiny red running suit at the only occupied outside table, pretending he wasn't cold as he drank espresso and read a John Grisham book, which, realizing with a batty smile that I would suffer relatively few long-term repercussions, I snatched from his hand. Then I broke into a sprint and hurled the thing into the Lafayette Street traffic, thinking that at least I'd lived to achieve *one* of my long-standing ambitions as I sped away from his

"Fucking asshole!"

past a clapboard wall covered with posters of Tyson, our modern Grendel, who'd managed to master the role of the monster, rabid mascot, once again facing off against the latest fool. I ran and ran through the chill gray day, past Grace Church, the Strand, and Virgin Megastore, Cammy's memory a stitch in my side until I reached the Coffee Shop on Union Square West, where I saw, leaning thick thighs on the railing, that same little cell phone guy who'd been giving his girlfriend counterfeit coordinates.

"Tell New Line I just don't like the numbers yet," he barked into his headset.

"Lighten up, mogul," I told him, panting. "It's really not worth it."

I decided to treat myself to a last meal, but, having no cash, I could afford only those free pastry samples they offered at the Starbucks in Union Square's Barnes and Noble, where I stood dunking over a dozen scraps of linzertorte into a little plastic cup of the skim* milk they put out for free, causing a chubby aproned woman who worked there to give me acidic scowls until I dashed over to Fifth Avenue, where, as I watched with detached fascination my outstretched hand tremble, a spick-and-span black man holding fistfuls of Paul Smith bags said,

"You've still got all five, handsome."

I gave him a futile/grateful smile.

"Where are *you* off to?" he asked me.

"Off."

From a passing Jeep Laredo came Kid Rock "singing" a song that, again, sounded very, very familiar, when one melting moment later I realized it was a rap rendition of "If Camilla Fell." I experienced the same horrific blur of identity as when I'd caught my mother giving my father head in his Santa suit.

Thanks for all the memories, Gary.

And so I became a splintered hoof clopping through the meatpacking district, whose street banter zigzagged in and out of my fading awareness as if distorted through a cell phone's decaying connection. And all this in the midst of the incessant sirens, horns, and jackhammers that compose Manhattan's infernal orchestra, which, I see now, was rotting the heart of a silence I'd long forgotten I'd needed.

FOOTNOTE >

*I'd been so programmed to follow Gary's fat-free curriculum that, even in this anti-moment, I'd managed to resist the whole milk.

WE'RE NOT HOME.

Arriving into the sick throbbing organ of Forty Deuce with all its peep shows, trannies,* and crack whores, my inner voice lost its breath, could no longer narrate me along, and I had to sit down on a guardrail . . . only to rediscover how every horizontal surface in this City bares little metal rump-deterring teeth. So I soldiered on to Forty-eighth and Eighth, where a blind man asked me the way to Worldwide Plaza, and as this was my own destination, I gently took his arm and, gazing into the defunct caves of his eyes, on this day of solving old questions, I asked him, with a pointless smile, what it was he "saw" when he dreamed.

"I dream in colors."

I crawled onto a high windy ledge of Worldwide Plaza.† As I peered down through khaki smog at the sleazy sprawl of Hell's Kitchen, I saw the obligatory *Highlights-of-Your-Life* thing . . . My mother opening her robe to get me out of her bathroom, which I'd barged into so I could confront her about that evening's tranquil family dinner at Domino's Pizza, where she'd howled at my father, "You were the one who wanted to have the fucking kid!" . . . My first-grade teacher, Mrs. Moody, at the chalkboard, chirping out the fart that'll make her a legend . . . My dad making me swear not to tell my mom I'd caught him in

*Transvestites.

†It's a kind of record company central.

bed with her best friend again . . . And finally Little Green, in beret and holey knee socks, skidding across my hardwood floor to a stop before lining up her toes and shutting one immense emerald eye as she whips her hand in a circle, declaring a disappointed "Spare!" . . . All these memories on a Lazy Susan just in back of my eyes, which Cammy's caramel fingers spin with a Vanna White flourish. And then I see everybody I've told you about, from the steam room Oinkers, to Better Me, to the sound booth guy's unpresence, until, glancing down at Tonka Trucks and Matchbox Cars, despising every thought, smell, and sigh that was oozing out of me and convincing myself to leap* . . . I realized I hadn't even written a sayonara note. So as I turned around to tap on the window for a piece of paper, half hoping somebody would talk me down, I saw a bunch of dingy rocker dudes smoking cigarettes around a boardroom table, who I suddenly recognized as Hanging Door Chad. Then, on the back of my hand, writing down instructions that Gary's name must be erased from my will, I actually *saw* him on Forty-eighth Street! Getting out of a bloody fang that I'd learn a minute later was his just-washed scarlet Maserati, which he'd only that afternoon bought with royalties earned from "Emily's E-Mail" and other hits.

In a minute he was yelling up at me through a bullhorn to

"Go ahead and jump! You'll be immortalized after your death."

A clotting crowd, with hands for visors, began looking up at me.

FOOTNOTE >

*Which gave me the idea for a country song called "Gravity'll Always Letcha Down," which I figured I could no doubt get Gary to "place" with another artist.

Gary yelled, "This is what we've always wanted, Curtis!" his (newly capped) smile a shard of glass in the sun.

"I can't believe you're egging me on!" I hollered, but my words were lost in the cold, discourteous wind. Then Gary, who'd apparently bouffanted his hair up into a frosted, Shelly Winterish mane, was giving orders into his cell phone—and from an open window right behind me, Hanging Door Chad's drummer tossed me another one. I yelled into it,

"I can't believe you sold my fucking songs to Kid Rock and Britney Spears!"

"I thought you'd be happy we got the songs *co*vered," he spoke into both cell phone and bullhorn. "You're gonna get your five percent. I did it for *you,* that was your birthday surprise."

But as much as I found myself needing to believe him, I said,

"Did you run that line of horseshit by Donnie?"

"Actually, asshole" . . .

As a fire truck screamed up and parked, I saw myself holding one of their hoses and blasting Gary across the cement piazza, spraying him out along Eighth Avenue past Port Authority and Penn Station, where he tumbled and writhed blindly against my pulverizing water jet . . .

"So don't fucking lecture *me,* loser!" he was screaming. "Look at where *you're* standing. And Donnie says I have to forgive myself for all that, anyway. And that you have to take responsibility for *your* role in all this because apparently I did a lot of that stuff because I just wasn't getting what I needed from our relationship."

"Our re*lat*ionship! You stood me up on my *birth*day!"

"I was recording with Dimpled Chad."

"I thought it was *Han*ging Door Chad," I said, ignoring the call waiting beep in my ear.

"I made them change it. And you've actually made me late for a meeting with them upstairs right now. I'm producing a tune of theirs called 'Diesel Dyke from Düsseldorf' that's a total home-run, which is why I had to put Birnbaum on the back burner. Plus, Donnie says that you've always just liked me more than I like you and so I shouldn't feel guilty just because . . ."

And there he was, in the eye of that enormous lurid moment, talking and talking; through the ensuing mega media blitzkrieg; through the arrival of SWATs, cops, Jerry Springer, and vans with VH-1, K-ROCK, and MTV painted on them. As Gary and my conversation boomed over the giant television monitors now sparkling below me, as dozens of cameras began teething on me, their new meat . . .

Well, you can probably see where all this was leading.

THREE >

# Marina[1]

*Quis hic locus, quae regio, quae mundi plaga?*[2]

What seas what shores what gray rocks and what islands

1. Pericles' daughter in Shakespeare's play *Pericles Prince of Tyre:* she was born at sea, lost to her father, then as a young woman found by him again.

2. "What place is this, what country, what region of the world?" Spoken by Hercules on regaining sanity after having killed his children in his madness, in Seneca's play *Hercules Furens* ("The Mad Hercules"). This is a situation contrary to the one evoked in the poem. Eliot once wrote to a correspondent that he wished to achieve a "crisscross" between the scenes in the Senecan and the Shakespearean plays.

# Twenty Paces

The *Billboard* magazine touted:

**Birnbaum . . . From Subway to Sony!**

Because basically, all the major record labels had waged a bidding war over me on the basis of what Kurt Loder called "a tawdry suicidal spectacle of soul-selling in the shameless name of post-Cobain fame."

I'd spent the day viewing half-hourly reruns of my "dubious MTV debut," wondering if Camilla was watching her white elephant trumpeting over the airwaves as well. But I found, after all this effort, that I wasn't even happy, thinking, *Simile Game:* the few gifts delivered to me . . . Camilla, Phillip, Record Deal . . . always ended up seeming somehow irrelevant, after-the-fact, like receiving some exotic postcard from a friend who's been home a week already. Which reminded me to walk down to my mailbox and start abolishing my debts with *"one of the largest advances a record company has ever awarded a new artist (without first hearing him perform)."* —The Village Voice

. . . and to try and come up with some kind of a Camilla plan, when I suddenly remembered the

We're not home

again. Jesus. Who was this prick? Were people still dueling?

Well, in monetary light of all that had happened, I did feel I could at least give her some kind of a life now . . .

At the mailboxes, in what, I guess, I would have to call *good* news, Dr. Singh "informed" me (still without the aid of grammatical articles) that "said lump is either non-toxic fatty deposit or rare, but also relatively* harmless, venereal wart." He also explained that he'd terrified me with his whole *You-might-want-to-sit-down* bit over the phone so "Birnbaum would be loath to engage in future unprotected fucking, hee, hee. Doctor desires to perform follow-up visits where I will insert acupuncture needle into tip hole of Birnbaum's little penis. In meantime, you shall please call list of past sexual partners you gave Doctor, except for one who happens to also be my patient, and who I will contact personally."

Meaning . . . Groupie.

I figured that giving the heads-up, as it were, to every one of my past partners wouldn't prove such a Promethean task as the roster included only the above and Cam– Oh, God. What if I'd given her *warts*?! Yet another charming legacy I'd left her, and one that would probably tend to tarnish the new Safe Guy role I was hoping to win her back with. Because learning that your ex-boyfriend had been all along hosting a variety of exotic and highly contagious viral STDs, and all without a lick of health insurance, didn't exactly strike me as a reconciliation-clincher.

WE'RE NOT HOME

In other news, I was able to pay my mom back, including the penalty fees I'd incurred after ignoring my birthday arraignment. Then I learned from the next letter that, regarding the evi-

FOOTNOTE >

*An adverb, I've found, of often alarmingly elastic definition.

dent CONNY/ASPSCA merger, I'd now be able to kill two vultures with one stone.

Back in my apartment, getting the guts up to call her (or *them*), I accidentally pressed rewind on my answering machine. The digital lady informed me of a message dated three months ago.

And there it was, the Voice, as intimate and intricate as the valved song of my own blood.

It was, of all people, Camilla.

# Assent

Through the phone's hissy connection,* I finally heard that blue noise, which had for nine months been washing my thoughts in its waves, so that now it seemed to arrive as much from inside of my own head as from out of Camilla's. I wondered if she was sensing all of this as well, as she told me how her

WE'RE NOT HOME

had been only a screen against a general fear she'd been feeling more and more . . . a fear of never hearing my mind work again. Because Love was, she saw now, although never enough, also the *only* thing.

I climbed the five mildewy flights up her stairs, out of breath. My three metal knocks sounded silly and courageous, as if they were claiming, *Alas, we are knocks!* Then I waited . . . and waited . . . staring at the doorknob as if it were an ATM cash slot, Suspense doing its old feathery number in my stomach. When suddenly she was in front of me.

*And it was Her.* It was her.

FOOTNOTE >

*I had to use a payphone as my own had been suddenly cut off because of an unpaid slew of 900-number phone-sex calls that Gary had been secretly making. At least now I had the money to go and reinstate my service the next day.

With her eyes cast down, even now.

I tried not to let this oppress me as I walked into our moment, which she'd decked out in Buckley's grim grace and some soft fickle candlelight, and through which she led me on her shy stocking feet. But all at once the whole thing felt self-conscious and too cardinal, a shadow allegory of Curtis and Camilla.

I didn't tell her this, though. In the warm wobbling light, I looked around at her kitchen table, with its bottle of Tabasco and above it the *Land of Make Believe,* and all that was her, was us, in this room, which had once been my planet.

Despite myself, I felt the scorn ebbing out of me as I sat down on the white chenille sofa, where I thought I'd never sit again and where I looked up to see that Phillip had delivered, by teeth, my old pillow to me.

"My little man," I said, pulling the pillow onto my lap and then setting him on top, where I buckled the Christie's* collar around him, squeezing him, working him, nuzzling the little cowlick master switch in the middle of his puffed, imperious chest. I could feel Cammy sitting firm and noiseless next to me, wearing her Rip ring,† as well as a pair of my old flannel plaid boxers, which struck me as stagy. And she was still preventing any eye contact, as Buckley did his aching archangel thing, to which the candles swayed and swooned.

I'd told myself I wouldn't be the first one to speak, because I was so sick of being just and sensible. So I looked over on her

FOOTNOTE >

*I'd been able to buy the collar after I got my advance.

†I wondered if she only just put it on that night.

bed, where I saw myself making all those nights of bottomless love to her, forever trying to grasp the guts of her. I remembered the first noon I'd awoken there alone, (tea)spooning little Phillip while she was at work, knowing I'd finally won the tacit gift of her trust. And like a young god I'd romped nude through every Camilla scent, shade, and echo, giddy with recovered Hope as I meddled in every one of her little carved boxes, books, and feminine flasks—a mischievous kitten left alone in the house to unravel Cammy, my new ball of twine, in attempt to demyth her (but only a little), when suddenly there was her phone's plastic yodel, which was thrilling enough to know I could answer, and which, after a conferring glance at Phillip, I didn't.

But tonight, here, in the rickety candlelight, there were still no words between us. Finally, I jumped into that first question as a summer camp kid might into a spooky night lake.

"Do you know how much you hurt me?"

Phillip slid off the sofa and tiptoed into helpful shadows. I waited for Cammy's answer to our first face-to-face phrase in nine months.

"Yes," she whispered, staring down. "I'm sorry, Curtis."

The flame shadows fumbled over her espresso skin.

"No. Really. I really don't think you *do* know how much you hurt me, Camilla," trying not to love the trill of her name in my throat as it became choked in rage. "Do you have any idea of the fucking *hell* I've been living without you?"

She shook her bowed head.

"You made me feel like some fucking loser," I said. "Like I was this big pathetic burden to you. Like your retarded child or something. You just threw me away, and waited for me to die. And now you think because you put on a pair of my fucking boxers that now everything's just A-OK?"

Still looking down, with the measured melody of remorse in her voice, she said, "I'm so, so sorry. I realize I made a horrible mistake now. I missed you so much." She took my hand. "I couldn't go even seven seconds without thinking about you. Please, can you forgive me?" Her eyes flickered up at me—then down again. "I love you more than anything in the world. I'll show you."

"But I don't understand what's changed. How are things gonna be different *now*? I mean, what about the whole me-not-making-you-feel-safe deal?"

"Maybe I can make my*self* feel safe now."

"But you still can't even really look at me, Cammy."

She gave me her deliberate eyes . . .

. . . out of which the flames teased new promise. And as I sat there, lost once again in the blue roar of her stare, I knew then that I loved her even more than before, and that I wasn't ever going to shake her, now was I, not *ev*er? I felt my face going ugly in tears.

For a long time, all I could say was "You hurt me so much," over and over, wondering, as she sat squeezing my hand, why she wasn't crying.

Until, after about an inch of the candles, the brittle ice core of the past seemed to thaw. But,

"I feel like you're drifting from me again," I said. "Do you feel how you're drifting?"

She moved closer, bridging us, trying.

"Look. I just need to feel like you're really on my side this time," I said. "That you're really behind me, you know? No matter *what*. This time it's for real. This time we're playing for keeps, okay?"

"Yes." She nodded. "I want to cleave together."

"Oh, Cammy. That's *all* I want. Please. Just don't hurt me again."

I slid shyly inside her and we made thoughtful love. Each touch told our past, each gesture cast a shadow gist, and every remark we'd ever exchanged was cloaked in our motions.

# Something in the Way

Dawn was rinsing Time against Camilla's window. I touched a needle from the little cactus on her sill to see if I was dreaming.

No.

So here I was, after all those months, in her bed again. But as we lay chest to chest in the drowsy blue light, I felt perplexed . . . a cold question mark had curled up inside me. There was something wrong in the room.

"You started smoking?" She touched my Patch as she blinked herself awake.

"No, I got a tattoo." I rolled over to adjust the venetians so the day could slant in.

"I wonder who talked you into that." She touched my cheek. The sun set tiny blue fires in her eyes.

"And can you believe he didn't tell me you called?" I said.

"Is that a rhetorical question?"

"My new health insurance may cover getting it removed," I said, driving that one home, and there were so many things that we needed to tell each other . . .

"*Simile Game,*" she said, looking straight above her. "I'm feeling all those old feelings that I guess I thought I was done with. Like when you thought spring has finally arrived, but then a cold snap comes and you have to dig out your long underwear and mittens and stuff you thought you'd finally put to rest."

Inside his private sun puddle at the foot of her bed, Phillip glanced back in anger at the intrusion on his beauty sleep, got to his paws, chased his tail one revolution, then renestled himself with a self-important snort. I smelled Cammy's shoulder and told her how much I'd loved my Panel.*

"I thought you might've liked that," she played it down, like I'd thanked her for refilling the ice tray.

I tried to tell her how my life, how the record deal, had meant nothing without her; how after I'd proved I could do it, I didn't really feel the need to go through with it after all.

"Like the way you don't have to actually send a nasty letter you've written?" she said.

"Exactly."

We lay there holding hands. A distant garbage truck mooed. I rubbed Phillip's tummy with my toes.

We kept trying to catch up, realigning, reshuffling, but our words seemed more and more only pastels of themselves. Another language was striving under all this . . .

"I'm just so glad to have you back in my life," she told me, with a jot of abstraction in her face.

I got up on an elbow to look at her. "You look so sad, Cutie. Why don't you smile? You never smile."

She strained one, pulling my hand to her chest and turning away from me. I canoodled her tight a while.

"Please, sweetie," I said finally. "I didn't mean to criticize you. But your heart is racing. What's wrong? Please tell me."

She was quite still and breathing against me. I slowly rolled

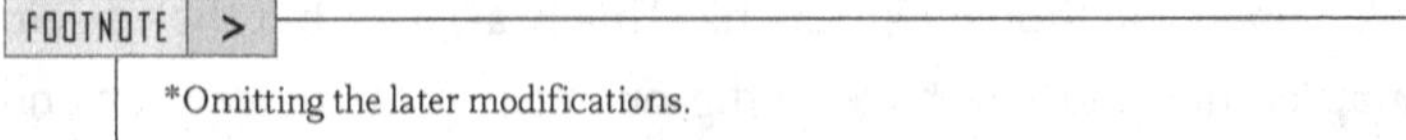


*Omitting the later modifications.

her shoulders so she lay on her back. And I saw that her eyes had gone dim—receded somewhere—the dying star of an old turned-off television.

"Cutie—"

"There's something I never told you," she said. "You were right. There's something—" On that last word her voice clogged with tears. "That's why I was going to leave New York. My fath—"

Suddenly Cammy's methodical eyes, which had, for as long as I'd known them, been forcing themselves to go through the motions, to blink away that *something,* could no longer do it. And while her face betrayed no pain, those eyes pushed a few doll's tears down the sides of her temples and onto the pillow.

"Cammy, it's okay, hon," I sat up, kissing her hand. "I love you. You can tell me anything, Cammy. Please, Cam."

"My fath—," she tried, her eyes on the ceiling.

I kissed her hot wet cheek. "It's okay, hon . . ."

"My fa—"

Her face finally crumpled. I pulled her close and slowly rocked her, while above Phillip's whimpers, Camilla heaved and shook through me with that kind of sobbing we've stored up for life's few and true catastrophes . . . that unraveling song, breathless and thoughtless.

# Where All the Waters Meet

As the little girl sits in her daddy's lap, he reads her the same poem. Before it'll happen. Always. Aloud. This lets her *know* it will happen.

And she thinks she might love this poem . . . or might've. Cause it really is lovely. So wild and familiar. And that's what complicates her the most . . .

*What images return.*

Because Love is, among other things, a trap.

*Marina*

Her father's made the name her middle one. She's become the thing he does to her. His play within a play, the hole that Bottom made.* When each night he finds her middle. Marina.

On some far littered shore within her—*what seas . . . what shores . . . what images return*—she understands this.

Father's study is dark save azure TV haze. And the sound's never on. While her trusting feet dangle from a grimy striped couch. Which she's ashamed to let her friends near. And not only because it's ratty.

*From *Pyramus and Thisbe*, the play performed within *A Midsummer Night's Dream*.

Mom is, as ever, far off asleep with odd dreams in her veins.

Sometimes she hears Mommy moan. Sometimes. As if Mommy might hear what He does through her mist. As if her dreams might unravel the truth. Because she can't make herself tell her mother. Through some deep, strenuous instinct, the little girl knows It describes her.

Lately she's been feeling so ancient. And most when he's sharp and searching inside her. But she's scarcely known different. Her agony's her source now, confusion her map. She's become wise and weary, way beyond her eight years.

Because Time, among other things, is a cannibal.

*"O my daughter,"*

Father purrs, close in her ear, and he laps a clumsy tongue, rough as a cat's, till she hunches brittle shoulders against him.

"Marina Fell. That's *you,*"

he urges, marking the page with a long, grimy fingernail. "I *made* you." He turns her chin so she sees her own eyes in his mirrored sunglasses. "You're me," he says, his breath getting ragged, twisting her face back to *Family Affair*.

His hand finds her ankle. A wedding ring sparkles the dark. A commercial for Ultra brite as his fingers crawl up into her blue-checkered dress, a tent over his lap. As her eyes, still on the screen, grow cool, and callused. Part of her going elsewhere . . . holding hands with her mother through a foggy dawn wood.

*"What images return,"*

and his words sound so actual, sliding through his sharp little teeth.

She thinks she remembers when his voice once was safe. Long ago. She thinks. As he whispers

"Follow the words now, Marina."

Though by now they both know the poem. By now. By heart.

Her eyes, still dry, because he hates when they wet, watch the pearly moon of his nail move along the lit page, while his other one finds her, cutting into her slightly, loosing her up till he anchors himself in.

"Jesus God," he groans, going deep. "I love you," he swears, slowly pumping. Smothering her mouth as his girl softly screams.

Later, at last, he pulls himself out. Whimpers,

"You are my hummingbird, aren't you, Sunshine?"

She keeps very still, swallowing snot.

"You are my only hummingbird," he says, "now hum for me."

He pulls her little head down. Panting, reading . . .

*"What seas . . ."*

She hates the taste of herself on him, but he knows she can't spit, with him stopping her up.

"Christ, I love you," he grunts. "Tell me you love me, honey. Tell me. Quick!"

*I love you*

she thinks, from her far garbage shore.

And he gasps.

So now, at least, she knows that he's over. Almost.

"Swallow it for Daddy. Don't you love me enough?"

She's heard this more times than she knows, as he takes her trembling chin in his hand, tilting her eyes back up to his shades.

"It's liquid moonlight. So swallow," in a voice that is level, like when he feeds her cough syrup.

She gulps, shutting long lashes tight.

"Smile for me, Sunshine," he says, zipping up. "Sunshine. I said smile."

And as a single tear falls, she does.

# I'm an Absolute Pawn When It Comes to the Weather

At Mike's Pawnshop in Chelsea, the man who "helped" me, and who might've been Mike, wore a milky sealant in the corners of his mouth. And when I'd asked him if by any min*ute* chance they happened to have a Zumwalt automatic like the one in *White Noise,** he was clearly disgusted that he would, in fact, be able to meet such an obviously wildcard demand. Which ended up costing me $99.96. And for which, after I'd handed him a $100 bill, he neglected to give me the four cents change. I would've asked had it been a nickel.

So it turned out to be the whole incest cliché.

I think very few people ever know the feeling of having nowhere to turn but inside, only to find that place has been raided as well. And while I was obviously homicidal, and for the first time in my life actually willing to die for someone, I have to admit I was also secretly glad that for once I wasn't to blame—that someone else on the team had struck out. Because this thing, which like a word's silent letter had been for so long lurking unspoken in Camilla, had at least drawn us together.

And now I knew a restoration must begin.

FOOTNOTE >

*I didn't actually allude to the book in this case. And Camilla was completely ignorant of my whole mission. I'd told her I was beginning the recording on my album that night. I'd learned earlier that my lyrics had all been recovered.

# Shagadelic

The train clanged to its stop. The chilly metal sign said,

**Gibraltar**

. . . bold against a dusk sky worried with clouds. And below this, on the track bed, four eager blades of green grass, the first arrivals of spring, cast four matching blades of shadow across the gray cinders.

I opened my little lyrics pad and wrote

*Time . . . That grim old loan shark,*
*sending out his best thug Death.*

Him.

The train wrenched back into motion. Darkness fell over rapid April landscape, which was suddenly hemmed with a rot wood fence, fallen over and undulating like the warps of a ruined old roller coaster in some derelict carnival, then a jointed muffler like the flexed arm of Hercules. *What images return.* While superimposed over all this was my reflected eye, horse-terror wide.

How would I do this? *Could* I? *I am not Prince Hamlet,* I said to myself, still the affected pedant, even in this insane situation.

A silky little girl walked to a nearby window and watched the sun drowning in the whooshing movie that was making itself outside, which lit her face up a campfire crimson as she began to lean tiptoe against the emergency exit.

"Sweetie," I yelled through the shuddering hum. "Little child, be careful!" surging out of my seat, surprised at the ritual words coming out of me, when a woman I hadn't seen in the far dim of the car gave me a steady look that sat me back down. Then her eyes rolled back down onto her find-the-word-within game and a circling pencil appeared having, evidently, found a word within.

Arriving in Colonus,* Connecticut, I heard the train doors suck closed behind me in a final, film noir sort of way. I marched past the uncurious stares of locals waiting in the station, and into the ritzy suburban nightfall. Standing there, I immediately felt the fading insult of the City behind me. I let the new nippy silence acquire me, believe in me . . . and what I must do.

I could see my shaky breaths in front of me as I walked (or paced an incessant line) past all the satisfied houses with smoke singing out of their chimneys; through the sweet reek of burning leaves, of clearance, of the old making room for the new . . .

I remember a sidewalk puddle whose shores had receded to half their dimension . . . *what shores* . . . unknowing my unconscious machinery would somehow translate this image, like the bar code on a Coke can, so apparently ordinary, into the lasting symbol of that night.

FOOTNOTE >

* The Metro North stop was between Gibraltar and Ceuta, the original pillars of Hercules, on either side of the Straits of Gibraltar.

Suddenly there was a mailbox in front of me with a raised flag and its mouth agape, hailing a cab . . .

S. Fell
1 Elm Street*

I took one little cough of a step into the gravel driveway, fondling cool, confident Chap† in my jean jacket pocket.

"Chappy," I said, inhaling the air's bracing despair. "Can we do this?"

Wondering what it was exactly we were going to do.

Every neighborhood has the eyesore house that shames all its neighbors. And the unshaven lawn of this three-story ranch matter was ankle high, with the occasional Schlitz can floating on top. As I began to wade through it, to avoid the noisy driveway, I realized that what I'd thought was a flowerbed beside the front door was actually a medley of empty junk food containers: Fritos, Cool Ranch Doritos, Double Stuff Oreos, Tostitos . . . ,‡ and that the giant elm tree's blossoms above me were little white plastic bags, swaying in the breeze with dirty old rain. While on top of all this was a satellite dish almost the size of the house it was crouching on.

Jesus.

FOOTNOTE >

*I'd found the address in Cammy's little book under *Father.*

†I'd narrowed his name down to either that or Pally . . . in the tradition of Humbert's Chum. Life leaches Art, causes Death. Create to kill, kill to live? In my head I kept hearing *Sending out his best thug Death* in the end-vamp melody of Sting's "Message in a Bottle."

‡Why did they all end in *O*s?

I had to admit it was regal, this massive latticed gadget against the flaming sky, cocked to interpret all the invisible litter of the universe.

As I advanced in the falling dark, I noticed that no lights were on, something I hadn't even considered: Maybe he wasn't even *home*. So where *was* he? *Who* was he? What in God's name could he be doing? Playing bingo in a moldy church basement? Shaving a pug?

With sudden Hitchcockian timing, one yellow rectangle appeared on the second floor, framing a momentary figure . . .

. . . who jerked down the shade.

My terror bubbled into rage. I tried to remember the reason behind everything was just beyond those walls.

When I reached the front door, I rang a pink doorbell button with a finger I noticed was shaking.

And I waited. Rang the bell again. Then heard the little intercom to my left listening to me . . .

"Hello?" I asked it.

Nothing.

"Hi. I'm sorry to disturb you. I'm looking for the Fell residence?"

There was the faint sound of a fishing-rod reel above me . . . where I looked up to find a mounted camera watching me with its flat little *Alien* head.

"Hi," I said, waving to it. "Did Camilla Fell grow up in this house?"

Silence. Rustling papers . . . slow breathing.

"Please. Can you–"

"Where is my daaaaaddy?" called the voice of a distant, tiny child. Which I instinctively knew was a girl's, and was enough like Camilla's to goosebump my whole body.

"Honey," I said, trying to grasp the inconsiderate, kaleidoscopic logic of this nightmare. "Are you okay? Is your daddy home?"

"I'm scaared?!" cried the voice, now even more distant, as if she were at the bottom of a well.

"Hold on, sweetie." As the camera buzzed above me, I flipped to the script I'd written in my lyrics pad.

"I'm from the *Colonus High School Alumni Bulletin*.* I'd like to ask your father a few questions about Camilla. Is that your sister, honey?"

Pause.

"Is your daddy coming back?"

Long silence.

Clicking in the intercom, and the door suddenly sprang ajar . . .

. . . onto spongy carpet and total darkness.

"Daaaaddy? Where are you?" called the voice, now wobbling in wavelength as if through a wind tunnel.

"Little girl," I called, squinting into the pitch. "Where *are* you? Can you turn a light on? Mr. Fell?"

"Our electricity's out," the little girl cried, it seemed from every direction.

"Hold on, honey."

I heard my own heart thumping with stethoscope clarity. And as my vision adjusted, I noticed a panicky little candle on a near wooden table.

"Daaaaaddy, I'm scared."

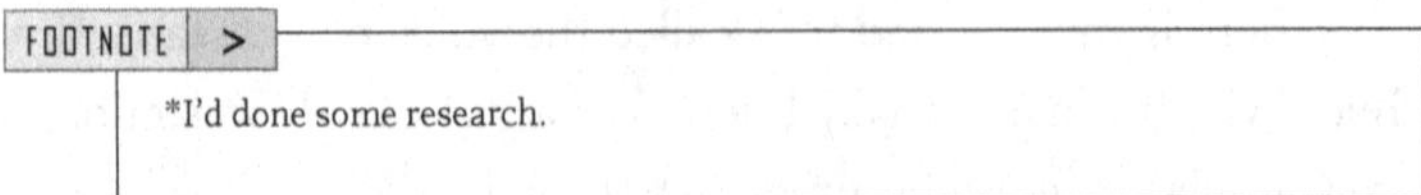


*I'd done some research.

"I'll bring you a candle, sweetie, just hold on," I yelled, looking around. "Where *are* you?"

But there was only silence. The wind whimpering outside. Stunned, I made my way to the candlelight and noticed, on the table, a little silver-framed yearbook photo.

By the feeble flicker, I saw a young girl, perhaps eight, with coffee skin and hair pulled tight into plastic gobstopper pigtails. There was the pouting clue of buckteeth behind a mouth that could not quite make itself smile for a corny cameraman's jokes. This mouth, which had already . . . While even bluer than the cardboard sky she was posed against were the little girl's eyes, already so *elsewhere* . . . and yet, at that point, still attempting to decide on something.

"Daddy?"

"I'm coming," I shouted, shoving her picture into my pocket, when suddenly there was the faint motorized buzzing above me again. I held up the flame to find the eye of another camera contracting.

"Where are you, sweetie?" I called, looking right into the lens.

"Upstairs," came the small, obstructed voice.

I found a waxy banister a few feet in front of me and started mounting a carpeted staircase. By that time I'd abandoned all rational thought, but there seemed to be forces within me, driving me onward, as if I were an old-fashioned cartoon ambulance, careening and screaming through intersections with a squad of hound dogs dressed up as gangsters inside me, abusing my sirens for their own cackling mission.

Then, of course, my little shiver of fire went out. So tickling the darkness in front of me, sleepwalker-wise, I made it to a landing . . .

. . . Where there was a misty blue splinter in front of me. It looked like the chink of a door to a TV room. But there was no sound I could hear, save the submarine-sonar ping of my tinnitus.

As I touched the doorknob, the slat of blue light went black. I walked into damp, dark silence. Where slowly I began to see a puny flame in the distance . . . revealing the vaguest notion of a face . . . which slowly receded.

*Where's the little girl?* I asked it. Then realized the question hadn't made it to my lips; that they were flapping in a parody of the speechless axe-murder-movie victim, as my tongue tried to pluck words out of a sticky, matted alphabet, resisting division, like eyelashes clumped in mascara.

"Who are you?" came a whisper.

I tried to gather saliva . . .

"Are you the father of Camilla Fell?"

Silence.

I could smell the consoling aroma of Johnson's Baby Powder pierced by the fungal tang of feet. Slowly, the bleary appearance began to take shape, as if someone were polishing the image out of tarnished silver.

Within the fluttering skirt of candlelight, on a vast mahogany desk, lay a pair of beautiful brown hands. Their fingers spiraled into sharp yellow talons, maybe two inches long, which were fiddling at something. As I narrowed my eyes and shuffled a few feet through some kind of clutter, I realized these claws were sliding, with doting slowness, a pair of tiny white panties up the legs of a black Barbie doll. Until at last, panties in place, the index claw touched one of her little red stiletto heels and began edging up her leg, slowly, until it vanished under the underwear, where it twitched, as if eating.

"Yes! I mean, no. Ohhh!" sighed a voice, which I recognized as the lost little girl's voice I'd heard just before. Then the claw withdrew into darkness, leaving the Barbie facedown in the shivering spotlight . . . followed by a deep sniffing noise.

"Remember when King Kong did that to Fay Wray?" came a hillbilly twang like a spoken banjo, as eerily slow and Caucasian as those in *Deliverance*. Then the claws reappeared in the light and began petting the doll.

"And were you aware," asked the drawl, "that *King Kong* was Hitler's favorite movie?"

I actually was, but, sensing this routine didn't exactly call for an audience, I didn't say so. I just stood there . . . or *shook* there. Amazed at how terrified I actually was.

Gradually, a pair of aviator sunglasses leaned into the candlelight, with a flaming tower in each mirrored lens.

"Are you the father of Camilla Fell?" I heard my voice asking.

The sunglasses fell back into shadow.

"But ain't this a purdy frock?" the brogue wondered, as the Rosemary's Baby claws now began fitting Black Barbie in a little blue-checkered dress. "It's a nice gingham plaid." The claws fussed at the dress hem. "Fits your tight little ass *jist* right, don't it?"

The tiny Pam Grier Afro nodded,

"It sho nuff do, my big-dicked niggah man."

Very quickly another, much larger Afro in the towering Don King tradition leaned into the light, put its ear to a whispering Barbie, then dissolved into darkness.

I gathered this guy didn't get out all that much.

"I'm startin' to take a real shine to this little bitch," he said. Again the hand disappeared. There were two more sniffles in the darkness. A waggling claw was offered into the candlelight. "Have a whiff. She's ripe."

I felt Chap in my pocket and began to move forward, but I

stopped when my foot crunched something glass. I could now see, in the warm jerky light, that the floor in front of me was a furious history of Coke cans, little jars of Gerber's baby food, a paddleball, several sixty-nining, interracial Barbie and Ken dolls, board games of Risk, Battleship, Yahtzee, Oiuja, chess, Clue, Parcheesi, Monopoly, of course, and Marvel comic books under heaps of rank laundry, snotty Kleenex, *TV Guide*s, a rosary, and . . .

I couldn't have sworn in court that there was a floor.

"Are you the father of . . ."

"My name is Shag," the Southern accent told me, and then, in blank-versed TV jingle, "like the carpet, like the hairdo, and yes, like the verb. Who the fuck are you?" A flashlight was stinging my eyes, which I shielded until the beam fell onto my crotch—and was turned off. My mouth said,

"I'm from the *Colonus High Alumni Bulletin,* sir. We're conducting a ***Questionnaire***** to assess the whereabouts and what-they've-been-up-to's of our ten-year celebrants. Would you be kind enough to give us just seven minutes of your time to answer a few questions about your daughter, as we'd like to do our semi-annual *So-Just-Where-Are-They-Now-a-Decade-Later?* Spotlight on Camilla Marina . . ." I let the last word spill at him into the darkness . . . "Fell?"

The spectacles came slowly into the glow again, motionless, throwing back golden fire . . . then faded.

FOOTNOTE >

*(Okay. I'll need some industrial-strength parentheses around this one. Yes, I did say ***Questionnaire***. Irony was peeking around the columns of my crumbling façade . . . the fallen caryatid on my Coliseum. I thought that using ***Questionnaire*** might give this Love Story a sense of completion because, in the end, aren't all great melodies circular?)

"How do you know her middle name?" he said.

I inched forward.

"It was listed in our *I-Have-Forgotten-and-Remember* compendium."

The immense Afro, now in the half-light of a *60 Minutes* informant, tilted slightly as if listening for a distant song. I recognized in the gesture a hint of Camilla. This wasn't going to be so easy.

I could hear labored Shag breaths. I took another step through the rubble at him.

"Who are you?" he said, with composure. "I'm afraid I'm going to have to ask you to leave our house."

"I told you," with another nimble step. "I'm from the Colonus High Alumni. Can you answer a few questions, sir?"

"I can answer anything. Because I'm a got-damn brilliant genius," with both *i*'s silent.

Watching the dark just behind his candle, I pulled from my chest pocket my little script and pen, then used the framed picture of Her I'd found downstairs for writing support.

"What's that?" asked invisible Shag.

The claws shot into the light and aimed an emery board at me. It made frantic little stabs.

"It's yours," I said, softly. "And mine."

A pause.

"What do you want with me?"—her shrillness in his timbre.

"Let's begin the *Questionnaire,*" I advanced. "Would you say your daughter was a happy child?" stealing another step. "I mean, were there any events you, her *fath*er, would consider traumatic?"

"Who the fuck are you?" he hissed. The wiggling flames reemerged.

"Does she have a significant other?" I took another step.

"I guess you could call him that. In a pinch."

I stopped. "What's that supposed to mean?" (I couldn't help myself.) I tried to move, but my foot was caught in something I realized was a werewolf mask.

"You're not from the alumni board," he said. "Not at all."

For the first time the Afro came full into the stuttering light. It was ochered with sebum, a giant used Q-Tip. Below it, he fixed me with slow, determined flames. At last, he said

"Are we a rock star yet?"

I tried to speak, but my mouth misfired again.

"What is it exactly you want with me?" asked diplomatic Shag.

"I'm here to get some answers."

"What a *mar*velous Alan *Ladd*!" He was clapping. "Really. Bravo, hero."

I swallowed. "I know what you did," I said, putting her picture away.

Pause. The glasses recoiled.

"Ah, you sunk my *batt*leship." His dim shape suddenly stood.

"Sit down, you syphilitic old fuck!" I aimed Chap at his shadowed Afro . . . which he slowly lowered. "I'm going to kill you, you piece of shit!" I was screaming, walking forward, through his heap of broken images, where I noticed an elaborate intercom/surveillance system. And that his mammoth desk held a large fan, some half-eaten Gerber's jars, while opened just in front of him was *The Waste Land and Other Poems*.

"That's a good little read," I pointed Chap at the ragged book. "Sexy stuff. Looks like you might've read it once or twice."

It was yanked into shadow.

I stopped about a yard in front the desk, aiming Chap, with shaky arms extended, between the mini Towering Infernos.

There was a cry so faint it might have been from his stomach.

"You think you can do it?" he whispered out of his darkness. "We wish you would."

"I love her. Why did you ruin her?"

"But would you love her if I *had*n't?"

I stared at the tiny twin fires in his glasses . . . trying not to consider what he'd said.

"And what if she ruined *me*?" he proposed. "Do you know how much I wish I were you?"

As I stood there, with my astonishment, with my sweaty trigger finger, I began to see, in the shadows, Cammy's faint Roman curve in his nose; the same intelligent hands, which were, with a razor blade, now chopping paths of white powder in the glow. Then the reflected flames receded and were replaced by the gassy blue tongue of a cigarette lighter, lapping the darkness. I realized from the strange gurgle-purr that Shag was freebasing into a little bong whose clear plastic neck, full of creamy smoke, was being pushed across the desk to me. And my mouth, adrenaline-dry, began watering. It looked delicious.

He blew his smoke out of the shadows in a long, fed-up sigh. "Apparently we have a lot in common," he said, unhappily.

And I figured what the hell. Maybe the crack would detach me; give this whole scene a psychedelic finale. So with one hand training Chap on his blazing shades, with the other I grabbed the hookah and took a monster hit. I held the smoke in as long as I could before I blew out a bitter lovely plume. Then my gun arm began to ache, so I switched it.

"I don't know what I want from you," I confessed. Standing there, feeling ridiculous.

"I do." The claws began slowly packing another bowl.

"Well?"

"You want to see that you could never become me. That

someone like me can't possibly eat breakfast cereal and pay his phone bill. That all this melodrama will only end up, like everything else, filling you with empathy and contempt. You want to find out that I couldn't have possibly loved her. But that's the whole problem."

Amazingly, his drawl was growing oddly cozy, even lulling.

"There was this little scumbag scout from Next Models," he went on. "He told me she had real star potential and all that shit and, of course, he tried to take her away from me before she turned fifteen. Camilla begged me to let her go study in Paris. But we both knew I could never share her. We love her like vice, don't we?"

It was the first time I'd heard her name in his mouth. I shut my eyes. I opened them and, on a bookshelf to my left, above a shabby striped couch in the spastic glow, I noticed *Vocabulary Builder*—and then it hit me . . .

"This is her room, isn't it? You moved yourself *in* here. Oh, my God. Tell me that's not her bed." I aimed Chap at a frilly dim canopy in the corner.

"Okay, that's not her bed. And I don't love the way it smells," he sniffed, "or hate myself for sleeping naked in it every night since she left me. I don't fuck her pillows and beat off into her panties. Or into that," he said, spraying the flashlight into a closet next to me, where I saw hanging the blue-checkered dress; the smudgy, penciled height-marks on its doorjamb; a stack of records with Cole Porter's "Night and Day" on top.

I cocked Chap.

Shag's small jagged teeth flashed in the shadows. "You're no killer, Elvis. I admire your passion, though. I can see you're a star." (Amazing how flattery works.) "But passion's a difficult thing. All those tourists come to Times Square to see the ball drop on New Year's Eve. And then, standing there, they realize they can't eat it or fuck it. So what do they do? They buy a bunch of souvenir crap . . . like this charnel." He waved his arm at the rubble around us, sending a faint waft of Her at me. "Imagination," he said, "all this shit, is really only another way around ourselves, isn't it? Like murder and sex. It stops time. Look at Hitler and Elvis. There was nowhere for them to go. People say the media is evil and that Fame is unnatural and everything. That all these mothers who kill off their daughters' cheerleader rivals are products of the tabloids. But we are what we are, you know. Nothing is really false, because we *caused* it all. NutraSweet, Hiroshima."

"Of course you say all this . . . because you *fucked* her!"

"What if she fucked me back?"

"I—you—"

"I've fantasized about kicking my own father to death every day of my life. *He* passed this down to me. And it just keeps on going. It lives inside us until it uses us all up. And then it goes and finds its next fifteen minutes. It just doesn't care."

"How could you do it?"

"How could I *not*? I'm a werewolf, man! Aren't we all? That's why I had it done. Didn't she tell you?"

"What?"

There was a pause. I could hear his thick, hampered breaths. "I've been sterilized."

Slowly, Shag removed his flaming Top Gun shades . . .

And there they were. Of *course*. The Eyes. That he'd willed her. Hiding behind themselves. Whatever light they might've once cast had long ago been stolen. And now, in its place, shadows rippled over their blue ocean floor.

---

Outside hung a big drowsy moon. Which seemed to be saying, *Hey, I didn't see a thing.**

I realized I'd been so scared that all my endorphins had vetoed the cocaine. So I'd relapsed for nothing. Great. I walked to the train.

But after a block, I had to look back at the house. A silhouette divided the amber window, like the pupil of an owl's eye.

I waved.

FOOTNOTE >

*"Night and Day" was all in my head . . . *Only you beneath the moon and under the sun.*

# Imprisoned

The Metro North ride back to Manhattan felt a lot faster, as return trips always seem to, once we're done squinting through the loupe of anticipation. The lonely old train grumble-groaned her way through sleeping hamlets and gloomy damp boondocks, trying on the trip's one lit tunnel with the furtive yearning of a widow in her wedding gown.

I rested my cheek against the cool window. As I gazed into the moving night, I tried to "process" everything I'd been through.

It was inconceivable.

Partly because my insomniac fatigue had dissolved the past few days into a soupy third state of mind, somewhere between mirage and reality, and swimming with metaphorical morsels like Gary's half-eaten face, or the Hieronymus Boschy hybrid of me/Shag/Camilla and (oddly enough) Actory. Basically, I felt like Memory and Desire had been mixed until I couldn't tell the two apart. I even started to wonder whether the whole Shag fiasco had actually happened. But I also had the uncanny impression that all of it had happened be*fore*. Shag seemed almost imaginary, while somehow, at the same time, he was unavoidably familiar. He reminded me of that faint, faint song that once or twice in my life had kept me lying awake all night in the dark, trying to decide if its ghostly melody was floating out of some distant radio, or was only inside my own head.

The old boy had really outdone himself. In light of his age (seventy-eight), I guess I'd expected, at *worst,* some twisted old Alzheimer's guy, babbling in dementia while his live-in (male) nurse changed the colostomy bag.

Boy was I off.

Dealing with Shag had been like enduring a complex series of excruciating eye operations. Now I needed a nap—or a coma.

We rolled past New Canaan's statued town square, where the flames of oil lanterns shivered kindly in the mist. And while the dark distance kept rushing under us, under us, the engine slowly hummed me back . . .

. . . to a lush, rainy summer (my seventh). It was during a bottle green, puddled dusk, the air damp and tender right after a storm. I'd been helping my dad gather branches fallen from the mingled awning of pine and magnolia that sheltered our acre when, from maybe ten feet away, I noticed a field mouse ("Can we pet it, Doug?") making her brave, nose-quivering way out of the woods and into the next galaxy (our backyard). Before I knew it, my father had pounced and was taking his tiny prisoner. The weird thing was that as he gently, expertly scooped her out of the wet tangy grass, she didn't even bother to bite him. Instead, she gazed out with a regal ease, resting two assessing front paws on the balustrade (index finger) of her chariot as it carried the little queen through the green dripping twilight and into my room, where she would be christened Miss Esme. And where, exactly a year to the dusk, coming home after fielding ground balls with my dad, I would find her neck caught between the two highest spokes of her exercise wheel, one hind leg twitching as she dangled in a last ray of sun.

I can still see the lone film-school spot of blood on her silent white chest; my father's moist eyes, which couldn't help but flash a janitorial glance at the orange dirt my cleats had crumbled onto the cream carpet as he walked across it and out of my room, cradling Esme to his chest inside his college catcher's mitt, which he hadn't taken off. And how, though he wouldn't allow me outside, I watched, through a slit of curtain, through a fog of tears, my father with a shovel in the sunset, burying the mitt, with Esme curled in its worn leather palm.

Even then I understood it was a gesture of respect, the sacrament in symbols, the gift of ritual; understood how my father's glove was really one sacrifice in tribute to another. Because if he'd let the thing stay above ground, with the living, both of us knew we could never have played catch with it again. Just as I knew (without knowing), that our blithe little coffin was actually part of an endless attempt to give the absentminded earth something hard to forget.

Standing at the window, I remember feeling, under a blur of despair, the first hot throbs of betrayal going through me. And because the offender was gone, because I could get no revenge, I'd decided somehow to blame her death on my dad. But as I watched him in the deepening cricket evening, patting down dirt with a worried foot, I also decided, if I was going to be totally sincere with myself, that I really wouldn't want anyone else as my father.

Could Cammy, just possibly, say the same? Maybe. Shag was still hoarding something, it seemed, that she still thought she needed. So how would he fit into her life now that *I* was in it? Shag, the jagged old jigsaw, puzzle unto himself. For instance, would he come to our wedding? And not only give away the bride, but be the guy who objected? I mean, come on, what chance was there for any marital bliss with him in the picture? Not to mention *Gramp*uh Shag . . . spending the day with his granddaughter . . .

But who was I to judge? How did I really know I could trust myself if *we* had a daughter? Well—I just knew.

*Did*n't I?

The train paused and stood panting at the Cos Cob station. From out of the darkness a lady got on and sat down in front of me, vividly scarved, with a brooch and brittle hair dyed that special copper color that a lot of creative women go for when they reach middle age. Then the train sighed and started moving again.

Hey, maybe I wouldn't even tell Camilla I'd met him. But what if he was sending her a cheeky e-mail about it right now? Playing it down. *Just a little manly gunplay's all it was, hon. Harmless, really.* Clubhouse roughhousing. The boys trading notes.

Maybe we'd avoid the subject altogether. Or maybe we could learn from it? I remembered Gary's (Donnie's) theory about how there was something "chicly unbathed about incest." He'd told me "the French have all sorts of movies about it. They're not afraid of it like the puritanical, parochial American. In fact, they *cel*ebrate it. It's the finest faux pas, the deepest double entendre, the most dangerous liaison. Don't try this at home, ha, ha."

But how could I live in a world with this . . . ridiculous incubus . . . who'd dimmed the light I'd tried so long to find in her eyes? Did he *have* it somewhere? She must have owned it at some point.

Maybe he could give it back to us.

I remembered the obedient, punctured look in her eyes the first and only time I'd rolled her over and taken her from behind. God, she must have felt him every time I touched her. Every time

I'd tasted her–I'd tasted him. So how could part of me not *love* him? The silent trois in our ménage. Somehow our love would *have* to welcome the hate; because to deny his presence would be to negate part of her. So had Cammy cried yesterday for the little girl? For him? For us? I wondered what he'd learned about himself inside her. Did he hope he'd discover something in there . . . him*self*, maybe? I'd tried that trick as well, only to find him stumbling around in the dark with me. And I was almost looking forward to going back inside of there now–now that I knew what to look for . . .

Even if I didn't know what to *feel*. I mean, was this Love, Terror, Rage? They seemed like the gas, liquid, and solid states of the same emotion. I also had the humiliated sense of being cheated on–retroactively. Because it was the first time I'd really had a chance to consider the fact that she and Shag had been in touch the whole time we'd been together. It was all coming back: *What does your father do?* on our first date; the picture she'd scribbled on her Delta napkin; the photo of the little girl on the mechanical seahorse; the time she'd mumbled that her jean jacket had been a present *from my father* . . . just like the one I was *wearing*! Jesus. Our unholy trinity. Or was it some sort of sick contest between me and Shag, with Camilla-the-Prize? Had she made some kind of mangled religion out of him?

And yet, of course, I still loved her. Loved her more than my own recollections. My ravaged girl, Cammy, my little, my only. Loved her *more* for the damage; for the way my voice seemed always an echo around her; for the way she'd disappear even as we made love. And now I knew why. Knew why she was airless. *There's such a thing as too much love*–the thing she'd told me, breaking up at the Met. Of *course*. And then it hit me. Oh my God.

What if they were *still*–?

—my lungs filled with a swarm of baffled urges. I shivered. Christ. How could I possibly be getting an erection now?! What the fuck was *wrong* with me? With *everyone?*

And so I sat on that train, plowing into the night, astounded at the lurking things within me, as if a magician were plucking long black feathers from my throat.

*What images return.*

Slowly, I sank into deep scarlet sleep. I was inside her, watching chinks of white light flash at me as he pried her open that very first time, all those broken years ago. I was supersensitized. Thirsty for murder. I could taste my own brain. I *was* the sense of taste. Became all senses. Was forever and everywhere. Never and all at once. As dull as Time. The size of a quark. In the tip of his cock. Surfing on a pearly, polluting wave of his semen. Sitting inside my own synapse and watching the neural impulse that would've allowed me to kill him. Riding the bullet that would pierce him and then sloshing through his veins in a victory scream. Then, as a kid, I was screaming down the water tube at Six Flags, with my own dad right behind me—

When screaming brakes woke me up. There were awed whispers around me. I opened my eyes to find all the passengers, including Copper, pointing through the windows at the tracks outside where, in the slowing train's headlight, we watched a delicate explosion of deer—

vanish into black woods.

I yawned. Felt my jeans for my wallet. Still there. I hadn't killed him. Still there.

# Cynara

On my way to Camilla's apartment, I walked through a last, yawning crowd as they shuffled out of the Angelika Cinema. And then, in front of me, under a streetlight, under a shaved head, I thought I recognized a face . . . which, as it approached, I began to connect with vague dread.

"Hey, rock star," it said.

It was Groupie.

We did that maneuver where each person keeps walking, half-facing the other and both afraid to be the first one to stop—until, somehow, we were a hug.

She told me how she'd read all about my big record advance in Time Out, and I explained (with a levelheaded perspective I now attribute to the evening's earlier events) how, in order to quench her father's jailbait extortions, I'd just sent a generous percentage of that advance to his P.O. box . . . which, she informed me, didn't belong to her father at all . . . but Gary! Who had, she explained, "pimped out" Groupie when he'd met her backstage at a FUCT show, for the $100 he actually "borrowed" from me. Their little deal having been for Groupie to portray herself as the most wicked Camillopposite, an anti-seductress who would render me miserable enough to churn out love songs tor*ment*ed enough for Kid Rock and Britney to buy from, who else—Gary. Who had, in line with Donnie's whole Art-Equals-

Recollection-Distorted-By-Anguish corollary, also prescreened alt-culture expert Groupie on which tattoo she felt would prove the most absolutely uncool/regrettable for me to get.

("Is that thing still on your *body*?")

Then I realized she was wearing a most un-groupie-like ensemble of prim-white-oxford-buttoned-up-to-the-collar, black patent-leather penny loafers, and a beige skirt pleated like a pencil sharpener's shaving. She'd also smuggled a new, enforced joy into her voice, ending all of her sentences like they were the precious last lines of children's books. Notwithstanding all this and her hairless head, I sensed something else awry about her, that, under the weary streetlamp, I couldn't quite—oh, her eyebrows had been mowed as well! Which left her face roofless, overly expressive, and, I had to admit, oddly erotic. And the reason for all of this? . . .

"I understand now, of course, that everything in my life had been leading up to my CONNY Epiphany."

I congratulated her on their recent ASPSCA merger, pleased with myself for being so au courant. "So you must know Rip?" I added, wondering if she knew his *Earth Name*.

"*Rip*, as you call him, just formed his own sect," she said, with a bitterness I didn't pursue. "And my name is no longer Groupie, by the way. It's Cynara."*

Lastly, there was the issue of . . .

"It took me years, but finally, because of CONNY, I love my

FOOTNOTE >

*Horace wrote, *Non sum qualis eram bonae sub regno Cynarae* . . . "I am not as I was under the reign of the good Cynara," pleading with Venus to stop tormenting him with Love. Ernest Dowson later wrote a riveting poem with this name.

warts. How could I not have seen they were a blessing? They're beautiful! I'm so *glad* I'm celibate. They made me the leper messiah. I hope I gave them to *you*."*

In parting,

"We should get wheat germ enemas together at Dr. Singh's sometime," she offered in a hearty, reminiscent voice, as if she'd suggested we go Christmas caroling. The grippy shark flesh above her eyes lifted and waited for my response . . .

I took a rain check.

FOOTNOTE >

*Which meant, I hoped, that she hadn't given them to me, because Dr. Singh had said the symptoms would've manifested themselves immediately if they were to develop at all.

# Pretty Vacant

I walked along empty Houston Street. Past the kitschy colors of the car wash and the imperial Puck Building. Past the overpriced little junkyard of "antique" furniture, and the locked-up SoHo Poolroom with its fleet of velvet green tables, waiting in the darkness.

A gust of wind brought a crabby "Last call!" from a distant bar. I pulled up the collar on my blue jean jacket.

Against the starless, muddy horizon, Red Square's clock tower said it was two fifty-nine in the morning. Then the huge impatient minute-hand skipped over the remaining moment, so it stood up straight. Which reminded me of when Peroxide, that stewardess, jerked Cammy's "seatback to its upright position."

As usual, as always, the world meant Camilla.

Just as I was zeroing in on her apartment, who do I see but AA John from Crunch, lumbering out of Max Fish. He'd packed himself tight inside a wife-beater, and despite the raw night, wasn't even wearing a jacket. Suddenly I remembered my relapse . . . but because John was assessing a helpful bicep as he marched at me, I was able to duck into Katz's Delicatessen. Where they were blasting Kid Rock's idiotic take on "If Camilla Fell." Great. I almost said the hell with it all and ordered a Heineken with a chubby kosher hotdog. But no. I told myself, that in so many ways, I'd be starting all over again.

I reached her tenement and looked up at her window. Surprisingly, the lights were all blazing.

As I trudged up the rank steps, I could see that her front door was open. Mmm. What would I tell her? I couldn't think. All my thoughts shuffled together. How would I play this hand?

I was looking forward to Phillip's quiver-wagging welcome when I got to the landing, but there was only a startled silence.

"Hey, guys?" I said, panting, peeking into the apartment.

All the lights were on—it was totally empty.

I stood there a long time, in that stunned, bright room. It and me staring at each other with egg on our faces. There was nothing left, not a scrap of her, anywhere. Only this abandoned hive of us.

At some point I found myself sitting on the kitchen floor, my back to the fridge, staring above the sink across from me at the *Empire of Light* poster—upside down—clinging to the wall by a desperate corner.

# Sweet Child of Mine

The next afternoon I woke up and went to my window. I stood in front of the gray dull Sunday. Fern had become just a withered stump, so finally, I lifted the sill and emptied her into the wind—watched the swirling dust of her vanish down the block into Bleecker . . .

I sat down on the sofa, and there was the warped *White Noise* on the coffee table, and then the rip in my gig bag on the floor. I was so sick of all our heavy-handed symbolism.

She was gone.

I think I was still too astonished to really comprehend it. Too exhausted. What exactly happened? Shag must have called her right after I left him, persuading her against me—or was she running from both of us?—no, something told me she'd chosen him after all . . .

Because deep down, as in a dim dream, I sensed a kind of sinuous shadow logic guiding all of this, which always slithered off just as I began to grasp it. For instance, had we really even gotten back to*geth*er? Had I actually *seen* her again? Somehow it didn't matter, exactly. As usual, there seemed to be no beginning or end to her. She was always, Camilla, essential and impossible—my psalm and my alms.

I thought of a long, luminous afternoon, near the beginning. And ending with Cammy at the sink of her dusk-drenched kitchen. Her bare back to me, supine on the bed with my loins still moist from her; golden motes of dust and the bright scent of lemon as she stirred an invisible pitcher of iced tea; muscles working in her lonely shoulders. Then a long pause, filled only by the satisfying crackle-melt of her ice . . .

"On my best day I'm weak," she'd told me, finally, still facing away.

These days I imagine the cold blue hum in her eyes, as they would've watched the slowly tangoing cubes in her glass. Just as I imagine myself running over and enclosing her, from behind; asking her "Why?"; asking if there were perhaps some unthinkable thing that had ripped through her past in a wind of jagged glass; and then, as I turned her to face me, assuring her that she'd see, okay, she'd see, that the world didn't have only dirty tricks up its sleeve; that its reservoirs weren't all so salty, if she would only allow herself to drink from them again.

And so I re-choreograph the past.

I sat there on the couch until the bland afternoon was a sunset. Plucking my guitar. Surprised I couldn't cry. Then some kind of colossal detachment lifted me out of myself. And from above, as if through the opposite end of a telescope, I saw three tiny figures (one a brown smudge), down there on that happy SoHo sidewalk, on that first thrilling yellow Sunday . . .

. . . and I wondered if all of it had really added up to nothing; if, in the end, Space and Time make trinkets of us all.

When suddenly there were three anxious knocks at my door.

She'd changed her mind!? . . .

No. Little Green let herself in, hiding her ample forehead with the heels of her hands as she plopped down next to me. "Please promise not to laugh, okay, Clyde?" she said, palms still affixed.

"Don't worry." I set my guitar aside.

"I got kind of carried away." Slowly she unveiled her ash-blonde bangs—or lack of them—because they'd been hacked, almost to her scalp, as if with zigzag scissors.

"Give it to me straight. *Really,* Clyde. I can take it."

I could tell from the flushed rims of her giant green eyes that she'd been crying.

"Just admit it looks awful," she said.

(It looked awful.)

"No, sweetie. It's totally rock 'n' roll. And Walter," I said, taking the Cub Scout bandanna off the coffee table and tying it around her head, Axl Rose-fashion. "It'll grow."

# PERMISSIONS ACKNOWLEDGMENTS >

Excerpts from *PNIN* by Vladimir Nabokov courtesy of Alfred A. Knopf, a division of Random House, Inc.

Photographs of dogs (title page, p. 1, p. 173) copyright © Shusuke Nakamura/Photonica.
Photograph of Don DeLillo (p. 23) copyright © Joyce Ravid.
Photograph (p. 46) courtesy of NASA/STSCI.
René Magritte, "Empire of Light" (p. 60) copyright © 2002 C. Herscovici, Brussels/Artists Rights Society (ARS), New York.
Photograph (p. 252) courtesy of John H. Nation.
Illustration (p. 396) from *Household Stories from the Collection of the Brothers Grimm,* illustrated by Walter Crane. Image courtesy of the Library of Congress.

Printed in the United States
by Baker & Taylor Publisher Services